Praise for

GREEN GRASS,
RUNNING WATER

"An irresistibly funny novel. . . . King blends myth, folklore and contemporary events to create his satirical look at society."
—*Toronto Star*

"*Green Grass, Running Water* is a novel novel. In many ways it's a groundbreaker in an area that needed it. . . . Once you catch on to the style, it's hard to get the book out of your hands. I read it in one sitting, accelerating through the pages, laughing out loud several times, silent with admiration at others."
—*Ottawa Citizen*

"Original, witty and stylishly executed, and all adding up to more than a little bit of truth."
—*Maclean's*

"A witty, wild, wooly romp of a story; wonderful is the best way to describe it. . . . *Green Grass, Running Water* is a sharp-witted and warm-hearted novel fuelled by oral storytelling traditions. Its pages brim with titillating In(dian)-jokes and sparkle with puns, pokes and post-modern plot polkas. It may well be one of the most significant novels of the past two decades."
—*The Edmonton Journal*

"Elegant and outrageous: a richly rewarding saga from a first-rate talent."
—*Kirkus Reviews*

"This is storytelling in the best tradition, with plot lines and people that wander in and out of things, ravelling and unravelling themselves to the rhythms of musical language. . . . The humour here is crackling dry."
—*The Vancouver Sun*

GREEN GRASS, RUNNING WATER

THOMAS KING

HARPER
PERENNIAL

Originally published in hardcover by
HarperCollins 1993. First Harper*Perennial*-
Canada paperback edition 1999. This
Harper*Perennial* edition 2007.

HARPER PERENNIAL®
is a registered trademark of HarperCollins
Publishers Ltd.

Part title calligraphy in Cherokee by Chris
Costello

HarperCollins books may be purchased
for educational, business, or sales promotional use through our Special Markets
Department.

HarperCollins Publishers Ltd.
2 Bloor Street East, 20th Floor
Toronto, Ontario, Canada
M4W 1A8

www.harpercollins.ca

National Library of Canada Cataloguing
in Publication

King, Thomas
Green grass, running water

ISBN-10: 0-00-648513-8
ISBN-13: 978-0-00-648513-1

I. Title.

PS8571.I5298G77 1999   C813'.54
C99-931151-4
PR9199.3.D4422G77 1999

RRD   40 39 38 37 36 35 34

Printed and bound in the United States
Set in Sabon

JUST FOR HELEN

*who will not think less
of me for having written it*

ACKNOWLEDGMENTS

My thanks to the Jerome Foundation for a summer travel grant that allowed me to roam around southern Alberta and points west to talk with people about oral literature, and to the Ucross Foundation, which provided me with a month-long residency where the first draft of this novel was written.

Thanks to Buzz and Judy Webb for the generous use of their oceanfront studio, where parts of the novel rolled in and rolled out.

Special thanks to Martin Heavyhead, Leroy Littlebear, and Narcisse Blood for their friendship over the years and for the hospitality they have always afforded me.

And to Alan Kilpatrick and Ada:lagh(a)dhí:ya, wado.

So.

In the beginning, there was nothing. Just the water.

Coyote was there, but Coyote was asleep. That Coyote was asleep and that Coyote was dreaming. When that Coyote dreams, anything can happen.

I can tell you that.

So, that Coyote is dreaming and pretty soon, one of those dreams gets loose and runs around. Makes a lot of noise.

Hooray, says that silly Dream, Coyote dream. I'm in charge of the world. And then that Dream sees all that water.

Oh, oh, says that noisy Dream. This is all wrong. Is that water we see? that silly Dream says to those dream eyes.

It's water, all right, says those Dream Eyes.

That Coyote Dream makes many sad noises, and those noises are loud and those noises wake up Coyote.

"Who is making all that noise and waking me up?" says Coyote.

"It's that noisy dream of yours," I says. "It thinks it is in charge of the world."

.   .   .

{ 1 }

I *am* in charge of the world, says that silly Dream.

"Perhaps you could be a little quieter," says Coyote. "I am trying to sleep."

Who are you? says that Dream. Are you someone important?

"I'm Coyote," says Coyote. "And I am very smart."

I am very smart, too, says that Dream. I must be Coyote.

"No," says Coyote. "You can't be Coyote. But you can be a dog."

Are dogs smart? says that Dream.

"You bet," says Coyote. "Dogs are good. They are almost as good as Coyote."

Okay, says that Dream. I can do that.

But when that Coyote Dream thinks about being a dog, it gets everything mixed up. It gets everything backward.

"That looks like trouble to me," I says.

"Hmmm," says Coyote. "You could be right."

"That doesn't look like a dog at all," I tell Coyote.

"Hmmm," says Coyote. "You could be right."

I am god, says that Dog Dream.

"Isn't that cute," says Coyote. "That Dog Dream is a contrary. That Dog Dream has everything backward."

But why am I a little god? shouts that god.

"Not so loud," says Coyote. "You're hurting my ears."

I don't want to be a little god, says that god. I want to be a big god!

"What a noise," says Coyote. "This dog has no manners."

Big one!

"Okay, okay," says Coyote. "Just stop shouting."

There, says that GOD. That's better.

"Now you've done it," I says.

"Everything's under control," says Coyote. "Don't panic."

. . .

Where did all that water come from? shouts that GOD.

"Take it easy," says Coyote. "Sit down. Relax. Watch some television."

But there is water everywhere, says that GOD.

"Hmmmm," says Coyote. "So there is."

"That's true," I says. "And here's how it happened."

TAROT

454

"WHAT DO YOU THINK, LIONEL? Maybe something in blue?" Norma began pulling pieces of carpet out of her purse and placing them on her lap. She stuck the larger pieces on the dashboard. "I like the green, too."

Lionel could feel his eyes start to settle. The radio would have helped him stay awake, but it had stopped working months before.

"What color do you think your mother will choose?"

"Wouldn't hold my breath."

"Band council's already voted the money."

"They've done that before," said Lionel, and he reached up and pinched his cheek.

"Well, I'm going to order the blue. It reminds me of the sky. Going to get money to paint the house, too."

"Wouldn't hold my breath."

"Council is even talking about paving the lease road. Asphalt, all the way. I was at the meeting."

"What happened? Council run out of dirt and gravel?"

Norma shook her head. "Lionel, if you weren't my sister's boy, and if I didn't see you born with my own eyes, I would sometimes think you were white. You sound just like those politicians in Edmonton. Always telling us what we can't do."

Lionel lowered the visor. It didn't help. "Blue is probably the best, auntie."

"I don't know," said Norma. "The green's nice too. Don't want to make a mistake, you know." She ran her hand over the carpet. "You make a mistake with carpet, and you got to live with it for a long time."

"Everybody makes mistakes, auntie."

"Best not to make one with carpet."

THIS ACCORDING TO THE LONE RANGER:

"*Okay,*" said the Lone Ranger, "is everybody ready?"

"Hawkeye doesn't have a nice shirt," said Ishmael.

"He can have one of mine," said Robinson Crusoe.

"The red one?"

"Yes."

"The red one with the palm trees?"

"Yes."

"Don't forget the jacket," said Ishmael.

"I won't."

"You forgot it last time."

"Did I?"

"What about the light?" said Robinson Crusoe.

"We'll turn it on later," said Ishmael.

"And the apology?" said Hawkeye.

"Coyote can do that," said the Lone Ranger. "Okay, are we ready now?"

"Whose turn is it?" said Ishmael.

"Mine," said the Lone Ranger.

"Are you sure?" said Robinson Crusoe. "Maybe it's Hawkeye's turn."

"No," said the Lone Ranger. "Hawkeye has already had a turn."

"Maybe it's Ishmael's turn."

"Ready," said the Lone Ranger. "Here we go."

"Once upon a time . . ."

"What are you doing?" said Hawkeye.
    "Okay, I'll begin again," said the Lone Ranger.
    "Okay," said Ishmael.
    "Okay," said Robinson Crusoe.
    "Okay," said Hawkeye.

"A long time ago in a faraway land . . ."

"Not this again," said Ishmael.

"Okay, I'll begin again," said the Lone Ranger. "Are we ready?"

"Yes. We are all ready."

"Okay?"

"Okay."

"Many moons comechucka . . . hahahahahahahahahahahaha."

"Perhaps Hawkeye should tell the story."
  "Perhaps Ishmael should tell the story."
  "Perhaps Robinson Crusoe should tell the story."
  "I'm okay now," said the Lone Ranger.
  "Do you remember how to start?"
  "Yes, I remember."
  "Can we begin?"
  "Yes. We should begin."

"*In the beginning, God created the heaven and the earth.* And the earth was without form, and void; and darkness was upon the face of the deep—"

"Wait a minute," said Robinson Crusoe.

"Yes?"

"That's the wrong story," said Ishmael. "That story comes later."

"But it's my turn," said the Lone Ranger.

"But you have to get it right," said Hawkeye.

"And," said Robinson Crusoe, "you can't tell it all by yourself."

"Yes," said Ishmael. "Remember what happened last time?"

"Everybody makes mistakes," said the Lone Ranger.

"Best not to make them with stories."

"Oh, okay," said the Lone Ranger.

"Gha!" said the Lone Ranger. "Higayv:ligé:i."

"That's better," said Hawkeye. "Tsane:hlanv́:hi."
  "Listen," said Robinson Crusoe. "Hade:lohó:sgi."
  "It is beginning," said Ishmael. "Dagvyá:dhv:dv:hní."

"It is begun well," said the Lone Ranger. "Tsada:hnó:nedí niga:v duyughodv: o:sdv."

"Okay?"
  "Okay."

DR. JOSEPH HOVAUGH SAT AT HIS DESK and rolled his toes in the soft, deep-pile carpet. The desk was large, one of his wife's auction discoveries, a rare example of colonial woodcraft. She had had it stripped, repaired, stained blond, and moved into his office as a surprise. He was delighted, he said, and he praised her eye for having found so massive a piece of wood. It reminded him of a tree cut down to the stump.

He had of late cultivated the habit of sitting behind his desk and staring out the window onto the grounds of the hospital. It was a way to collect his thoughts, a way to get ready for the week. Every day, he sat a little longer. There was no harm in it. He was tired, getting older, becoming reflective.

The front of the hospital was a long expanse of white stucco, brilliant and warm. Behind the wall, the willows were beginning to get their leaves, the cherry trees were heavy with pink and white blossoms, the evergreens stood dark and velvet against the stone. Yellow daffodils lined the front of the flower beds, and the wisteria and the lilacs around the arbors were greening up nicely. Dr. Hovaugh sat in his chair behind his desk and looked out at the wall and the trees and the flowers and the swans on the blue-green pond in the garden, and he was pleased.

The knock, a sharp rap, barely gave Dr. Hovaugh time to swivel back toward the door and bring Mary into focus.

"Good morning, Mary. What do we have for today?"

"The police are downstairs."

"The police?"

"Yes, sir . . . the Indians."

"The Indians?"

"Yes, sir."

"Again?"

Dr. Hovaugh turned back to the window. He stretched both his hands out on the desk and pushed down as if he expected to move it.

"Look at that, Mary. It's spring again. Garden looks good, eh? Everything's green. Everything's alive. You know, I thought I might get a pair of peacocks. What do you think?"

Mary stood in the middle of the room unsure of what to do. Dr. Hovaugh seemed to shrink behind the desk as though it were growing, slowly and imperceptibly enveloping the man.

"The Indians," he said.

"They're just gone," said Mary. "Like before. They'll be back."

Dr. Hovaugh turned away from the window. Perhaps he should move the desk out and get another that didn't seem so rooted and permanent.

"I shall probably need John, Mary." Dr. Hovaugh leaned on the desk and spoke each word slowly, as if he were trying to remember exactly what he wanted to say. "Find me John."

ALBERTA FRANK LEANED ON THE PODIUM and watched Henry Dawes fall asleep.

"In 1874, the U.S. Army began a campaign of destruction aimed at forcing the southern Plains tribes onto reservations. The army systematically went from village to village burning houses, killing horses, and destroying food supplies. They pursued the Cheyenne, Kiowa, Comanche, and the Arapaho relentlessly into one of the worst winters of the decade. Starvation and freezing conditions finally forced the tribes to surrender."

"Professor Frank, what was that date?"

"Eighteen seventy-four."

"Who were the tribes again?"

"The Cheyenne, Kiowa, Comanche, and Arapaho."

"How do you spell Arapaho?"

"Look it up in your book. Now, as the tribes came in, the army separated out certain individuals who were considered to be dangerous. Some were troublemakers in the eyes of the army. Some were thought to have been involved in raids. Others were simply leaders opposed to the reservation system.

"The army identified seventy-two such individuals, and when the rest of the people were sent to reservations, these Indians were chained to wagons and taken to Fort Sill in what is now Oklahoma. There they were put on a train and sent to Florida."

"Florida?" said John Collier. "That doesn't sound too bad."

"They were imprisoned at Fort Marion, an old Spanish fort in Saint Augustine."

"Oh, bummer."

"The man responsible for the Indians at Fort Marion was an army lieutenant, a Richard Pratt. As a way to help to reduce the boredom of confinement, Pratt provided the men with drawing materials, ledger books, and colored pencils. Some of the prisoners began producing drawings that depicted the battles that they had fought with the army and with other tribes. They also drew pictures about their life on the plains, and some even drew pictures of their life in prison. Collectively, these drawings are known as Plains Indian Ledger Art."

Alberta pressed the button and the first slide flashed on the screen. "This is a drawing by Little Chief, a Cheyenne. It's titled 'Chasing Two Osage.'

"This is one by Squint Eyes, another Cheyenne. It depicts a battle between the Cheyenne and the army.

"Here's a drawing by a Kiowa artist, a man named Etahleuh. This drawing shouldn't need an explanation."

Alberta worked her way through the slides. Henry Dawes was sound asleep at the back of the room, his head wrapped up in his arms. Mary Rowlandson and Elaine Goodale were bent over, their heads locked together. Hannah Duston and John Collier had moved their desks together again, and were virtually in each other's laps. Helen Mooney was sitting in the front row, writing down every word Alberta uttered.

"This drawing is called 'On the Warpath.' It was done by a Cheyenne called Making Medicine." Alberta raised her voice sharply. "Some of these will probably be on the test."

Henry Dawes's head rolled out of his arms. Mary and Elaine glanced up from their conversation.

"Mr. Dawes, do you see anything unusual in these drawings?"

Henry blinked his eyes like an owl caught out in the light. "Well . . . I don't know exactly what you want . . . Those slides, huh? Well, they're not very well done."

"How so, Mr. Dawes?"

"Well, I mean, they're kind of like stick figures. You know, like kids draw."

"Thank you, Mr. Dawes."

"Sure. And the colors are kinda unusual too."

"The colors?"

"The browns, I mean. Seems like everyone liked to use browns and reds a lot. Together, I mean. All the time. Maybe it was traditional or something like that."

Alberta sighed. Friday afternoon. She showed the last two slides, one by White Horse and another depicting the meeting of Indian and white culture by a Kiowa named Wohaw.

"What might we deduce from these drawings? Do they tell us anything about the people who did them or the world in which they lived?"

There was a wonderful, rich silence. Alberta looked at her watch. "Well then, do you have any questions?"

"These Indians. Did any of them escape?"

"From Fort Marion?"

"Yeah. Did any of them get away?"

"No."

"They just sat around and drew pictures?"

"Not all of them drew. So far as we know, none of the Comanche produced any drawings. Of the seventy-one prisoners, only twenty-six are known to have drawn."

Helen Mooney raised her hand, her head glued to her notepad. "I believe you said there were seventy-two prisoners?"

"That's right," said Alberta. "There were seventy-two to begin with. However, on the trip to Fort Marion, a Cheyenne named Gray Beard was shot and killed."

Henry Dawes was still awake. "Did he try to kill a guard or something?"

"No, he jumped out of the window of the train."

"So, one of them did try to escape."

"Not exactly."

"But he jumped out the window."

"He had chains on his hands and legs."

"And they shot him?"

"That's right."

"Oh, bummer."

"I should mention, too," said Alberta, "that one of the prisoners was a woman. But she didn't do any drawings."

"What did she do?" said Elaine Goodale. "I mean, why did they throw her in prison?"

"She was the wife of one of the prisoners. Any other questions?"

Mary Rowlandson rolled her lips together and slid a pencil under her nose. "Do we have to know all these guys' names? I mean, will they all be on the test?"

"There's always that chance, Ms. Rowlandson."

"But what if we know who they are but can't spell their names exactly right?"

"You probably won't get exactly all the points."

Alberta closed the folder and turned on the lights. "We'll finish this on Wednesday. Don't forget, next week we're back in Canada with the Métis in Manitoba and Saskatchewan. I'm sure I don't have to remind you that Monday is a holiday. Have a good weekend."

Helen Mooney had her hand in the air. The rest of the class was in flight toward the doors. "Professor Frank," Helen said, "the seventy-one Indians. The ones at Fort Marion. I was wondering."

"About what?"

"Well, for one thing, what happened to them?"

"WHAT HAPPENED TO THE TREES? said Hawkeye.

"Well, this isn't exactly what I had in mind," said the Lone Ranger.
    "But there are no trees," said Hawkeye.
    "It was my turn."
    "Could we get on with this?" said Ishmael.
    "I'm really going to miss the trees," said Hawkeye.
    "It is a beautiful sky, however," said Robinson Crusoe.
    "Yes, it is a beautiful sky," said Ishmael.
    "Are we in Mexico?" said Hawkeye.
    "No," said the Lone Ranger. "I believe we are in Canada."
    "Canada," said Ishmael. "What a good idea."
    "Yes," said Robinson Crusoe. "We certainly enjoyed ourselves the last time we were here."

BABO JONES SAT IN THE STAFF ROOM and looked out the window. She could see the green Dumpster at the back of the west wing of the hospital and the string of smaller, green plastic garbage cans lined up near the staff door, looking as though they were waiting to get in. Babo could see her car too, the red Pinto she had bought from her brother-in-law. She could see the muffler drooping down like a ripe brown fruit. A yellow dog was sniffing at the rear tire. Go ahead, Babo thought, pee on it. Won't hurt a thing.

"Jimmy." Sergeant Cereno gestured to the uniformed policeman standing at the door. "Find an outlet for the extension."

Babo licked at her cup of coffee. Sergeant Cereno pushed the buttons on the tape recorder. "Okay, Jimmy, it's working now." Cereno folded his hands and leaned forward in the chair. "Well, Mrs. Jones. Pretty busy morning. You been working here long?"

"Ms."

"What?"

"Ms. Jones. I'm not married."

Sergeant Cereno smiled and tapped the tips of his fingers together. "Right. How long have you been working here, Miss Jones?"

"Ms. I've got four kids."

"Right. How long have you been working here?"

"Sixteen years."

"Sergeant Cereno."

"What?"

"Sixteen years, Sergeant Cereno."

"You're kidding."

"This is a serious matter, Ms. Jones."

"You can call me Babo."

Sergeant Cereno leaned back in the chair, pressed his hands together under his nose as if he were smelling the tips of his fingers. "So, you've been working here sixteen years."

"Some people think that Babo is a man's name."

"Working here must get dull sometimes."

"But it's not. It's tradition."

"I mean, getting up every morning, eating breakfast, driving across town, punching in."

"Firstborn gets named Babo."

"But you must have ways to liven up the day."

"Are you recording this?"

"Yes, I am, Ms. Jones."

"You watch a lot of television?"

"Why don't we let me ask the questions."

Babo picked up her coffee cup and looked out the window. The Pinto was sitting in a puddle of water. The rear tire was half submerged. The yellow dog was gone.

"Sure. I'll tell you just what I told Scotty. He's the guy who called you. Maybe you should talk to him. He watches a lot of television, and he's got a tape recorder just like yours."

"We'd rather talk with you right now, Ms. Jones."

"Suits me. What do you want to know?"

"Everything," said Sergeant Cereno.

Babo wondered where the water had come from. She hadn't remembered parking in a puddle. Babo smiled at Sergeant

Cereno and Sergeant Cereno smiled back. No teeth. Just a shallow bowl of lips.

"It was six o'clock," Babo began. "Like it always is on the days I work, which is six out of seven. I'd work seven if they let me. Kids give you lots of energy. You got kids?"

Babo paused for a moment and watched Sergeant Cereno slide his index fingers into his nose. "I'll bet you guys only work five days a week. Am I right?"

"So you got to work at six, Ms. Jones."

"I got three girls and a boy."

"What happened when you got to work at six?"

"Allison is the oldest. She looks like me. I've got some pictures."

"So you drove to work."

"That's right. I drove to work. I pulled into my parking space, looked at the back side of old 'Rancho Deluxe' here, and decided that today was the day I stopped smoking."

"So you pulled into your parking space."

"That's right. Threw my smokes on the dash. They're still there. You can almost see them. You guys came in through the front gates. Am I right? Nice and white out front. Well, the back side is pretty grimy. I see it every morning. Looks like those pictures Dr. Eliot has stuck up in his office. Smoking does that. To lungs, I mean. Gets them all grimy and shriveled up like raisins and prunes."

"So you pulled into your parking space."

"I don't know what gets the back of the hospital looking like that. You smoke, Mr. Cereno?"

"Sergeant Cereno."

"Is that Italian or Spanish or what?"

"What happened then?"

The tire of the Pinto wasn't sunk into the puddle. Babo could see that now. She had been deceived by the reflection off the water. The tire was flat.

"So today was going to be the day. Would have been, too. I was feeling strong. Real strong. Had four rolls of Life Savers with me. Got to have them when you try to stop. Cold turkey is okay. My brother-in-law tried it. Real tough, that. You got to have something to take up the slack."

"This is very interesting, Ms. Jones."

"Would you believe that I've smoked for over thirty years? I still feel good, too. Don't cough much. It was my kids got me to stop."

"That's very interesting."

"The other cop smoke?"

"No."

"Damn."

Where was the water coming from? The radiator was new—at least that's what Martin had told her. The muffler was under water now.

"Well, it was early." Babo began again. "I always get here early. Grab that parking space right there. You get here half an hour later and you got to walk in from the other lot. I should stop smoking tomorrow, you know. This thing has me upset. Maybe I should get a pack."

"Perhaps you could do that later, Ms. Jones."

"I'm not going to smoke them. They're for temptation. Martin says you carry them around with you, but you don't smoke them. That sort of thing is what makes you strong."

"I'm sure you're a very strong woman, Ms. Jones."

"Raised four kids all by myself. What's your first name? Let me guess. Is it Ben? That's my boy's name."

"Ms. Jones . . . The hospital?"

"He didn't make it."

"What?"

"Not your fault. Martin's just weak. I told Zolla when she married him. 'He won't stop smoking,' I said. I'm always try-ing to help."

"Ms. Jones—"

"Bought that car off him. Always trying to help."

"The hospital?"

The puddle had spread, grown wider and deeper. From a distance, the Pinto looked a little like a ship. Babo squeezed her eyes and looked again. "So, the back door is locked, just like it always is, and I unlock it. Like I always do."

"When was that?"

"Six o'clock."

"Exactly six o'clock?"

"Maybe a couple of minutes before."

"You unlocked the door at six o'clock?"

"Maybe a few minutes after."

"And?"

"The place was dead. You ever been in a hospital in the morning? Not like those regular hospitals. I used to work at General. Busy, busy, busy. Emergency ward was always stacked with bleeders and screamers. A crazy hospital is the place to work. Crazy people don't get many visitors, and they don't wander around much after nine. Pills. That's what does it.

"So I unlock the back door and go to my room to hang up my coat and see if Dominic has left me a wet mop in the bucket again. Everything is okay, so I go down to the coffee machine. I don't start getting paid until six-thirty, so I have some coffee and look around."

"For what?"

"What do you mean?"

"What do you look for?"

"Nothing. I walk around. Sometimes I read the magazines. Then I check out the messes I got to clean up. You know, look the area over. See where I'm going to start."

No, thought Babo, not exactly a ship. The red paint on the door was beginning to bubble. There were brown spots all along the wheel wells. The antenna was bent over on its side. Not a ship at all.

"That's what I'm doing. Drinking my coffee and walking and looking. You know, this is an important job and today I said to myself, Babo, you got no business smoking because no one takes you serious these days if you smoke."

Babo finished her coffee. Sergeant Cereno still had that nice smile on his face. He had folded his fingers on top of his lips. The Pinto was moving now, floating toward the far lot.

"So, it's just like I told Scotty," said Babo. "When I got here, they were gone."

THE LONE RANGER, ISHMAEL, ROBINSON CRUSOE, AND HAWKEYE stood by the side of the highway and looked around.

"So," said Hawkeye. "Here we are."

"Yes," said the Lone Ranger. "Here we are."

The land curved out, full and flat. From where they stood, the old Indians could see the edges of the world in all directions.

"That is a very nice sun," said Ishmael.

"Yes, it is."

"And the grass is a beautiful color."

"Yes, it is."

"And the wind feels good on my face."

The old Indians walked around in a circle, looking at the sky and the grass, feeling the wind on their faces.

"So," said Ishmael. "Are we lost again? Have we made another mistake?"

Lionel had made only three mistakes in his entire life, the kinds of mistakes that seem small enough at the time, but somehow get out of hand. The kinds that stay with you for a long time. And he could name each one.

The first mistake Lionel made was wanting to have his tonsils out. It had happened when he was eight, and in many ways it was more a simple error in judgment. Several of the kids at school developed sore throats, and Lois James wound up having her tonsils out. What Lionel noticed most about Lois's tonsils was that she got to stay home from school for over two weeks, and you couldn't even tell she had had an operation. Then, too, the teachers treated her like she was royalty or something. Mrs. Grove brought Lois a sucker, the kind with a hard candy shell and a chewy fudge center. Green, Lionel's favorite. So when Lionel developed a sore throat, he began thinking about Lois and her tonsils. When his throat didn't improve, his mother took him to the band office to see Dr. Loomis.

"You know," said Norma, "we haven't had new carpet since the houses were built. I remember 'cause you went to Calgary that winter to have your throat cut."

"Tonsils, auntie."

"Can't believe my own sister let them do that to you. Got no more sense than a hubcap."

"They didn't do anything."

"Letting them cut you like that."

Dr. Loomis was a skinny old man with a huge pile of white hair and eyes that looked as though they would pop out of his head. His tongue was inordinately long, and as he talked, he would run it around his face, catching the sides of his mouth and the bottom of his chin. Once a week, he came out to the reserve to doctor the sick. There was no formal clinic, and he seldom had any patients. Most of the people on the reserve went to see Martha Old Crow or Jesse Many Guns, who were the doctors of choice. Dr. Loomis generally spent his time in the board office cafeteria drinking coffee and talking about the hospital in Toronto where he had trained just after the turn of the century.

Lionel's mother had taken Lionel to see Martha first, and after Martha was done feeling his ears and shoulders and looking in his eyes, she said, "Simple thing, this. Maybe take this boy to see the Frog doctor. No one comes to see him last week. Maybe his feelings are hurt, that one."

So on Wednesday Lionel's mother arrived at the band office with Lionel in tow. Dr. Loomis shook Lionel's mother's hand and touched his nose with his tongue and told her that her boy was in the best of hands. "I studied in Toronto, you know," he said.

Lionel told him that his throat hurt something awful, that it was hard to swallow or move his head, and that he kept making mistakes on his math homework. Dr. Loomis pursed his lips and nodded gravely. He squeezed Lionel's neck and face and shoulders and had Lionel suck in air in quick, noisy gulps.

Lilly Morris, who worked behind the snack bar, got on the phone, and by the time Dr. Loomis got around to thumping Lionel on the chest and feeling under his armpits, there were about twenty people in the cafeteria.

"Does it hurt here?"

"Something awful."

"Does it hurt here?"

"There too."

"Does it hurt here?"

"Ohhhhh . . ."

Charlie Looking Bear, who was two years older than Lionel and related through a second marriage, grabbed his crotch and asked in a high voice, "Does it hurt here?" But Dr. Loomis ignored Charlie and continued to prod Lionel with his bony fingers. Finally, he took a flat stick out of his jacket pocket and stuck it down Lionel's throat. "Say 'Ahhhhhh.' "

Lionel almost choked.

"Well," said Dr. Loomis, "the boy has a sore throat. Pretty bad one, too. Can't do much about it. Best thing is a little crushed aspirin mixed up with some honey and lemon. Give him lots of fluids. Maybe keep him in bed for a couple of days."

"It hurts real bad!" said Lionel.

"Course, the tonsils are inflamed and they don't look all that healthy. Wouldn't hurt to get them out sometime. They can just keep getting inflamed. Always better to get them out when the child is young."

Lionel could see the distress in his mother's face. "Don't think we need a hospital," she said. "We should wait and see."

"I can't even eat!" said Lionel.

"It's an easy operation," said Dr. Loomis.

"See!"

Lionel's mother shook her head. "He's not doing too well in school right now. If he had that operation, how much school would he miss?"

This was where, as Lionel remembered, the idea began to fall apart.

"Actually," said Dr. Loomis, "there's no need to miss any school at all. We could do it this summer."

"Summer?" said Lionel. "I don't want no operation during the summer."

Charlie was grinning. "What would John Wayne do?" he whispered, and he grabbed his hair and pulled his head off to one side and made cutting motions across his throat.

"We don't want you missing any more school, honey."

"I don't mind missing school. Lois had her tonsils out, and she missed school, and she still gets good grades."

Dr. Loomis laughed, and his eyes bugged out of his head even more, and his tongue went looking for his chin. "Why don't you think about it and let me know. See how the throat does. He'd have to go to Calgary to have it done."

In the car, on the way home, Lionel sulked in the front seat and stared out the window. "I know I can't do any homework with my throat like this."

For the rest of the week and the next, Lionel shuffled around the house, coughing and complaining, until finally his mother called Dr. Loomis and asked him to arrange for an operation as soon as possible.

Norma held the piece of green carpet up to the light. "Martha told your mother to leave them tonsils alone. But oh, no, Camelot's progressive, you know. Indian doctors weren't good enough."

"Long time ago, auntie."

"Latisha goes to see Martha. Ought to pay attention to your sister."

"You can't change the past."

"Your sister is the smart one in the family, that's for sure."

"What about George Morningstar? Real smart choice, that one."

"Thought you were dead for sure."

"What about George Morningstar?"

"Letting them cut on you like that."

And so, in early February, Lionel and his mother drove the two hundred and ten kilometers to Calgary. One of Lionel's aunts lived in Calgary. "I'm going to stay with Jean," his mother told him, "so I can come and see you every day."

There were no beds available in the children's ward, and Lionel was given a bed in another wing. "It's just for the night," the nurse said. "After the operation, we'll move you in with the other children."

To his delight, Lionel discovered that the nurses were much too busy to bother with him, and he was free to roam the hospital. The cafeteria was his favorite stop. His mother had given him three dollars in case of an emergency, which Lionel decided, after thinking about it, included the purchase of doughnuts. Later in the evening, a tall, blond woman came into the room.

"Hi," she said. "You must be the lucky young man who won the free plane ride."

Lionel liked playing these kinds of games. "That's me," he said. "When do we go?"

"Well," said the blond woman, "we're almost ready. Have you ever been on a plane?"

"No!"

"Well, you certainly are lucky."

An hour later, a nurse came in with a wheelchair, and Lionel was put into a red and white ambulance, driven to the airport, and placed on a plane.

"Is my mother coming on the plane?"

"Don't worry, kid," said the ambulance driver. "Nurse said she's going to meet us in Toronto."

"Toronto!" said Lionel. "I've never been to Toronto!"

"Pretty exciting, huh?"

"It sure is."

When Lionel arrived at Sick Children's Hospital, everyone was so friendly. An older nurse who reminded him of his Auntie Louise took him to his room and told him all about the doctor who was going to perform the operation. This doctor had three children of her own, and heart operations, the nurse said, were a very common thing these days.

"Nothing wrong with my heart," said Lionel. "It's my tonsils that hurt."

"You don't have to worry," said the nurse. "A heart operation like yours is really very simple."

"My heart is just fine."

"And it'll be even better tomorrow."

Lionel thought the nurse was kidding, and he laughed, and then he looked at her face. "Where's my mother?"

"She'll be here tomorrow, sweetheart. She'll be right here when you wake up. You better hop into bed now and get some sleep."

In that instant, Lionel knew that some horrible mistake had been made, that he was alone in Toronto, that his mother was in Calgary, that, in the morning, some doctor with three kids was going to cut his heart open. And he began to cry.

"My heart's good. There's nothing wrong with it. My tonsils are rotten, that's all."

The nurse tried to calm him down, told him she would see if the hospital could get in touch with his mother, and in the meantime, why didn't he watch some television in the lounge, which was just down the hall to the left. At the last moment, the nurse must have realized her mistake, because she called to him as he got to the door. "Wait a minute, honey," she said, "I'll go with you."

But it was too late. Lionel turned right and bolted down the hall. He found a set of stairs going down, crashed into the main lobby, and before anyone could do anything, he was out the front door and into the night. He got as far as a video arcade on Yonge Street and was trying to call home when the manager noticed that there was a barefoot Indian kid in what looked to be a hospital gown in his arcade and called the police.

By the time Lionel was dragged back to the hospital, insisting the entire way that his heart was just fine, the resident on call had had the good sense to phone Calgary and discovered that the patient they had been expecting was a ten-year-old white child named Timothy and not an eight-year-old Indian boy named Lionel.

The next day he was on a plane, his heart and tonsils intact, and by the time they got back to the reserve, Lionel's throat felt fine.

But that wasn't the end of it. Fourteen years later, when he applied for an insurance policy, Lionel discovered that while he had almost forgotten the incident, the original error had somehow worked its way into a file. The insurance company wanted him to have a physical with a separate evaluation of his heart condition.

"You know who you remind me of?" said Norma.

"Uncle Eli," said Lionel.

"You remind me of your uncle Eli."

Norma set the piece of green carpet on the dash next to the blue piece.

"He didn't believe in Indian doctors, either."

Lionel could feel his eyes curling up. He gripped the wheel harder and shook himself back and forth ever so slightly.

"Eli went to university, just like you. Only he graduated. With a Ph.D." Norma let the *D* rattle around in her mouth, as if she was clearing her throat. "Used to dress up, just like you. You know, Eli would polish his shoes so you could see the sky when you looked down."

Lionel stretched his face in an effort to keep his eyes open.

"Your uncle wanted to be a white man. Just like you."

Lionel could see the sun and he could see the road and he could see the steering wheel. Norma was talking to someone. He could hear her voice. It sounded very warm and very far away.

A year later, Lionel applied for a car loan, and when he went back to check with the loan manager, the man sat Lionel down, smiled, and asked him if he had had any more trouble with his heart.

Six months after that, he was turned down for a part-time job driving a school bus because of his health, and for years the Heart Foundation sent him letters about tax-deductible donations.

Three years ago, a woman from Calgary called to say that a group was forming to help heart patients in outlying towns such as Blossom and asked if Lionel would like to come to their first meeting in March and share his experience.

"A white man," said Norma, and she shook her head. "As if they were something special. As if there weren't enough of them in the world already."

WHERE DID ALL THE WATER COME FROM? says that GOD.
  "I'll bet you'd like a little dry land," says Coyote.
  What happened to my earth without form? says that GOD.
  "I know I sure would," says Coyote.
  What happened to my void? says that GOD. Where's my darkness?
  "Hmmmm," says Coyote. "Maybe I better apologize now."
  "You can apologize later," I says. "Pay attention."

Okay. There are two worlds, you know. One world is a Sky
World. One world is a Water World.

"Where do the Coyotes live?" says Coyote.
  "Forget the Coyotes," I says.

That Sky World has all sorts of things. Sky things. They got
Sky Moose. They got Sky Bear. They got Sky Elk. Sky Buffalo.

"And Sky Coyotes?" says Coyote.
  This is all wrong, says that GOD. Everybody knows there is
only one world.
  "Listen up," I says. "I only want to do this once."

                        .   .   .

In that Water World, they have all sorts of water things. Water Turtles. Water Ducks. Water Fish. Things like that.

So, in that Sky World is a woman. Big woman. Strong woman. First Woman.

First Woman walks around, says, straighten up, and she says, mind your relations, and she walks around that world with her head in the trees, looking off in the distances, looking for things that are bent and need fixing. So that one walks off the edge of the world.

So that one starts falling.

Oh, oh, First Woman says, looks like a new adventure. And she is right.

Down below in that Water World, those water animals look up and they see that big, strong woman falling out of the sky. Those Ducks shout, look out, look out. And they fly up and catch that woman and bring her to the water.

What's all that noise? says grandmother Turtle, and when grandmother comes up to see what all the fuss is about, those Ducks put First Woman on her back.

Ho, says grandmother Turtle when she sees that woman on her back. You are on my back.

That's right, says First Woman. I guess we better make some land. So they do. First Woman and grandmother Turtle. They get some mud and they put that mud on grandmother Turtle's back and pretty soon that mud starts to grow.

That's a pretty good trick, says Old Coyote, who comes floating by on that air mattress. Maybe I can help.

Straighten up, says First Woman.

Mind your relations, says grandmother Turtle.

So that mud gets big and beautiful all around.

That is beautiful, says Old Coyote, but what we really need is a garden.

Exactly, says that backward GOD.

"Look, look," says Coyote. "It's Old Coyote."

"Calm down," I says. "We got lots to do."

A garden is the last thing we need, says grandmother Turtle.

No, no, no, says Old Coyote. A garden is a good thing. Trust me.

Oh, oh, says First Woman. Looks like another adventure.

"So that's the way the story starts," I says. "That's the way it is beginning."

No, no, says that GOD. That's not the way it starts at all. It starts with a void. It starts with a garden.

"Stick around," I says. "That garden will be here soon."

Hallelujah, says that GOD.

"Is Old Coyote going to make that good garden?" says Coyote.

"Not likely," I says. "Can we continue?"

First Woman's garden. That good woman makes a garden and she lives there with Ahdamn. I don't know where he comes from. Things like that happen, you know.

So there is that garden. And there is First Woman and Ahdamn. And everything is perfect. And everything is beautiful. And everything is boring.

So First Woman goes walking around with her head in the clouds, looking in the sky for things that are bent and need fixing. So she doesn't see that tree. So that tree doesn't see her. So they bump into each other.

Pardon me, says that Tree, maybe you would like something to eat.

That would be nice, says First Woman, and all sorts of good things to eat fall out of that Tree. Apples fall out. Melons fall out. Bananas fall out. Hot dogs. Fry bread, corn, potatoes. Pizza. Extra-crispy fried chicken.

Thank you, says First Woman, and she picks up all that food and brings it back to Ahdamn.

Talking trees! Talking trees! says that GOD. What kind of a world is this?

"Did someone say food?" says Coyote.

"Sit down," I says. "Boy, this story is going to take a long time."

So that good woman brings all that food back to Ahdamn. Ahdamn is busy. He is naming everything.

You are a microwave oven, Ahdamn tells the Elk.

Nope, says that Elk. Try again.

You are a garage sale, Ahdamn tells the Bear.

We got to get you some glasses, says the Bear.

You are a telephone book, Ahdamn tells the Cedar Tree.

You're getting closer, says the Cedar Tree.

You are a cheeseburger, Ahdamn tells Old Coyote.

It must be time for lunch, says Old Coyote.

Never mind that, First Woman tells Ahdamn. Here is something to eat.

Wait a minute, says that GOD. That's my garden. That's my stuff.

"Don't talk to me," I says. "You better talk to First Woman."

You bet I will, says that GOD.

So. There is that garden. And there is First Woman and Ahdamn. And there are the animals and the plants and all their relations. And there is all that food.

"Boy," says Coyote, "that food certainly smells good."

They can't eat my stuff, says that GOD. And that one jumps into the garden.

Oh, oh, says First Woman when she sees that GOD land in her garden. Just when we were getting things organized.

WHEN ALBERTA GOT BACK TO HER OFFICE, there was a note on her door that said a Mr. Looking Bear had called and would call again at four. Alberta stood by the window and looked out at the grove of Russian olives banked against the coulees. She could feel the wind lean against the building, could see the yellow prairie grass rolling down the cutbanks. Off to the west, the chinook arch had raised its back like a cat stretching.

Alberta let the phone ring four times before she picked it up.

"Hey, Alberta. It's Charlie. We keep missing each other."

"Hi, Charlie."

"So, you're coming up this weekend."

"Charlie, you know I have to go home."

"You can go home next weekend. This is the long one. Catch the plane to Edmonton. Think of it as an adventure. Dinners, shows, shopping, you know."

Alberta knew. "Charlie, it all sounds nice, but it's Lionel's birthday, and I told him I would be there."

"Lionel? You're joking. I mean, he's a nice guy, but you're not serious about him, are you?"

"No," said Alberta, sitting on the edge of her desk and watching the light shift on the grass. "And I'm not serious about you, either."

"Hey, I'm all for that. So catch the plane. Tell Lionel you changed your mind. He'll understand."

"Maybe next month, Charlie."

"Okay, I'll come down."

"I told Lionel I'd have dinner with him."

"I'll fly down and we'll all have dinner with Lionel. We'll sing 'Happy Birthday,' and then you and I can drive back to Calgary."

Alberta laughed. "Charlie, you're really an ass sometimes. How would you like it if I brought Lionel along when I came to Edmonton?"

"You hardly ever come."

"I've been busy. I work, remember?"

"Hey, nothing personal, but you're not sleeping with John Wayne, are you?"

"God, Charlie."

"Seriously, Alberta. I know Lionel is a friend. Hell, he's my friend, too. He's more than a friend, he's family. But you can't be serious about him. I mean, he sells stereos and televisions for Buffalo Bill Bursum, and he's what . . . forty-six?"

"Thirty-nine. Forty tomorrow."

"Really?"

"Charlie!"

"Okay, nice is nice and Lionel is nice. He just never made it."

"You used to sell televisions and stereos at Bursum's, too."

"Yeah, and there's the difference. I used to sell that crap. But I don't anymore. I got out and made something of myself. Lionel's never going to get out. Hell, another couple of years and he'll be back on the reserve running for council. Besides, you know how I feel about you."

"It's one of the reasons I'm going to Blossom."

"Come on, Alberta."

"This is costing you a fortune, Charlie. Let's look at something next month."

There was a long pause on the phone. Alberta picked up a

pen and made herself a note to drop off her coat at the dry cleaners before she left town.

"Okay. If you want to watch a forty-five-year-old television salesman blow out his candles, go ahead."

"I'm glad I have your permission."

"I really like you."

"And so romantic."

The sky was deepening, slate gray and coral. The last thing in the world Alberta wanted was a three-hour drive. And right now, the next to the last thing she wanted was to spend a three-day weekend with Lionel or anyone else for that matter. What she really wanted was a large bowl of cream of mushroom soup, a hot bath, two pieces of cinnamon toast, and a good mystery.

Alberta liked having two men in her life, especially when they were both over two hundred kilometers away. And it was most enjoyable when they came to Calgary. Her city, her house, her terms. She was not happy chasing after them, suffering bathtubs ringed with hair and grit, and refrigerators organized around hamburger, frozen corn, white bread, french vanilla cookies, and beer. With prehistoric vegetables turning to petroleum in plastic sacks.

She especially hated watching the videos that Lionel and Charlie picked up for a romantic evening, videos where everyone shot at one another from moving cars. Once she had suggested that she'd like something without guns and cars, machines that exploded, or killer robots gone wild, and Lionel had come back from the store with *Rocky III*.

What she hated most were the cold, polished cotton sheets. No man she had ever known owned a single flannelette sheet, and it was only her false sense of pride that kept her from taking a set along when she went visiting. Charlie had satin sheets. If anything, they were colder than cotton, and they showed every drip and stain.

But having both Lionel and Charlie relieved her of the anxiety of a single relationship in which events were supposed to rumble along progressively, through well-defined stages. First dates, long talks, simple passion, necking, petting, sex, serious conversations, commitment, the brief stops along the line to marriage and beyond. Alberta had just gotten beyond sex with both men before derailing the social locomotive on a grassy shoulder of pleasant companionship and periodic intercourse. Some women would see two men as an embarrassment of riches. But Alberta knew that apart from no men in her life, two was the safest number.

When Charlie began talking commitment, Alberta phoned Lionel. When Lionel started hinting about spending more time together, Alberta would fly to Edmonton for two or three weekends in a row. Men wanted to be married. More than sex, Alberta was convinced, men wanted marriage. So far, she had been able to maintain the balance. The distance helped.

But there were complications. Complications that called for decisions, decisions Alberta did not want to make.

"YOU KNOW I CAN'T make that kind of decision on my own."
Dr. John Eliot smiled over the top of his glasses. The sun was
coming in through the window at Dr. Hovaugh's back, and
John had to squint to make out the shadow of the man behind
the desk. "Besides, they'll be back. They always come back.
Remember when they disappeared the last time?"

"Yellowstone," said Dr. Hovaugh.

"Joe . . . Joe, we've talked about this."

"It's in the book," said Dr. Hovaugh. "I didn't make it up.
The Indians disappeared on July eighteenth, 1988."

"Yes," said Eliot, "but that doesn't prove anything."

"By the end of the month, Yellowstone was in flames."

"Coincidence."

"Mount Saint Helens. They disappeared on May fifteenth,
1980, and on the eighteenth, Saint Helens explodes."

"Joe," said Eliot, "you've got to stop doing this."

Dr. Hovaugh thumbed through the book. "October twenty-
sixth, 1929. They disappeared in October of 1929. Do you see
what's happening?"

"Nothing's happening," said Eliot.

"Makes you wonder where they were in August of 1883."

"Eighteen eighty-three?"

"Krakatau," said Dr. Hovaugh. "August twenty-seventh, 1883."

John couldn't see Dr. Hovaugh's face, but he hoped that Joe was smiling. "A little compulsive, don't you think?" And John chuckled for his friend's benefit.

"What?"

"The dates. Knowing those dates. I mean, knowing them exactly."

"They're all in the book. Occurrences, probabilities, directions, deviations. You can look them up yourself."

John slid forward in the chair and tried to find his friend in the circle of bright light. "I can't sign the certificates."

"They're dead, John."

"I need bodies."

"Sign the certificates, John. You've been expecting them to die for years. You said yourself that they couldn't live much longer. Isn't that what you told me?"

John crossed one leg over the other. "I said they were old. Hell, Joe, both of us know that. And they should have died . . . a long time ago."

"If you believe the stories."

"If you believe the stories. But they haven't, and I can't sign a death certificate until they do die."

"They're dead," said Dr. Hovaugh. "I can feel it. All four of them. We just need the certificates. Heart attack, cancer, old age. I don't care. Be creative."

John uncrossed his legs. "Joe, what if they come back? This isn't the first time. It isn't even the second time."

"Thirty-seven times." Dr. Hovaugh held up the book. "Thirty-seven times that we know of."

John pushed the glasses back against his face. "I'm sorry, Joe. Show me four dead Indians, and I'll sign the certificates."

Dr. Hovaugh could feel the desk swelling, growing larger. "For Christ's sake, John. If I had four dead Indians, I'd give them to you."

It was the sound that startled Eliot, hard and quick like breaking ice. Dr. Hovaugh raised his hand as though he wanted to say something more. Both men waited in silence.

"Look, Joe . . . didn't the Indians disappear in 1969 and 1952?"

"That's right," said Dr. Hovaugh. "And 1971, 1973, 1932 . . ."

"Okay, okay," said Eliot. "And what were the disasters that were supposed to occur on those dates?"

"It's a pattern, John."

"Maybe there wasn't one," said Eliot. "You see what I mean? Maybe nothing happened on those dates. Or maybe something good happened on those dates. You ever think of that?"

Dr. Hovaugh looked across his desk and considered John. Eliot was talking, saying something about the Indians, but Dr. Hovaugh couldn't quite hear him. It was curious how they just disappeared like that. John didn't understand. That was it. He must think it was all a game. Hide-and-seek. Cowboys and Indians.

"It's just one of those mysteries, Joe." Eliot got to his feet. "I better go and see if the police have found anything. You going to be okay?"

So the Indians were gone again. Dr. Hovaugh watched John gesturing and smiling. He envied the man his easy manner in the face of disaster.

Eliot paused at the door. "What I can't understand is how they escape. And where do they go? Have you ever thought about that, Joe? And why, in God's name, would they want to leave?"

THE LONE RANGER LOOKED DOWN THE ROAD AGAIN. It ran out on a straight line and disappeared in the distance.

"Are we waiting for something?" said Ishmael.

"A ride," said the Lone Ranger.

"How long do we have to wait?" said Robinson Crusoe.

"Not long," said the Lone Ranger.

"Are you being omniscient again?" asked Hawkeye.

"I think so," said the Lone Ranger.

"I was afraid of that," said Robinson Crusoe.

"What else would you like to know?" said the Lone Ranger.

"WHAT ELSE WOULD YOU LIKE TO KNOW?" said Babo. The tape recorder was making squeaky noises, as though something deep in the mechanism was slipping.

Sergeant Cereno sighed and pushed his fingers into the sides of his nose. "This thing has happened before, hasn't it?"

Babo looked at Cereno. "You'd have to ask Dr. Hovaugh. He keeps track of those kinds of things."

"But you know a lot of things, too."

Babo shook her coffee cup. "You guys want some more coffee?"

"No, thanks."

"You sure?"

"I'm sure."

"You drink coffee?"

"Maybe you could tell us some of the things you know."

Babo swirled the remains of the oily brown coffee around in the cup. "I don't know much."

Sergeant Cereno closed his eyes and motioned to Jimmy. "Get Ms. Jones a cup of coffee. You like it black, Ms. Jones?"

Babo smiled. "When you put the money in and it starts up, make sure a cup drops down straight. Sometimes it drops crooked. Makes a big mess."

"You want it black, Ms. Jones?" asked Jimmy.

"Little cream, one sugar. Watch that cup! You know who has to clean up the messes around here. Don't be like that boy of mine."

Sergeant Cereno leaned back in the chair and slowly swung it from side to side. "All right, Ms. Jones. These four Indians . . . what did they look like?"

"Like I said. They were Indians. Old ones."

"How old would you say?"

"I don't know . . . four, five hundred years . . ."

Sergeant Cereno took his fingers out of his nose and made a long, hollow sound, like a horse blowing air.

"Course I don't know for sure," said Babo. "And it's kind of hard to tell, once you get past seventy or eighty."

"The Indians tell you that?"

"Nope," said Babo. "Heard Dr. Eliot and Dr. Hovaugh talking."

"No one is that old."

"I figure they're older." Babo pushed her lips forward. "Come on . . . How old do you think I am?"

"Tell me about the Indians."

"No, go ahead. You won't hurt my feelings."

"You're forty-six, Ms. Jones."

"Well, I'll be!"

"It's in your personnel file."

Babo scratched the side of her head and looked out the window. The Pinto was gone. "I'll bet you're . . . forty-two," she said, smiling at Sergeant Cereno.

Sergeant Cereno put his fingers back under his nose. "About the Indians."

"You got their files there, too?"

"Yes, I do."

"Was I close?"

"I'm thirty-six, Ms. Jones."

"No, I meant the Indians."

Sergeant Cereno ran his fingers alongside his nose, across his forehead, and into his hair. "Ms. Jones, we need to let me ask the questions."

"Thirty-six! Police work must be hard."

Jimmy arrived with two cups of coffee. "The machine worked fine," he said. "No problems with the cups. I spilled a bit on the floor, but I wiped it up. This okay?"

Babo took a sip. "Just right. You make good coffee."

"The Indians, Ms. Jones?"

"Well, they were old. All of them."

"Did you ever talk to them?"

"Sure. All the time."

"They were in the security wing, weren't they?"

"That's right. Don't know why, though. They were real nice."

Jimmy leaned against the wall and sipped the coffee. "I had a grandfather like that once," he said. "He was crazy but real nice, at least to me."

"They sure didn't seem crazy to me," said Babo.

"But they did escape," said Sergeant Cereno, "didn't they? You can see our concern."

"Well, you got me there." Babo caught a glint of something red in the lilacs at the far edge of the parking lot.

"Can you think of how they might have gotten out?" Sergeant Cereno continued.

"Nope."

"No idea? Someone could have forgotten to lock the door."

"Is that how they got out?"

"Someone could have helped them escape."

It was the Pinto. It was hung up in the bushes and leaning dangerously to one side.

Sergeant Cereno cleared his throat and opened the file in front of him. "Were you friends with . . ."—he squinted at the file and held it up to the light—"Mr. Red, Mr. White, Mr. Black, and Mr. Blue?"

"Who?" said Babo.

"The escapees."

Babo frowned and drank some of the coffee.

"What's wrong, Ms. Jones?"

"Nothing, I guess," said Babo. "Never heard of those names. We still talking about the Indians?"

"We're talking about the four Indians who escaped from this hospital at . . . Jimmy?"

"Yes, sir," said Jimmy, putting down his coffee and pulling out his book, "between four and six this A.M."

"The Indians in F Wing?"

"Jimmy?"

"Yes, sir. F Wing."

"What were those names, again?"

"Mr. Red, Mr. White, Mr. Black, and Mr. Blue."

Babo laughed and shook her head. Sergeant Cereno had stopped smiling. "I never heard of those guys," she said. "The Indians in F Wing had different names. Weren't any Reds or Whites or Blacks or Blues, or any other colors for that matter."

"I see."

"Hey, I'll bet you watch those cop shows. Am I right?"

"Ms. Jones, I'm sure you can see that this is a serious matter. What can you tell me about the escapees?"

"Well, they were old. No crime in that. They didn't hurt anyone. And they were women, not men."

"Women?"

"That's right. We used to talk, you know, life, kids, fixing the world. Stuff like that. We'd trade stories too, the Indians and me. That's what I could do, you know, tell you one of the stories they told me."

"Are you sure?"

"Sure, there was a great one, all about how things got started, about how the world was made . . ."

"No. Are you *sure* they were women? You must be mistaken."

"Pretty hard mistake to make. How about that story?"

"The files say the Indians were men."

"Suit yourself," said Babo.

Sergeant Cereno turned to Jimmy, who was making teeth marks on the Styrofoam cup. "That doctor show up yet?"

"Yes, sir. Secretary said he could see you in half an hour."

Cereno turned back to Babo. "Okay, Ms. Jones. Why don't you tell us what the Indians told you."

Babo finished the rest of her coffee. "Now you got to remember that this is their story. I'm just repeating it as a favor. You understand?"

Sergeant Cereno closed his eyes and nodded. "Go ahead, Ms. Jones."

"Sure," said Babo. "Just got to remember how to start."

"Start at the beginning."

"No, you don't understand. There's a way . . ."

The tape recorder made a whirling, squeaky sound, followed by a loud click. Sergeant Cereno looked over and held up a hand. "Just a moment, Ms. Jones."

Cereno stood up and walked to the door. "Jimmy," he said in a loud voice, "put in a new cassette and make sure you mark the old one. And take good care of Ms. Jones." Then Cereno leaned in, his back to Babo, his mouth close to Jimmy's cheek. "Enough of this dog and pony show," he said in a whisper. "I'm going to see the doctor." Cereno's voice was low and hard. "You finish up with Aunt Jemima."

"Take your time," said Babo. "Can't remember how to start the story anyway."

"YOU AWAKE?" Norma put out a hand and pushed at Lionel's ribs. "Maybe it's time for me to drive."

"I'm awake. I was just thinking."

"Thinking with your eyes shut up tight like that will land us in a ditch."

"I was just thinking."

"Had me fooled."

"Some people think when they sleep," said Lionel. "I think when I drive."

"Long as you know the difference," said Norma.

The second mistake Lionel made was going to Salt Lake City. He was in his second year at university and working for the Department of Indian Affairs at the time. Duncan Scott, Lionel's supervisor, was supposed to give a paper at a conference on Indian education, but couldn't go. So he asked Lionel if he would give the paper for him.

"It's already written, Lionel. All you got to do is read it."

"Sure."

"We'll pay all your expenses plus per diem."

"Sure."

The occupation of Wounded Knee was in its second month,

and when Lionel got to the room in the Hotel Utah where he was to give his talk on "The History of Cultural Pluralism in Canada's Boarding Schools," he found, not the twenty-five or thirty teachers and bureaucrats whom he had been told would be there, but a room jammed with Indians dressed in jeans and ribbon shirts. All the chairs were taken, and half the crowd was standing or leaning against the walls or sitting on the floor. Most everyone had a beaded leather headband.

Lionel felt out of place in his three-piece suit, but he hitched his pants, marched to the lectern with an authoritative swing to his arms, and began to talk about the history of boarding schools. He had hardly gotten through the opening joke when one of the women at the back of the room, a woman who surprisingly reminded him of his sister Latisha, stood up and shouted, "What does this crap have to do with our brothers and sisters at Wounded Knee?" And before Lionel could think up a good answer, several people pushed their way to the lectern and crowded him away from the microphone. He was left in a most awkward position, standing just to the left of the lectern with the paper in his hand. There was no place to sit and no easy path through the people on the floor to the door.

Norma put the pieces of carpet back in her purse. "What you need is a job."

"I've got a job."

"Selling them televisions is not a job for a grown man. Too bad about that government job."

"Wasn't my fault, auntie."

"Government pays good. You got free trips all over the place, too."

"Just bad luck."

"Look at your sister. She makes her own luck."

"What about George Morningstar?"

"That restaurant of hers is going to make her a rich woman."

"What about George Morningstar? He used to beat hell out of her."

"Nice to have a real Indian restaurant in town."

"She sells hamburger."

"People come from all over the world to eat at the Dead Dog Café."

"She sells hamburger and tells everyone that it's dog meat."

"Germany, Japan, Russia, Italy, Brazil, England, France, Toronto. Everybody comes to the Dead Dog."

"The Blackfoot didn't eat dog."

"It's for the tourists."

"In the old days, dogs guarded the camp. They made sure we were safe."

"Latisha has time to come out to the reserve and visit us, too. Always helps with the food for the Sun Dance. Helps out with other things, too."

"Traditional Blackfoot only ate things like elk and moose and buffalo. They didn't even eat fish."

"Music to my old ears to hear you talking traditional, nephew."

"They sure didn't eat dog."

"If you had a real job, maybe you would come out and visit us like Latisha and Alberta."

"The Dead Dog Café. Some of the elders might find that insulting all by itself."

"Maybe then you wouldn't be ashamed of us."

So he stood there, feeling vulnerable, as each speaker talked about the people at Wounded Knee and the FBI and the general condition of Native people in North America. Every so often someone would remind the crowd that this was their chance to stand up for the people. Lionel stood there for two hours, nodding his head occasionally, shifting from one leg to the other, putting his hands behind his back, putting his hands in front of him, pushing his lips out, sucking his lips in.

After the speeches, one of the men who had been at the lectern, a man about Lionel's age, turned and shook Lionel's hand and thanked him for his remarks and for his generosity in sharing the podium with the people. And he invited Lionel to a rally that was to take place at the state capital later in the day.

"It's going to be at the state capital near the statue of Massasoit."

"That's good."

"Massasoit was the Indian who greeted the Europeans at Plymouth Rock."

"I'm Canadian."

"Every Indian in Salt Lake is going to be there. We need your support."

"I'm from Blossom, Alberta."

"You got some other clothes?"

"I'm not sure I'll be able to make it. I have to fly back. I've got a reservation."

The man took Lionel by the shoulders, looked at him hard, and said, "Some of us don't."

There were more than sixty people at the statue when Lionel arrived. The man who had thanked him at the hotel was standing near the base of the statue with a bullhorn in his hand. A woman in a beaded jean jacket had just finished singing a song and was shouting something about donations. Lionel could see four other women moving through the crowd with a blanket between them. People threw dollar bills and loose change onto the blanket, and as it came nearer to where Lionel was standing, he reached into his pocket and realized that he had left his wallet in his suit jacket back at the hotel. As the women and the blanket passed, Lionel jammed his hands deeper into his pockets, smiled, and rocked back and forth on his heels. His black wing-tip shoes were covered with dust and the new jeans he had hurriedly bought at ZCMI felt embarrassingly stiff.

There were more songs, and some of the people held hands.

The man with the bullhorn and four other men went through the crowd, asking who had a car.

"You got a car, brother?"

"No," said Lionel. "I'm just visiting."

"You can ride with Cecil."

"I'm from Canada."

"Cecil is the guy with the horn. You see him? The green van over there is his."

Lionel was never quite sure how he wound up in Cecil's van, sitting on a large pillow in the back, stuffed between canned goods, rifles, and boxes of ammunition.

"Just throw the thirty-thirty on the mattress," Cecil told him. "I don't want the scope getting dinged."

Lionel must have known that the van and the six cars that were following close behind were headed to Wounded Knee, but he could not recall knowing. Still, all the details were there. Cecil was driving the van. Eddie was in the passenger seat. Billy and Rita were stretched out on the mattress in the back, and Lionel Red Dog, Canadian citizen, government employee, and status Blackfoot Indian, was sitting cross-legged among the groceries and the guns. There was a box of bumper stickers that said "American Indian Movement" and a margarine container half full of red buttons that just said "AIM."

"Put one on," said Eddie. "Red and proud!"

The police stopped the van just outside Green River. Lionel could remember the flashing lights and the loudspeaker telling them to get out of the van with their hands on their heads. Cecil told them all to stay put and wait for the television trucks, which were no more than five minutes behind the police. Everybody got out, but as Lionel stepped from the van into the bright Wyoming sun, he hooked a wing tip through the sling of one of the rifles and pitched forward into a policewoman who shouted, "He's got a gun," deftly stepped to one side, and hit Lionel across the head with something long and hard.

It took eleven stitches to close the wound. Lionel spent a day in the hospital, four days in jail until the police could verify his identity, and despite his pleas, another five days in jail for disturbing the peace. He called Duncan to tell him what had happened, how the whole thing was one very funny mistake.

Duncan was sympathetic and told Lionel not to worry about anything. Talking with Duncan made Lionel feel much better, and it was only after he hung up that he remembered that he was in Green River, Wyoming, and that he was broke. He went back to the phone and dialed the D.I.A. office in Blossom.

"It's a collect call."

"Your name?"

The operator told the secretary who answered that she had a collect call for Duncan Scott from Lionel Red Dog and would he accept the charge. The secretary put the operator on hold and came back a minute later to say that Mr. Scott had left the office for the day and wasn't expected back until the middle of next week. Lionel tried three more names, but the secretary said that they were out of the office too. The operator asked him if he would like to try back later. Even before he hung up the phone, Lionel realized that no one at the office was going to talk to him. Not today. Not tomorrow.

It was a long, hot walk from town to the highway, and Lionel had to stand there with his thumb out for over three hours before he caught a ride. The man was nice enough, but he was only going as far as Little America. The next ride got him just outside Lyman. The next dropped him off in downtown Evanston. It was the next day before he got out of Wyoming, and through a succession of starts and stops he arrived in Salt Lake City at two the next morning. Lionel walked the four miles from the gas station just off the highway to the Hotel Utah.

The man at the front desk was young and blond, and Lionel had to explain the situation to him twice.

"I was in room two forty-six."

"Are you checking out?"

"Not exactly. I need to get my clothes and my suitcase so I can pay the bill."

"Where are they?"

"In the room."

The young man smiled and looked at the computer. "We don't have a Lionel Red Dog in two forty-six."

"That's right. I was supposed to check out nine days ago."

"But you decided to stay."

"No, I was in Green River."

"You checked out and left your clothes and suitcase?"

"No," said Lionel, keeping up his good spirits, "I didn't check out. All I want to do is to get my clothes and suitcase and check back in."

"I see," said the blond man. "Why don't you give me a minute to look into this."

The lobby of the hotel was an inventory of draperies, columns, paintings, tapestries, and chandeliers. Lionel felt important sitting there in the wingback chair surrounded by blond men in blue uniforms with gold braid who moved effortlessly back and forth through the lobby bringing drinks, cleaning ashtrays, carrying luggage.

At the far end of the lobby, under the decorative pilasters, cornices, and coves, was a painting of the Battle of the Little Bighorn. George Armstrong Custer stood at the center of the drama, looking splendid in a fringed leather jacket, matching gloves, and black riding boots. He wore a broad-brimmed cavalry hat and carried shining guns in both hands, and even from where Lionel sat, he could see Custer's blue eyes flash while all around him Indians and soldiers swirled in a whirlpool of color and motion.

Lionel considered the painting for a time, remembering the convoy of police cars that had descended on the van. He was still shaken and embarrassed by the whole episode. Maybe that's how Custer had felt when he discovered his mistake. Embarrassed.

Sitting there, Lionel realized he was hungry. Once he got back in the hotel room, he decided, he'd call up room service and treat himself to a large steak with a baked potato, some vegetables, a thermos of coffee, and something chocolate for dessert. And after that, a long, hot bath.

"Maybe you should run for council," said Norma. "Try to do some good."

"I don't want to run for council."

"Charlie's father ran for council and he was famous."

"Charlie's father was in a few movies. He wasn't famous."

"If you ran for council, you'd be on the reserve and you could see your parents before they die."

"I see them all the time."

"They don't have that many more years left. Your father just set up his lodge at the Sun Dance. Said he hoped he would see you there this year."

"I see them all the time."

"Course I'm not sure I'd vote for you." Norma cleared her throat and looked at Lionel. "You know who you remind me of?"

"Not again."

"Your uncle Eli. He went to Toronto. He taught university there. Did I ever tell you that?"

"Hundred times at least."

"Married a white woman. Brought her out to the Sun Dance one year. Should have seen him."

"White shirt and slacks and fancy shoes."

"White shirt and slacks and fancy shoes."

"And now he's a hero."

"And now he's a hero," said Norma.

Lionel yawned. "He can't hold that dam back forever."

"Ten years, nephew," said Norma, "and he's still there. Coming to the Sun Dance is what did it. Straightened him right out and he came home."

"He went back to Toronto. He went back to Toronto after the Sun Dance. He came home after Granny died. That's all that happened. And he came home then because he had retired."

"He came home, nephew. That's the important part. He came home."

Lionel was just getting really comfortable in the chair when two large men in tight suits came over and introduced themselves.

"I'm Tom, and this is Gerry."

"We're with the hotel."

Lionel told Tom and Gerry what had happened and then he told the story again to the two policemen who drove him to the Salt Lake City jail.

"It was all sort of an adventure," said Lionel.

"Nothing to worry about," said Chip. "Everything'll get straightened out in the morning."

"Things like this happen all the time," said Dale.

At the arraignment, Lionel went through the whole story once again. The judge ordered the hotel to return Lionel's clothes, and Lionel paid the outstanding bill with the traveler's checks in his jacket. The hotel manager apologized for any inconvenience and hoped that Lionel would visit them again in the future. The judge gave Lionel thirty days for leaving town without paying the bill.

"Seeing as you're Canadian, I'll reduce it to ten days," the judge told him. "If it was your first offense, I could let you off with probation."

"It *is* my first offense."

"That's not what Wyoming says."

One day less than a month after he left for Salt Lake, Lionel was back in Blossom, an unemployed ex-con. He explained everything to Duncan.

"It was all a big mistake."

"My hands are tied, Lionel."

"If you had been there, you would have laughed."

"You're probably right."

The new Woodwards store in the mall was hiring. Lionel didn't mention the incident in Wyoming and he got a part-time job as a salesclerk. Three weeks later, the police arrived to question him about a rally that the American Indian Movement had planned for the following weekend.

"I don't know anything."

"Is that what you told them in Green River?"

"That was a mistake."

"Always a mistake to get caught."

"I don't know a thing about AIM."

"Report we saw says you were one of the leaders."

The police talked to him for over an hour, and by the time they left, Lionel was unemployed again.

"You look like a smart fellow," one of the officers told him. "Get your life together. With your record, you're running out of options."

THERE WAS THE MATTER OF CHILDREN. Alberta wanted at least one, perhaps two. And, as she saw it, she had several options.

Option one was to ignore her anxieties and good sense, swallow her fears, and marry Lionel or Charlie.

Option one was obscene.

Option two was to sit down with Lionel and/or Charlie, explain to them her desire to have children, and see if either would be willing to help, without seeing their role as anything more than a considerate donor. Of course, she told herself, she could manage option two *without* the excruciating heart-to-heart talk. She could simply forget her diaphragm. Or she could neglect to put it in. Option two was inviting but fraught with pits and traps. Both men would want to know who the father was, a sort of masculine muscle-flexing contest. And she knew herself well enough to know that she would have trouble lying about something like that. As soon as Alberta said the name, the winner would insist that he marry her on the spot and the loser would disappear. There she would be with one man instead of two and back to the first option.

Option three was to get dressed up and go to one of the better bars in town, pick out a decent-looking man, and use him as a willing but uninformed father. Option three, Alberta reasoned, should be the answer to her dilemma. But even putting the question of disease to one side, she found just the thought of crawling into bed with a strange man paralyzing. Where would they go? Certainly not to her house. What would he expect her to do? Would he be content simply crawling around under the covers or would he expect something more elaborate and spirited? What would she say to him after they had finished? Would he want her phone number? Would he want to see her again?

What if he offered to use a condom?

And worst of all, how many times would she have to do it? She knew of married friends who had been trying for years to have children.

Still, option three was the lesser of two evils, and when she turned it over in her mind, the merits seemed to outweigh the problems. So five months ago, fourteen days into her cycle, Alberta got dressed and caught a cab to the Shagganappi, an upscale lounge in the financial district. She put on her good green silk dress. High heels, nylons, perfume, lipstick, gold bracelets, eye shadow. The cab dropped her off across the street. Through the bank of windows she could see the people leaning over the tables in their fine clothes, and she imagined herself floating among the ferns and the brass fixtures, smiling, laughing, touching.

It was cold on the street, yet Alberta felt as though her whole body were on fire. As she waited for the light to change, she caught her reflection in the glass building behind her. She was surprised at how good she looked. Dark, sleek, luxuriant hair, thin ankles, good legs, nice smile. It would be all right.

The night sky was cobalt and black. The lights of the city were amber and warm. She turned back to the corner and waited as the light changed to green. It changed to yellow and then to red and back to green again. When the light got to green for the third time, Alberta crossed the street and hailed a taxi.

She cried for a long time that night in her bed, and in the morning, for all her trouble, she was back to option one.

"BOY," says Coyote, "that silly dream has everything mixed up."

"That's what happens when you don't pay attention to what you're doing," I says.

"It's not my fault," says Coyote. "I believe I was in Toronto."

So that GOD jumps into that garden and that GOD runs around yelling, Bad business! Bad business! That's what he yells.

You got to put all that stuff back, that GOD tells First Woman.

Who are you? says First Woman.

I'm GOD, says GOD. And I am almost as good as Coyote.

Funny, says First Woman. You remind me of a dog.

And just so we keep things straight, says that GOD, this is my world and this is my garden.

Your garden, says First Woman. You must be dreaming. And that one takes a big bite of one of those nice red apples.

Don't eat my nice red apples, says that GOD.

I'll just have a little of this chicken, if I may, says Old Coyote.

Your apples! says First Woman, and she gives a nice red apple to Ahdamn.

Yes, says that GOD, and that one waves his hands around. All this stuff is mine. I made it.

News to me, says First Woman. But there's plenty of good stuff here. We can share it. You want some fried chicken?

"Fried chicken!" says Coyote. "That certainly looks delicious."
"Never mind the chicken," I says. "We got to see what happens."

What bad manners, says First Woman. You are acting as if you have no relations. Here, have some pizza.

First Woman and Ahdamn eat those apples and that pizza and that fry bread. Old Coyote eats those hot dogs and the melon and the corn. That GOD fellow doesn't eat anything. He stands in the garden with his hands on his hips, so everybody can see he is angry.

Anybody who eats my stuff is going to be very sorry, says that GOD. There are rules, you know.

I didn't eat anything, says Old Coyote.

Christian rules.

I was just looking around.

Is that chicken I see hanging out of your mouth? says that GOD.

No, no, says Old Coyote. It must be my tongue. Sometimes it looks like chicken.

What a stingy person, says First Woman, and that one packs her bags. Lots of nice places to live, she says to Ahdamn. No point in having a grouchy GOD for a neighbor.

And First Woman and Ahdamn leave the garden.

All the animals leave the garden.

Maybe I'll leave a little later, says Old Coyote.

You can't leave my garden, that GOD says to First Woman. You can't leave because I'm kicking you out.

But First Woman doesn't hear him. She and Ahdamn move west. They go looking around for a new home.

"Maybe I should stay in the garden with Old Coyote," says Coyote. "Somebody should keep that GOD and Old Coyote and all that food company."

"We can eat later," I says. "Right now, we got to catch up with First Woman and Ahdamn."

So First Woman and Ahdamn go west and they look all over and pretty soon they find a really nice canyon and at the bottom of the canyon are a bunch of dead rangers.

Oh, oh, says First Woman to Ahdamn. Here we go again.

And she is right. There is that canyon. And there are those dead rangers.

What are we going to do with all these dead rangers? says Ahdamn.

Better yet, says First Woman, what are we going to do with all those live rangers?

What live rangers? says Ahdamn.

First Woman is right. Pretty quick a big bunch of live rangers ride into the canyon. All of those live rangers have guns.

Yes, says those live rangers. We are live rangers, and we have guns.

Now what are we going to do? says Ahdamn. Maybe we should have stayed in the garden.

So, those rangers ride up, and those rangers look all around. They look at the canyon. They look at the dead rangers. They look at First Woman. They look at Ahdamn.

Say, they says, Who killed these dead rangers? Who killed our friends?

Beats me, says First Woman. Maybe it was Coyote.

"Ah, excuse me," says Coyote. "I was asleep at the time."

"What time was that?" I says.

"When were the rangers killed?" says Coyote.

It looks like the work of Indians, says those live rangers. Yes, they all say together. It looks just like the work of Indians. And those rangers look at First Woman and Ahdamn.

Definitely Indians, says one of the rangers, and the live rangers point their guns at First Woman and Ahdamn.

Just a minute, says First Woman, and that one takes some black cloth out of her purse. She cuts some holes in that black cloth. She puts that black cloth around her head.

Look, look, all the live rangers says, and they point their fingers at First Woman. It's the Lone Ranger. Yes, they says, it is the Lone Ranger.

That's me, says First Woman.

Hooray, says those rangers, you are alive.

That's me, says First Woman.

Boy, says one of the live rangers, that's good news. I'll just shoot this Indian for you.

No, no, says First Woman. That's my Indian friend. He helped save me from the rangers.

You mean the Indians, don't you? says those rangers.

That's right, says First Woman with the mask on. His name is Tonto.

That's a stupid name, says those rangers. Maybe we should call him Little Beaver or Chingachgook or Blue Duck.

No, says First Woman, his name is Tonto.

Yes, says Ahdamn, who is holding his knees from banging together, my name is Tonto.

Okay, says those rangers, but don't say we didn't try to help. And they gallop off, looking for Indians and buffalo and poor people and other good things to kill.

"What happened to that GOD?" says Coyote.

"He's still in the garden," I says.

"He's missing all the fun," says Coyote.

"That's the truth," I says.

Boy, says First Woman, that was close. And she takes off the mask.

Yes, says Ahdamn. But who is Tonto?

Just then, some soldiers come along, and before First Woman can put on her ranger mask, those soldiers grab First Woman and Ahdamn.

You are under arrest, says those soldiers.

What's the charge, says First Woman.

Being Indian, says those soldiers.

Not another adventure, says Ahdamn.

Yes, says First Woman, and it looks like a very nice day for one, too.

THE TROUBLE HAD STARTED IN THE SPRING, seven years before. There had been a blight and all the elm trees in the garden had died. Even the huge oak that stood at the center of the grounds had been affected. Several large branches had turned gray, and though the tree was still alive, the leaves were sparse and dull.

It had grieved Dr. Hovaugh to watch the men in yellow uniforms with their silver and purple chain saws slice each of the elms into short, round blocks and cart them away. The branches were fed into a square leaf green machine and ground into sawdust. It made a terrible wailing noise. The stumps were ripped out of the ground, and in two days you could hardly tell that the elms had ever been there. New trees, thin and fragile, were brought in to complete the illusion, but the death of the old trees, which were almost as old as the garden itself, left Dr. Hovaugh burdened with inexplicable remorse and guilt.

"Dr. Hovaugh, Sergeant Cereno is here to see you."

Dr. Hovaugh pressed the button on the intercom and braced himself behind the desk, hooking his feet under the crossbar. "All right, Mary." He placed his hands on the desk, folded his fingers together, consciously willed his shoulders to drop. "Show him in."

Sergeant Cereno was wearing a green polyester suit. It was the first thing that Dr. Hovaugh noticed about him. Dr. Hovaugh couldn't recall ever seeing one quite so green. It reminded him of outdoor carpet.

"Dr. Hovaugh, I'm Sergeant Cereno." And Sergeant Cereno opened a leather case that had a badge inside and placed it on the desk. "I'll be handling the investigation."

Dr. Hovaugh motioned Cereno into a chair, looked at the badge, nodded, and pushed it back toward Cereno. He pushed it too far, and it slithered over the edge. But Sergeant Cereno reacted with surprising quickness, uncrossing a leg, lurching forward, and catching the badge before it hit the floor.

"I'm terribly sorry."

"Not at all," said Sergeant Cereno, and he flipped the case shut. "I know you're busy."

Dr. Hovaugh extended his hands, palms up. "How may I help you?"

Sergeant Cereno pulled his coat open and took a pen from his pocket. As he did, Dr. Hovaugh saw the handle of a gun. "I see you carry a gun, sergeant."

"We have to carry them," said Cereno. "It's the rules. Don't let it bother you. I don't like them myself, but there you are."

"I suppose there is a certain amount of danger in your work."

"It's a Smith and Wesson," said Sergeant Cereno. "Thirty-eight caliber. It's not your standard issue." Cereno pulled the gun from its holster and held it against the light.

"I'm sure it's very nice."

"It's just a tool. I load my own ammunition. You can't be too careful."

"Of course, we don't see many guns in the hospital. My father had a gun. Actually it was a rifle. It was black, I think. Yours is so shiny."

"Stainless steel."

Sergeant Cereno was still looking at the gun. The handle was rather large, more a club, Dr. Hovaugh thought, and there was a bright red dot on the front sight. He wondered how it felt to have such a thing tucked under your arm. He wondered how Cereno would describe the sensation.

Sergeant Cereno put the gun back in its holster. "Are they dangerous?"

"The Indians? I don't think so."

"But there might be some danger?"

"These are very old men, patrolman."

"Women," said Sergeant Cereno. "And it's sergeant."

"Sorry," said Dr. Hovaugh. "What's this about women?"

"Ms. Jones said that the Indians are women."

"Who?"

"The Indians."

"No, no . . . Ms. . . . ?"

Sergeant Cereno crossed his left leg and flipped a page in his notebook. "Ms. Jones."

"Ah . . . yes . . ." said Dr. Hovaugh. "Secretary?"

"Janitor."

"Ah . . . yes . . . janitor."

Sergeant Cereno uncrossed his left leg and crossed his right leg. "So they're not women?"

"We hardly ever make that mistake."

Sergeant Cereno uncrossed both legs. The leisure suit crackled and shimmered. "What were they being treated for?"

Dr. Hovaugh winced. "Well, now, that is a little complicated."

"Are they senile?"

"It would be difficult to discuss the specific prognosis in lay terms. I suppose I should say at the start—"

"Are they women?"

". . . that many of the problems we face are those created by the divisions in the medical sciences and the social sciences, particularly in the—"

"Are they dangerous?"

". . . areas of gerontology and cultural anthropology and the lack of—"

"And they just walked away from the hospital?"

". . . any substantive crossover research . . ."

Sergeant Cereno raised his head from his notebook. There was a light wet sheen on the doctor's face. Sergeant Cereno scribbled something in his notebook. "So, what exactly were they being treated for?"

"Depression," said Dr. Hovaugh.

"Are they sociopaths?"

"Good heavens, no."

"But you said they might be dangerous."

"Did I?"

Cereno leafed back through the notebook. "Question: Are they dangerous? Answer: The Indians?"

Dr. Hovaugh pushed down on the desk. "I see."

"So, they could be dangerous."

"Anything is possible." Dr. Hovaugh swiveled back and forth in his chair. "The escape *is* a mystery. The door is always locked and there's that heavy mesh on the windows."

"The door is always locked?"

"Yes . . . Well, most of the time."

"But always at night?"

"Oh, yes," said Dr. Hovaugh. "Always at night."

Sergeant Cereno leaned forward in the chair and stared at Dr. Hovaugh without blinking. He stayed like that, staring, until Dr. Hovaugh had to turn away. "Why do you lock the door?" he said finally.

"What do you mean?"

"If these Indians aren't dangerous, why do you lock the door?"

The desk swelled slightly. Dr. Hovaugh pressed down hard with his hands and feet. His eyes felt surprisingly heavy. "I'm afraid, sergeant, you'll have to talk with the government about that."

"State or federal?"

"Federal. As I'm sure you know, Indians come under their jurisdiction. We simply provide the services they need."

"The government?"

"The Indians."

"Ah."

"The lock was their idea."

"The government?"

Dr. Hovaugh closed his eyes for a moment and felt his body begin to relax. He could picture the desk he wanted—black slate and brass, thin and sleek. A desk with drawers that opened and closed regardless of the weather.

"Yes," said Dr. Hovaugh, trying to think of something else to say. "Yes."

"Yes?" said the Lone Ranger.

"What I would like to know," said Ishmael, "is when we are going to eat."

"Yes," said Robinson Crusoe. "I am very hungry."

"It would be nice to have a warm meal and a nap," said Hawkeye.

"Oh, yes," said Ishmael. "A nap is a very good idea."

The Lone Ranger nodded and got down on his knees. He put his ear to the asphalt and listened. "Stay awake," he said. "Our adventure is about to begin."

"LIONEL! LIONEL! STAY AWAKE! You think any harder, you'll be snoring. You better let me drive."

Lionel blinked. The car was straddling the yellow line. "I'm okay," he said. "Wind is blowing pretty hard. Steering's tricky."

Norma snorted. "Want to get back to the reserve in the same condition I left. I got other nieces and nephews besides you."

Lionel opened his eyes wide and blinked them several times. "Boy, if it weren't for the clouds," he said, "you could see all the way to the mountains."

"You could see the mountains real good if you came out to the reserve once in a while."

"I can see the mountains from Blossom."

"You could see your parents, too."

"I see them all the time."

Norma folded her arms across her chest. "Sad thing for a son to be ashamed of his parents."

"I was out there two or three weeks ago."

"Parents know these things, Lionel. Waste of breath to lie. Alberta gets out regular."

"She works at the university. She has more free time."

"Latisha comes out regular, too. Nothing to do with time, nephew. Has to do with pride."

{ 79 }

"What about Charlie? You never see Charlie on the reserve anymore."

"Listen, nephew, maybe you should talk with Eli or your father, get yourself straightened out."

"You should stop by the store and see the display that Bill and I built."

"Alberta's not going to wait forever, you know. And she's not going to marry a city Indian who sells appliances."

"It takes up an entire wall."

"Eli wanted to be a white man, but he got over it."

The third mistake Lionel made was taking the job at Bill Bursum's Home Entertainment Barn. Bursum owned the largest television and stereo store in Blossom, and he had the best selection of movies in the area. Lionel was returning a video when Bill caught him.

"Hey, Lionel. How you doing? I heard about the job. Bad break. Government's got no sense of humor."

"Way things go, I guess."

"Hey, how could you have known the van was stolen."

"It wasn't stolen."

"Some people get more than their fair share of bad luck. You got plans?"

"Go back to school, I think."

"School's expensive. You got money saved up?"

"The band will probably help me out."

"That's right, you guys get all that free money. Hey, you know Charlie Looking Back, don't you?"

"Looking Bear. Sure, Charlie's my cousin."

"That's right. All you guys are related."

"Doesn't Charlie work for you?"

"Used to. Good man. Brought in a lot of business from the reserve. But he left. Went to Edmonton. I'm looking for someone to replace him."

"I'll probably go back to school."

Bill unbuttoned his gold jacket and leaned on the counter. "You know, in a good year Charlie would make thirty-five, forty thousand dollars. You ask him next time you see him. Damn good opportunity for the right Indian."

"Sure."

"I think I've got a gold jacket that'll fit you."

"Probably go back to school."

"Hey, school's the way to go, all right."

That evening Lionel went out to the reserve. His mother was trying out a new recipe from the Italian cookbook his father had given her at Christmas. "It's Tortino de Carciofi with Ribollita," his mother told him as he came in the door.

"What is it?"

"Vegetable soup and an artichoke omelet."

"Where'd you get the artichokes?"

"I had to substitute."

"So, what's in it now?"

"Elk."

Even Lionel had to admit it was tasty. Not exactly Italian, but tasty.

"I'm thinking about going back to university."

"Good idea," said his father. "Maybe you want to give me a hand this weekend."

"You know if the band has any money for school?"

"Going to go to the mountains and cut some new poles."

"Bill Bursum offered me a job at his store."

"The old ones are pretty shot."

"Televisions and stereos. Pretty easy to sell."

"Sun Dance is coming up. Got to get the poles fixed up before then."

"Charlie used to work for him. Made forty, fifty thousand last year."

"Take part of a day. That's all."

"I told Bill I was probably going to school."

Lionel's father settled back in his chair and finished his

coffee. "Some of our young people are getting jobs with that university degree, I hear. Alberta just got a teaching job in Calgary."

"But I figured that it wouldn't hurt to work for a while."

"Course, Everett James and Maggie Plume and Jason Whiteman got university degrees, too. But they don't have jobs."

"You know, get some money ahead."

"Jason says that no matter what your education, whites don't want to hire Indians unless the government makes them."

"Make some firm plans."

"But that doesn't sound like the government, does it? Making whites hire Indians."

"You and Mom should come down and see the store."

"Sure, son," said Harley. "But me and your mother don't need a new television right now."

Lionel called the band office the next morning, and Morris told him that all the money for the current year had been given out.

"Lots of kids going to school, Lionel. Not like the old days."

That afternoon, he called Bill. The money wasn't as good as Bill had said, but it was enough to allow Lionel to get some new clothes and a couple of credit cards. The next year came and went. So did the next one. Each year, Lionel swore he was going to get back to university, and each year he put off the application until it was too late.

"If you're going to go," his father told him, "you probably better get going."

"No real rush. Get some of the bills paid off first."

"Maybe they got an age limit at that university."

"I'm only thirty-two. Don't plan to sell televisions the rest of my life."

"When your grandfather was thirty-two," his father said, "he was dead."

Lionel had almost stopped promising himself that next year would be the year when Charlie Looking Bear walked into the store one evening. Bill came out of his office and threw an arm around Charlie. "Lionel," he shouted, "look who's here."

"Hey, cousin," said Charlie, "how you doing? Buffalo Bill treating you right?"

"Can't complain. Haven't seen you for a while."

"Just signed on with Duplessis International Associates. Got an office overlooking the river."

"Charlie's into the big bucks," said Bill. "You ought to sell him that new twenty-eight-inch set for his penthouse."

"Next time you're in Edmonton, cousin, I'll take you to lunch."

"Hey, I'll bet you get all that easy Indian business," said Bill. "Listen, you guys go ahead and catch up. Show him that new stereo system with the remote."

Charlie looked around the store. "Place hasn't changed much. How long you been here now?"

"Not long."

"Thought you were going back to school."

"Next year."

"Hey, if I can do it, so can you. Look at me. You believe it? Come on outside. I got something to show you."

It was a red Porsche. The license said "L Bear."

"What do you think?"

"Porsche is a good car."

"The best. It flies down the highway. You know what? They threw in a radar detector." Charlie slid in behind the wheel and put the key in the ignition. "Listen to this."

"Sounds great." Lionel squatted by the side of the car.

Charlie shook his head. "Bill's an asshole, and the job is shit. You can do better."

"It's just temporary until I pay off some bills."

"Smart move, John Wayne." Charlie put on his driving gloves and turned on the headlights. "Mind the paint."

Lionel watched Charlie spin the car around and roar off down the street. Lionel watched him go, watched his taillights flash, disappearing into the dark. The night was alive with stars, and as Lionel looked west, he imagined he could see the outline of the Rockies reflected in the ocean of sky.

Lionel sighed.

Inside, through the plate glass windows, past the video posters and the clearance sale banners, he could see Bill, all smiles in his gold jacket, talking to a young couple and patting the new Panasonic.

Outside, the night air was cold, but standing there, looking back at the store, Lionel felt exhilarated, intoxicated. For a long time, he stood there in the dark, smiling and swaying until the edges of his ears began to burn and he started to shiver. And as he came back through the darkness and into the light, he caught a glimpse of his own reflection in the glass.

ALBERTA LIKED TO DRIVE. She liked to drive her own car, and she liked to drive alone. She didn't like the idea of a trip, but once she was on her way, once the lights of the city were behind her and the road narrowed into the night, a feeling of calm always came over her, and the world outside the car disappeared. She rarely flew, hated planes, in fact. In a plane, she was helpless, reduced to carrying on an inane conversation with a total stranger or to reading a book while she listened for the telltale vibration in the engine's pitch or the first groan of the wing coming away from the fuselage. And all the time, that faceless, nameless man sat in the nose of the plane, smiling, drinking coffee, telling stories, completely oblivious to impending disasters. Marriage was like that.

Alberta had made the mistake of getting married young. She knew that. But there were those driving expectations that hemmed her in and herded her toward the same cliffs over which her mother, her brothers, sisters, cousins, and friends had disappeared.

And of course there was Bob. Handsome and witty. They met at university. She had resisted at first, delighted with the attention, but fearful even then of being lost in someone else.

Bob teased her, said that their relationship was a slow burn, like igniting a peach. Alberta was sure Bob hadn't thought that up, but she liked it. It was clever, and the idea of a soft, fuzzy peach, full of juice and sparkling flesh all aglow in flames, was intellectually erotic.

They were married that same year. There was love, good times, wonderful and consuming passion, and at the edge of her hearing, the slight change of pitch, the gentle tearing barely audible over the hiss of the flames.

Bob wanted her to finish her degree. It was the way he started when he wanted to explain to her why she didn't need to finish it right away. Why didn't she wait on her degree and help put him through? Sociology was a good investment. She could go back later, when the children were older, after Bob had established himself in a good government position.

It was, to Alberta's mind, a ridiculous request. Bob just wasn't looking at it properly. And she said no. Bob kept on smiling and talking. They should move into a larger apartment, he said. They should buy a car, too.

"We don't have the money for those things."

"One of us could get a job."

"But we don't need them."

"Nobody needs those things. But everyone wants them. You want them. I want them. You don't want to spend the rest of your life in a tepee, do you?"

Bob meant it as a joke, and Alberta tried to laugh.

"I don't want to drop out of school. Why don't you go to work and put me through? Then you can go back and finish."

"And who's going to have the children?"

"The children can wait."

The following year they were divorced, and the only apparent casualty was the semester Alberta missed trying to convince Bob that there wasn't another man.

After it was over, Alberta tried to remember the long, intimate conversations that they had had before they were married, conversations about their dreams and expectations. But she couldn't remember ever saying or even hinting that she wanted to stay at home, and she didn't think she had ever suggested that she would be willing to put him through university. And children at twenty-one? Where in the world had he got such an absurd idea?

Whenever Alberta went on a long drive alone, her marriage, its demise, and the aftermath were the first things she worked out. And she always came to the same conclusions. Bob wanted a wife; he did not want a woman. All of this was confirmed the year she graduated and Bob married a second-year history major who promptly dropped out of university and went to work for one of the large oil companies.

Just before she left graduate school, Alberta met Bob for coffee. They talked about the good old days, the fun they had had, and the plans he and Nancy (was that her name?) were making. He chattered on about their new apartment and how Nancy was anxious to start a family. The conversation hurt, but sitting there talking with Bob, she had never felt so free.

Alberta opened a bag of potato chips on the seat beside her. Calgary disappeared behind her, and the road ahead rolled out onto the prairies. The stars were everywhere and they reminded her, once again, of the last night her father came home.

There was no moon the night Amos slid his pickup down the reserve roads and drove into the outhouse. Alberta remembered the sound of the crash and the boards snapping and the tires spinning in the mud and the snow. Her mother went to the door and stood on the porch and looked out, but it was too dark to see much. Alberta and the rest of the kids gathered at the windows and in the doorway. The light from the house shone on her mother's back, and Alberta could see her mother's shoulders bunch and her fists clench.

Then the cursing began and the smashing and the laughter, high-pitched and wild.

"He's just got bad times," her mother said. "You kids go on to bed."

But nobody moved. Alberta stood in the doorway behind her mother and listened as Amos called out to them from the darkness.

"Daarlink," he shouted. "I'm stuck in the shit, Ada. God, I'm in the shit again." There was more laughter and smashing. "They're right behind me, Ada. You better come quick if you want to take a crap. You better come quick, 'cause it's coming down. God damn it, yes, it's coming down."

Alberta's mother didn't move. She stood on the porch in the yellow light, blocking the entrance to the house.

"I can see you, Ada. I can see your ugly cow face. Get out here and help me!"

The smashing stopped, and there was no sound at all.

"Go to bed, you kids. Nothing to see here. It's just your father had too much to drink. He's just fooling around. Go to bed. He don't want you should see him like this."

It was then that Amos appeared out of the black, just on the edge of the light. There was a bottle in his hand, and he was naked from the waist down, his shirttails hanging on his bare thighs, his jacket pulled off his shoulders. His underpants and his trousers were bunched down around his ankles, and he moved forward like a horse hobbled, dragging his pants in the snow.

"Ada," he called out. "You still mad at me, honey? Am I in the shiiiit again?" And he laughed. "'Cause there ain't no shit house, anymoooore. Nothing but a hole. A shit hole. You hear me?"

He was fully in the light now, swaying, struggling, as if his pants were hooked on something. "Can you hear them? Can you hear them, Ada?"

Amos stopped and tried to shield his eyes from the light. "You hear me calling? You hear me calling you?"

"I hear you," Alberta's mother called out.

"I'm drunk, Ada."

"Whole world knows that."

"I can't piss. I tried, but I can't do it."

"You're just drunk."

"No. It won't work. I can't walk, either."

"Pull up your pants."

Amos looked down at the ground. "My pants are full of shit!" he shouted. "Come out here and help me, you old cow. Help me. Give us a kiss, daaarlink!"

Alberta's mother stepped back into the doorway and set her feet.

"God damn cow! Come here! Come here and help me!"

Alberta saw her father stagger forward, and the bottle came flying out of the dark and smashed against the side of the house. It must have been then that he saw the children at the windows, for Alberta remembered him stopping, and he shouted even louder, his voice beginning to crack.

"They're right behind me, Ada." And he sat down in the snow. His jacket fell further off his shoulders, trapping his arms at his sides. "I can't stop them." He tried to stand but pitched forward onto his face, lay there not moving, as if he had been shot.

Alberta's mother watched him, and then she came back into the house, shut the door, and threw the bolt. "Go to bed now," she said. "All of you. Everything's okay."

"What about Dad? He'll freeze out there."

Alberta's mother took off her apron and sat down on the sofa. She didn't say a word. She just sat there, her hands in her lap, her eyes fixed on the wood stove. Finally she stood up and put on her heavy wool sweater. "Alberta," she said, "you and Grace and Sonny help me get him. The rest of you, go to bed."

Amos was lying in the snow, unconscious. Alberta's mother rolled him over and pulled his underpants up. She grabbed him under one arm, and Alberta and Grace took the other. Sonny got the feet, and they dragged him onto the porch.

"Leave him be," said their mother. "Throw that old blanket over him, and leave him be."

In the morning, before the sun was up, Alberta went outside. The blanket was folded and waiting on the wood table. The pickup was sitting in a small lake where the outhouse used to be, the water above the wheels and the doors. The air was clear, and Alberta could see all the way to the mountains and across the prairies until the land outran itself.

When Alberta got to Claresholm, she stopped for gas. Her back was sore and she found herself wishing she had stayed in Calgary. Men. In the end, Charlie and Lionel weren't much different from Bob and Amos. They all demanded something, insisted on privileges, special favors.

Amos never came back. The pickup sat there in the water for years, slowly rusting and sinking into the depths. Her mother never said a word about the truck or the lake, never seemed to wonder where he had gone to or where the water had come from.

"THERE WAS JUST WATER," said Babo, rolling the empty coffee cup around in her hands. "That's what they said . . . nothing but water. Now, there were some animals, but they didn't live on the water. They lived in the sky."

"Heaven?" asked Jimmy Delano.

"I don't think so. No, it was just another place. Like the moon or Mars. Wherever it was, this other place was getting crowded, and the animals had this meeting and decided to see if they could do something about all the water."

"Maybe it was Venus."

"Sure. Well, anyway, they had this meeting, and these four ducks volunteered to go down and see what could be done. So they swam around for a while . . . I don't know, couple of months, maybe a year . . . just swimming around and looking things over. But after a while, they got bored. You ever do any swimming, Jimmy?"

"Yes, sir," said the patrolman.

"Laps," said Babo. "I used to swim laps. You ever swim laps?"

"You bet. I used to swim a lot, but the stuff they put in the pool gives me a skin rash and makes my hair go funny."

Babo's eyes brightened. "That's right," she said. "My grandmother had some stuff she put on her hair to protect it.

They were barbers. You know, my whole family. All the way back. They knew about hair."

"No kidding."

"My great-great-grandfather was a barber on a ship. Sailed all over the place, cutting hair, shaving people."

"Wow!"

"That other cop, the old guy . . . I'll bet his wife does his hair."

"How did you know that?"

"You can see it around the ears. And that rash on his neck. I'll bet he uses a cheap electric razor, too."

"That's right. One of those cordless models."

"Straight razor," said Babo. "It's the only thing to use. Good blade, good strop, and you can get the best shave in the world. Now, my great-great-grandfather could handle a blade. Have I got stories—"

"Those things are pretty dangerous, aren't they?"

Babo waved her hand. "Nothing to it. Just practice. Got to be careful under the nose and around the neck."

"I use a safety razor," said Jimmy. "What about those ducks?"

"What ducks?"

"You know, the ducks in the story."

"Oh, yeah . . . almost forgot. Well, those ducks swam and swam all over the place, just like swimming laps, and finally they had it with swimming, and one of them says, 'Let's make some dry land' . . . No, wait. I messed it up. There's this woman."

"Was she nice looking?"

"Must have been. So, this woman falls from the sky."

"Same place as the animals?"

"I guess. Now, how did that go. So, there was this woman and four ducks, and this woman was sitting on the back of a giant turtle—"

"Boy, Ms. Jones," said Jimmy, "you can sure tell a story."

"You following this, Jimmy?"

"Yes, ma'am."

"So this woman says that they could create some dry land, and the ducks, who are tired of swimming laps, say, 'Sure, let's do that.' Anyway, one of the ducks dives down to the bottom, and she's gone for a long time. But pretty soon she bobs back up looking half dead, and the rest of the ducks crowd around and ask her if she found any land."

Babo looked out into the parking lot. There was no sign of the Pinto. "That's not right either. I keep getting it wrong. I better start at the beginning again."

"Sure," said Jimmy. "We got lots of tape."

"Okay," said Babo, and she leaned back and closed her eyes. "In the beginning, there was nothing. Just the water."

SERGEANT CERENO SAT in the white wingback chair, all green and glowing. Dr. Hovaugh leaned forward and cleared his throat. Cereno's eyes were shut. "Sergeant . . . Sergeant . . . ?"

Cereno opened his eyes. "I was just reflecting."

"About the Indians?"

"No, just reflecting." Cereno opened his notebook again and wrote something on the page. Could you describe the Indians?"

"Isn't all that in the files?"

Cereno held up the folders and nodded. "Yes, it is. But it's rather vague."

"Vague?"

"Yes, doctor. You know. . . height, weight, distinguishing marks. That sort of thing."

"Well, they were all about five foot three to five foot five, I would guess . . ."

Cereno stopped writing and held up his hand. "No, no . . . *that's* in the files. I'm more interested in your impressions, your observations. For instance, was one of the Indians more or less their leader? How did they like to dress? What did they like to eat? Who were their friends? Did anyone come to visit them? Were they on drugs? Did they drink?"

"Oh."

"Did they talk about escaping? Were they unhappy?"

"I see."

"Did they have any friends on the hospital staff? Could someone have unlocked the door for them?"

"Why would someone do that?"

"Who, Dr. Hovaugh?"

Dr. Hovaugh squeezed his hands together. "Perhaps you would like some tea, Detective Cereno."

"Sergeant."

"Certainly."

Sergeant Cereno adjusted himself in the chair so that his jacket fell free and the bulbous handle of the revolver poked out from his armpit. "Dr. Hovaugh, perhaps you can tell me exactly why these Indians were in this hospital."

"Ah," said Dr. Hovaugh. "That is a rather long and a rather boring story."

"How long?"

"Well, I'd have to start at the beginning, I guess, with my great-grandfather and his vision. That's how this hospital started, you know, with a vision."

"But this story has to do with the Indians?"

"Oh, yes."

"Do you mind if I record this?"

"Not at all."

Sergeant Cereno set the tape recorder on the edge of the desk. He pushed the buttons and settled back in the chair. "Okay, you can start."

Dr. Hovaugh leaned back. He was feeling better now. Tired, but better. "Well . . . let's see. I never know where to start. I suppose I should begin by saying that in the beginning all this was land. Empty land. My great-grandfather came out here from the Old World. He was what you might call an evangelist. It wasn't how he made his money. There was very little money in evangelism in those days. Not at all like now. He made his money in real estate. He bought this land from the Indians."

"Our Indians?"

"No, no. He bought the land from a local tribe. They're extinct now, I believe."

"When was that?"

"Eighteen seventy-six."

"And the Indians?"

"I believe they were all killed by some disease."

"Not those Indians, our Indians."

"Of course. Well, according to the old records, the Indians arrived in January of 1891."

Sergeant Cereno held up a hand and looked at the ceiling. "That would make them at least one hundred and one years old."

"Hardly, sergeant. They were old when they arrived."

"How old?"

"I don't know."

"Could you guess?"

"Doctors don't like to guess."

"So, you're saying that they were old."

"Yes, that's safe to say."

"Maybe you better start at the beginning, Dr. Hovaugh."

Dr. Hovaugh looked out the window. The grass near the wall seemed unusually dry and the leaves on one of the new elms appeared yellow and curled. The big oak wasn't showing any signs of improvement, either.

"Well," he said, locking his fingers together and leaning back in the chair, "in the beginning, there was nothing. There was just the water."

NORMA STARTED HUMMING a round-dance song. The car was warm, and Lionel closed his eyes again. He wondered if Dr. Loomis was still alive. Maybe Cecil made it to Wounded Knee after all. And he remembered that night in the parking lot, standing there, watching himself in the window.

"Wake up, nephew," said Norma. "Company up ahead."

Lionel opened his eyes in time to see four old Indians standing by the side of the road.

"Better give them a ride," said Norma, easing the car off the road. "They look about as lost as you."

It wasn't until Norma had stopped the car completely and Lionel had opened the door and stepped out that he noticed two things. The first was that he was standing ankle deep in a pool of water. The second was that one of the Indians was wearing a black mask.

"Where did the water come from?" said Alberta.

"Where did the water come from?" said Patrolman Delano.

"Where did the water come from?" said Sergeant Cereno.

"Where did the water come from?" said Lionel.

"FORGET THE WATER," says Coyote. "What happens to First Woman and Ahdamn?"

"They go to Florida," I says.

"Florida," says Coyote. "Can I go too?"

So those soldiers take First Woman and Ahdamn to a train station. And then they take them to a train. And then the train takes them to Florida.

"I always wanted to go to Miami," says Coyote.

"We're not going to Miami," I says.

"Fort Lauderdale is okay too," says Coyote.

"We're not going there either," I says.

So First Woman and Ahdamn are on that train and there are a bunch of Indians on that train with chains on their legs. First Woman and Ahdamn have chains on their legs, too. Everybody is going to Florida. We are going to Florida, those Indians tell First Woman. Yes, says First Woman, I can see that.

So they get to Florida and First Woman and Ahdamn and all the Indians sit around and draw pictures.

Boy, says Ahdamn, this is fun, and he draws a buffalo. I am

having a good time, says Ahdamn, and he draws a horse. Look at me, says Ahdamn, and that one draws a refrigerator.

And Ahdamn becomes a big star. People from New York and Toronto and Chicago and Edmonton come down to Florida to watch Ahdamn draw pictures.

I am famous, Ahdamn tells First Woman.

We better get going, says First Woman. Lots of work to do.

But I am famous. Ahdamn says that again.

This world is getting bent, says First Woman. We got to fix it.

Lots of time for that later on, says Ahdamn.

Okay, says First Woman, and she puts on her black mask and walks to the front gate.

It's the Lone Ranger, the guards shout. It's the Lone Ranger, they shout again, and they open the gate. So the Lone Ranger walks out of the prison, and the Lone Ranger and Ishmael and Robinson Crusoe and Hawkeye head west.

Have a nice day, the soldiers say. Say hello to Tonto for us. And all the soldiers wave.

"Wait, wait, wait," says Coyote. "Who are those other people walking out the gate with the Lone Ranger?"

"We'll meet them later."

"But what happens to Ahdamn?"

"Who cares."

"But what happens to First Woman?"

"Oh, boy," I says. "You must have been sitting on those ears. No wonder this world has problems."

"Is this a puzzle?" says Coyote. "Are there any clues?"

"We are going to have to do this again. We are going to have to get it right."

"Okay," says Coyote, "I can do that."

"All right," I says, "pay attention. In the beginning there was nothing. Just the water."

JSθ6T

ОЛЕ

THIS ACCORDING TO THE LONE RANGER:

"Wait a minute. Wait a minute," said Hawkeye. "You just had a turn."

"That's right," said Robinson Crusoe. "Whose turn is it now?"

"I'm not tired," said the Lone Ranger. "I can keep going."

"It's Ishmael's turn," said Hawkeye. "I remember."

"Okay," said Robinson Crusoe. "But let's keep going."

"Okay?"

"Okay."

THIS ACCORDING TO ISHMAEL:

All right.

In the beginning there was nothing. Just the water. Every-where you looked, that's where the water was. It was pretty water, too.

"Was it like that wonderful, misty water in California," says Coyote, "with all those friendly bubbles and interesting stuff that falls to the bottom of your glass?"

"No," I says, "this water is clear."

"Was it like that lovely red water in Oklahoma," says Coy-ote, "with all those friendly bubbles and interesting stuff that floats to the top of your glass?"

"No," I says, "this water is blue."

"Was it like that water in Toronto . . ."

"Pay attention," I says, "or we'll have to do this again."

So.

There was water everywhere, and when Changing Woman looked out over the edge of the Sky World, she could see her-self reflected in that beautiful Water World.

Hmmmm, she says, not bad.

Every day, Changing Woman goes to the edge of the world and looks down at the water and when she does this, she sees herself.

Hello, she says.

And each day, Changing Woman leans a little farther to get a better look at herself.

"If she leans out any farther," says Coyote, "she's going to fall."

"Of course she's going to fall," I tell Coyote. "Sit down. Watch that sky. Watch that water. Pretty soon you can watch her fall."

"Does Changing Woman get hurt?"

"Nope," I tell Coyote. "She lands on something soft."

"Water is soft. Does she land in water like First Woman?"

"No," I tell Coyote. "She lands on a canoe."

"A canoe!" says Coyote. "Where did a canoe come from?"

"Use your imagination," I says.

"Was it a green Royalite Old Town single," says Coyote, "with oak gunnels and woven cane seats?"

"No," I says, "it wasn't one of those."

"Was it a red wood-and-canvas Beaver touring canoe with cedar ribs and built-in portage racks?"

"Not one of those either," I says. "This canoe was big canoe. And it was white. And it was full of animals."

"Wow!" says Coyote.

So Changing Woman falls out of that sky. And she falls into that canoe. And she lands on something soft. She lands on Old Coyote.

"Oh, no!" says Coyote.

"Oh, yes," I says. "Stick around. This is how it happens."

"IS THAT OUR RIDE?" said Hawkeye.

"Yes, I believe it is," said the Lone Ranger.

"So, what happens now?" said Ishmael.

"In that car?" said Robinson Crusoe.

"The newer ones don't have as much room," said the Lone Ranger.

"We were better off standing," said Robinson Crusoe.

The Lone Ranger and Ishmael and Robinson Crusoe and Hawkeye stood by the road and watched a man get out of the car and open the back door.

"Is that him?" said Ishmael.

"I think so," said the Lone Ranger.

"We were better off standing," said Robinson Crusoe.

Hawkeye shielded his eyes and looked at the man and the car. "Why is he standing in a puddle of water?"

"Toilet's backed up again!"

Latisha straightened the menus and watched the bus hit the pothole and lurch into the parking lot. "Bus coming," she shouted back to Billy. "How bad is it?"

Billy began whistling "Ebb Tide." Latisha could hear a mop sliding through water.

"Enough water here to make a dryland farmer grin."

The bus had Montana plates. Tourists. Rita stuck her head out of the kitchen. "How many puppies you think?"

Latisha could feel an itch settling in behind her ear. "Start with fifteen."

"What's the flavor?" Billy sang out from the bathroom.

"American."

"We got enough menus and cards?"

"What about the water?"

"We got plenty of that," Billy shouted.

American tourists were the best. They almost never ordered the special, and they almost always bought the menus and the postcards.

Cynthia came out of the back room. "A guy called for you."

"Who was it?"

"Didn't say."

"Lionel? Eli?"

"Don't think so. Said he'd be in town on the weekend. Said he'd probably catch you at the Sun Dance. He sounded cute."

Latisha nodded and wiped the blackboard. "What are we going to call the special today?"

"What did we call it yesterday?" said Cynthia.

"I forget."

"Rita," shouted Latisha, "what'd we call the special yesterday?"

"What difference does it make?"

"How about Old Agency Puppy Stew?" said Cynthia.

"Rita," shouted Latisha, "it's Old Agency Puppy Stew, again."

One of the secrets of a successful restaurant was to keep things simple. Every day Rita cooked up the same beef stew, and every day Rita or Billy or Cynthia or Latisha thought up a name for it. It wasn't cheating. Everybody in town and on the reserve who came to the Dead Dog Café to eat knew that the special rarely changed, and all the tourists who came through never knew it didn't.

"Toilet's working." Billy let the door swing shut behind him. "You want me to change the gas on the dispensers?"

"No, get dressed. We may need help out front."

"Plains, Southwest, or combination?"

The itch was more persistent. "What'd you do yesterday?"

"Plains."

"Do Southwest." Something was coming. Latisha could feel it.

The food at the Dead Dog was good, but what drew tourists to the cafe was the ambience and the reputation that it had developed over the years. Latisha would like to have been able to take all the credit for transforming the Dead Dog from a nice local establishment with a loyal but small clientele to a nice local establishment with a loyal but small clientele *and* a tourist trap. But, in fact, it had been her auntie's idea.

"Tell them it's dog meat," Norma had said. "Tourists like that kind of stuff."

That had been the inspiration. Latisha printed up menus that featured such things as Dog du Jour, Houndburgers, Puppy Potpourri, Hot Dogs, Saint Bernard Swiss Melts, with Doggie Doos and Deep-Fried Puppy Whatnots for appetizers.

She got Will Horse Capture over in Medicine River to make up a bunch of photographs like those you see in the hunting and fishing magazines where a couple of white guys are standing over an elephant or holding up a lion's head or stretching out a long stringer of fish or hoisting a brace of ducks in each hand. Only in these photographs, it was Indians and dogs. Latisha's favorite was a photograph of four Indians on their buffalo runners chasing down a herd of Great Danes.

Latisha had some of the better photographs made into postcards that she sold along with the menus.

"What do you want?" Cynthia was holding up several tapes. "Chief Mountain Singers or that group from Brocket?"

The tourists milled around in front of the restaurant. Latisha stood at the window and watched them as they pointed at the neon sign of a dog in a stewpot and took pictures of each other.

"Chief Mountain, I guess. But keep the volume down."

Trouble, thought Latisha, scratching at her ear. That's what was coming. Trouble.

ELI STAND ALONE STOOD at the window of the cabin and watched the water slide past the porch. It was getting higher, but they had done that before, open the gates just a little and let the stream come up over the sides of the channel and wash against the logs. A lot of trouble for nothing.

He took his cup of coffee out on the porch and sat down in the easy chair and looked back to the west. Four hundred yards behind the cabin, he could see the dam, an immense porcelain wall, white and glistening in the late morning light.

Eli could also see Clifford Sifton walking down the streambed, and he waved to Sifton and Sifton waved back.

"You want some coffee?" Eli shouted, though he knew Sifton couldn't hear him above the rush of the water. Sifton raised his walking stick and shouted back, but Eli couldn't hear him either.

Eli brought the coffeepot out and put it on the table. The water was still rising, and Sifton was having difficulty wading through the thigh-deep, gray-green water as it tumbled over the granite riprap. The water buffeted Cliff's legs, and Eli could see the man rocking and balancing as he stepped from rock to rock, picking his way across the stream.

"Guess they're mad as hell about the new injunction," Eli said.

"Guess you're right," said Sifton, making the porch and looking at the coffeepot. "Brewed or instant?"

"Always make brewed. You know that. You always ask me that, and it's always brewed."

"That one time it was instant."

"You guys flooded me in for two weeks. What'd you expect? Besides, that was seven years ago."

"Always pays to ask." Sifton pulled a package out of his knapsack. "Here," he said. "Where do you want it?"

He poured a cup of coffee and leaned his walking stick against the porch railing. "How you think the fishing is going to be this year?"

"Should be good. Be better if your dam wasn't there."

"Not my dam, Eli. And you know it."

"So you say."

Sifton sat on the railing and squinted at the sun. "That's the beauty of dams. They don't have personalities, and they don't have politics. They store water, and they create electricity. That's it."

"So how come so many of them are built on Indian land?"

"Only so many places you can build a dam."

"Provincial report recommended three possible sites."

"Geography. That's what decides where dams get built."

"This site wasn't one of them."

Sifton rolled his lips around the cup. "Other factors have to be considered too."

"None of the recommended sites was on Indian land."

Sifton swirled the coffee in the cup until it sloshed over the rim. "I just build them, Eli. I just build them."

"So you say." Eli settled into the chair. "What do you figure? Now or later?"

"Now, probably," said Sifton. "No sense wasting good coffee and a beautiful day. You know, we haven't had any wind for almost a week."

"Weather pattern," said Eli. "It'll change."

"I know it'll change. I just want to enjoy another day without that damn wind."

Eli leaned over the arm of his chair and watched the water. "Looks like it's going down."

"Just before I left, I told them to back off."

"Came pretty close this time."

"We know our business."

"Guess they'll be turning on the light again, too," said Eli.

"We know our business," said Sifton.

"So ask the question."

Sifton put his coffee cup down and pulled a white card out of his jacket pocket. He looked out over the stream, cleared his throat, and began to read.

Eli's mother died while he was living in Toronto. No one told him about her death until his sister called.

"Mom died," Norma said.

"When?"

"Couple of weeks ago."

"What? Why didn't you phone me?"

"Last time we saw you was twenty, thirty years ago."

"Norma—"

"Haven't written in four or five years, either."

"It hasn't been that long."

"Thought you might have died."

"I could have helped."

"Didn't need you. Camelot and I took care of everything. I was going to call, but then I forgot. I remembered today, so I called."

"I could have helped," Eli said.

"You can help now," said Norma.

There was the matter of their mother's house, Norma told him. No one could live in it because it was right in the middle of the proposed spillway for the Grand Baleen Dam, but Norma thought Eli might want to see the place or take a picture of it before it was flooded or torn down or whatever they did to things like that that were in the way of progress. There was even some furniture in the house that Eli could have if he wanted.

"You were born there before you went off and became white," Norma told him, "so I thought it might be of senti-mental value. I hear if you're a famous enough white guy, the government will buy the house where you were born and turn it into one of those tourist things."

Eli hung up before Norma could really get rolling. The next day he caught a plane to Blossom, hired a car at the airport, and drove all the way to the reserve without stopping.

It was morning when he walked out of the trees and across the meadow to his mother's house. Off to the west, he could see bulldozers and semitrucks and a couple of portable offices. There was smoke coming from one of the offices.

His mother had built the house. Log by log. Had dragged each one out of the small stand of timber behind the house, barked them, hewn them, and set them. He and Norma had been too young to help, and Camelot was only a baby then. So they looked after their sister while their mother coaxed the trees into place.

Clifford Sifton had come down from the dam site that day, the morning sun in his eyes, and walked the length of the meadow, his walking stick stabbing at the ground. He had stood at the bottom of the porch and looked up at Eli. "Morning," he said, shading his eyes. "Saw you drive up."

"Morning," Eli repeated.

"You must be Eli Stands Alone."

"That's right."

"Your sister says you teach in Toronto. At the university?"

"That's right."

"What do you teach?"

"Literature."

"Don't suppose you have any coffee?"

Eli couldn't put a name to it, but he didn't like Sifton. He didn't want to make him any coffee. And he didn't want the man on his mother's porch.

"Looks like you're thinking about building a dam."

"That's right," said Sifton. "She's going to be a beauty."

"This is my mother's house."

"Your sister said you might want some things out of it before we tore it down."

"She built it herself, log by log."

"If there are any big pieces, sing out, and I'll send some of the boys to give you a hand."

Eli ran his hands along the railing, feeling for the carvings that he and Norma had cut into the wood. In the distance, he could hear a diesel motor turn over.

"Don't know that I want anyone tearing this house down."

"Construction starts in a month."

"Maybe it will," said Eli. "And maybe it'll have to wait."

Sifton looked at Eli, and he looked back at the bulldozers and the semis and the portable offices. "Nothing personal," he said, smiling and extending his hand.

Eli took Sifton's hand and held it for a second with just the fingers, the way you would hold something fragile or dangerous. "Okay," he said, "nothing personal."

WHEN CHARLIE LOOKING BEAR got off the phone with Alberta, he fixed himself a sandwich and sat on the balcony. Somewhere to the west, in the suburban roil of apartments, houses, motels, restaurants, churches, and car lots, was the West Edmonton Mall. Beyond that, out on the horizon piled high with deep-bellied, blue-gray clouds, was Jasper and the Rockies.

So, Alberta was sleeping with Lionel. Mr. Television. Mr. Stereo. Mr. Video Movie. The idea galled Charlie more than he would have expected. Lionel's birthday. Hardly a major holiday. Poor Alberta. She would drive all the way to Blossom, take a good, close look at Lionel all trussed up in the ratty gold blazer that Bill Bursum made his salespeople wear, and decide that she had made a terrible mistake.

Charlie munched on his sandwich and replayed the conversation.

"Hey, nothing personal, but you're not sleeping with the guy, are you?"

"God, Charlie."

"I really like you."

"And so romantic."

Okay, so he wasn't romantic. And he wasn't monogamous. But he wasn't a television salesman, either. He loved Alberta.

He was reasonably sure of that. And she loved him. Lionel was simply a diversion. Like Susan had been. Or Carol. Or Laura.

Charlie respected Alberta. She was smart. She was educated. Best of all, she was employed, albeit not in a profession Charlie would have chosen for her.

"You should be in law," Charlie had told her. "It's where the action is."

"You mean where the money is."

"Same thing."

"I like teaching."

"Money's better."

"Some of my students may be dumb, but they're not sleazy."

"Christ, Alberta, lawyers aren't sleazy. They're slick. There's a big difference."

It was always the same argument. Always the same topic. *Stands Alone v. Duplessis International Associates.* The case was ten years old, had started before Charlie had even been accepted to law school. And the way things were going, it would be in the courts for another ten years.

Duplessis had hired him right out of law school. *Stands Alone* v. *Duplessis* was his first case. It was his only case. He didn't make the decisions, of course. Those were made by big-shot corporate lawyers in Toronto or London or Zurich. He was just the front, and he knew it. After all, they hadn't hired him because he was at the top of his class. He hadn't been. They hired him because he was Blackfoot and Eli was Blackfoot and the combination played well in the newspapers.

"Charlie, how can you work for Duplessis? You know that the tribe isn't going to make a cent off that dam. And what about all that waterfront property on the new lake—"

"Parliament Lake."

"Parliament Lake. What happened to all those lots that the band was supposed to get?"

"The government made some changes."

"That's a new way to describe greed. You know that the tribe isn't going to make any money off the entire deal."

"Then some of us should, don't you think?"

"God, Charlie."

"Look, where's the harm? The case will probably be in the courts long after we're dead. I mean, the dam is there. The lake is there. You can't just make them go away."

The dam was there all right. Anyone who wanted to could drive along the river to the small recreation area and have lunch in the shadow of the dam. Or you could walk along the lakeshore and enjoy the panorama of water and sky. Or you could drive across the top and look down the spillway into the concrete channels that were clogged with spongy moss and small plants.

The dam was there. It just wasn't working. The lake was there. But no one could use it.

Eli had fought Duplessis from the beginning, producing a steady stream of injunctions that Duplessis countered. After the fourth year, the company hired Crosby Johns and Sons Inc., a slick public relations firm in Toronto, to mount a publicity campaign to convince the Indians that the dam was in their best interest, a campaign that culminated with a story in *Alberta Now* demonstrating rather conclusively, with graphs and charts and quotes from various experts on irrigation and hydropower, that after only one year of the dam operating at full efficiency, the tribe would make in excess of two million dollars. White farmers and white business would profit, too, the article conceded, but the Indians would be the big winners.

Two days after the article appeared, Homer Little Bear called an emergency council meeting to discuss ways to spend the money. At the meeting, Homer tried to read the article out loud, but had to give up, he was laughing so hard. Someone suggested that they rename the dam the Grand Goose or the Golden Goose because of the promised fortune and because, as Sam Belly put it, that's about all Indians ever got from the government, a goose.

"It's nice to see a company like that lose some money."

"Duplessis isn't losing money, Alberta."

"The dam is just sitting there. They can't use it. And no one can use the lake or build on the lots until the case is settled."

"Most of the money was put up by the province. The company gets to write the losses off their taxes."

"That's sick, Charlie."

"I don't call the shots."

The irony, Charlie mused, was that once Duplessis started construction on the dam, nothing stopped it. Environmental concerns were cast aside. Questions about possible fault lines that ran under the dam were dismissed. Native land claims that had been in the courts for over fifty years were shelved.

"Once you start something like this," Duplessis's chief engineer had told an inquiry board, "you can't stop. Too damn dangerous."

So Duplessis built the dam. But the day after it was completed, after all the champagne, the speeches, the pictures, just as the chief engineer, the premier of the province, and the federal minister for natural resources were set to throw the switches that would open the gates for the first time and send the rushing water down the channels to where the farmers, the businessmen, and the Indians waited, Eli Stands Alone finally got an injunction that stuck.

Well, the dam wasn't his fault. Alberta knew that. In her heart, Charlie told himself, she knew that he was doing his job. But being right didn't seem to be very persuasive. Maybe, Charlie thought, he should give his father's method a try.

"If you want to get a woman interested in you," Charlie's father had told him, "act helpless."

"Is that how you got Mom?"

"Absolutely."

While she was alive, Charlie's mother would laugh and tell his father that he had never had to act about that.

Charlie brought out his address book. The long weekend.

And Alberta was actually going to Blossom. He started with the *A*'s.

"Hi, Jennifer."

"Jennifer's not here."

"Will she be back later?"

"Is this Ted?"

It was a beautiful day. Between calls, Charlie watched the sun heading west. He worked his way through the *J*'s and *K*'s and was into the first of the *L*'s before he realized that he had lost his enthusiasm. Rita Luther was home, but by then Charlie was no longer interested.

"Hi, Rita."

"Charlie?"

"Yeah. Thought I'd call and say hello."

"Charlie Looking Bear?"

"I was thinking of calling you sometime next week. Maybe we could catch lunch. Or something."

"You okay?"

Charlie closed the book. Apart from the mountains, which you really couldn't see, the sky was the best part of the landscape. One of his teachers at law school had said that the sky in Alberta reminded her of an ocean.

"A deep, clear ocean," the teacher had said, "into which you can look and see the soul of the universe."

"Look again," Charlie had said under his breath, but loud enough for everyone in the class to hear.

Even the teacher had laughed.

What Charlie saw when he looked up was . . . sky, not some clever metaphor. Sky and clouds. Subtle colors. Shifting angles of light. That was it. Physics and refractions.

In the west, the cloud towers climbed high above the mountains and moved in front of the sun, momentarily capturing the light, while at the edges and along the seams, bright shafts and delicate fans burst from cover high above the prairie floor.

Charlie leaned back in his chair and stretched. Farther to the north, clusters of darker clouds drifted into the foothills. Charlie could hear the soft rumble of distant thunder, could see the low, banking mist and the sudden rains slanting onto the plains. It reminded him of movies.

Alberta and Lionel. She couldn't be serious. Charlie picked up the phone.

"Time Air. When you fly with us, you fly on time. How may we help you?"

Charlie looked out at the clouds and the light. Yes, he could see how people might think of it as magnificent, spectacular. "Yes," he said, turning back to the matter at hand. "When's your next flight to Blossom?"

LIONEL PULLED HIS FOOT OUT OF THE PUDDLE and shook the water out of his shoe. The old Indians watched him.

"Pretty good puddle," said the Indian in the mask.

"Yes," said the Indian in the Hawaiian shirt with the red palm trees. "You stepped in that pretty good."

"Lionel," Norma called from the car. "Mind your manners."

Lionel put his weight on the wet shoe. It made a soft, squishy sound that was not altogether unpleasant. "Evening," he said, looking at the four Indians. "You headed for the reserve? We can take you as far as Blossom."

"That's where we're going all right," said the Lone Ranger. "Blossom is where we want to be."

"Come on, then," said Norma. "Hop in."

Lionel opened the back door for the Indians and sat on the edge of the front seat and took off his shoe. The sock was soaked. He angled the shoe and let the water collect in the heel. Lionel had remembered reading somewhere that if leather shoes get wet they have the tendency to shrink and that the best thing to do is to stuff them with newspapers.

Lionel wrung out the sock and laid it on the dash next to the piece of blue carpet.

"We got any newspaper?"

"Newspaper?" said Norma. "What do you want a newspaper for? You know when you read in the car, you get sick."

"It's for my shoe. To keep it from shrinking."

Norma put the car into gear, checked her rearview mirror, stuck her arm out the window, and waved it up and down. "Put your foot back in it. Now," she said, half turning toward the Indians, "let's get acquainted."

When Lionel found out that Alberta was seeing Charlie, he was confused. It didn't make any sense. Charlie was a nice enough guy. He was good looking and he had a good job and a great car, but he was, well, sleazy. He had been sleazy as a kid and he was sleazy now. Some women probably liked sleazy, but not Alberta. She was solid and responsible. She had a good education and a good job.

"Charlie? Charlie Looking Bear?"

"I go out with you."

"Why are you going out with Charlie?"

"I ask myself the same question about you."

Lionel hadn't liked the way the conversation was going, so he changed the subject. "I've been thinking about us."

"And?"

"Just thinking."

"About what?"

"Us."

Which turned out to be even a worse topic of conversation. After that, Lionel didn't see Alberta for a month.

Norma leaned her head toward Lionel. "This is my nephew Lionel. I'm Norma."

"Yes," said the Lone Ranger. "I'm the Lone Ranger."

Lionel snorted. Norma whacked him in the ribs with her free arm. "Nice to see our elders out on vacation," she said.

"Oh, we're not on vacation," said Ishmael.

"No," said Robinson Crusoe.

"We're working," said Hawkeye.

"Working, huh?" said Lionel, and he dropped his arm to protect his side.

"That's right," said the Lone Ranger. "We're trying to fix up the world."

Norma glared at Lionel. "Sure could use it. I was just telling my nephew that the world could sure use some help."

"That's true," said Hawkeye.

"But these young people just don't listen to us."

"Yes," said Ishmael, "that's true, too."

Lionel was trying to hide his smile in his hand. "So, you're hitchhiking to Blossom, and once you get there, you're going to fix up the world ?"

"Oh, no, grandson," said the Lone Ranger. "It's too big a job to fix it all at once. Even with all of us working together we can't do it."

"Yes," said Robinson Crusoe, "we tried that already."

"Things are too messed up," said Ishmael.

"We let it go too long."

Lionel shifted around so he could see the Indians. "So you're going to start with Blossom and go from there?"

"Well, you have to start somewhere," said Norma, glancing at Lionel to see if she could get at his ribs.

The Lone Ranger shook his head. "No," he said. "That's too big a job, too."

"We're not as young as we used to be," said Hawkeye.

"And even when we were younger," said Ishmael, "we couldn't have done it."

"When we were younger," said Robinson Crusoe, "we tried. That's how we got into this mess in the first place."

Lionel looked at the four Indians. Now that he could see them clearly, he was surprised at how old they looked, perhaps eighty or ninety years old. Perhaps older. And there was something about them that made Lionel's ear itch.

·   ·   ·

It was Norma who had given Lionel the key to Alberta. After Alberta disappeared for a month, his auntie took him aside and gave him a short lecture. "Babies," she said. "That's all you need to know."

"What?"

"You deaf? Alberta wants children."

"All women want babies."

"That's what men like to think. Makes them feel wanted. Not much good for anything else, I can tell you."

"She's never mentioned it to me."

"Of course she's never mentioned it to you. She doesn't want to put up with a man. A woman who gets married and has a child winds up with two babies right off the bat. You get the picture?"

Lionel said he did just to keep Norma from shifting into high gear.

"You don't get the picture at all, nephew."

Norma took Lionel by the arm and sat him down on the couch. She pulled up a chair right in front of him, and she reached out and took his face in her hands and held it there so she could see his eyes.

"You ready?"

Lionel nodded that he was.

"First of all," Norma said, "Alberta wants children. Most women want children. Why do you think there are so many human beings in this world? You think women are that crazy about men? You think women are that crazy about sex? Day after we find some other way to get pregnant, you guys will be as attractive as week-old fry bread."

Lionel smiled and nodded some more. He could feel Norma's fingernails at his ears.

"Second, stop talking about cars and other guys and sex and start talking about babies. Maybe borrow one. Got enough of them around. Tell her you can't go out because you're watching a baby for a friend. Invite her over. Let her hold the baby. Stuff like that."

Lionel's neck began to stiffen up. He wet his lips and blinked his eyes.

"Don't go to sleep on me, nephew. We're almost done."

Norma let go of Lionel's face and wiped her hands on her skirt. "Last," she said, "don't ask her to marry you. Don't get all dressed up and take her out to a fancy dinner. Don't get her a ring and crawl around on your knees. Don't say squat about marriage. She'll make up her own mind about that, and if she's interested, she'll let you know."

Norma sat back and sucked on her lips. "You get all that?"

"Sure."

Norma looked at Lionel and shook her head. "You're my nephew, and I love you," she said. "But I don't think it's going to help."

"So," said Lionel, "how do you figure you're going to help?"

The Lone Ranger looked at Robinson Crusoe and Robinson Crusoe looked at Ishmael and Ishmael looked at Hawkeye and they all looked at Lionel.

"I mean, it's a big world. And even if you split Blossom up four ways, it would be a lot of work, I guess." Lionel could feel Norma measuring the distance to his ribs. "I mean, maybe you could use some help."

"That's real nice, grandson," said the Lone Ranger. "But we made this mess and we got to clean it up."

"But we're going to start small," said Ishmael.

"Real small," said Robinson Crusoe.

"And once we get the hang of it," said Hawkeye, "we'll move on to bigger jobs."

"That sounds smart," said Norma. "Start small and work your way up."

"So," said Lionel, chuckling to himself and watching the prairie disappear through the rear window of the car, "where are you going to start?"

BILL BURSOM STOOD AT THE FAR END of the store and looked back at the wall. It was magnificent, spectacular, genius. Oh, Eaton's and the Bay had similar kinds of displays, but nothing of this size, and size, Bill reminded himself, was everything.

"What do you think, Minnie?"

Minnie Smith looked up from sorting the videos that had come in overnight.

"Ms. Smith," Minnie corrected.

"Whatever," said Bursum.

"Ms. Smith," said Minnie.

Bursum stood in front of the "fantasy" section and held his arms out wide. "It's done. What do you think?"

The far wall was filled with television sets. They ran from corner to corner and were stacked right to the ceiling, all shapes and sizes.

"Is it just that it's crooked?" said Minnie.

"It's not crooked," said Bursum.

But it wasn't exactly square, either. On the lower right-hand side, several twelve-inch televisions hung down like a tail. The entire left side was uneven, moving in and out as it rose to the roof. Even the top row dipped and peaked as it ran the length of the wall.

"Or is it just that it isn't square?" said Minnie.

"It's not supposed to be square," said Bursum.

Minnie shrugged her shoulders. "What does it do?"

Bursum strode across the store, swinging his arms as if he were marching in a parade. "Watch." And he picked up a remote control. For a moment there was nothing, and then each set blinked and a soft dot of gray light swelled to fill the screen.

All two hundred screens glowed silver, creating a sense of space and great emptiness at the end of the store. Bursum smiled back at Minnie.

"Now watch this." Bursum pushed a tape into a VCR at the corner of the display and waited while the machine whirled and clunked and buzzed. Suddenly the screens came alive with brilliant colors.

"Yes!" Bursum shouted, and he looked back to see if Minnie was impressed.

"That's very nice, Mr. Bursum," said Minnie.

"It really catches your eye."

"Do all the sets have to show the same movie?"

Lionel had helped him build the display, had assisted with the layout and the framing, but it had taken longer for Bursum to make the final connections and get everything running. Now that it was working, Bursum was anxious to see what Lionel thought of the finished product, not because he put a great deal of stock in Lionel's opinion but because Lionel understood, to some degree, the difficulties of the logistics, the intricacies of the wiring, the spatial arrangements that had to be considered in conceiving the overall plan.

"Do you see it?"

"Sure," said Minnie. "You can't miss it."

"No," said Bursum. "Do you *see* it?"

Bursum smiled and moved in front of the televisions. He spread his legs and extended his arms. "It's a map!"

Minnie cocked her head to one side.

"Of Canada and the United States."

Minnie cocked her head to the other side.

"Here's Florida," said Bursum, pointing to the tail. "And here's Vancouver Island and here's Hudson's Bay."

"Where's Blossom?" asked Minnie, her head still bent to one side.

"Someplace around there," said Bursum, and he pointed at a thirteen-inch Sony Digital Monitor high on the wall.

Minnie cocked her head back to the other side.

Bursum raised his arms over his head and extended his fingers. "I call it . . . The Map!"

"Is it just for display?" asked Minnie.

Bursum doubted that even Lionel understood the unifying metaphor or the cultural impact The Map would have on customers, but that was all right. Lionel, at least, would be able to appreciate the superficial aesthetics and the larger visual nuances of The Map.

The Map. Bursum loved the sound of it. There was a majesty to the name. He stepped back from the screens and looked at his creation. It was stupendous. It was more powerful than he had thought. It was like having the universe there on the wall, being able to see everything, being in control. Yes, Lionel might just appreciate it.

And then again, he might not.

"Now that's advertising," said Bursum, adjusting his gold blazer. "Do you know what something like that is worth?"

Minnie nodded and smiled.

"It has no value," said Bursum. "It is beyond value. Have you read *The Prince* by Machiavelli?"

Minnie nodded and smiled.

"It's all about advertising. If you're going to succeed in this business, you better read it."

Lionel, at Bursum's insistence, had read *The Prince*, and so had Charlie Looking Bear for that matter, but Bursum was sure that neither of them had understood the central axiom. Power and control—the essences of effective advertising—

were, Bursum had decided years before, outside the range of the Indian imagination, though Charlie had made great strides in trying to master this fundamental cultural tenet.

Minnie leaned on the counter. "I suppose its advertising value compensates for its lack of subtlety."

"That's right," said Bursum, turning around completely. "It's like being in church. Or at the movies."

"I'VE BEEN ELECTED SPOKESPERSON FOR OUR TABLE, said the woman, folding the map and putting it back in her purse. "My name is Jeanette, and this is my friend Nelson. This is Rosemarie De Flor and her husband, Bruce."

Latisha nodded, hoping she could keep this short. Tourists loved to talk. Latisha guessed it was part of the lure of travel, the chance to tell someone who didn't know you the stories everyone who did know you was tired of hearing.

"Don't let her fool you," said Rosemarie, spearing a Deep-Fried Puppy Whatnot. "Nobody elected her anything. She's just bossy."

"Damn straight," said Nelson, and he and Bruce fell to giggling behind their coffee cups.

"And as spokesperson," Jeanette continued, ignoring Rosemarie and the two men, "I get to ask all the questions everyone else is too embarrassed to ask." Jeanette waited to see if there were any objections. Latisha shifted her weight and sighed. Jeanette looked like a woman just warming to a lengthy task.

"Now," said Jeanette, "may we assume that you are Indian?"

"Jesus, Jeanette," said Nelson, reaching out and patting Latisha on the arm. "Any fool can see that."

"Never hurts to ask."

"I'm Blackfoot," said Latisha.

"Damn fine tribe," said Nelson, leaving his hand on Latisha's arm and trying to reach her hip with his thumb.

"Ah," said Jeanette. "And you are the owner?"

"That's right."

Jeanette glared at Nelson. "And here at this restaurant that you own," she said, raising her voice a notch, "you serve dog?"

"That's correct."

Nelson took his hand off Latisha's arm and looked at his Saint Bernard Swiss Melt. "Jesus! You're kidding. It's not really dog?"

"Of course she's kidding," said Bruce. "I used to work for the RCMP—"

"We all know that, honey," said Rosemarie.

"Twenty-five years I was a sergeant with the RCMP, and if we had heard of anyone cooking up dog and selling it in a restaurant, we would have arrested them. It's beef, right?"

"Are you married?" asked Jeanette.

"No."

"Very wise," said Jeanette, leaning her head in Nelson's direction.

Then again, Latisha reflected, she wasn't single, exactly. But she definitely wasn't married.

Nelson had lifted the top piece of bread off his sandwich and was examining the meat with his fork. "Looks like beef to me." And he reached out to try to pat Latisha's butt. "You were kidding, right?"

"Black Labrador," said Latisha, avoiding Nelson's hand. "You get more meat off black Labs."

"Jesus!"

"But you have been married," said Jeanette. "Every woman makes that mistake at least once."

George Morningstar. Latisha had even liked his name. It sounded slightly Indian, though George was American, from a small town in Michigan. He had come out west to see, as he put it, what all the fuss was about. Tall, with soft light brown hair that just touched his shoulders. Best of all, he did not look like a cowboy or an Indian. Even at eighteen, Latisha had already tired of skinny men with no butts in blue jeans, pearl-button shirts, worn-at-the-heel cowboy boots, straw hats with sweat lines, driving pickups or stacked up against the shady sides of buildings like logs.

"We got to get this dog-meat thing straight," said Nelson, his arm still hanging out in space.

"It's a treaty right," Latisha explained. "There's nothing wrong with it. It's one of our traditional foods."

"I've never heard of that, either," said Bruce, "and I was a sergeant with the RCMP for twenty-five years."

"We raise them right on the reserve," Latisha explained. "Feed them only horse meat and whole grain. No hormones or preservatives."

"Jesus," said Nelson. "I had a black Lab when I was a kid. He was a great dog."

George had come out to the reserve for Indian Days. Latisha could still remember what he had been wearing—tan cotton slacks and a billowy white cotton shirt that was loose in the body and tight at the cuffs. He had on oxblood loafers and patterned socks, and he had stood at the back of the gawking crowd and watched. At the end of the day, he was still there, watching, listening, looking for all the world like the most intelligent man in the universe.

"His name was Tecumseh," said Nelson. "After the Indian chief. And you know what?" Nelson motioned for Latisha to come closer. "He could sing."

"You're not eating Tecumseh," said Rosemarie. "Did I tell you I was in opera?"

"Yes," said Jeanette, "we all know you were in opera."

Nelson laid his head back and pointed his lips at the ceiling. "When I'm calling you, oo-oo-oo, oo-oo-oo!"

Billy stuck his head out of the kitchen and looked at Nelson. Latisha waved him off and shifted her weight to the other leg.

"He lived to be fourteen years old," said Nelson.

"Once they get past two or three," Latisha said gravely, "the meat's too tough to eat."

"That dog wasn't singing, Nelson," said Rosemarie, "he was just howling. Now, I could sing, isn't that right, Jeanette?"

"And," said Jeanette, trying to regain control of the conversation, "were you born on the reserve?"

That was one of the things George had asked her that first evening, had been pleased that she was, as he said, a real Indian. And he had been so attentive. It was his one great quality. He made you believe that he was listening, made you believe that what you had to say was important, made you believe that he was interested.

"You know, Country," George told her on their third date, "talking to you is better than sex or good food."

And Latisha had talked, poured her life out, a great flood of dreams and enthusiasms, and George had sat there and waited and listened, his mouth set in a pleasant smile, his blue eyes never blinking.

Jeanette put her napkin on the table. "Most interesting pictures," she said, gesturing to the photograph of two Indians holding up the ends of a pole strung with dachshunds. "The waitress tells us that you sell recipes for dog."

"Yes, that's right."

"That is very clever of you. I suppose we'll have to buy one for Nelson."

Latisha was beginning to like the old woman. Nelson was

back to nibbling at his sandwich again. Jeanette pushed her chair back and struggled to her feet.

"Could you help me, dear," she said. "These days, I have a little trouble getting going."

Latisha took her arm. "Where to?"

"She has to go to the bathroom," said Nelson. "She's always going to the bathroom. Has a bladder problem."

Jeanette smiled back at Nelson and Rosemarie and Bruce. Latisha felt the old woman's grip on her arm tighten and realized that the woman was strong, could probably break Nelson's neck.

"He'll die before I do," Jeanette said under her breath as Latisha helped her down the hall. "There's some consolation in that."

George had kept his hands in his pockets. After fighting off the local cowboys and Indians, it was nice to be with a man who didn't think that her shoulder or her waist or her butt was part of the public domain. For the first month he didn't touch her at all. They walked and talked, had cheap, wonderful dinners, went to the movies. One night George took her to the Blossom library. Latisha had never even been inside the building. He led her into the record section, and they spent the evening listening to classical music on headsets.

He had seemed vulnerable then, almost girlish, always looking off into space. To commemorate their third month together, he gave her his copy of Kahlil Gibran's *The Prophet*.

She had felt the itch early on and thought it was love. Six months later, they married, and before the first year was out, Latisha realized that the reason George wondered so much about the world was because he didn't have a clue about life. But by the time she figured out that the itch was really trouble and not love at all, it was too late. She was pregnant.

Jeanette paused at the door. "This is fine, dear. I can make it the rest of the way myself." She let go of Latisha's arm and leaned on the door handle. "How long were you married?"

"Nine years."

"Children?"

"Three."

Jeanette shook her head. "Did you kill the bastard?"

Latisha laughed. "No, he's still alive. I threw him away."

"Splendid," said Jeanette, opening the door. "I love stories with happy endings."

"Watch the toilet," Latisha called after her. "Sometimes it overflows."

"Don't they all," Jeanette called back, sounding very far away. "Don't they all."

FROM WHERE ELI SAT on the porch, he imagined he could see the cracks that were developing near the base of the dam. Stress fractures, they called them, common enough in any dam, but troublesome nonetheless, especially given the relatively young age of the concrete. Of more concern was the slumping that had been discovered.

"It's a beauty, isn't it?" said Sifton, swirling the remains of the coffee around in the cup. "You know, if your cabin faced west, you'd have a great view of the dam from your front window."

"View is fine as it is."

"It's nice in the morning. Sort of white. Like a shell."

"Reminds me of a toilet," said Eli.

"But the evening is best. Soon as the sun gets behind it, the whole face turns purple. Sometimes I'll walk down the streambed just to be able to see it in evening light."

"Hear they found some more cracks in the dam."

"You know," said Sifton, "I could have had the big project in Quebec."

"Hear they think the earth is moving under the dam."

"But I said no. I want to do the job in Alberta. That's what I said."

The clouds to the northwest were filling up the sky. They had been slowly organizing and gathering all day. Eli turned his face into the wind. Rain.

Sifton set his coffee cup on the railing. "You know, I always thought Indians were elegant speakers."

"Storm's coming."

"But all you ever say is no. I come by every day and read that thing those lawyers thought up about voluntarily extinguishing your right to this house and the land it sits on, and all you ever say is no."

"Be here by tonight."

"I mean, no isn't exactly elegant, now is it?"

"Maybe get some hail, too."

"It's hard work walking down here every day, and it would help if sometime you would tell me why."

Every July, when Eli was growing up, his mother would close the cabin and move the family to the Sun Dance. Eli would help the other men set up the tepee, and then he and Norma and Camelot would run with the kids in the camp. They would ride horses and chase each other across the prairies, their freedom interrupted only by the ceremonies.

Best of all, Eli liked the men's dancing. The women would dance for four days, and then there would be a day of rest and the men would begin. Each afternoon, toward evening, the men would dance, and just before the sun set, one of the dancers would pick up a rifle and lead the other men to the edge of the camp, where the children waited. Eli and the rest of the children would stand in a pack and wave pieces of scrap paper at the dancers as the men attacked and fell back, surged forward and retreated, until finally, after several of these mock forays, the lead dancer would breach the fortress of children and fire the rifle, and all the children would fall down in a heap, laughing, full of fear and pleasure, the pieces of paper scattering across the land.

Then the dancers would gather up the food that was piled around the flagpole—bread, macaroni, canned soup, sardines, coffee—and pass it out to the people. Later, after the camp settled in, Eli and Norma and Camelot would lie on their backs and watch the stars as they appeared among the tepee poles through the opening in the top of the tent.

And each morning, because the sun returned and the people remembered, it would begin again.

"Look, it's not my idea." Sifton raised his arms in surrender. "It's all those lawyers and the injunctions and that barrel load of crap about Native rights."

"Treaty rights, Cliff."

"Almost as bad as French rights. Damn sure wish the government would give me some of that."

"Government didn't give us anything, Cliff. We paid for them. Paid for them two or three times."

"And so because the government felt generous back in the last ice age, and made promises it never intended to keep, I have to come by every morning and ask the same stupid question."

"And I say no."

"You know you're going to say no, and I know you're going to say no. Hell, the whole damn world knows you're going to say no. Might as well put it on television."

"So why come?"

Sifton looked at Eli and both men began to chuckle. "Because you make the best damn coffee. And because I like the walk."

"Answer will be the same tomorrow."

Every year or so, a tourist would wander into the camp. Sometimes they were invited. Other times they just saw the camp from the road and were curious. Most of the time they were friendly, and no one seemed to mind them. Occasionally there was trouble.

When Eli was fourteen, a station wagon with Michigan plates pulled off the road and came into the camp just as the men were finishing their second day of dancing. Before anyone realized what was happening, the man climbed on top of the car and began taking pictures.

Eli saw the man and told his uncle Orville, who quickly gathered up his two brothers and their sons and descended on the car. The guy must have seen the men coming because he slid off the car, climbed into the driver's seat, rolled up all the windows, and locked the doors.

The men surrounded the station wagon. Orville motioned for the man inside to roll down his window. There was a woman sitting in the passenger seat and a little girl and a baby in the back. Orville tapped on the glass, and the man just smiled and nodded his head.

Things stayed like that for quite a while. The dancers finished, and as word went around, a large part of the camp moved in on the car. The baby in the car began to cry. Finally the man stopped smiling and began to wave at Orville, motioning for him and the rest of the people to get out of the way.

"Roll down your window," Orville said, his voice low and controlled.

Instead, the man started his engine, revved it, as if he were going to drive right through the people. As soon as the man started the car, Orville's brother, Leroy, went to his truck and grabbed his rifle off the rack. He walked to the front of the station wagon and held the gun over his head. The man in the car looked at Leroy for a moment, yelled something at his wife, and turned off the engine.

Then he rolled the window down just a crack. "What's the problem?"

"This is our Sun Dance, you know."

"No," said the man. "I didn't know. I thought it was a powwow or something."

"No," said Orville, "it isn't a powwow. It's our Sun Dance."

"Well, I didn't know that."

"You can't take pictures of the Sun Dance."

"Well, I didn't know that."

"Now you know. So I have to ask you for the pictures you took."

The man looked over at his wife, who nodded her head ever so slightly. "Well," he said, "I didn't take any pictures."

"You got a camera," Orville said.

"We're on vacation," said the man. "I was going to take some pictures of your little powwow, but I didn't."

Orville looked at Leroy, who was still standing in front of the car, the rifle cradled in his arms. "Is that so?"

"Yes," said the man. "That's the truth. Take it or leave it."

Orville put his hand on Eli's shoulder. "My nephew here says he saw you taking pictures."

The man's wife suddenly leaned over and grabbed her husband's arm. "Give them the pictures, Bill! For God's sake, just give them the pictures!"

The man turned, shook her arm off, and pushed her against the door. He sat there for a moment, looking at the dash, his hands squeezing the wheel. "I got pictures of my family on that roll," he said to Orville. "Tell you what. When I get them developed, if there happen to be any pictures of your thing, I'll send them to you along with the negatives."

Orville took out a handkerchief and blew his nose. "No," he said very slowly. "That's not the way it's going to work. I think it's best if you give us the film and my brother will get it developed. We'll send you the pictures that are yours."

"There are some very important pictures on that roll."

"Yes, there are," said Orville.

Eli had never seen someone so angry. It was hot in the car and the man was sweating, but it wasn't from the heat. Eli could see the muscles on the man's neck, could hear the violent, exaggerated motions with which he unloaded the camera and passed the film through the window to Orville.

Sifton pushed off the railing and snapped to attention, lowering his voice to a deep growl. "I am required by law to respectfully request that you relinquish your claim to this house and the land on which it sits and that title to this property be properly vested with the province of Alberta."

Sifton quickly sat down in the chair next to Eli and smiled up at the character he had just created.

"No," Sifton said, imitating as best he could Eli's soft voice.

Eli laughed and shook his head. "That's pretty good, Cliff. Real soon now you'll be able to do it all by yourself. You won't need me at all."

Sifton stayed in the chair. "You know what the problem is? This country doesn't have an Indian policy. Nobody knows what the hell anyone else is doing."

"Got the treaties."

"Hell, Eli, those treaties aren't worth a damn. Government only made them for convenience. Who'd of guessed that there would still be Indians kicking around in the twentieth century."

"One of life's little embarrassments."

"Besides, you guys aren't real Indians anyway. I mean, you drive cars, watch television, go to hockey games. Look at you. You're a university professor."

"That's my profession. Being Indian isn't a profession."

"And you speak as good English as me."

"Better," said Eli. "And I speak Blackfoot too. My sisters speak Blackfoot. So do my niece and nephew."

"That's what I mean. Latisha runs a restaurant and Lionel sells televisions. Not exactly traditionalists, are they?"

"It's not exactly the nineteenth century, either."

"Damn it. That's my point. You can't live in the past. My dam is part of the twentieth century. Your house is part of the nineteenth."

"Maybe I should look into putting it on the historical register."

Sifton rubbed his hands on his pants. "You know, when I was in high school, I read a story about a guy just like you who didn't want to do anything to improve his life. He just sat on a stool in some dark room and said, 'I would prefer not to.' That's all he said."

"'Bartleby the Scrivener.'"

"What?"

"'Bartleby the Scrivener.' One of Herman Melville's short stories."

"I guess. The point is that this guy had lost touch with reality. And you know what happens to him at the end of the story?"

"It's fiction, Cliff."

"He dies. That's what happens. Suggest anything to you?"

"We all die, Cliff."

Orville took the man's name and address. The people pulled back from the station wagon and let it pass. Halfway out of the camp, the man gunned the engine and spun the tires, sending a great cloud of choking dust into the air that floated through the camp. Then Leroy went for his pickup, but Orville stopped him.

"Come on, Eli. You're a big city boy. Like me. There's nothing for you here. You could probably get a great settlement and go on back to Toronto and live like a king."

"Nothing for me there."

"Nothing for you here, either," said Sifton. "One of these days we're going to open the floodgates, the water is going to pour down the channels, the generators are going to start producing electricity, and this house is going to turn into an ark."

"This is my home."

"Hell, what this is is a pile of logs in the middle of a spill-way. That's what it is."

The film was blank. The people at the photo store told Leroy that it had never been used. Orville wrote the man, but the letter came back a month later marked "Address Unknown."

Leroy had copied down the man's license number. He called the RCMP and explained what had happened, but there was little they could do about it, they said. The man hadn't broken any laws.

Eli stretched and pushed his glasses back up his nose. "When I figure it out, I'll let you know."

Sifton stood and leaned over the railing. The water had receded into the channels. "Time for me to get back. You need anything?"

"Nope. Probably go into town the next day or so." Eli walked with Sifton to the edge of the water. "What happens when it breaks?"

"The dam?"

"What happens when it breaks ? You can't hold water back forever."

Sifton jammed his walking stick into the gray-green water. "It's not going to break, Eli. Oh, it'll crack and it'll leak. But it won't break. Just think of the dam as part of the natural landscape."

"Just thought I'd ask."

Eli watched Sifton work his way into the stream. As he climbed out on the opposite bank, Sifton turned and raised his stick over his head. Eli could see the man's mouth open and close in a shout, but all the sound was snatched up by the wind and drowned in the rushing water.

"OH, NO!" says Coyote. "Changing Woman has landed on Old Coyote."

"Yes, yes," I says. "Everybody knows that by now. And here's what happens."

Changing Woman falls out of the sky. She starts way up high, so she can see all around the water. And what she sees is all that water, and what she sees is a canoe.

Hello, she says, I can see a canoe. And she could. A big canoe. A big white canoe with lots of animals in it. There were elephants and buffalo and rabbits and alligators in that canoe. There were frogs and mosquitoes and hawks and monkeys and spiders and worms in that canoe too. There were snakes and pigs and dogs and honey-bees and many other interesting things in that big white canoe.

It must be a party, says Changing Woman as she falls through the sky. But as she gets closer, what she sees is poop. There is poop everywhere. There is poop on the side of the canoe. There is poop on the bottom of the canoe. There is poop all around the canoe. That canoe isn't all white, either, I can tell you that.

Oh, dear, says Changing Woman. I don't know that I want to land in poop.

.   .   .

"Well, I know I wouldn't want to land in poop," says Coyote.

"Well, neither would I," I says.

So. There is Changing Woman falling out of the sky. And there are those animals. And there is that canoe full of poop. Watch out for the poop, all those animals shout.

But just as Changing Woman comes falling into that canoe, Old Coyote wakes up and that one rolls over and that one stretches. And Changing Woman lands on Old Coyote.

Pssssssst, goes Old Coyote. He makes that sound. Like something that has gone flat.

What was that? says one of the Pigs.

Sounded like a fart, says one of the Raccoons.

Okay, says one of the Moose, who farted?

No one farted, says Changing Woman. It was only me. I landed on Old Coyote. But before Changing Woman can apologize to Old Coyote, before she can give him some tobacco or some sweetgrass, a little man with a filthy beard jumps out of the poop at the front of the canoe.

Who are you? says the little man.

I'm Changing Woman, says Changing Woman.

Any relation to Eve? says the little man. She sinned, you know. That's why I'm in a canoe full of animals. That's why I'm in a canoe full of poop.

Are you all right? Changing Woman asks Old Coyote.

Psssst, says Old Coyote.

Why are you talking to animals? says the little man. This is a Christian ship. Animals don't talk. We got rules.

I fell out of the sky, says Changing Woman. I'm very sorry that I landed on Old Coyote.

The sky! shouts the little man. Hallelujah! A gift from heaven. My name's Noah, and you must be my new wife.

I doubt that, says Changing Woman.

Lemme see your breasts, says Noah. I like women with big breasts. I hope God remembered that.

Don't do it, says one of the Turtles. He'll just get excited and rock the canoe.

I have no intention of showing him my breasts, says Changing Woman.

Talking to the animals again, shouts Noah. That's almost bestiality, and it's against the rules.

What rules?

Christian rules.

"What's bestiality?" says Coyote.

"Sleeping with animals," I says.

"What's wrong with that?" says Coyote.

"It's against the rules," I says.

"But he doesn't mean Coyotes," says Coyote.

For the next month, Noah chases Changing Woman around the canoe. Noah tries balancing along the railing, but he falls in the poop. Noah tries jumping across the backs of the animals, but he falls in the poop.

He tries to wade through the poop to get at Changing Woman. But every time he works his way to the front of the canoe, she dances to the back. And every time he works his way to the back of the canoe, she dances to the front.

Hahahahahahahahahahahaha.

Then, one morning, they find an island.

Time for procreating, shouts Noah, and that one leaps out of the boat and begins chasing Changing Woman up and down the beach. All the animals line up on the beach and watch Changing Woman and Noah run back and forth.

Five dollars on Changing Woman, says those Kangaroos.

Who's got any of that good Noah money? says those Bears.

Odds, says those Trout. Who will give us odds?

After a while, that Noah gets tired and that one has to sit down. Well, this is certainly a mystery, he says. I better pray.

. . .

"Boy, is he going to be surprised," says Coyote.

"We're going to have to sit on that mouth of yours," I says.

"I didn't say anything," says Coyote.

Well, pretty soon Old Coyote comes over to where Changing Woman is resting. Old Coyote is still sort of flat. He walks flat. He talks flat. He thinks flat. Boy, says Old Coyote, I feel kind of flat.

Hello, Old Coyote, says Changing Woman. What are you doing on this voyage?

It all started when the waters rose, says Old Coyote. The waters rose, and we had to get into Noah's canoe.

That was nice of him, says Changing Woman.

Oh, no. He tried to leave us behind, says Old Coyote. Then he tried to throw us into the water. But his wife and children said no, no, no. Don't throw all our friends into the water.

Wife? says Changing Woman. Children?

Noah threw them into the water instead, says Old Coyote. It's the rules.

Rules, says Changing Woman. What rules?

Well, says that Old Coyote, Noah has these rules. The first rule is Thou Shalt Have Big Breasts.

And Noah's wife had small breasts? says Changing Woman.

No, says Old Coyote, she had great big breasts.

Ah, says Changing Woman.

It makes sense when you think about it, says Old Coyote.

We got to get rid of those rules, says Changing Woman.

"Rules?" says Coyote. "Rules?" Coyote says that again. "Is this that contrary dream from the garden story?"

"Of course," I says. "It's all the same story."

"That makes sense," says Coyote.

Rest period is over, shouts silly Noah, and that one jumps to his feet. Time for procreating!

So Noah and Changing Woman run back and forth along the beach. They run back and forth for a month. And then Noah gets sweaty, and that one gets angry and that one stops running back and forth.

No point in having rules if some people don't obey them, says Noah. And he loads all the animals back in the canoe and sails away.

This is a Christian ship, he shouts. I am a Christian man. This is a Christian journey. And if you can't follow our Christian rules, then you're not wanted on the voyage.

"Oh, oh," says Coyote. "Changing Woman is stuck on the island all by herself. Is that the end of the story?"

"Silly Coyote," I says. "This story is just beginning."

"INITIAL HERE that you've read the rules, here that you don't want the special no-deductible insurance waiver, and sign at the bottom."

Charlie signed the rental-car form while the clerk behind the counter chirped away about the points of interest in and around Blossom. There were old Indian ruins and the remains of dinosaurs just to the north of town and a real Indian reserve to the west. She stuffed a bag full of restaurant guides, maps, two-for-one coupons, several pens, a copy of the local paper, and a Welcome-to-Blossom litter bag. She announced each item as if it had intrinsic value over and above the cost, and as one thing disappeared into the bag, another would magically appear at her fingertips.

It was much too late to be that cheery. Charlie felt under assault as he waited for some computer in Toronto or Vancouver to verify his credit. All he wanted was to get the car, drive to the hotel, and fall asleep. He would find Alberta in the morning.

As he waited for the woman to finish, he decided, not for the first time, that flying to Blossom and chasing after Alberta was truly stupid, on a par with watching television and smoking. What was he going to say?

"Hi. I was just in the area."

"Hi. I was in town on business."

"Hi. I was just passing through on my way to Waterton for the weekend."

"Hi. I didn't want to miss Lionel's birthday."

Act helpless. On the flight down from Edmonton, Charlie had turned his father's advice over once again. Easier said than done.

"You're not a movie star or something like that, are you?"

Charlie didn't hear the woman at first.

"I mean, you look . . . you know, sort of familiar."

"No," said Charlie, trying to work up a smile. "That was probably my father."

"Oh, wow!" said the woman, and she handed him the keys to the car, the rental agreement, and the white and orange bag stuffed with advertising debris. "Have a nice stay."

Portland Looking Bear had been a movie star. After Lillian got sick and was confined to her bed, Charlie would sit with her after school and listen to the stories about how she had run off with Portland, how they had borrowed her father's pickup and made it as far as Missoula before it bellied-up in a motel parking lot, and how, from there, they had worked their way through Montana and Idaho, Washington and Oregon, all the way to Los Angeles. Hard times and good times.

"This was long before your father changed his name to Iron Eyes Screeching Eagle."

"You're kidding."

"Oh, yes. Iron Eyes Screeching Eagle. What an imagination!"

Hollywood had not even noticed them arrive, but Portland had been persistent, and a few roles as an extra in crowd scenes turned into some bit parts. Within two years, Portland was in almost every B Western that the studio made.

"Did he ever play the lead? You know, the hero."

"He could have," Charlie's mother told him. "But that was back before they had any Indian heroes."

"I mean, did he ever play a lawyer or a policeman or a cow-boy?"

"A cowboy." And his mother had laughed. "Charlie, your father made a very good Indian."

After the fourth year of playing minor roles, C. B. Cologne, a red-headed Italian who played some of the Indian leads and ran the extras for three or four of the studios, told Portland he should think about changing his name to something more dramatic. Portland and Lillian sat around one night with C.B. and his wife, Isabella, and drank wine and tried to think of the most absurd name they could imagine.

"Iron Eyes Screeching Eagle. It still makes me laugh."

But before the year was out, Portland was playing chiefs. He played Quick Fox in *Duel at Sioux Crossing*, Chief Jumping Otter in *They Rode for Glory*, and Chief Lazy Dog in *Cheyenne Sunrise*. He was a Sioux eighteen times, a Cheyenne ten times, a Kiowa six times, an Apache five times, and a Navaho once.

"We were on top of the world then. We lived in an apartment that had a pink swimming pool. Can you imagine? And if you stood on the toilet, you could see the ocean."

"Did you know any of the big movie stars?"

"All of them," Charlie's mother told him. "We knew them all."

"So what happened? Why'd you leave Hollywood?"

When Charlie had first asked that question, his mother said she was tired and that she should rest. And for weeks after that, while she continued to delight Charlie with stories of life in Hollywood, she did not touch on the subject of their leaving Los Angeles and coming home to the reserve.

Then a few days before she slipped into a coma, Lillian had Charlie sit very close to her and said in a whisper that Charlie could barely hear, "It was his nose, Charlie." And she laughed, the effort sending spasms through her thin body. "It was your father's nose that brought us home."

. . .

Charlie dragged his bag to the parking lot. The woman at the desk had said that the rental car would be waiting at the far end of the lot, that he couldn't miss it. So far as Charlie could tell, there was nothing at the end of the lot. But as he walked away from the lights and the terminal, he began to make out a ghostly form in a dark corner, tucked in against some bushes.

As he got closer, the first thing that Charlie noticed about the car was that it was red, a color he hated. The second thing was that it was old; in fact, as he got up to the car itself, he realized that some of the red was, in reality, rust. Charlie looked around the lot again. Nothing. He tried the door key. The door opened.

The walk back to the terminal was even longer than Charlie remembered. It had just been a mistake. No one rented cars like that, not even the secondhand outfits. Charlie was halfway to the building when the terminal lights went out. By the time he got to the door, it was locked. He leaned against the glass to see if he could spot the young woman at the rental counter, but the counter was in shadows. As he stood by the door, he felt the wind freshen, and as he debated his options, it began to rain.

Portland's nose wasn't the right shape. As long as he had been in the background, a part of the faceless mob of Indians falling off their ponies in the middle of rivers or hiding in box canyons or dying outside the walls of forts, things had been okay. But now that he was center stage, playing chiefs and the occasional renegade, the nose became a problem.

The matter came to a head when Portland auditioned for the Indian lead in *The Sand Creek Massacre* starring John Wayne, John Chivington, and Richard Widmark. The director, a slight man with a sparse blond mustache that made his upper lip look as if it were caked with snot, told Portland that he could have the part but that he would have to wear a rubber nose. Portland thought the man was kidding and told him that the only professionals he knew who wore rubber noses were clowns.

The next day, it was announced that C. B. Cologne had been signed to play Chief Long Lance in the movie. There were two other Westerns that were casting, and Portland tried out for them.

"He brought the nose home with him," Charlie's mother told him.

"What'd he do with it?"

"It was the silliest thing you ever saw. Portland put it on and chased me around the house. He only caught me because I was laughing so hard."

"What'd he do with it?"

"He nailed it to the wall in the bathroom."

The desk clerk at the Blossom Lodge was a thin, older man. He had on a dark blue blazer and a gold name tag that said "N. Bates, Assistant Manager."

"I have a reservation. Charlie Looking Bear." And Charlie handed the man his credit card.

"Is that one word or two?"

"Two. Looking and Bear."

"Ah, yes, here it is. Mr. and Mrs. ?"

"Just me."

"Certainly," said the clerk, never taking his eyes off the computer. "Does the gentleman have a major credit card?"

"I already gave it to you."

"Ah, yes, so you did. Here we are. Does the gentleman have a car?"

Charlie looked out the window. The Pinto was leaning to one side. "The red thing."

The clerk leaned over the counter. "The Pinto?"

"It's a rental."

The parts dried up completely after that. Portland held out for six months. Then one morning, when Lillian came into the bathroom to brush her teeth, the nose was gone.

Everyone loved the nose. C.B. and Isabella swore it made him look even more Indian. And the parts began to open up again. But the nose created new problems. Portland couldn't breathe with the nose on, had to breathe through his mouth, which changed the sound of his voice. Instead of the rich, deep, breathy baritone, his voice sounded pinched and full of tin. Then too, while the nose looked dramatic in the flesh, it looked rather bizarre on film. Under the lights, in front of the cameras, it seemed to grow and expand, to dominate Portland's face. And Portland found that he was constantly bumping it or hooking it on a cup of coffee. Worst of all, it stunk, smelled like rotting potatoes. People began to measure their distance. And the parts dried up again.

Charlie dumped his bag on the dresser and went to the window. Outside, in the parking lot, he could see the rain falling. What should he say to Alberta? What did he want to say to her?

The Pinto was sitting in a low depression that was fast becoming a puddle. He'd call in the morning and see about an exchange. In the meantime, maybe it would just float away.

THE SECOND WAVE OF TOURISTS arrived just before five. Latisha got off the stool and took a deep breath. Dinner was the toughest shift. At lunch, everyone was still energetic, looking forward to what lay ahead. After five, tourists tended to sag, get grouchy. Food was never quite right. Service was always too slow. The adventure of the day had floated away, and all they had to look forward to was a strange bed in a strange motel.

"Bus in," Latisha shouted into the kitchen.

"What flavor?" Billy shouted back.

The bottom half of the bus was crusted with dirt, as if it had spent part of the morning wallowing in a mud hole. Latisha couldn't see the license plates.

Billy leaned around the doorway. "Not Canadian, I hope."

As the people got off the bus, Latisha could see that they all had name tags neatly pasted to their chests. They filed off the bus in an orderly line and stood in front of the restaurant and waited until they were all together. Then, in unison, they walked two abreast to the front door, each couple keeping pace with the couple in front of them.

"Canadian," Latisha shouted.

. . .

Early on in their marriage, George began to point out what he said he perceived to be the essential differences between Canadians and Americans.

"Americans are independent," George told her one day. "Canadians are dependent."

Latisha told him she didn't think that he could make such a sweeping statement, that those kinds of generalizations were almost always false.

"It's all observation, Country," George continued. "Empirical evidence. In sociological terms, the United States is an independent sovereign nation and Canada is a domestic dependent nation. Put fifty Canadians in a room with one American, and the American will be in charge in no time."

George didn't say it with any pride, particularly. It was, for him, a statement of fact, an unassailable truth, a matter akin to genetics or instinct.

"Americans are adventurous," George declared. "Canadians are conservative. Look at western expansion and the frontier experience. Lewis and Clark were Americans."

What about Samuel de Champlain and Jacques Cartier? Latisha had asked.

"Europeans." George laughed, and then he gave her a hug. "Don't take it personally, Country."

The woman at the near table held up her hand and waited. Her name tag said "P. Johnson."

Latisha took four menus with her. "Good evening."

"Yes, it is," said the woman. "And your name is?"

"Latisha."

"That's a lovely name," said the other woman, whose name tag said "S. Moodie." "My name is Sue and this is my good friend Polly."

The two men nodded as Latisha passed out the menus. They smiled and stuck out their chests so Latisha could read their tags: "A. Belaney" and "J. Richardson."

"Could you tell us what the special is?" asked Polly.

"Everything smells so wonderful," said Sue.

"Old Agency Puppy Stew."

"And how much is it?"

"Six ninety-five."

Polly looked at Sue and the two men. "Archie? John?" Both men nodded. "Excellent. We'll all have the special."

"Four specials."

"Does the special come with a vegetable?" asked Archie.

"Vegetables are in the stew," said Latisha.

"And bread?" asked John.

"Bread comes with it."

"I don't suppose dessert is included," said Sue.

"Ice cream or Puppy Chow. Coffee comes with it too."

"Wonderful," said Polly. "We'll all take the special."

"Four specials," said Latisha, holding her tongue between her teeth.

It hadn't bothered Latisha at first. But as George made these comparisons a trademark of his conversations, Latisha became annoyed, then frustrated, and then angry. After a while, she began to lay in wait for him.

"All the great military men in North America," George began, "were Americans. Look at George Washington, Andrew Jackson, George Armstrong Custer, Dwight D. Eisenhower."

"What about Montcalm?"

"He was French, and he got beat by an American."

"Wolfe was British."

"Almost the same thing."

"What about Louis Riel? What about Red River and Batoche?"

"Didn't they hang him?"

"Billy Bishop!" Latisha almost shouted the name.

George put his arms around her and kissed her forehead. "You're right, Country," he said. "There's always the exception."

. . .

"With the exception of Archie," said Sue, "we're all Canadians. Most of us are from Toronto. Archie is from England, but he's been here for so long, he thinks he's Canadian, too."

"It's nice to meet you."

"None of us," said Polly, looking pleased, "is American."

"We're on an adventure," said Sue.

"We're roughing it," said Archie.

"That last motel was as rough as I want it," said John, and Polly and Archie and Sue laughed, though not loud enough to disturb the other people at the other tables.

"Well, there's lots to see around here."

"What we really want to see," said Archie, "are the Indians."

"Mostly Blackfoot around here," said Latisha. "Cree are a little farther north."

Sue reached over and put her hand on Polly's arm. "Polly here is part Indian. She's a writer, too. Maybe you've read one of her books?"

Latisha shook her head. "I'm sorry, I don't think I know them."

"It's all right, dear," said Polly. "Not many people do."

It was a stupid game, but Latisha had to will herself not to play it. The baby helped. After Christian was born, Latisha had little time for George's nonsense. It was a stage, she told herself. But if anything, George's comparisons became even more absurd. The United States had more doctors, more lawyers, more writers, more motels, more highways, more universities, more large cities, and had fought in more wars than Canada.

Americans were modern, poised to take advantage of the future, to move ahead. Canadians were traditionalists, stuck in the past and unwilling to take chances. Americans liked adventure and challenge. Canadians liked order and guarantees.

"When a cop pulls a Canadian over for speeding on an open road with no other car in sight, the Canadian is happy.

I've even seen them thank the cop for being so alert. What else can I say?"

In the end, simple avoidance proved to be the easiest course, and whenever George started to warm up, Latisha would take Christian into the bedroom and nurse him. There, in the warm darkness, she would stroke her son's head and whisper ferociously over and over again until it became a chant, a mantra, "You are a Canadian. You are a Canadian. You are a Canadian."

Latisha shook hands with Polly and Sue and Archie and John as they left the restaurant. None of them bought menus. Latisha got the trolley from the kitchen and began clearing the dishes off the tables.

"Thank God they're not all Canadians," said Billy.

"You sound like George," said Latisha.

"And how many specials did we serve?"

Latisha laughed. "Okay, so they all had the special."

"Twenty-six specials. Baaaaaa," said Billy. "It was like feeding cheap sheep. Oh, Cynthia said that that guy called again."

"He leave a message?"

"Nope."

Latisha began clearing the tables. She was finishing up when she saw it. Sitting on a chair under a napkin. For a moment she thought someone had forgotten it, and she tried to remember who had been sitting at the table.

The Shagganappi.

Under the book was a twenty-dollar tip.

EVEN BEFORE ELI OPENED THE PACKAGE Sifton had brought, he knew it was books. Sifton always brought books. Sifton's brother-in-law, Arthur, owned a book store in Calgary. From time to time, Arthur would get in an uncorrected proof or an advance reading copy or a free promotional book. Some of them he would keep. The others he passed on to Cliff, who passed them on to Eli.

"Don't read anything over four pages anymore," Sifton told Eli. "Here, you used to teach literature and that sort of stuff."

Over the years, Eli had stocked several shelves in the kitchen with books Sifton had brought by and stored the rest in boxes under the bed.

There were three books this time. Eli hefted each one and decided on the Western. The cover featured a beautiful blond woman, her hands raised in surrender, watching horrified as a fearsome Indian with a lance rode her down. There was a banner stamped across the front that said, "Based on the award-winning movie."

He stacked the other two books on the floor and settled into the sofa. He paused for a moment, looked around the room to make sure he was alone, and then he opened the book. Even after all this time, Eli could still feel Karen looking over his shoulder.

He had met Karen in his second year at the University of Toronto. After a few weeks of repeated hellos, casual conversations, coffee at Murray's, and several brisk walks around Queen's Park, Karen had asked him if he had read any good books lately. Eli had not been prepared for the question. It was the first time a woman had asked him anything like that. Not having an answer he was sure of, he asked her what she was reading, and Karen promptly pulled a copy of Sinclair Ross's *As for Me and My House* from her pack.

"It's a wonderful novel," she said, and she lowered her voice. "All about a woman who almost dies of boredom on the prairies."

Eli hefted the book, turned it over once, smiled, and nodded.

"So," said Karen, "what are you reading?"

At that moment, all Eli could see was the reading list for the Victorian novel class he was taking.

"Just finished Wilkie Collins's *Bleak House*."

"You mean Dickens."

"Right."

"What else?"

"Ah . . . *The Woman in White* by . . ."

"Wilkie Collins."

"Right."

"Is this for a class?"

After that, Karen began lending him books. Some of them were interesting. He rather liked the one about the Halifax explosion.

"Penny's a New Woman," Karen told him after he had read half the novel. "Don't worry. She gets her baby back."

Others were not as interesting. "These are about Indians, Eli. You should read them."

"Okay."

"This one is about a kind of mythic character who comes out of the ground. He fights a bear. You'll like that. This one is by that painter in Vancouver or Victoria who does totem poles. You know, the one with all the animals."

"I think it's Vancouver."

"Here's one by a Native writer on Indian legends. My father heard her speak once. Said she was very good."

Eli found a copy of Stephen Leacock's *Arcadian Adventures of the Idle Rich* at a used-book store. "You ought to read it," he told Karen. "It's funny as hell."

"A little on the light side," Karen told him. "Here," and she gave him a thin volume by Dorothy somebody. "Imagist poetry. It's a little tough going at first, but worth the effort."

Most of the books that Karen brought by were about Indians. Histories, autobiographies, memoirs of writers who had gone west or who had lived with a particular tribe, romances of one sort or another. Eli tried to hint that he had no objection to a Western or another New Woman novel, and Karen would laugh and pull another book out of her bag. Magic.

"You have to read this one, Eli. It's about the Blackfoot."

What amazed Eli was that there were so many.

Eli settled into the couch and opened the novel. The plot was simple enough. A young woman from the east, who had lived a sheltered life, had come west to join her fiance, only to find that the young man had been killed by Indians. Distraught, she threw herself on his grave, had a good cry, packed her bags, and headed back east. Just beyond the town, where the road wound its way through a narrow pass, the stagecoach was attacked by Indians led by the most notorious Indian in the territory, the Mysterious Warrior. The Indians killed the driver and the guard and one of the passengers, an older man who, perceiving the young woman to be in danger, drew a pistol in her defense. Trembling and alone, the woman, whose name was Annabelle, huddled on the ground waiting for death. But instead of being scalped as she had supposed, the Mysterious Warrior picked her up, put her on his horse beside him, and galloped away.

Eli got up and put a pot of water on. The light was beginning to fade. It was junk and he knew it, but he liked Westerns. It was like . . . eating potato chips. They weren't good for you, but no one said they were. Beyond the river and through the trees, Eli could see the prairies, and he chuckled as he imagined for a moment galloping through the tall grass on a glistening black horse with Karen flung across the saddle. At first, she lay there, looking up at him with wondering eyes, and then she was laughing and throwing books into the air and shouting, "Read this one, read this one."

And then the horse stumbled.

Eli poured the water over the teabag and went back to the couch. He took off his shoes and stretched out, a large pillow behind his shoulders, and opened the book.

Chapter four.

Karen liked the idea that Eli was Indian, and she forgave him, she said, his pedestrian taste in reading, and at the end of the summer, after Karen had come back from an extended vacation in France with her family, she and Eli moved in together.

Actually, Eli moved in with Karen. It had always been obvious that Karen had money, and moving from his fourth-floor studio walk-up into Karen's brownstone just off Avenue Road reminded him of the distance the two of them had crossed. The flat was simple enough and there was no conspicuous show of wealth, but even Eli could tell that the rugs on the floor were Persians and the paintings and prints on the walls were not the cheap reproductions that the university bookstore sold.

"That one is by A. Y. Jackson. The other is by Tom Thomson. What do you think?"

"They're great."

"It's the light. It makes the land look . . . mystical."

"They're great."

That first night in bed, surrounded by the rugs and the paintings and the books, Karen rolled on top of Eli, straddled him, and held his arms down by the wrists. "You know what you are?" she said, moving against him slowly. "You're my Mystic Warrior." And she pushed down hard as she said it.

The Indian's name was Iron Eyes, and his family had been killed by whites. He was sworn to stop western expansion onto his people's land and he had spared Annabelle's life because he wanted her to see that Indians were human beings, too.

"Iron Eyes will not hurt you. You will go free. Tell the chiefs who watch the sun set that Iron Eyes wishes to live in peace."

But before she could be released, Annabelle had to spend some time in the camp. At first she thought it was the dirtiest place on earth. The tepees smelled, the people smelled, the food smelled, the dogs smelled. The Indian women resented her and the men kept casting lewd glances in her direction. After a few weeks in camp, her dress was in shreds and her hair, which had been delicately piled on her head, was hanging across her face in matted lumps. Worse, she began to smell.

Finally, Iron Eyes's sister, a beautiful woman named Hist, took Annabelle under her wing, showed her where she could bathe in the river, gave her some buckskin clothes to wear, and combed and braided her hair for her. When Annabelle and Hist came back into the camp that evening, Iron Eyes, who was practicing hand-to-hand combat with some of his men, stopped what he was doing, walked over to where Annabelle and Hist were standing, and took Annabelle's hands in his.

Eli closed his eyes for a moment and rubbed his stomach. He was going to sleep. Not a good sign. He rolled off the couch and went back to the kitchen. The water was still hot, and he poured himself a second cup. As he came back into the living room, he caught a glimpse of himself in the mirror. Tall, dark, overweight, gray. He smiled at his reflection and tightened his chest muscles for a moment. It didn't help.

Eli adjusted the pillow, sipped at the hot tea, and opened the book.

Chapter eight.

They had lived together for two years before Eli met Karen's parents. Karen assured him that her mother and father would love him as much as she did, and Eli was sure that she was wrong.

"Mom and Herb are going to the cottage we have in the Laurentians. You'll love it."

Eli knew he was not going to love it, but he smiled and pretended that he was looking forward to the trip.

The cottage was not a cottage at all. It was a four-bedroom house set on a lake. When Eli and Karen arrived, Karen's father was up on a ladder painting a shutter.

"Go on in," he shouted. "Maryanne's waiting for you. I'm Herb. You must be Eli. Nice to meet you."

Karen's mother greeted him as if he were a long lost son, and while Karen helped her mother in the kitchen, Eli wandered back outside and watched Herb touch up the corners of the shutter.

"Looks good," he shouted.

"Thought you Indians had keen eyes." Herb laughed, and he hung the bucket on the ladder and came down.

Karen had told Eli that they would probably have to have separate rooms. Her parents knew they were living together, but at the cottage they might have to compromise.

And that was another pleasant surprise. Not only did Karen's father seem like a regular guy, but when Eli took the bags upstairs, he found Karen in a large, airy room with a view of the water, sitting in the middle of a bed.

"Nice. Where do I sleep?"

Karen patted the bed. "Here."

"What about your parents?"

"They're progressive. Mom said that this was the twentieth century."

Eli dropped the bags, climbed on the bed, and rolled Karen on her back.

"But we can't do anything."

"What?"

"God, Eli. My parents. What if they heard?"

Herb was an avid reader. The cottage was stuffed with books, most of them mysteries and Westerns.

"Maryanne indulges me. I mean, this stuff is junk, but, well, hell, I love it. You read Westerns?"

"You bet."

"Those sleazy little cowboy and Indian shoot-'em-ups?"

"Yes," Eli admitted. "Those are the ones."

Herb went to a shelf and took down a book. "Here, I'll bet you haven't read this one yet."

That evening, Eli snuggled against Karen and slid his hand under her nightgown. "I really like your parents," he said, finding her nipple. "They won't hear us."

"You're awful," she said, and she pulled Eli's shorts down in one decisive jerk.

Afterward, as Eli was on the verge of sleep, Karen kissed his chest and drew herself in against his body. "So," she said in a sleepy whisper that seemed to come from miles away, "when do I get to meet your parents?"

LIONEL PAID FOR THE GAS and slid behind the wheel. "I've got lots of options," he said.

"You ran out of options years ago," said Norma. "The boy can use all the help he can get."

"She's just kidding," said Lionel.

"No, I'm not."

"I don't need any help."

"You should see some of the mistakes he's made. Would make your teeth fall out."

Lionel tried to brush Norma off with a wave of his hand. "Doing just fine."

In the rearview mirror, Lionel could see the old Indians talking to each other, but he couldn't hear what they were saying.

"Okay," said the Lone Ranger. "We can do that."

"Look," said Lionel, "maybe you should save a whale or something like that."

"Whales don't need help," said Ishmael.

"No," said Robinson Crusoe. "It's human beings that need help."

"So we're going to help a human being," said Hawkeye.

"That's right, grandson," said the Lone Ranger. "We're going to help you."

Lionel opened his mouth just as the Lone Ranger leaned forward and patted his shoulder. "No need to thank us, grandson," he said. "Where do we start?"

"Well," said Norma, "you can start with his jacket. The one he has to wear to work is real ugly."

"Oh, boy," said the Lone Ranger. "That's a good start all right."

"Yes," said Ishmael. "And we have just the thing."

Actually, three mistakes wasn't so bad. Lionel had made a great many good choices. He had chosen Alberta. Nothing wrong with that choice. Even Norma liked her. Lionel could even remember the evening he had decided that Alberta was the woman for him.

It had been a Tuesday evening, four years ago in June. He had come home from work and called his mother to tell her about the big sale Bursum's had on stereos.

"Don't need a stereo, honey," Camelot said. "That RCA you gave us for Christmas still works real good."

Lionel couldn't remember giving his parents an RCA. "Is that the one that Grandpa had in his basement?"

"Oh," said his mother. "Maybe it is."

"It's getting kind of old."

"So are we," said Camelot. "Latisha was out this weekend. Said she hadn't seen you for a while."

"You know the television business."

"I'm making Hawaiian Curdle Surprise this Friday. You can't get food like this in town."

"What's in it?"

"It's a surprise. Your father can't wait to taste it."

"Alberta's coming out this weekend. We'll probably go over to Waterton. Or maybe Banff."

"Bring her out to the house. She's a wonderful woman. Wouldn't mind her for a daughter-in-law. Your father likes her, too."

"I think we're going to Banff."

"If you're serious about Alberta, you should bring her home so we can meet her."

"You've known her all your life."

"It's not the same."

Actually, it hadn't been a bad idea, after Lionel thought about it for a while. They could have dinner at his parents' house. Go for a walk on the prairies in the evening. The next day they could drive to Banff, maybe take in the hot springs. And at the right moment, Lionel could turn the conversation around to relationships and marriage. He had debated getting a ring, but decided there was no need to rush things. After all, Alberta might want to help pick it out. She was an independent woman. She might even insist on sharing the cost. But whatever happened, the dinner at his mother's would get things off to a good start.

"The jacket is a real good start," said Ishmael.

Up ahead, Lionel could see the sign for Blossom. He'd drop the old Indians off at the Lodge, take Norma home, go back to his apartment, and watch some television. Alberta might have phoned. She might even be in town. Tomorrow he would be forty, and by that evening, if everything went as planned, he'd have his life back on track.

"He sells televisions," Norma was telling the Indians. "His birthday is tomorrow. He's going to be forty, and he sells televisions."

"Birthday?" said the Lone Ranger. "I guess we got to sing that song."

"No need," said Lionel. "It's not until tomorrow."

"No," said the Lone Ranger. "We better start now. No telling what's going to happen tomorrow."

The turnoff for Blossom was just ahead. Lionel pressed down hard on the accelerator.

.   .   .

Things got off to a bad start. Alberta was happy enough to eat at his parents' house, but the minute Lionel stepped in the door, his father started in.

"You still working at that toilet store?"

"Television store."

"Don't see much of you."

"It's long hours, but it pays good."

"Don't see much of you."

The Hawaiian Curdle Surprise was a big surprise. Lionel didn't know exactly what was in it, but he was able to identify the pineapple and the fish.

"It's delicious," Alberta told his mother.

"I got the recipe out of the cookbook on Hawaiian cuisine that Harley gave me for Christmas. You're supposed to use octopus for the stock, but where are you going to find octopus around here?"

"It's really good."

Lionel fished around in the stew and found another piece of pineapple. "Bill's Fish Market might have octopus."

"Moose works just as well," said his mother.

By the time they had finished dinner, the wind had come up. Lionel could hear the dirt hitting the windows and the sides of the house.

"Harley and I are going for a walk," his mother said, looking at her husband. "Why don't you two just stay here and relax."

"A walk?" his father said.

"We always go for a walk after dinner."

"In this wind?"

"It's okay, Mom," said Lionel.

"No," said Alberta, "it sounds like a great idea. Why don't we all go."

"In this wind?" said Lionel.

By the time Lionel got to the Lodge, Norma and the Indians had sung four choruses of "Happy Birthday." Lionel had driven as fast as he could, run yellow lights, cut off corners, passed cars on two-lane streets. Whatever else the old Indians were, they weren't singers. All the way through town, their voices had twisted and turned, sounding for all the world like cats trying to get out of a tin can.

"Boy," said the Lone Ranger, "that was some good singing. That was a good way to start. It made me feel good all over."

"You sing real good," said Norma. "After you fix the world, maybe you want to come out and visit."

"That would be good," said the Lone Ranger.

"I'm going to be setting up my lodge tomorrow."

"That's a good idea," said Ishmael. "We should do that."

"Will our grandson be there?" said Hawkeye.

"What about it, Lionel?" And Norma stabbed him in the ribs again.

"Here's the Lodge," said Lionel, pulling under the canopy at the front door, jumping out, and opening the back door. "Sure was nice to meet you."

"You got a favorite color?" asked Ishmael.

"A color that makes you feel good?" said Robinson Crusoe.

"I like red, myself," said Hawkeye.

Lionel opened the front door of the Lodge for the Indians. "You have a safe trip. Maybe we'll run into each other again sometime."

"Tomorrow," said the Lone Ranger. And the Indians walked past Lionel single file into the lobby of the hotel.

"Tomorrow," said Lionel after they all got back from the walk and his parents had gone to bed, "I thought we could go to Banff." There were pieces of grit in Lionel's hair and in his nose. As he talked, he casually tried to scoop his ear out. "We could go to the hot springs or walk around or something. Anything you want to do." Lionel put his hand across the back of the sofa, the fingers almost touching Alberta's shoulder.

"Your parents are nice."

"Nobody cooks like Mom."

"That's mean. Your mother's very adventurous."

"No, I mean it. She's a great cook."

Lionel moved his hand so that he could rub Alberta's shoulder with one finger. "So, tomorrow we drive to Banff. Stay the night." Lionel leaned forward as if he was stretching and moved closer. "It'll give us a chance to talk."

By the time Lionel got up the next morning, his mother and father were sitting at the kitchen table drinking coffee.

"Thought you wanted to get an early start," his mother said.

"No rush."

"Tell Alberta when she uses the shower to watch the hot water handle. Harley hasn't fixed it yet."

"She like waffles?" asked Lionel's father. "I'm making waffles today. Belgian waffles. Camelot got this great recipe from Latisha."

"She had to go back to Calgary."

"Alberta?"

"She forgot about a meeting."

"Today's Saturday, son."

Camelot frowned at her husband. "You two have a fight?"

"Nope."

"That's too bad, honey. Banff is beautiful this time of year. And romantic, too."

Lionel's father got the waffle iron down and plugged it in. "You want some waffles?"

"Sure."

"Could use a hand around the house."

"Probably should get back," said Lionel, cutting a hunk of butter off the block. "Bursum's getting a big shipment today. I can always use the money."

"It's not much. Just a little plumbing and a hand with the front porch."

"We got any maple syrup?"

.   .   .

Lionel unlocked the door to his apartment. Inside, the air was cool, the room dark.

The old Indians.

Lionel could still hear their singsong voices in his head. Happy birthday. Happy birthday, as if something was coming apart, as if he had unknowingly made yet another mistake.

Lionel squeezed past the Formica table, fumbled his way into the easy chair, and found the remote control without ever having to turn on the lights.

BY THE TIME ALBERTA ARRIVED IN BLOSSOM, it was too late to drive out to the reserve. Another hour over two-lane roads in the dark was not the way she wanted to finish her evening. As she followed the off ramp, Alberta could see the big square sign for the Blossom Lodge. The only parking spot was next to an old red car that was tilted to the side at a funny angle. When she got out, she saw that one of its tires was flat. Even more annoying, there was a small lake around the car, and Alberta had to walk all the way out to the curb in order to get back to the lobby.

"I'd like a room for the night."

"Mr. and Mrs.?"

"No, a room for one."

The desk clerk looked over his glasses at Alberta.

"As I recall, you have a university discount," she continued.

"And does the lady work at a university?"

Alberta pulled out her university identification card and her driver's license.

The desk clerk smiled and handed her cards back to her. "You can't always tell by looking," he said.

"How true it is," said Alberta. "I could have been a corporate executive."

. . .

The receptionist at the clinic had been almost as unctuous.

Option four.

Artificial insemination.

When Alberta was small, she had seen cows artificially inseminated. There was nothing wrong with it, she guessed, for cows, but even there it had seemed . . . mechanical. The thought of crawling up on a table and putting her behind in the air while some doctor fiddled with a hose made her furious. She wasn't even sure that that was how they did it with humans, reasoned that it was not. But she remained skeptical and unconvinced, even by the articles that she was able to find on the subject, which dwelt, for the most part, on the successes and the failures and not the process itself. All that changed after the night she had stood across the street from the Shagganappi Lounge and watched the lights change.

But having made the decision, Alberta discovered she had no exact idea how to go about it. So one Saturday, greatly comforted by the fact that she could do the preliminary gathering of information by phone, Alberta sat down with the *Yellow Pages* and looked up artificial insemination.

Cows. Cows.

Horses.

Cows. Horses.

Cows. Cows.

"Does the lady have a major credit card?"

Alberta put her card on the desk.

"Does the lady have a car?"

"The blue Nissan parked next to the red thing."

"And does the lady require any help with her bags?"

Alberta smiled and leaned forward on the counter.

By the time she got to her room, Alberta was sorry she had been so rude. At least the room was pleasant. Alberta flopped down on the queen-size bed, stacked the pillows under her head, let her shoes drop off her feet, picked up the remote control, and aimed it at the blank screen. Then she got up, went to the bathroom, and flossed her teeth.

The next thing Alberta did was to call the general number for the Calgary hospital.

"Information."

"Yes. Could you transfer me to the Artificial Insemination Department."

The woman on the other end of the phone didn't say anything for a moment, and Alberta hoped she was running her finger down the directory, looking in the A's.

"Please hold," said the woman.

"Gynecology."

After that, Alberta got Obstetrics, and after that, Pediatrics. And after that, the main switchboard.

"Information."

"Ah . . . Artificial Insemination?"

"Please hold."

"Gynecology."

But the call hadn't been a total waste of time. As she hung up the phone, Alberta realized that the best place to start was probably with her own gynecologist. Dr. Mary Takai was a short Japanese woman, and while they were not exactly friends, they had, over the years, developed a professional relationship, and more important, Alberta felt comfortable talking with her.

"So that's the situation," Alberta said after she had explained her dilemma to Mary.

"Ah," said Dr. Takai.

"Given the options, I think that artificial insemination would be the best."

"Let me make some calls."

Alberta read the newspaper while Mary called Edmonton and several clinics in Calgary. "Okay," she said, "I have good news and I have bad news."

"Bad news?"

"Most of the clinics won't take single women. I think it's a question of morals."

"Morals?"

"One clinic will take single women. But you have to get a letter from me testifying to your physical health, your mental health, and your morals."

"Morals?"

"In the first instance, they figure that if you're not married, you're not trying. In the second instance, they figure that if you're not married but trying hard, you're not the kind of person they want to associate with."

"I just want a child. I don't want a husband."

"The Bennett Clinic in Edmonton." Mary wrote down the address and the phone number.

"Edmonton? Isn't there something in Calgary?"

"Foothills isn't taking any new patients. I'll write the letter today and you should hear from them in about six to eight months."

"Six to eight months?"

Mary smiled and crossed her legs. "It takes most couples longer than that just to get pregnant."

Alberta lay on the bed and touched the remote control. An old Western. Alberta changed to the next channel. Nothing. The next channel. Nothing. And the next. Before she knew it, she was back to the Western.

What men saw in these kinds of movies was beyond her. This one featured a white woman who was being held captive by Indians. Alberta watched the screen and thought about what she should get Lionel for his birthday. A book was the obvious answer, but Lionel, so far as she knew, didn't read. He could use a new jacket. That horrible gold thing that Bill Bursum made him wear was hideous enough in the context of the store, but Lionel insisted on wearing it on dates. She could always call Latisha in the morning, maybe even drop in for breakfast, and see if she had any ideas.

It was nine months before Alberta heard anything from the Bennett Clinic, and what she got was a form letter welcoming her interest in the services of the Bennett Clinic, a twenty-four-page form to fill out, and a chart on which she was to plot her body temperature and her periods for the next four months.

The woman who answered the phone was very friendly.

"Hi," said Alberta. "I just got a letter from your clinic—"

"And you're wondering why you have to wait another four months to get this thing rolling."

"Ah . . . well, yes."

"Everybody wants to know that. It's a real pain, isn't it."

"Well, inconvenient, I guess."

"I know just how you feel. You're probably regular as clockwork, eh?"

"Well, yes, I am. But I guess I don't mind filling in the form."

"If I got something like that, I'd be tempted to toss it out and forget the whole thing."

"No, no. I don't mind filling it out at all."

By the time Alberta got off the phone, the sweat was pouring down the sides of her breasts. That evening, she filled in all the questions.

Do you have frequent intercourse?

Are your periods painful?

Have you ever taken drugs?

Is there any mental illness in your family?

And later that month, when she started spotting, Alberta taped the chart to the wall and put a thermometer next to her bed.

The movie had run on ahead without her. Now the white woman was in love with the Indian chief and the soldiers were coming to rescue her. Just the sort of thing that Lionel and

Charlie would like. As Alberta watched, the chief, a tall man with a muscular chest and a large nose, sent the woman back to the fort and prepared to ambush the soldiers at the river.

Two months after Alberta sent in the questionnaire and the chart, another woman from the clinic called to tell her she was a blue priority patient and that they would call her for an interview as soon as they had an opening.

"Interview?"

"That's right. All of our patients have to see one of our staff psychologists. It's a rule."

"Blue priority?"

"It's based on age. Younger women get higher priority. You can see why."

"I'm not sure—"

"And when you get the interview, make sure your husband comes with you. We can't begin the interview process unless both the husband and the wife are here."

"I'm not married."

"A lot of people make that mistake."

"I'm sure."

"The women come and the men stay home."

"I don't have a husband."

"And then we have to start all over again."

Alberta readjusted the pillows and pulled the blankets around her shoulders. Lionel's birthday. What Lionel really needed, Alberta concluded as she fiddled with the remote control under the covers, was some help with his life. It had sort of drifted away from him. Lionel wasn't pushy and slick like Charlie. He was sincere and dull. And when she thought about it, Alberta wasn't sure that there was anything in between. Maybe all men were like that, Charlies and Lionels. Or worse. Maybe, in the end, they all turned into Amoses, standing in the dark, angry, their pants down around their ankles.

CHARLIE COULDN'T SLEEP. He rolled around in bed for an hour, rearranging the pillows, adjusting the blankets. Finally he sat up and turned on the lamp. There were color bars on channels two, four, and eleven, static on channel twenty-eight, and a Western on twenty-six.

Charlie shoved all the pillows behind his back so he could see the screen without having to sit up. A Western. The long flight down to save Alberta from herself. The mix-up with the car. Insomnia. And now a Western.

Lillian was three months pregnant when Portland packed everything in a pickup, and they came home from Hollywood. They stayed at Lillian's mother's place until after Charlie was born, and Portland went to work for the band council. Those were good years. Charlie and his cousins ruled the prairies, and if Portland missed the glamour of Hollywood, he didn't say. He stayed busy organizing tours, doing slide shows, writing articles for the travel magazines, and on the weekends he showed his son and the rest of the kids how to mount a horse without a saddle, how to ride bareback using just the mane and your hands, how to drop to the side of the horse so you couldn't be seen. How to fall off.

Charlie was fifteen when his mother got sick. He could remember her being sick. The trips to the hospital, the jars of pills, the machine next to his mother's bed that sounded as though it were breathing. But by the time he realized just how sick she was, she was dead.

A week after they buried Lillian, Portland stopped going to work.

At first, he simply stayed at the house and fixed things—the water pump, the fence, the door on the barn. Then he stopped fixing things and began to watch television. He would sit in the chair and flip through the channels, never watching any program for very long. Except for the Westerns.

"That one was on last week, Dad."

"I played a small part in that movie, but they cut it out."

"What else is on?"

"That's C. B. Cologne, Charlie. That Italian friend of mine I told you about. He got most of the good Indian parts in those days."

"What else is on?"

"You know what the *C. B.* stands for? You'll laugh. Crystal Ball. It was a perfume his mother was crazy about."

One afternoon, Charlie came home and found his father packing the pickup. Charlie stood at the gate and watched his father stuff a large suitcase into the camper.

"If you could go anywhere in the world," his father said, looking up in the sky, "where would you want to go?"

"What happens if I guess right?"

"Go ahead." Portland stood by the pickup, his hands stuck in the back pockets of his jeans. He had on his good boots. His hair was combed, and he had shaved. "Where would you want to go?"

Charlie wasn't sure he wanted to go anywhere, but as he looked at his father standing there, shifting his weight back and forth, smiling, Charlie knew the answer his father wanted to hear.

"Anywhere in the whole world," his father said.

"Hollywood?" said Charlie.

Charlie adjusted one of the pillows. He was sure he had seen the Western before. But after watching so many of them with his father, they all just ran together. There was a white woman in this one and an Indian chief and soldiers, and they ran around and shot at each other. Charlie recognized John Wayne, and one of the character actors was a man his father had known. The plot was boring, the acting dull, and Charlie was not any sleepier than before.

Lionel and Alberta. Lionel was his cousin, but even with the benefit of kinship, and allowing that women saw things in men that other men could not, Charlie was still at a loss to understand why Alberta would want to be seen with Lionel.

Charlie was better looking. It wasn't even close. Charlie had the better job, the better education. He made more money. Drove a better car. Better clothes. Better, better, better. Charlie rolled up on his side and turned the sound off. Damn. Damn, damn, damn.

All the way down through Montana and Idaho, Oregon and northern California, Portland retold the story about how he and Lillian had made their way to Los Angeles and into the movies. Sally Jo Weyha, Frankie Drake, Polly Hantos, Sammy Hearne, Johnny Cabot, Henry Cortez, C. B. Cologne, Barry Zannos, friends and rivals, a tight community of Mexicans, Italians, Greeks, along with a few Indians, some Asians, and whites, all waiting in the shadows of the major studios, working as extras, fighting for bit parts in Westerns, playing Indians again and again and again.

They stopped at a service station just outside Los Angeles. Portland slipped into the phone booth, dropped a dime in the slot, and dialed a number. Charlie had never seen so many cars, so much traffic. As they had come farther south, the traffic had increased, until now it was a steady flow, like a stream or a large river.

"Charlie," his father shouted, "you got a quarter?" Portland stood just outside the booth, the phone dangling from his hand. "It costs a quarter now. Would you believe it? When me and your mother were here, it was a dime."

"There sure are a lot of cars."

"You're going to love it here, Charlie. With your looks, you may even become a bigger star than me."

Charlie could hear the big trucks as they hissed across the overpass in the dark. There was a green highway sign in the distance, but it was too far away to read. Above the freeway lights and the headlights of the traffic pouring south, the sky was yellow and purple.

"Sky looks kinda funny, Dad."

"It'll be tough at first, but once we get rolling, nothing's going to stop us."

Portland winked and closed the door and the booth lit up. Charlie leaned against the truck and watched his father dial the number. There were no stars in the sky like home, and Charlie guessed it was because there were high clouds. Portland was talking to someone now, gesturing, smiling, laughing, rocking his shoulders backward and forward.

By the time Portland finished his call, Charlie had decided he wanted to go home and he told his father so.

"When are we going to go home?"

"We just got here. You're a little homesick right now, but you'll get over it."

"But if I want to go home, can we?"

"Sure," his father said. "You just say the word." And Portland started the truck, pulled onto the freeway, and they headed south.

That was it.

Charlie sat up in bed. His father had been right all along. Lionel was helpless. That's what Alberta saw in him. Helplessness. It was, Charlie admitted, the one area where Lionel had him beat. Lionel was helpless. Charlie was self-sufficient. Being better was suddenly worse.

Lionel was overweight, and Alberta felt sorry for him. Lionel had a lousy job, and Alberta felt sorry for him. Lionel had a mediocre education, barely earned minimum wage, owned a twelve-year-old car, and had to wear a gold blazer. And Alberta felt sorry for him. Damn. Damn, damn, damn.

C. B. Cologne and his wife, Isabella, insisted that Charlie and Portland stay in their basement.

"Rents are hell," C.B. told Portland. "Things have changed. The whole place has gone to shit. Remember how it was?"

"It was the best."

"Bet your sweet ass it was. You remember Frankie Drake?"

"Sure."

"He died."

"Shit!"

"Remember Henry Cortez? He played Montezuma in that little classic that what's-his-name directed."

"Me and Henry were like that."

"Dead, too."

Isabella went to bed at two. Charlie curled up on the couch and listened to his father and C.B. catch up on the years.

"I'm sorry as hell to hear about Lillian. Me and Isabella loved her, you know. Christ, you should have called. If I'd known, we'd of come up for the funeral."

"I need to get some work, C.B. Get back in the swing. Who's doing the Westerns these days?"

"Christ, Portland, things have changed. Not like the old days. Unions, rules, more asses to kiss. Who can predict it. It ain't like the old days at all. Hell, you don't even have to act anymore."

Act helpless. And Lionel didn't have to act. Charlie wasn't sure he could act as helpless as Lionel looked. Of course, there was the Pinto.

That was pretty helpless. Just seeing Charlie in that wreck should be enough to sweep Alberta off her feet.

Charlie laughed at the idea. In the old days, a man would bring in horses or perform brave deeds to impress the woman he loved. Now courtship had been reduced to displays of incompetence and junk cars.

The next morning, Portland and Charlie and C.B. piled into C.B.'s Plymouth and drove to the studio, and Portland spent the day meeting people, shaking hands, talking about the old days. C.B. showed Charlie around the different lots where movies were being shot.

"Hey, you know your father was the best. I mean it. Better than even Sammy Hearne."

"What are they doing over there?"

"Nobody played an Indian like Portland. I mean, he is Indian, but that's different. Just because you are an Indian doesn't mean that you can act like an Indian for the movies."

"Is that Jeff Chandler?"

"It's expensive down here now. You know what I mean? Me and Isabella do okay. But, hey, coffee costs a buck a cup. Who'd have guessed? What the hell are you supposed to do with that?"

C.B. and Portland spent the next night telling the same stories they had told the night before.

"You used to run the extras, C.B. What happened?"

"Hey, what can I say. They brought in some accountant type. A bean counter. He's the big cheese's nephew. And now they got computers."

"I need work, C.B. Couple more months, Charlie has to be back in school. We got to find our own place."

"Hey, maybe Remmington's is hiring."

"Oh, God!"

"Hey, hey, hey. Better than Four Corners."

The next day, they were at the studio again. The day after it was the same. Everyone remembered Portland. And everyone was glad to see Portland, all smiles and laughter. Charlie had never seen so many happy people in his life.

BILL BURSUM SQUEEZED PAST THE PACKING CRATES, turned on the light, unlocked the back door, and let Minnie out.

"Good night, Mr. Bursum."

"Good night, Minnie," said Bursum.

"Ms. Smith, Bill," said Minnie.

"Whatever," said Bursum, smiling. "My mother trained me."

"Try again," said Minnie.

"Good night," said Bursum.

"Good night," said Minnie.

Mrs., Miss, Ms. Bursum locked the door behind her. He just couldn't keep everything straight. At first it had been fun. Ms. For God's sake, it sounded like a buzz saw warming up. He had tried to keep up, but after a while it became annoying.

Indians were the same way. How many years had that old fart held up the dam? Some legal technicality. And the lake. A perfectly good piece of lakefront property going to waste.

And you couldn't call them Indians. You had to remember their tribe, as if that made any difference, and when some smart college professor did come up with a really good name like Amerindian, the Indians didn't like it. Even Lionel and Charlie could get testy every so often, and they weren't really Indians anymore.

The world kept changing and you had to change with it. Otherwise you could go crazy like that nut in Montreal. One bad apple and the next thing you know, everyone is screaming that the whole barrel is full of worms.

Make money. The only effective way to keep from going insane in a changing world was to try to make money.

Bursum walked back to his office and ran the totals. Not a bad day. Not a good day. He opened a drawer and pulled out a catalogue. How he wished he had been in on the video market from the beginning. He could have predicted the popularity of old movies. Ten years ago, all the movies that came through his store were new movies. Now more than half were old movies, made before video had even been invented. A gold mine.

Better yet, Bursum enjoyed old movies more than he liked the new videos, in which most of the action centered around weird machines and robots with rifles. Romance, that's what the new movies were missing. And the best romances were Westerns.

Bursum wandered through the displays of televisions, stereos, VCRs, speakers. Everything said money. It was a wonderful feeling. Bursum slipped the tape into the VCR and pushed a button. He pulled up a chair and sat down in front of The Map.

The screens glowed and flashed silver. One by one they came to full color. Bursum rocked back and forth in the chair, watching one screen and then another. Then taking in the panorama.

The Mysterious Warrior. The best Western of them all. John Wayne, Richard Widmark, Maureen O'Hara. All the biggies. He had seen the movie twenty times, knew the plot by heart. Even knew some of the lines.

"Yes!" Bursum whispered as the movie opened with a shot across Monument Valley, and he clutched his hands in his lap as if he was praying.

WHEN LATISHA GOT HOME, Christian was cooking something on the stove. Benjamin and Elizabeth were watching him.

"What's cooking?"

"Ssh!" Benjamin whispered, his hands clutched in his lap. "If you talk too loud, the food will burn."

"Yep!" said Elizabeth.

Christian pulled one side of his mouth up and looked at Benjamin. "It's just that they wouldn't stop talking. Where have you been?"

"Had to work late."

"You own the place."

"That's why I had to work late."

Christian stirred the pot with the yellow spatula. "Maybe we should come down to the restaurant to eat."

"What are you cooking, honey?"

"Spaghetti."

"You cooked spaghetti last night."

"I've cooked it every day this week."

"You should probably use a wooden spoon to stir it."

"They're all dirty."

"Well, you could wash them."

Christian stayed over the pot with his back to his mother. "I do everything already."

Latisha sighed. So that's the kind of evening it was going to be.

"It's okay, Mom," said Benjamin, rocking against his chair. "Elizabeth likes spaghetti."

"Yep," said Elizabeth.

She had stayed with George for nine years. That was how long it took to get the matter settled in her mind. Christian had been an only child for years before they decided that a second child would be good for Christian and would probably save their marriage. Benjamin and Elizabeth were two years apart. Elizabeth had been a surprise. The divorce was not.

At first, Latisha didn't believe it. It was one thing to know that George was worthless and quite another to act on it. It wasn't that George didn't have a job. He had had lots of jobs. Changed them four or five times a year. Each one was going to be *the* one.

"You got to move with the times, Country," George told her.

"Nothing wrong with a steady job. My brother does okay."

"Things that stand still, die."

And it wasn't the affairs, or as George called them, "lapses in judgment." In fact, she had grown tired of hearing about George's "lapses," had grown tired of forgiving George.

That was it. In the end, Latisha had just gotten bored. George was dull and he was stupid, bone-deep stupid, more stupid than Latisha could ever have guessed whites could be stupid.

"Quite a few men are like that, honey," Camelot told her daughter. "You ought to read the articles in *Cosmopolitan*."

So far as Latisha could tell, George's twinkling eyes, his wonderful smile, and his sparkling teeth were all painted on a balloon.

"I'm sorry I'm late, honey." Latisha gave Christian a hug. "You know how the place gets."

"I want a hug," said Benjamin.

"Me," said Elizabeth.

Christian spooned the spaghetti into three plates. It slid out of the pan with remarkable speed, bright red and quivering. "You want some, Mom?"

Latisha looked at the wad of noodles on the plate. Under the strands of spaghetti and the oily sauce were brown chunks. "What's in the spaghetti, honey?"

"Hot dogs," said Christian.

"Oh, God."

"Oh, Gawd," said Elizabeth.

"That's a bad word," said Benjamin. "You're going to have to have time out."

"No time out," Elizabeth shouted.

"How about it?" said Christian. "I don't want to stand here all night."

"No," said Latisha. "I'm not really hungry."

Elizabeth was sucking on her cup. "Yook, Mommy, yook," and she held it up. The liquid inside was brown.

"Christian, what's Elizabeth drinking?"

"Coke and milk."

"What?"

Christian tossed the spatula into the sink. It landed in a bowl of water and flipped specks of spaghetti sauce on the window. "It's the same thing as a milk shake."

"Look, guys," Latisha said, rubbing her forehead, "I could use some help around here, you know."

Christian ran his fork through the spaghetti. "What do you think this is?"

One day George walked into the restaurant wearing a fringed leather jacket. "What do you think?"

Latisha had looked and nodded and gone back to work. George stood there in the middle of the restaurant as if someone had turned him off.

"There's a hat and gloves that go with it," he said. "They belonged to one of my relatives. Now they belong to me."

"Nice jacket," Billy had told him.

"Damn right it is," said George.

"Thought you just liked new things," said Latisha, wiping down a table.

"It's history," said George, rolling his shoulders in the jacket. "Most old things are worthless. This is history."

"Guess you got to know which is which."

"There's a hat and gloves that go with it."

That night when Latisha got home, George was sitting in front of the television with Christian curled up on his lap. He still had on the jacket. Latisha hadn't even seen it coming. George turned the television off, got out of the chair as if he was getting up to get a cup of coffee, grabbed Latisha by her dress, and slammed her against the wall. And before she realized what was happening, he was hitting her as hard as he could, beating her until she fell.

"Don't you ever do that again," he kept shouting, timing the words to the blows. "Don't you ever do that again."

He stood over Latisha for a long time, breathing, catching his breath, his feet wide apart, his knees locked. And then he sat down in the chair and turned the television back on.

Latisha could feel blood running from her nose, but she stayed there on the floor. She could hear Christian sobbing, could see her son's thin body shaking as George took the boy in his arms to comfort him.

Benjamin and Elizabeth fell asleep on the couch, curled up against each other. Christian slouched over a pillow, his feet leaning against the wall.

"Mom, is this the one where the cavalry comes over the hill and kills the Indians?"

"Probably."

"How come the Indians always get killed?"

"It's just a movie."

"But what if they won?"

"Well," Latisha said, watching her son rub his dirty socks up and down the wall, "if the Indians won, it probably wouldn't be a Western."

On the screen, the chief and his men thundered across the river, yelling as they came. On the other side of the river, John Wayne stood up and waved his pistol over his head. He was wearing a leather jacket with fringe on it and a wide-brimmed hat. He stood in the sand, his feet set, challenging, ready. His gloves were stuck in his gun belt. On the ridge behind the Indians, a troop of cavalry appeared.

Christian took off one of his socks, smelled it, and threw it in the corner. "Not much point in watching it then."

"OH, OH," says Coyote, "I don't want to watch. Changing Woman is stuck on the island by herself. Is that the end of the story?"

"Goodness, no," I says. "This story is just beginning. We're just getting started."

Changing Woman is on that beautiful island by herself for a long time.

So.

One day she is watching the ocean and she sees a ship. That ship sails right to where Changing Woman is standing.

Hello, shouts a voice. Have you seen a white whale?

There was a white canoe here a while ago, Changing Woman shouts back.

Canoe? shouts the voice. Say, are you an able-bodied seaman?

Not exactly, says Changing Woman.

Close enough, says the voice. Come aboard.

Okay, says Changing Woman. And that one swims out to the ship.

I'm Ahab, says a short little man with a wooden leg, and this is my ship the *Pequod*.

Here says a nice-looking man with a grim mouth, and he hands Changing Woman a towel. What's your name?

Changing Woman, says Changing Woman.

Call me Ishmael, says the young man. What's your favorite month?

They're all fine, says Changing Woman.

Oh dear, says the young man, looking through a book. Let's try again. What's your name?

Changing Woman.

That just won't do either, says the young man, and he quickly thumbs through the book again. Here, he says, poking a page with his finger. Queequeg. I'll call you Queequeg. This book has a Queequeg in it, and this story is supposed to have a Queequeg in it, but I've looked all over the ship and there aren't any Queequegs. I hope you don't mind.

Ishmael is a nice name, says Changing Woman.

But we already have an Ishmael, says Ishmael. And we do so need a Queequeg.

Oh, okay, says Changing Woman.

"My favorite month is April," says Coyote.

"That's nice," I says.

"I also like July," says Coyote.

"We can't hear what's happening if you keep talking," I says.

"I don't care much for November," says Coyote.

"Forget November," I says. "Pay attention."

Pay attention, says Ahab. Keep watching for whales.

Why does he want a whale? says Changing Woman.

This is a whaling ship, says Ishmael.

Whaleswhaleswhaleswhalesbianswhalesbianswhaleswhales! shouts Ahab, and everybody grabs their spears and knives and juicers and chain saws and blenders and axes and they all leap into little wooden boats and chase whales.

And.

When they catch the whales.

They kill them.

{ 195 }

This is crazy, says Changing Woman. Why are you killing all these whales?

Oil. Perfume, too. There's a big market in dog food, says Ahab. This is a Christian world, you know. We only kill things that are useful or things we don't like.

"He doesn't mean Coyotes?" says Coyote.

"I suspect that he does," I says.

"But Coyotes are very useful," says Coyote.

"Maybe you should explain that to him," I says.

"Just around the eyes," says Coyote, "he looks like that GOD guy."

We're looking for the white whale, Ahab tells his men. Keep looking.

So Ahab's men look at the ocean and they see something and that something is a whale.

Blackwhaleblackwhaleblackwhalesbianblackwhalesbianblackwhale, they all shout.

Black whale? yells Ahab. You mean white whale, don't you? Moby-Dick, the great male white whale?

That's not a white whale, says Changing Woman. That's a female whale and she's black.

Nonsense, says Ahab. It's Moby-Dick, the great white whale.

You're mistaken, says Changing Woman, I believe that is Moby-Jane, the Great Black Whale.

"She means Moby-Dick," says Coyote. "I read the book. It's Moby-Dick, the great white whale who destroys the *Pequod*."

"You haven't been reading your history," I tell Coyote. "It's English colonists who destroy the Pequots."

"But there isn't any Moby-Jane."

"Sure there is," I says. "Just look out over there. What do you see?"

"Well . . . I'll be," says Coyote.

. . .

It's Moby-Dick, Ahab tells his crew, the gre...

Begging your pardon, says one of the c...
whale black?

Throw that man overboard, says Ahab.

Begging your pardon again, says another...
But isn't that whale female?

Throw that man overboard, too, says Ahab.

"Look out! Look out!" shouts Coyote. "It's Moby-Jane, the Great Black Whale. Run for your lives."

"That wasn't very nice," I says. "Now look what you've done."

"Hee-hee, hee-hee," says Coyote.

Moby-Jane! the crew yells. The Great Black Whale!

Throw everybody overboard, shouts Ahab.

Call me Ishmael, says Ishmael, and all the crew jumps into the boats and rows away.

This could be a problem, says Ahab.

That is a very beautiful whale, says Changing Woman, but I don't think she looks very happy.

Happy, happy, there you go again, says Ahab. Grab that harpoon and make yourself useful.

But Changing Woman walks to the side of the ship and dives into the water.

Hello, says Changing Woman. It's a good day for a swim.

Yes, it is, says Moby-Jane. If you'll excuse me, I have a little matter to take care of and then I'll be back.

And Moby-Jane swims over to the ship and punches a large hole in its bottom.

There, says Moby-Jane. That should take care of that.

That was very clever of you, says Changing Woman as she watches the ship sink. What happens to Ahab?

We do this every year, says Moby-Jane. He'll be back. He always comes back.

curious, says Changing Woman.

here are you going? says Moby-Jane.

Someplace warm, I think, says Changing Woman.

Come on, says Moby-Jane. I know just the place.

"I know the place she is talking about," says Coyote. "Italy."

"No," I says, "that's not the place."

"Hawaii?" says Coyote.

"Wrong again," I says.

"Tahiti? Australia? The south of France? Prince Edward Island?" says Coyote.

"Not even close," I says.

"Hmmmm," says Coyote. "How disappointing."

ELI OPENED THE BOOK AND CLOSED HIS EYES. He didn't have to read the pages to know what was going to happen. Iron Eyes and Annabelle would fall madly in love. There would be a conflict of some sort between the whites and the Indians. And Iron Eyes would be forced to choose between Annabelle and his people. In the end, he would choose his people, because it was the noble thing to do and because Western writers seldom let Indians sleep with whites. Iron Eyes would send Annabelle back to the fort and then go to fight the soldiers. He'd be killed, of course, and the novel would conclude on a happy note of some sort. Perhaps Annabelle would find that her fiancé had not been killed after all or she would fall into the arms of a handsome army lieutenant.

Chapter ten.

Eli opened one of his eyes. Then again, this one might be different.

Eli avoided the question of Karen's meeting his mother as long as he could. He wasn't sure why he was reluctant to take Karen with him back to the reserve, but he knew in his heart it was a bad idea.

At first, he didn't say anything, hoping that Karen would forget about it.

"When was the last time you were home?"

"Few years ago."

"You ever phone?"

Karen never came out and said that they should go to Alberta. She just let Eli know that she hadn't forgotten. Then one morning, as Eli was getting ready to go to class, Karen poked her head out of the shower.

"When am I going to meet your family?"

Eli waved at her and smiled.

"I mean," said Karen, leaning out and dripping water on the floor, "your mother's not an Indian or something like that, is she?"

Eli laughed and pulled a towel off the rack.

"Come on," Karen said, running her hands over her soapy breasts. "I showed you mine. You've got to show me yours."

Eli should have kept his eyes closed.

Chapter fourteen.

Iron Eyes and Annabelle were standing on the bank of a beautiful river. It was evening, and in the morning, Iron Eyes was going out with his men to fight the soldiers.

"It's such a beautiful evening," said Annabelle, brushing a wisp of hair from her glistening cheeks. "I don't want to leave," she said, trembling. "I don't want to leave this land. I don't want to leave you."

Eli shifted his body on the sofa. His left leg was going to sleep.

"Tomorrow is a good day to die," said Iron Eyes, his arms folded across his chest, etc., etc., etc.

Eli flipped ahead, trying to outdistance the "glistenings" and the "tremblings" and the "good-day-to-dyings."

Flip, flip, flip.

In April, Eli wrote his mother, suggesting that he might come out to Alberta in early July, that there was someone special he wanted her to meet. It was a long letter, eight pages to be exact, and the information on coming out and on Karen was buried in the middle.

At the end of May, he got a letter back from Norma that simply said, "We'll be at the Sun Dance, your sister, Norma."

"The Sun Dance!" said Karen. "I didn't even know you guys still practiced that. Is it true?"

"I guess."

"That's really nice of your sister. I mean, she doesn't even know me, and she invites us to the Sun Dance."

Eli agreed that it was nice of his sister.

"Can whites go? I mean, aren't some of those ceremonies closed?"

"No, you can go. It's no problem."

"I'll borrow my father's camera."

"You can't take a camera."

"Really? Well, I guess that makes sense."

Karen's father paid for the flight to Alberta. Said it would do them good to get away from the city, and they could think of it as a prehoneymoon.

"Isn't Herb progressive?"

At the Calgary airport they rented a car, a four-door De Soto, and drove the three hundred kilometers to the reserve without stopping. Eli liked being behind the wheel of the De Soto. There was no need for a car in Toronto, but if they ever got a car, this was the kind of car he wanted. It flew along the roads, floating over the landscape like a bird in flight.

Eli was having such a good time, he flew right off the asphalt and onto the lease road and the gravel and ruts before he had a chance to slow down.

From there, the De Soto became a different car. It lurched and wallowed through the potholes, slid on the gravel and the dirt. Karen had to brace her hands on the dash, the car pitching forward on its nose, as if it had been shot. Even slowing down didn't help a great deal. And behind the car, a huge, towering dust plume rose off the road into the night sky.

"How much farther?" Karen shouted over the bang and scrape and thump, thump, thump of the road.

The car windows slowly filmed over with dirt. Eli turned the windshield wipers on and cut tiny fans in the glass.

Just before dawn, Eli pulled the De Soto off to the side of the road. He got out and raised the hood to let the engine cool, and sat down on the bumper. Karen was asleep in the car, and Eli sat there for a long time and watched the circle of lodges in the distance slowly turn from blue to pink to white as first light gave way to the sun filling up the eastern sky.

The women's lodge was up. It had already started.

Smoke was rising from the tepees. There would be the horses moving on the prairies and the camp dogs nested beneath the wagons and the cars and the trucks, waiting for the day to begin. And the children. All the sounds and smells, all the mysteries and the imaginings that he had left behind.

It was cold still. Eli wrapped his arms around his chest and leaned against the radiator to stay warm. And as he sat on the bumper of the De Soto and watched the world turn green and gold and blue, he tried to imagine what he was going to say to his mother.

Eli flipped his way ahead almost to the end of the book.

Chapter twenty.

Iron Eyes was dressed in feathers and war paint and Annabelle was dressed in a beautiful white buckskin dress.

"Go," said Iron Eyes, stretching his arms out and pointing over Annabelle's shoulder.

"No," said Annabelle, flinging herself into his arms. "I want to stay with you forever."

Iron Eyes held her for a moment, and then pushed her away. "No," he said, his proud face turned toward the rising sun. "I am a warrior and a leader of my people. I cannot turn my back on them. I must fight and you must go."

"But I love you," said Annabelle, the tears forming in her eyes.

Just then, a runner came into the camp to say that the soldiers had been spotted, and the teakettle on the stove began whistling. Eli put the book down and got off the sofa.

It was a black, moonless night. Eli stood at the window and dipped the tea bag in and out of the cup, listening to the water swirl past the cabin in the dark.

Eli waited until Karen woke up.

"My God," she said. "That's beautiful. It's like it's right out of a movie."

It took a while for the De Soto to negotiate the track that led to the camp. As they got closer, Eli could see people moving among the lodges.

"It's enormous. There are hundreds of tepees." Karen leaned against the door as Eli swung around the circle. "What happens now?" she said. "You'll have to tell me what to do. I don't want to make a mistake and embarrass you."

His mother's lodge had always been on the eastern side of the circle. If it wasn't there, he would have to ask, but he wanted to avoid that if he could.

"It's like going back in time, Eli. It's incredible."

The lodges were six to eight deep, but he found his mother's lodge without difficulty. It looked deserted. As he pulled the car beside the tepee, the flap was drawn back, and Norma stepped out. She looked at the De Soto for a moment, shook her head, and went back inside.

"Who was that?"

"One of my sisters."

"I really want to meet her."

Eli opened the door of the car. It was getting warmer. The lodges cast long shadows on the land. Off to the right two dogs were arguing, and in the sky above a lone bird floated in the morning air.

"Is that an eagle?" asked Karen.

"No, it's a vulture."

Karen gestured toward the tepee. "Do we knock or something?"

"No, we just go in."

"Herb would like that."

Karen pulled the flap to one side and she stepped in.

Eli started to follow her. But for a moment, for just an instant before he stepped across the threshold and into the warmth of the lodge, Eli had an overpowering urge to lower the flap, get into the De Soto, and drive back to Toronto.

Chapter twenty-five.

The exciting part. Eli rolled up on the sofa with his tea. Iron Eyes and the other warriors rolled through the valley, driving the soldiers across the river, trapping them against a cliff. The scout, a tall man, stood up, took off his leather jacket, and waved his hat at the Indians.

Iron Eyes twisted around on his horse. The sun was at his back. As the light dropped into the eyes of the soldiers, Iron Eyes raised his rifle and swung his horse into the water.

Chapter twenty-six.

Eli's mother wanted to hear all about Toronto, what the city was like, where he lived. Norma took Karen around the camp and introduced her to Eli's relatives. Neither his sister nor his mother said anything about how long he had been gone or why he hadn't written.

Each day, friends and relations dropped by the lodge for coffee and conversation.

"Here's your boy all grown up," Eli's auntie told his mother.

"How's that Toronto, Eli?" his uncle wanted to know.

"When I get to Toronto, I'm going to come by and visit you," Eli's cousin Wilbur told him.

At first Karen was silent, content to listen as Eli's mother ran through the families. The babies who had been born, the young people who had gone away or come back, the elders who had died or were sick. Each one was a story, and Eli's mother told them slowly, repeating parts as she went, resting at points so that nothing was lost or confused. And then she would go on.

When Karen began to talk, she did so in short, abbreviated conversations that began apologetically and ended in mid-sentence. But by the third day in camp, just as the men began to dance, Karen found her voice, and Eli, who had been content to lounge on the blankets and drink coffee, was flushed from the lodge.

"Go on, Eli," Norma told him. "Go outside and chop some wood or chew some grass. Us women got talking to do."

There were other men outside, standing in groups, sitting in the grass. Eli stayed just outside the lodge. Every so often he would hear Karen's voice and the low muffle of laughter above the wind.

They stayed until the men finished dancing. And then Eli helped his mother take the lodge down.

"You going to marry her?" Norma asked him as he packed the suitcases into the De Soto.

"I'm sorry I haven't been back for a while."

"Rita Morley was asking about you."

"With any luck, we'll be able to get out here again next year."

"She wanted to know if you were married, and I told her I didn't know."

"Thanks for looking after Karen."

"You know Rita."

Eli's mother gave him a blanket and a braid of sweetgrass. She didn't ask him to write or to come back soon or to call. She kissed him, held him for a moment, and then she shook hands with Karen. Eli got into the car and started the engine.

Norma leaned in the window. "Camelot said to say hello. She couldn't make it over."

"Sorry I missed her."

Norma walked back to where their mother was standing, leaning on her cane. Both of them waved.

"We'll be here," Norma shouted over the roar of the engine.

Eli circled the camp. Most of the lodges were down. By nightfall the grounds would be deserted.

"It was wonderful, Eli. I've never been to anything like that." Karen drew her feet up on the seat and snuggled against the door. "Your mother and sister were great."

The De Soto made its way to the gravel road. Karen watched the camp through the rear window until the hills rolled up behind them.

"You must miss it." She put her head against his shoulder.

Eli drove the car through the gravel and the ruts and the washboards until he caught up with the main road to Calgary. And all the way across the prairies, he never looked back.

Chapter twenty-six.

CHANNEL TWENTY-SIX.

On the screen, the chief and the captive white woman were in each other's arms. It was standard stuff, but Charlie found himself watching the romantic tension that was building and wishing that Alberta were here in the room with him tonight. He suddenly felt lonely, terribly lonely. The kind of loneliness he hadn't felt for a long time. Not since his mother died. Not since he and his father had gone to Los Angeles to try to outdistance her death.

Portland had run into difficulties early. The matter was a simple one. No one would hire him as an actor. Or more properly, no one could hire him as an actor.

"You got to be a member of the union," Portland told Charlie.

"You going to join?"

"You have to have acting experience to join."

"You used to be an actor."

"Doesn't seem to count for much now."

There were a few nonunion jobs that Portland tried for, but everyone wanted young, muscular men with small butts and broad shoulders. Charlie had never thought of his father as middle aged or overweight. He wasn't. But he wasn't twenty, either.

"Remmington's is hiring," Cologne told Portland. "It's a shit job, I know. But, hey, the hours are flexible, and maybe someone sees you. Like the old days."

"Christ, C.B., I'm too old to do that."

"What about Charlie? Father-and-son team. They'd love it."

Portland continued to go to the studio, but each day he came back a little earlier. One day, Charlie came home and found his father sitting in front of the television. Portland had the remote control in his hand, but the set was turned off. He looked as if he had been sitting in the chair for a long time.

"You okay, Dad?"

"Sure, son."

"Maybe it's time for us to go home."

"You know how I got my start in the movies?"

"I mean, we've seen Disneyland already."

"Remmington's. I worked at Remmington's. I even worked at Four Corners for a while. I met C.B. when I was working at Four Corners."

"And there's nothing much for us here."

Portland put the remote control down and got to his feet. "It's how I started, and I can do it again."

"I'd like to go home."

"Come on," said his father. "We're just getting started."

Maybe what Charlie and Alberta needed to do was to start over. Charlie could see that he hadn't been as attentive as he might have been. Even cavalier. She was a professional, and he should treat her as such. Teaching was a fine profession, especially at the university level.

"My darling," the woman on the television was saying, "I don't ever want to leave your side."

"As long as the grass is green and the waters run," said the chief, holding her in his arms.

Charlie didn't need that kind of romance from Alberta, but it would be nice if she was more attentive, too. And supportive.

His job was tough enough without the woman he wanted to marry criticizing him. Sleazy. She hadn't meant it. Slick. Slick.

Charlie looked at the clock. It was two in the morning. The movie wasn't getting any better. And he wasn't any sleepier. Charlie closed his eyes, folded his hands across his stomach, and waited.

Remmington's was a steak house. It was done up to look like an Old West boardinghouse. The waiters all wore cowboy hats and cowboy shirts and chaps and cowboy boots. They all had bright colored bandannas tied around their necks and holsters hanging off their hips. Most of them wore mustaches. It was sort of like Disneyland with food.

"You friends with C.B., that right?"

"That's right," Portland told the man in the cowboy outfit.

"Okay, we can use a couple of guys. You worked here before, that right?"

"That's right."

"Check in with Doris. She'll give you your gear."

"Right."

"You dent any of the cars, it's out of your hide."

"Right."

The cowboy outfits weren't bad. Charlie hoped he'd get one with a blue shirt and a red bandanna. And like his father said, parking cars was an honest living. Lots of actors did it to get through the hard times.

"The cowboys work inside," Portland told him as Charlie squeezed into the flesh-colored tights. "It's the Indians who park the cars."

Charlie had to admit that he felt foolish standing around in front of Remmington's in tights, a beaded vest, and a headband with a brightly colored feather. The worst part was the fluorescent loincloth that hung down from his waist. "Remmington's" was written across the front.

"Remember to grunt," his father told him. "The idiots love it, and you get better tips."

At first the job was great. Charlie got to drive all sorts of really expensive cars—Mercedeses, Porsches, Lincolns, Jaguars, Ferraris. And the people were nice. Every so often a movie star would stop in. Once John Wayne came to Remmington's and Charlie got to get his car for him. Charlie grunted and handed Wayne the keys, and Wayne told Charlie not to order the prime rib and gave him a five-dollar tip.

After the second week, Portland caught him at the locker.

"I've got another job that pays better. But it's only for one."

"Where?"

"The Four Corners."

"Parking cars?"

"No, it's a strip joint." Portland smiled when he said it, as if he had just made a joke.

"You going to strip?"

"No, I just do some background dancing. Look, why don't you stay with this until school starts. The new job gives me more exposure. Probably pick up an acting job in no time."

"Sure."

For the rest of that summer, Charlie grunted and parked cars. On a good night, he could make up to fifty, sixty dollars, sometimes more. After work, on the weekends, he would walk over to the Four Corners and wait until his father finished his last set, and then the two of them would go out to Manny's and have breakfast.

Nothing happened. Charlie lay there and pretended to be asleep, and nothing happened. The white woman and the chief were still in each other's arms. Charlie put a pillow over his head and began counting horses, the kind of horses he and his cousins used to ride when he lived on the reserve.

In the background, filtered through the pillow, Charlie heard someone say something about soldiers and peace and love and then the white woman on the television began singing a song and all the horses in Charlie's head turned into dancing Indians.

.   .   .

The Four Corners was a burlesque theater. It was only about eight blocks from Remmington's, but the two were worlds apart. Remmington's was in the middle of an old neighborhood that had been gentrified into fashionable office complexes, upscale boutiques, and outdoor cafés. The Four Corners was in the same neighborhood, but in a section that had escaped urban beautification. There were no mosaic sidewalks outside the Four Corners. No decorator trees in natural clay pots. No little shops that smelled of cedar and rosemary, where all the prices were written on soft, cream cards and attached to the various objects with colored yarn.

On one side of the Four Corners was a bar. On the other side of the Four Corners was a bar. That was the block. The rest of the buildings were deserted, their windows either broken or boarded.

The first night Charlie went to the Four Corners to meet his father, he didn't know what to expect. He sat through three or four women who danced around on the runway and took off most of their clothes. It was smoky in the theater and so dark you could hardly see the dancers. There was a slightly pungent smell in the air, more than just the smoke, and as he shifted around in his seat, Charlie discovered that the floor was sticky.

Then a guy in a tuxedo came out, told a couple of jokes, and introduced the next dancer.

"And now, straight from engagements in Germany, Italy, Paris, and Toronto, that fiery savage, Pocahontas! Put your hands together for the sexiest squaw west of the Mississippi."

The woman, tall and good looking, was dressed up as if she were going to park cars at Remmington's. She walked around the stage as if she were lost, looked out into the audience with her hand shielding her eyes. And then, for no particular reason, she began to rotate her hips.

All of a sudden, Portland bounded onto the stage with a yell and grabbed Pocahontas. Charlie didn't recognize his father at first. He was wearing a black mask and he had done something to his nose and had painted it red. He looked silly, and he looked scary as he danced around waving his tomahawk and grimacing and sneering at Pocahontas and the audience.

At first Pocahontas pretended to be frightened, but as the two of them danced, things got friendlier. Halfway through the routine, Portland began to take pieces of Pocahontas's clothes off, first with his tomahawk and then with his teeth.

Just as Portland removed the last piece of clothing and the woman was standing on stage in just her pasties and G-string, another man, dressed up in a cowboy outfit, looking for all the world like one of the waiters at Remmington's, leaped onto the runway. The cowboy and Portland fought a short fight with the cowboy winning, and as Portland crawled off the stage in defeat, the cowboy began dancing with Pocahontas, their groins pressed together tightly, the cowboy's hands clutching the woman's buttocks.

"It's a dumb routine," his father told him as they walked to Manny's. "But that's acting."

"At least you don't have to take your clothes off."

"You're not embarrassed with me working there, are you?"

"No. Like you say. Maybe someone will see you."

Portland shoved his hands into his pockets and dropped his shoulders. "No one's going to see me, son."

A week later, Portland quit the Four Corners and went back to sitting in front of the television. In the mornings when Charlie got up, his father would be sitting in the chair in front of the television. When he left for work, his father would be there. Even after a long shift, Charlie would come home and find Portland sitting in the chair as if he had never moved.

C.B. took Charlie off to one side. "You know, your father isn't doing so well. I mean, hey, it's not really my place to say anything, but he's my friend."

"He just sits in front of the television."

"It's a young man's game. That's the problem. Portland left just as he was hitting the big money. No way he's going to get back in like before. It's a hard world, kid."

"Why'd they leave?"

"Your mom and dad?"

"Yeah."

"Don't know. Portland found out your mother was pregnant, and a couple of months later, bingo, he was gone. I guess that was it."

"What?"

"Maybe he didn't want to raise a kid in the city. Can't blame him."

The next evening Charlie packed their stuff in the pickup. His father stood on the sidewalk and watched his son lash the suitcases to the top of the camper.

"If you could go anywhere in the world," Charlie said to his father as he put the last bag on the truck, "where would you want to go?"

Portland looked at his shoes for a long time. When he finally looked up at Charlie, there were tears in his eyes.

"Anywhere in the world," said Charlie.

"Hollywood," his father said in a whisper. "I'd like to go to Hollywood."

The next day Charlie caught a taxi downtown, put his bags on the bus, and headed home alone.

Charlie took the pillow off his face. The white woman was nowhere to be seen. Soldiers were building a barricade of logs and saddles. More soldiers were running back and forth, shouting at each other. Charlie turned the sound off and lay there with his eyes open.

ALBERTA TURNED BACK TO THE MOVIE. The soldiers were trapped on one side of the river against a cliff face, and the Indians sat on their ponies on the other side. The chief whirled his horse around several times, held his rifle over his head, and all of the Indians began yelling and screaming, whipping their horses into the river. On the riverbank, four old Indians waited, their lances raised in the air.

Alberta hit the Off button. Enough. The last thing in the world she needed to do was to watch some stupid Western. Teaching Western history was trial enough without having to watch what the movie makers had made out of it.

But it was too late. As she closed her eyes, she could see Charlie mounted on a pinto, a briefcase in one hand, the horse's mane in the other, his silk tie floating behind him.

And Lionel mounted on a bay, naked, except for the gold blazer that billowed and flapped as he lay against the neck of the galloping horse, and his shiny wing tips glistening in the sun.

CHRISTIAN TOOK OFF THE OTHER SOCK and dragged it along the edge of the couch.

"Is it over, Mom?"

Latisha watched as the cavalry charged into the river bottom. John Wayne took off his jacket and hung it on a branch. All around him, the other men were starting to cheer as the soldiers bore down on the Indians.

"Yes," she said, "it is." And she touched the remote control. And the screen went blank.

LIONEL SETTLED INTO THE CHAIR. Norma hadn't let up, and Lionel had had to listen, once again, to his aunt's opinions about his life, about Alberta, about his job. Everybody wanted to run his life for him, as if he couldn't do it himself. Even the old Indians.

There was nothing on but a Western. Lionel settled farther into the chair and closed his eyes.

On the screen, an Indian danced his horse in the shallows of a river. On the bank, four old Indians waved their lances. One of them was wearing a red Hawaiian shirt.

But Lionel saw none of this. He lay in the chair, his head on his chest, the tumbling light pouring over him like water.

CHARLIE LIFTED THE REMOTE CONTROL and turned the sound on. The Indians were running their horses back and forth along the riverbank. On the other side, John Wayne and Richard Widmark waited behind a makeshift barricade of logs and saddles.

"Hear me, O my warriors," shouted the chief. "Today is a good day to die."

The chief spun his horse around in a circle, all the time grimacing and snarling into the camera, his long black hair flowing around his head, his wild eyes looking right at Charlie. But it was the voice that brought Charlie off the bed. He stood in the middle of the hotel room and watched as the chief rallied his men for the attack.

There on the screen, beneath the makeup, buried under a large rubber nose, was his father.

CHAPTER TWENTY-SIX.

Iron Eyes attacked the soldiers.

The cavalry came riding over the hill.

Etc., etc., etc.

Flip, flip, flip.

Eli tossed the book on the table, rolled up on his side against the cushions, and went to sleep.

BURSUM TOOK OFF HIS COAT and put it on the back of the chair. On the screen, John Wayne pulled his pistol out of his holster and raised it over his head and was shouting, "Hooray! We got 'em now, boys," as the cavalry came galloping into the valley.

Bursum stood in front of The Map and watched the spectacle of men and horses and weapons.

"Hooray," he shouted, waving the remote control over his head and turning the sound up. "Hooray!"

BABO PUT THE PLATE ON THE TABLE and eased herself into the recliner. The day had been exciting. The police and all. Sergeant Cereno had been especially entertaining. Sort of like Mike Hammer or maybe Perry Mason.

Those Indians. Boy, could they cause a stir. You'd think they had stolen a rocket and flown to Mars, the way people ran around.

Even Dr. Joseph God Almighty Hovaugh himself had come down to the lounge to talk to her. It was no big deal. The Indians would be back. They always came back.

Now her car *was* a big deal. She had no idea where it had gotten to, but Martin was going to hear about it. Cereno could have cared less, but that nice patrolman, Jimmy, had taken down all the information and promised to do the best he could to see that it was returned.

Babo turned on the television and flipped through the channels. Nothing. Nothing, nothing, nothing. Western. Nothing, nothing. It made the choices easier.

Babo put her feet up just as the chief spun his horse around in the river and raised his rifle to signal the attack. But it wasn't the chief that caught Babo's eye. In a small knot of Indians standing off to one side was an Indian in what looked to be a red shirt, and as Babo looked closer, she saw Hawkeye, Ishmael, Robinson Crusoe, and the Lone Ranger smiling and laughing and waving their lances as the rest of the Indians flashed across the river to where the soldiers lay cowering behind some logs.

"Well, now," said Babo out loud to herself. "Isn't that the trick."

DR. HOVAUGH SAT IN THE WINGBACK CHAIR and watched the chief spin his horse around and around in the water. Such a perfect symmetry of man and animal. Even though it was only a movie, Dr. Hovaugh was moved by the plight of the Indians, caught between the past and western expansion just as the soldiers were caught between the Indians and the sheer rock wall.

The horse must be an Arabian, Dr. Hovaugh reasoned, and the chief just might be an Indian. He knew that Hollywood used Italians and Mexicans to play Indian roles, but the man's nose was a dead giveaway. Probably a Sioux or a Cherokee or maybe even a Cheyenne.

As Dr. Hovaugh watched, the chief raised his rifle over his head and charged across the river, the rest of the Indians right behind him, while on the riverbank four old Indians raised their lances, encouraging their comrades, cheering them on.

It didn't reach Dr. Hovaugh all at once. When it did, he sat up in the chair.

"Oh, my God," he said, and he put down the remote control and reached for the phone.

THE LONE RANGER AND ISHMAEL lay on one bed. Robinson Crusoe and Hawkeye lay on the other.

"Oh, boy," said Robinson Crusoe, "it's a Western."

"But we have missed most of it," said Ishmael.

"Isn't this the one we fixed?" said Hawkeye.

"I believe it is," said the Lone Ranger.

"Yes, look," said Ishmael. "There we are."

As the old Indians watched, the chief led his men across the river. The soldiers behind the logs began shooting. One of the men stood up and waved his pistol over his head, and on the bluff overlooking the river, a cavalry troop appeared on the skyline.

Robinson Crusoe looked at the Lone Ranger.

Hawkeye looked at the Lone Ranger.

Ishmael looked at the Lone Ranger.

"Oh, oh," said the Lone Ranger. "Looks like we got to fix this one again."

I KNOW JUST THE PLACE TO GO, says Moby-Jane.

Where is that? says Changing Woman.

Florida, says Moby-Jane.

Is it warm?

Oh, yes, says Moby-Jane. That place is very warm and it is very wet. Just relax on my back, says that whale, and I'll take you there.

So, Changing Woman stretches out on Moby-Jane's back. Pretty smooth back, that one. Changing Woman presses herself against that whale's soft skin and she can feel those waves rock back and forth. Back and forth. Back and forth.

This is very nice, says Changing Woman.

Yes, it is, says Moby-Jane. Wrap your arms and legs around me and hold on tight and we'll really have some fun.

It is marvelous fun, all right, that swimming and rolling and diving and sliding and spraying, and Changing Woman is beginning to enjoy being wet all the time.

"Hey, hey," says Coyote. "That's not what I thought was going to happen. Hey, hey, hey. What are those two doing?"

"Swimming," I says.

"Oh . . ." says Coyote.

.   .   .

So.

Changing Woman and Moby-Jane swim around like that for a month. Maybe it is three weeks. Maybe not.

Then Moby-Jane sees some birds. Then that one sees some trees. Then she sees some land.

Oh, dear, says Moby-Jane. Here we are.

Perhaps we could swim some more, says Changing Woman.

That would be lovely, says Moby-Jane, but I have to get back and sink that ship again.

Moby-Jane and Changing Woman hug each other. Changing Woman is very sad. Good-bye, says Changing Woman. Have fun sinking that ship.

Changing Woman stands on the shore watching her friend swim away. So she doesn't see the soldiers.

Gotcha, yells those soldiers, and two of them grab Changing Woman. What have we here? says another.

Call me Ishmael, says Changing Woman.

Ishmael! says a short soldier with a greasy mustache. This isn't an Ishmael. This is an Indian.

Call me Ishmael, says Changing Woman again.

All right, says the short soldier. We know just what to do with unruly Indians here in Florida. And the soldiers drag Changing Woman down a dirt road.

Fort Marion, says the short soldier with the slimy mustache. Have a nice day.

Changing Woman looks around. There are soldiers with rifles everywhere. And there are Indians, too. There are Indians sitting on the ground drawing pictures.

This is quite interesting, says Changing Woman, but I'd rather be swimming with Moby-Jane.

"Fort Marion?" says Coyote. "The Lone Ranger is at Fort Marion."

"That's right," I says.

"Oh, good," says Coyote. "I love stories with happy endings."

"Happy endings?" I says. "You are one crazy Coyote."

"But I am very useful."

"Oh, boy," I says. "It looks like we got to do this all over again."

OSPET

ELI

"OKAY," I says. "Let's get started."

"Is it time to apologize?" says Coyote.

"Not yet," I says.

"Is it time to be helpful?" says Coyote. "I can be very helpful."

"Forget being helpful," I says. "Sit down and listen."

"Okay," said the Lone Ranger. "Whose turn is it now?"

"Well, who went last?" said Ishmael.

"You did."

"Then it's Robinson Crusoe's turn."

"What about me?" says Coyote. "I'd like a turn."

"That doesn't sound like a good idea," said Hawkeye.

"No," said Robinson Crusoe. "That sounds like a Coyote idea."

"Anyway," said Ishmael, "it's Robinson Crusoe's turn."

"Maybe Coyote can turn on the light," said Robinson Crusoe.

"Yes," says Coyote. "I can do that."

"Okay," said Hawkeye. "Let's get going."

"Watch me," says Coyote. "Watch me turn on the light."

THIS ACCORDING TO ROBINSON CRUSOE:

Thought Woman is walking. It is morning and Thought Woman is walking. So Thought Woman walks to the river.

Hello, says Thought Woman to the river.

Hello, says that River. Nice day for a walk.

Are you warm today? says Thought Woman.

Yes, says that River, I am very warm.

Then I believe I will have a bath, says Thought Woman.

That is one good idea, says that River, and that River stops flowing so Thought Woman can get in.

So that Thought Woman takes off her nice clothes, and that one gets into the River.

Whoa! says Thought Woman. That is one cold River. This must be a tricky River.

Swim to the middle, says that tricky River. It is much warmer there.

So Thought Woman swims to the middle of that River and it is warmer there.

This is better, says Thought Woman, and she lies back on the River and floats with the current. Thought Woman floats on that River, and that one goes to sleep.

I am very sleepy, says Thought Woman, and then she goes to sleep.

Hee-hee, says that River. Hee-hee.

"Hmmmmm," says Coyote. "I don't like the sound of that."

"Maybe that River reminds you of someone," I says.

"Who?" says Coyote.

"Never mind," I says. "More important things to worry about."

"Yes," says Coyote. "For example, what happened to Old Coyote?"

"Old Coyote is fine," I says. "But Thought Woman is floating away."

"Hmmmmm," says Coyote. "I don't like the sound of that."

When that River starts flowing again, it flows real fast. It flows around those rocks, and it flows past those trees.

Look out, says those Rocks, here comes Thought Woman. And those Rocks climb out of the River and sit on the bank.

Wake up, wake up, says those Trees. You are floating away.

But Thought Woman's ears are under water, and she doesn't hear those Rocks and she doesn't hear those Trees.

Oh, well, says those Rocks. Too bad. They say that, too. And those Rocks dive into the River and swim around until they find a nice spot to sit.

La, la, la, la, says that River, and it keeps going faster and faster. And pretty soon it is going very fast. It goes so fast, it goes right off the edge of the world.

Ooops, says that River. But it is too late. Thought Woman floats right out of that River and into the sky.

"Oh, no!" says Coyote. "Not again."

"Sure," I says. "What did you expect was going to happen?"

"How many more times do we have to do this?" says Coyote.

"Until we get it right," I says.

THE LONE RANGER, ISHMAEL, ROBINSON CRUSOE, AND HAWKEYE stood in the parking lot of the Blossom Lodge. Beyond the concrete and the asphalt and the cars, beneath the deep curve of the sky, the prairies waited.

"Good morning," shouted the Lone Ranger.

As the old Indians watched, the universe gently tilted and the edge of the world danced in light.

"Ah," said Hawkeye. "It is beautiful."

In the east the sky softened and the sun broke free and the day rolled over and took a breath.

"Okay," said the Lone Ranger. "Did Coyote turn on the light?"

"Yes," said Robinson Crusoe. "I believe he did."

"Are we ready?" asked Ishmael.

The light ran west, flowing through the coulees and down the cutbanks and into the river. In the distance, a star settled on the horizon and waited.

"Yes," said the Lone Ranger, "it is time to begin. It is time we got started."

"GHA! Higayv:ligé:i," said Robinson Crusoe.

"We've done that already," said Ishmael.
    "Have we?" said Robinson Crusoe.
    "Yes," said the Lone Ranger. "Page fifteen."
    "Oh."
    "See. Top of page fifteen."
    "How embarrassing."
    "Did you remember the jacket?" said Hawkeye.
    "How very embarrassing."

As the white convertible took the crest of the hill, Dr. Hovaugh caught sight of the squat dark buildings in the distance. He pushed back from the steering wheel and adjusted himself in the bucket seat. He had forgotten how uncomfortable the Karmann-Ghia was on a long trip, how every bump telescoped up through the steering wheel, shaking his arms and shoulders, how road noise rattled about the cavity of the car, leaving him with the vague feeling of being trapped inside a castanet.

"Wake up," he shouted over the race of the wind. "We're here."

Babo opened her eyes. "What happened to the trees?"

"Never mind the trees," said Dr. Hovaugh. "And let me do all the talking."

Babo settled against the door and watched the morning light flood the prairies. It rose and floated over the road, catching the Karmann-Ghia at angles and washing the car down the hill to the border. In the distance, at the edge of the horizon, Babo could see a point of light, a star in the morning sky.

"I'll bet they'll be happy to see us," said Babo.

"Remember," said Dr. Hovaugh, fishing his dark glasses out of his pocket and hooking them over his ears and nose, "let me do all the talking."

The Canadian border station was a low brick building with a long overhang that reached across the road and a tall flagpole that leaned against the sky. From where Babo sat, the pole looked as if it was not quite straight, as if it fell slightly to the left.

"Good morning," said the border guard.

"Good morning," said Babo.

"Hummph," said Dr. Hovaugh.

Babo turned in the seat. The American border station looked exactly like the Canadian border station. It was low. It was brick. It had an overhang. And it had a flagpole.

"Did you notice," Babo said to the Canadian border guard, "that your flagpole is crooked?"

"Destination?" said the border guard.

"North," said Dr. Hovaugh.

"The American one is crooked, too. See how it leans a bit to the right?"

"Purpose of your visit?" said the guard.

"Business," said Dr. Hovaugh.

"We're looking for Indians," said Babo.

"Any firearms or tobacco?"

"No," said Dr. Hovaugh.

"Four Indians," said Babo. "Really old ones."

"Citizenship?" said the guard.

"Maybe you've seen them," said Babo. "They're trying to fix the world."

Inside the border station, Babo could see three men leaning against the counter drinking coffee. On the wall behind them was a large picture of a woman in a formal with a tiara.

"Are you bringing anything into Canada that you plan to sell or leave as a gift?" said the guard.

"Nothing," said Dr. Hovaugh.

"What about her?" said the guard.

"She's with me."

"Nonetheless, you'll have to register her," said the guard.

"I see," said Dr. Hovaugh.

"All personal property has to be registered."

"Yes," said Dr. Hovaugh. "Of course."

"It's for your protection as well as ours," said the guard.

Babo looked back at the American border station and then at the Canadian border station. "Where did you say we were?" she said.

"Welcome to Canada," said the guard, and she handed Dr. Hovaugh her clipboard. "Sign here," she said, "and here."

"Thank you," said Dr. Hovaugh.

"Have a nice day," said the guard.

"Hey," says Coyote, "look who's back."

"Just ignore him," I says.

"But maybe they'll give us a ride," says Coyote.

"No time for that," I says. "We got to get back to the other story."

"By the way," says Coyote, "where are we?"

"Canada," I says. "Come on."

"Canada," says Coyote. "I've never been to Canada."

"Canada," said Babo. "I've never been to Canada."

"Let me do all the talking," said Dr. Hovaugh, and he slid the car into first and rolled away from the border. "Watch for the Indians."

Babo could see the light better now. It hung in the sky, low on the horizon. As the road ran out onto the prairies, dipping and rising, following the body of the land, Babo imagined that the light began to glow stronger, brighter.

"What do you think?" said Babo, gesturing toward the light with her chin.

"What?" said Dr. Hovaugh.

"There," said Babo.

Dr. Hovaugh slowed the car and pulled off the road. He stood on the seat and shielded his eyes.

"Maybe it's an omen," said Babo. "Or something like that."

"In ancient times," said Dr. Hovaugh, reaching behind the seat and pulling out a pair of binoculars, "primitive people believed in omens and other superstitions."

"Not like today," said Babo.

"What they thought were omens," said Dr. Hovaugh, adjusting the binoculars, "were actually miracles."

"No kidding," said Babo.

"When we get back," said Dr. Hovaugh, "I'll lend you a book I have."

Dr. Hovaugh stood on the bucket seat and watched the light in the distance.

"What do you think?" said Babo. "Omen or miracle?"

"Wow!" says Coyote. "Omens and miracles. We haven't had any of those yet."

"Get your head down," I says. "He's going to see you."

"Here I am," says Coyote. "Here I am." And that one dances around and jumps around and stands around. "Here I am," says that standing-around Coyote.

"You are one silly Coyote," I says. "No wonder this world is a mess."

Dr. Hovaugh blinked his eyes and looked through the binoculars again.

"Well?" said Babo. "What do you see?"

"Well . . ." said Dr. Hovaugh, letting the binoculars rest against his chest, "I . . . thought—"

"Let me look," said Babo. Babo slipped the strap over her neck and looked through the lenses at the light in the distance. "Well, now," she said, "isn't that the trick."

LIONEL GROANED HIS WAY to the edge of the bed, found the floor with his feet, and sat up. It was black out, dead black. He could hear the clock radio making its click, click, click insect sound as it built up the energy to flip the next minute placard over. Why was it so black? What time was it? Lionel rubbed his eyes and discovered that they were still closed. Well, it wasn't so dark out after all.

Happy birthday. Forty years old. Lionel sat on the edge of the bed and watched his stomach settle comfortably on his thighs. If he sucked hard, he could still pull it back to the outer limits of his groin.

Life, Lionel mused as he felt his chest slide on top of his stomach, had become embarrassing. His job was embarrassing. His gold blazer was embarrassing. His car was embarrassing. Norma was right. Alberta wasn't about to marry an embarrassment. Lionel sucked his stomach in for the fourth time and lurched to a standing position.

Happy birthday. Forty years old. Lionel padded his way to the bathroom. He had gotten into the habit of not turning the bathroom light on in the mornings. It hurt his eyes, but mostly he did not want to look at what he had become—middle aged, overweight, unsuccessful. But today he flicked out a hand like a whip and snapped the light on. The effect was startling and much worse than he had imagined.

"Today," he shouted at the mirror. "Today things change." And he whacked himself in the stomach and grabbed his saggy chest for good measure. He stood there naked, glaring into the mirror, pleased with the fire that burned in his eyes. Just above his left nipple, Lionel spotted the mole with the single long hair growing out of it.

All right!

He opened the medicine cabinet and threw out his tooth-brush and opened one of the new ones that had, over the years, piled up at the back. The tube of toothpaste was almost gone, but he wasn't going to wait and use up the last little drop, squeezing and rolling the zinc until all he could get were little white bubbles that popped out and popped in as you worked the tube.

Into the trash. Along with the tiny motel soap squares he had been saving for years. Lionel opened a new tube of tooth-paste. He unwrapped a large bar of soap, a green one with white stripes that smelled like lemon spice. A new blade for the razor. Deodorant. Aftershave.

Tomorrow, he would begin to floss.

Lionel pinched the end of the hair, pulled it taut, and snipped it off with the scissors. Defiantly, he turned his back to the mirror and looked over his shoulder at his butt.

Jesus!

After he showered and dressed, Lionel felt better. What the blazer needed, he concluded, looking at himself in the mirror, was a good cleaning. The cuffs were beginning to thin out and the polyester had rolled up into hard balls that hung off his wrists like tiny ornaments. And a new tie. The brown knit had seen better days and was probably out of style. Red. Bright red in silk. With little ducks or something like that.

And this year would be his last year at Bursum's. University. Of course, it was the key to everything. He had always known that. Alberta had a degree. Charlie had a degree. Eli had a degree. He'd ask Alberta to pick up a calendar for him. Law, Lionel thought as he buttoned the blazer, or maybe medicine, though perhaps he was a little too old for medicine. Doctor, lawyer, Indian chief. Doctor, lawyer, television salesman.

John Wayne.

By the time Lionel was six, he knew what he wanted to be.

John Wayne.

Not the actor, but the character. Not the man, but the hero. The John Wayne who cleaned up cattle towns and made them safe for decent folk. The John Wayne who shot guns out of the hands of outlaws. The John Wayne who saved stagecoaches and wagon trains from Indian attacks.

When Lionel told his father he wanted to be John Wayne, his father said it might be a good idea, but that he should keep his options open.

"We got a lot of famous men and women, too. Warriors, chiefs, councillors, diplomats, spiritual leaders, healers. I ever tell you about your great-grandmother?"

"John Wayne."

"Maybe you want to be like her."

"John Wayne."

"No law against it, I guess."

One of the cereal companies offered a free John Wayne ring for three boxtops and fifty cents handling charge. When the ring arrived six weeks later, Lionel put it on and showed it to Charlie.

"So, what does it do?"

"It's a John Wayne ring."

"My father knew John Wayne."

"It's got this secret compartment."

"My father knew all the big stars."

"Watch this." And Lionel slipped his thumbnail under the crest of the ring to pop it open.

It took a while to find the crest in the prairie grass. One part of the hinge had broken, and now the crest wouldn't stay on.

"Way to go, John Wayne. You broke your ring."

"Did not."

"Some secret compartment."

"That's the way it's supposed to work."

"So how you going to get it back together?"

"That's part of the secret."

Later that day, Lionel used his father's white glue to try to fix the hinge, but it wouldn't hold, and Lionel was stuck with gluing the crest down so that it couldn't open at all. The next week the adjustable band broke.

Lionel sucked his stomach in and tightened the belt. He'd talk to Bill next week or so about the future, give him some warning, so Bill wouldn't be caught unaware when Lionel resigned later. But he'd tell Alberta about his plans today, make sure she understood that he could make decisions. Happy birthday.

Things were coming together, Lionel told himself. Happy birthday. Happy birthday to you.

The morning air was damp. The clouds were arching above the Rockies, and Lionel could feel the wind coming in. By noon it would be rattling the plate glass windows at Bursum's and swirling the dirt up into a storm.

The reserve was just across the river. His parents would have set up their tepee at the Sun Dance by now.

"Be nice if you came out for your birthday," his mother told him.

"Give it a try."

"It would really please your father, you know."

"Sure."

"We're right next to Norma. You can't miss us. Wait till you see what I'm cooking."

"Alberta's coming down."

"Wonderful, honey. Bring her along."

Lionel started for his car and then stopped. No. He'd walk today. It wasn't that far to the store, and it would be a good way to start the day, a good way to start his new life.

That's what you did when you began again. That's what John Wayne would do.

LATISHA LAY IN BED with her eyes closed and listened to Elizabeth climb out of her crib. Christian, when he was small, had stood up in his crib and shouted "Mummy" until Latisha came and picked him up. Benjamin had sat up in a corner of the crib and cried until she arrived. Elizabeth was silent and determined. The first time she tried to get out of the crib, she had fallen and hurt herself. Latisha had thought that the experience might make her more cautious. It hadn't. The next morning, Elizabeth fell again, and the next morning and the next. She cried only the first two times, and by the end of the week, she had stopped falling.

Latisha kept her eyes closed. If she was lucky, Elizabeth would crawl into bed with her and fall asleep. Just another hour, Latisha prayed. Let me have one more hour.

"Mummy."

Latisha tried breathing deeply, hoping the breathing and the rhythm would have a soothing effect on her daughter.

"Mummy."

Somewhere in the room, someone was unwrapping a piece of gum or opening a plastic bag. For a moment, Latisha couldn't place the sound. Then she heard the diaper hit the floor, a heavy, full splat.

Latisha cracked one eye. Elizabeth was naked. She had shed her pajamas and her diaper and was standing next to Latisha's head, looking right at Latisha's face.

"Get up, Mummy."

"Mummy's very tired, honey."

"Get up!"

"Why don't you crawl into bed with Mummy? We can play Mummy and baby ground squirrel."

"Poopy, Mummy, poopy," said Elizabeth.

"Well, go jump on the toilet."

"You."

"Show Mummy what a big girl you are now."

"You."

One year, after he had left yet another job, George announced that he was going to stay home and look after the kids.

"It's no problem, Country," George told her. "We'll have a great time."

Latisha had thought it was a crazy idea, couldn't see how it was going to work.

"I'll cook dinner each night. Hell, you work all day at the restaurant. It's the least I can do."

"You don't cook."

"That's right now. But I'll learn. After all, the best cooks in the world are men."

Latisha didn't say yes. And she didn't say no. And she figured it would last a week.

The first week, Benjamin stayed in day care while George ran around Blossom, collecting everything he was going to need to assume his new duties. When Latisha got home that first night, George was in the kitchen setting up a pasta machine.

"What do you think, Country?" he said. "It's a beauty."

"We don't need a pasta machine."

"There's nothing like fresh pasta. Look, I got the flour and Sam Molina's book on pasta."

"The stuff in the packages is just as good."

"The stuff in the packages takes twenty minutes to cook. Fresh pasta takes about a minute and it's healthier."

Latisha had stood there and watched George screw the clamp onto the kitchen counter. He seemed so happy, so enthusiastic.

"One minute," he said. "That's all. I'll bet you didn't know that."

By the time Latisha got out of the shower, the kids were all downstairs eating breakfast. Christian was sitting at the table, stretched over a bowl of Cheerios. Benjamin was perched on the edge of the chair; his cereal hadn't been touched. Elizabeth was in the high chair, slapping at the bowl with her spoon.

"Stop it, Elizabeth," said Benjamin. "You're getting me all wet."

"Yes, I can," said Elizabeth.

Christian was staring at his bowl as if he had found something interesting floating about among the little O's.

"Thanks, honey."

"For what?" said Christian, never taking his eyes off the bowl.

"For getting the kids' breakfast."

"I always get the kids' breakfast."

"I know, and I appreciate it."

"Elizabeth is splatting milk all over the place," said Benjamin.

"It's okay, honey," said Latisha.

"Well, she is," said Benjamin.

"Yes, I can," said Elizabeth.

"You going to be home late again tonight?" said Christian.

Elizabeth was running the spoon through her hair. One hand was leaning on the edge of the bowl. Latisha watched as the milk and the cereal dribbled over the side, like water over a dam.

"Elizabeth is making a mess, Mummy."

Latisha grabbed Elizabeth's hand and rescued the bowl. She willed herself not to squeeze her daughter's hand too hard. Benjamin's cereal was still untouched.

"Eat your cereal, honey," said Latisha. "We have to get going."

"I'm full. Let Elizabeth eat it."

"Yes, I can," said Elizabeth.

The next day George brought home a blender and a heavy-duty mixer. The third day he found a juicer at Woodwards. Toward the end of the first week, whisks, bowls, large wooden spoons, pepper grinders, ravioli molds, bread pans, and matched measuring spoons and cups began appearing. When Latisha came home on Friday, she found an undercounter convection oven waiting for her.

"It'll cook the bread in half the time."

"What bread?"

"It was on sale, and they gave me a great discount on David Karaway's cookbook on breads."

"George, we don't need any of this stuff."

"Wait until you smell those loaves coming out of the oven."

The following week George started his new duties in earnest, and when Latisha arrived home, there was a meal waiting for her.

"You're late," George said.

"It looks wonderful."

"If I'm going to cook, you have to be here on time."

"What is it?"

It was pasta, and all things considered, it wasn't bad, though not all the pasta had come through the cutter cleanly. Some sections of the pasta were very good. Other sections were lumped together like knots in a rope.

"You might try making the dough a little drier. It'll come through the machine cleaner."

"Come on," said George. "Is that all you can do, criticize?"

"I'm not criticizing. This is wonderful. It's really wonderful."

· · ·

Latisha stacked the dishes in the sink. Elizabeth was lying on her stomach on her jacket. Benjamin had hold of one of the arms and was sliding Elizabeth around on the floor.

"Whee!"

"Honey," said Latisha, trying to knock the edge off her voice, "you'll get her jacket dirty."

"But she likes it."

"I like it," said Elizabeth.

"I suppose you want me to walk Benjamin to school," said Christian.

"You always walk Benjamin to school."

"Sure," he said, "take me for granted."

"You always walk me to school," said Benjamin.

"Then come on, you little drip," said Christian.

"Mummy, Christian called me a little drip."

Benjamin leaned back and dragged the jacket around in a quick circle. Elizabeth laughed, lost her balance, and tumbled over backward, hitting her head against the wall.

"Ooops," said Benjamin, not looking at Latisha. He took Christian's hand and headed for the door.

Elizabeth picked herself up, rubbed her head, and pushed her lip out. There were tears in her eyes.

"I like it," she said.

"See," said Benjamin, "she's all right. I don't know what you're getting upset for. Cheez."

The next night there was a large pot on the stove. George was standing next to a tray of what looked to be biscuits.

"Biscuits?"

"Croissants."

Latisha picked up one of the croissants and turned it over. The bottom had a brown, rock-hard coating that glistened in the light. There was the smell of burned onions in the air.

"Looks good," said Latisha, putting the croissant back on the tray. "What's in the pot?"

"Spanish ratatouille."

"Smells good."

"It's my own version."

The croissants were a three-layer affair. The first layer was crusty and somewhat flaky and somewhat resembled a croissant. The middle section was doughy and uncooked. The bottom was ceramic tile.

"Well, that's one recipe I won't use again," said George as he scraped the bottom of the croissant. "I hate it when you can't count on the recipes being right."

The ratatouille was better.

"What's that smell?" said Christian.

"That's the way it smells," said George.

"It smells like something's burned," said Christian.

"Really, honey," said Latisha, "that's the way ratatouille smells."

That night Christian woke up with stomach cramps. The next day Benjamin had diarrhea.

The next week George left. Just left. There was a long letter that said he was going home to get his life together. To find his roots. To Michigan first. Then to Ohio, where he was born.

"When I find what I'm looking for, I'll know it."

It was a long letter, filled with emotion and excitement. He was sorry for leaving, but he planned to be back. In each paragraph, he said he'd be back.

At first Latisha was angry, and she spent the next two weeks at the restaurant burning eggs and banging pans until the rage passed.

Then she discovered that she was pregnant with Elizabeth, and for a while she was numb. Then the letters began arriving.

They were long letters, longer than the first one, but filled with the same enthusiasms and plans and dreams. There were poems, too, all about love and the moon and the stars and the seasons. They came at regular intervals, and for a while Latisha looked forward to them.

Then she began to laugh.

And then she began to take them to work.

"Listen to this," she told Rita and Cynthia. "'I feel my spirit grow each day more clear and powerful.'"

The letters continued to come, and Latisha became bolder and bolder in her readings.

"'How I yearn for the simplicity of the west and the perfect clarity of sunrise and sunset. I remember you always as my sunrise and know that you will forever be a part of my heaven.'"

And finally they became boring. Just like George. Even the poetry dulled. After Elizabeth was born, Latisha stopped reading them altogether, stuffed them into a brown grocery bag in her closet instead, leaving them to collect like dust in a corner.

Latisha watched Christian and Benjamin walk down the street. Elizabeth stood at the window and waved until they were out of sight.

"Come on, honey," Latisha said. "Time for school."

"No way," said Elizabeth.

"You like school," said Latisha, forcing her daughter's arms into the jacket. "You want to see Ms. Alice and Sarah and Daniel and Agnes, don't you?"

"No way."

Latisha zipped Elizabeth's jacket and pulled up the hood. "Are you fooling me? Are you just looking to make trouble?"

Under the hood tied tightly under her chin, Elizabeth was smiling. "Yes, I can," she said.

CHARLIE SAT IN THE COFFEE SHOP of the Blossom Lodge and watched a mother try to coax her three-year-old into a high chair. The woman was smiling.

"Sit down for Mummy." The woman laughed, digging her fingers into the backs of her daughter's knees. "We can't sit down if we don't bend our knees."

In the far corner, three men were signing forms and passing papers back and forth as they ate. Across the room, under the canopy of ferns and green latticework, four old Indians were discussing the menu. One of the Indians was wearing a red Hawaiian shirt. From the back, the Indian reminded Charlie a little of C. B. Cologne.

Or was it Polly Hantos?

"Good morning," said the server. "Have you decided or would you like a little more time?"

Charlie glanced at the menu. "Maybe a couple of eggs and some toast. Hash browns."

"You're not a movie star or something like that, are you?"

Charlie didn't hear the server at first.

"I mean, you look . . . you know, sort of familiar."

"No," said Charlie, trying to work up a smile. "That was probably my father."

{ 251 }

"Oh, wow!" said the server. "You want some coffee?"

Charlie nodded and handed the server the menu. "Is there a pay phone around?"

"Out through the lobby and to your right. You want whole wheat or white?"

The old Indian in the Hawaiian shirt was looking at him, grinning.

As Charlie stood, the Indian said something to the other Indians, and they all looked at him, too.

Barry Zannos? Sally Jo Weyha?

"Hello, Charlie," said the Indian in the Hawaiian shirt. The other Indians smiled and waved.

As he passed the table, Charlie nodded and smiled back, as if he knew them, and it was only after he was in the lobby that he realized that one of the Indians was wearing a black mask. Definitely Hollywood.

Johnny Cabot?

The line was busy. He checked his watch and tried the number again. Busy.

Of course, the old Indians couldn't be from Hollywood. Now that he thought about it, it made better sense that they were probably from the reserve, were friends of the family, perhaps even relatives. Uncle Wally from Browning. Auntie Ruth from Brocket. Something like that.

Charlie put the phone on the cradle and walked back into the coffee shop. He'd say hello. Ask how the folks were, and if he was lucky, someone would drop a name and everything would come together.

The table was empty. The old Indians were nowhere to be seen.

"Your food's up," said the server.

"The Indians who were sitting here. Do you know where they went?"

"What Indians?"

"They were fairly old. One of them was wearing a mask."

"No kidding," said the server. "You want me to keep your breakfast under a heat lamp until you're ready?"

Charlie went back into the lobby. Nothing. He walked to the plate glass window and looked out. No Indians. Maybe they had gone to the bathroom. Maybe they had gone back to their room. Maybe he would see them later. No big deal.

Charlie stood at the window, thinking about what he was going to say to Alberta, when he noticed, quite by accident, that the car he had rented was missing.

At first, he thought he had forgotten where he had parked it, but as he looked from car to car, he remembered the flat tire and the puddle.

The puddle was still there. The car was not.

ALBERTA STOOD IN THE SHOWER and let the water rise around her calves. It was a trick she had learned at university. Take a quick shower, soap, shampoo. Put the plug in the bathtub. Turn the hot water on until you could hardly manage it. Stand under the spray until the tub filled up. If you did it just right, the bathroom would fill up with warm steam, and you could slide into the water and disappear.

Most times Alberta would close her eyes and dream of having a baby in the tub with her. Of course, the water was too hot for a baby, but that was the nice thing about dreams. The baby would be all wet and slippery and it would slide about on her body. She would wash its head as it nursed, and they would stay there forever. It was generally a short dream. Alberta would conjure up the baby, and just as she got it settled on a breast, she would discover that the baby had somehow turned into Lionel.

Or Charlie.

Sometimes she could block out both men, but even then there was always the sense of impending disaster, of something gone horribly wrong, and she found she could not look at the child in her arms for fear of discovering that it had died or been cooked or had disappeared beneath the water and drowned.

Showers were safer. But today Alberta let the water rise, and she turned off the shower and sat down in the tub and leaned back.

Alberta's father was a great believer in dreams. As a young man he had gone to the mountains to dream. If he dreamed, he never talked about it, but he liked to tell stories about the coming and going, as if these journeys were fishing trips or hunting trips. Or vacations.

"It's all forest, right up until you get to the mountains. There's deer and elk all over the place."

"What do you do, Dad?"

"Why, hell, you walk. That's half the doing, the walking."

"What do you see?"

"Deer and elk. Isn't that what I said? Sometimes you see a coyote or two."

"No. I mean, what do you see?"

"The world. You can see the whole world."

Women didn't go to the mountains, so Amos told her, and as she got older, her father stopped telling her and her sisters the stories and began taking the boys for trips into the trees.

Alberta asked her mother about the mountains and the dreaming, and her mother shook her head and went back to what she was doing.

"But why can't women go to the mountains?"

"No reason why they can't."

"Dad says they can't."

"Your father has his ideas on the subject."

"What if I wanted to go?"

"Pack a lunch," said her mother. "It's a long walk."

This time Alberta didn't dream at all. Not about the baby. Not about Lionel. Not about Charlie. Not about Amos. She soaked, lay in the tub until her skin bubbled up white and the water ran cold.

Lionel would be at work. There was no rush. She would have a leisurely breakfast, maybe stop by the Dead Dog and see Latisha, and wander over to Bursum's in the early afternoon. Actually, what she really felt like doing was going back to bed. She felt exhausted, drained, nauseous. As she pulled her slip over her head, she went over the plans for the day to see if there was any real reason why she should not go back to bed.

Lionel could wait.

Charlie was in Edmonton.

As she held that thought, she found that she felt better already. Smiling, Alberta closed the curtains, took off her slip, and slid back into bed.

When Alberta was thirteen, the family went across the line to Browning. Just south of Cardston, Amos pulled into the border crossing. The American border guard was a young kid, skinny, a student probably, someone they had hired on for the summer. He stood at the window of the pickup and then walked around the side of the camper, while Alberta's brothers and sisters pressed their noses against the windows.

"You want to park your truck over there and come inside," said the kid.

"We're just on our way to Browning," said Amos.

"Park it there," said the kid, and he pointed to a spot along the chain link fence. "And bring everyone in with you."

The inside of the building was air conditioned. Alberta roamed around the room looking at the brochures in the wood racks, at the magazines on the tables, at the pictures of serious-looking men hanging on the walls. Her father and mother talked to an older man at the front counter.

"Where you folks headed?"

"Browning," Amos told the man.

"You got any presents for your friends in Browning? You know, cigarettes. Maybe a little something to drink?"

"Nope."

"You folks Indians, that right?"

"Blackfoot."

"You aware we got laws that cover certain things . . . for instance, parts of animals."

Amos shrugged. Alberta's mother shook her head.

"Certain kinds of feathers. They're covered, too."

Amos didn't say a thing.

"What about feathers?" said the guard, looking past Amos. "What about it, kids? Your parents got any feathers in the truck?"

The older guy and the skinny kid made Amos take everything out of the truck. They unwrapped the dance outfits and laid them on the asphalt.

"Shouldn't put the outfits down like that," said Amos. "It isn't right."

"Guess we're the ones to say what's right and what's not right," said the guard. "Isn't that right?"

"That's sacred stuff," said Amos.

"No," said the guard. "What we have here are eagle feathers."

"Sure," said Amos. "That's what we use."

"Know an eagle feather when I see one."

"Sometimes we use prairie chicken for certain parts."

The border guard took a small camera out of his pocket and began taking pictures of the outfits. The skinny kid began writing on a clipboard.

"We'll be confiscating all of these materials," the older man said, sweeping his hand across the outfits.

"We need our outfits," said Amos. "We can't dance if we don't have our outfits."

The older guard moved in close to Amos, smiling as he came. "I can always put you in jail, if that's what you'd like. Is that what you'd like?"

"We need our outfits."

"Jail or home. What's it going to be?"

. . .

Alberta was fully awake now. She was in a wonderfully warm bed. She had nowhere to be. And she was wide awake. Worse, she was hungry. Alberta closed her eyes and imagined what it would be like to be asleep.

It didn't work. She had already begun working out what she was going to say to Lionel. What she would say to Charlie. The tension ran through her body, stiffening her back and bringing on a low-level headache. And the nausea was back.

Reluctantly, Alberta sat up and got dressed.

AT FIRST ELI SUPPOSED it was the dawn that woke him, but as he rolled away from the light, he saw that the sky out the front window was still black.

The floodlight.

They had turned the damn thing on again.

Almost as soon as the construction of the dam began, Duplessis brought in half a dozen generators and hung a series of floodlights that allowed crews to work in shifts right through the night. As the dam took shape, the smaller floods were exchanged for larger floods until the entire array was reduced to a single floodlight, a giant metal ball that floated above the dam on struts and guy wires like a miniature sun.

Eli thought they would take it down when the dam was completed, but for reasons known only to corporate vice presidents and lawyers, it remained in place, and as the litigation around the dam ebbed and flowed, the floodlight, like the water, became a calculated annoyance.

"It's there for safety," Sifton told him.

"Feel safer in the dark."

"Not your safety, Eli," said Sifton. "Ours."

"Dam's a dangerous thing all right."

"You want to talk dangerous, let's talk coal-burning plants."

"It's the idea," said Eli.

"Let's talk nuclear power."

"It's the idea of a dam that's dangerous."

Along with the injunction that forbade Duplessis from raising or lowering the level of the river beyond a certain point, Eli also got an injunction that forbade them using the flood-light after ten o'clock.

"You started it, Eli," said Sifton. "Once you get courts and lawyers involved in a simple matter, the whole thing goes to shit."

"It's real simple," said Eli. "You can't flood me out, and you can't turn on that light at night."

"Guess you better talk to your lawyer."

Eli had to admit that after all the years of arguments and threats and injunctions, he had won very little. The dam was there. It wasn't going to go away. And, at some point in the future, Eli had no doubt that they would find a way to maneuver around him. The sluice gates would open, the turbines would begin to turn, and Eli and the house would be washed out onto the prairies.

But not now. Not tomorrow.

And in a rather perverse way, Eli had come to enjoy the small pleasures of resistance, knowing that each time Duplessis opened the gates a little too much or turned on the light a little too late, it was because he was there.

When they returned to Toronto, Karen was full of enthusiasms and plans. They would go back next year. Early. Before the people put up the tepees. They would stay for the entire time, eat in the camp, sleep in the camp. Karen would help Eli's mother and sister.

"You can hang out with the guys," Karen told Eli.

"It's hard to plan that far ahead. I may have to teach in the summer."

"I don't mind. I really don't mind."

"If I don't teach, maybe your parents will want us to come up to the cottage."

"You know what I remember most?"

"It's a long trip. I'd like to go back. But it's a long trip."

"All those tepees. That's what I remember."

What Eli remembered were the people. Aunties, uncles, cousins, in-laws, friends. People he hadn't seen in years. People who greeted him as if he had never left. People who looked at him suspiciously, as though he were a stranger, a tourist who had somehow sneaked into the camp.

And he remembered the afternoon when the men came out of the double lodge at the center of the camp and danced for the first time, how, as they moved in the circle, Eli began to recognize them, boys he had grown up with who were now men. Jimmy, who had gone away to law school. Marvin, who had drowned a basketball scholarship in a bottle. Sweet, who had been sent to prison for robbery and assault before he was out of high school. Floyd, whose family was one of the wealthiest on the reserve and rigorously Catholic. Leroy, who had gone to work for PetroCan and was now, as Eli's mother told him, a big shot.

Rudy, Clarence, Cecil, Joe, Alex, Simon, Norbert, Eugene, Henry, Ray, Dayton, Buddy, Russell, Wilton, D'Arcy, Everett.

Eli measured the coffee carefully, set the pot on the stove, and put the can back in the refrigerator. There was a note stuck to the door. "Lionel's birthday." Norma had left it there. "Lionel's" was written in large, neat black letters, and Norma had circled everything with a heavy black line, drawing thinner lines out from the edges of the circle, so that the note looked like a child's stick sun or a bright idea going off.

"He's forty," Norma had said. "About time you had a talk with him."

"About what?"

"He's your nephew. You got responsibilities, you know. Look at what he's become."

"Sounds like he's doing fine."

"Sounds like you're not listening."

Eli sat down and waited for the coffee to brew and looked about the house at what he had become. Ph.D. in literature. Professor emeritus from the University of Toronto. A book on William Shakespeare. Another on Francis Bacon. Teacher of the Year. Twice.

Indian.

In the end, he had become what he had always been. An Indian. Not a particularly successful one at that. The cabin was hardly bigger than his office at the university. No electricity. No running water. A wood stove. An outhouse that was at least a hundred yards away. The great improvements he had made when he arrived and decided to stay had been the installation of a butane tank that backed up the wood stove and helped to heat the cabin in the winter and a small generator that allowed for some reading light in the evening and the luxury of a radio.

Not that he had a radio, but if he did, with the generator, he could have listened to it.

An Indian back on the reserve.

At first there had been the sensation of being home, of being in his mother's house, of reliving the memories. Then there had been the plotting, the schemes to slow the dam down, intrigues that became court cases, that began a long run of injunctions, that ended with the dam finished and silent. Eli could no longer remember what he had in mind when he moved into the cabin, could remember only the emotion he felt when Sifton told him that they were going to tear the cabin down.

"Don't have to stay home if you don't want to," said Norma.

"I'm not going to stay."

"Probably don't have all the fancy things here you have in Toronto."

"I just came back to see the place."

"Of course, being as you're the oldest, you can stay as long as you like."

"It's just a visit."

"Everybody should have a home."

"Probably stay a month or two."

"Even old fools."

Looking back, Eli could see that he had never made a conscious decision to stay. And looking back, he knew it was the only decision he could have made.

Karen told all their friends about the trip, and for months afterward, she found ways of working the Sun Dance into the conversation.

"A Sun Dance?" said Charlie Catlin. "You guys really went to a Sun Dance?"

"I just went along with Eli," said Karen.

"So tell us about it."

"It was wonderful," said Karen. "But you'll have to ask Eli."

At first Eli enjoyed the attention, but he quickly discovered that he didn't have the answers to the questions that people wanted to ask.

"When they do that piercing thing, do they go in under the muscle or just under the skin?"

"You saw that movie with Richard Harris, didn't you? Just how real was that ceremony?"

"What happens if it rains?"

When Karen told her parents about the Sun Dance and how she and Eli were going to go back next year, her father asked if they could come along, too. "That is, if it's okay," he said.

"No problem," said Eli.

"Did you get any pictures?" said Karen's mother.

"Mom," said Karen, "they don't allow photographs."

"That's probably wise," said her mother.

"Sounds like one hell of a vacation," said her father.

Karen was disappointed when they didn't go back the next year. Or the next. Each year, around May, Eli would get a letter from his mother. How was his health? How was Karen? Were there any grandchildren? Norma was fine. Camelot was fine. She was fine.

"Eli," Karen asked, "you're not embarrassed or something like that?"

"About what?"

"I don't know. Do you want to talk?"

"About what?"

"I don't know."

Eli poured a cup of coffee and set the pot on the table. What was he supposed to tell Lionel? Happy birthday. That's about all he could tell him. About all he wanted to tell him. But Norma expected more. In the old days, an uncle was obligated to counsel his sister's son, tell him how to live a good life, show him how to be generous, teach him how to be courageous.

"You're a teacher," Norma told him. "So teach."

Off in the distance Eli could see Clifford Sifton coming along the riverbank, his walking stick waving at the rocks.

Not today.

Eli finished his coffee and rinsed the cup. Today was Lionel's birthday. The least he could do was take the boy out for lunch.

Eli let Sifton get almost all the way to the cabin before he walked out on the porch, waved at the man, and then got in the pickup. In the rearview mirror Eli could see Sifton raise his arm in frustration, but Eli hardly gave the man a glance as he drove the truck through the shallows and up onto the road.

BILL BURSUM STROLLED AROUND THE STORE putting tapes into VCRs. Action drama for the thirty-two-inch Panasonic. A mystery for the row of Sonys. Cartoons for the thirteen-inch Hitachis. Family entertainment for the twenty-one-inch RCAs and the JVCs. A Western for The Map.

Bursum stopped by the blank videotape display and listened. This was the best time of the day. Everything was quiet. Everything was potential. Everything was imagination. In an hour or so, the doors would open and people would begin walking around the store, poking at the buttons, turning the knobs, asking the same questions they always asked.

"How's the picture quality?"

"How's the sound quality?"

Bursum dusted a Kenwood stereo tower and made a mental note to talk to Minnie and Lionel about keeping the equipment polished.

"What's the warranty?"

"Is it on sale?"

The knock on the door was so faint that Bursum was not sure that he had heard anything at all. The second knock was louder. No, thought Bursum, not a knock exactly. More like scratching.

"Not open yet," Bursum sang out, shuffling the headphones on their wire hangers so they hung straight.

Scratch, scratch.

"We don't open until ten," Bursum shouted. "Thank you."

Scratch.

Bursum walked to the back door very quietly and put his eye to the security viewer.

Nothing.

He opened the door a crack and looked out. Nothing. He held the door open, stepped over the threshold, and looked up and down the alley.

Nothing.

"Hey," says Coyote, "that was fun."

"You got to stop doing that," I says.

"I wasn't doing anything," says Coyote.

"You've done plenty already," I says.

"Let's go around to the front and wait," says Coyote.

"Wait for what?" I says.

"For the store to open," says Coyote.

Bursum put his feet up on his desk, leaned back in the chair, and looked at the large picture on his wall of Parliament Lake with the red circle around the piece of lakefront property that Bursum had bought just after the dam was announced. Just before Eli Stands Alone had come home.

Parliament Lake. Bursum had been one of the first people to buy a lot at Parliament Lake. Even before the dam had been started, before the contours of the lake were actually realized, Bursum had looked at the topographical map that Duplessis provided and picked out the best piece of property on the lake. A small, treed peninsula with lake frontage on three sides, southern exposure, with a dense stand of trees to the north to protect against the wind, and an unobstructed view of the mountains. Secluded. Exclusive. Valuable.

All the lot needed was a modest cabin, a boat landing, a low stone wall to discourage hikers and rubberneckers, and a satellite dish.

Eli's cabin was another matter. Tucked in under the face of the dam, it was in the wrong place. It was too small. There were no utilities. But because of the cabin, because of the injunction, because of Eli, no one could build on the lake itself until the matter was settled.

"Wouldn't be hard to move the cabin," Bursum had told Eli. "Probably get the government to move it to higher ground for free."

"Cabin's just fine right here."

"Might even be able to get a lot on the lake in exchange. What do you think of that?"

"Like the place right where it is."

"Can't stay there forever."

"As long as the grass is green and the waters run."

As long as the grass is green and the waters run. It was a nice phrase, all right. But it didn't mean anything. It was a metaphor. Eli knew that. Every Indian on the reserve knew that. Treaties were hardly sacred documents. They were contracts, and no one signed a contract for eternity. No one. Even the E-Z Pay contracts Bursum offered to his customers to help make a complete home entertainment system affordable never ran much past five or ten years. Even with the balloon payment.

Indians. Bursum had lived with Indians all his life. He had gone to school with Eli, known his mother. He had eaten at Eli's niece's restaurant and had given Lionel a job when no one else would because of his criminal record and his heart problem. Bursum considered himself part of the family, always doing what he could to help. He had been one of the leading voices in getting the city to declare February Indian month. Each year he sponsored the basketball team from the Friendship Centre, and hardly a week went by when he wasn't taking out advertisements in the local Indian newspaper.

Parliament Lake. The way things were going, he might as well give the lot back to the deer and the bears.

Bursum looked at the clock. Nine-forty-five already. Where was Lionel? Bursum hated opening the store, had of late cultivated the habit of sitting behind his desk and watching the early morning customers come into the store. It was a way to collect his thoughts, a way to get ready for the day. Each day he sat a little longer. There was no harm in it. He was tired, getting older, becoming reflective.

Parliament Lake. Bursum could picture his cabin. A long expanse of barked logs, soft yellow, glowing and warm. There were evergreens on the peninsula, dark and velvet against the lake and the mountains and white-trunked aspens and Saskatoon bushes.

Bursum sat in his chair behind his desk and looked out at The Map and dreamed about the lake and the cabin, the trees and the bushes, and he was pleased.

He was not pleased about Lionel being late. Already he could see people at the front door. Indians, it looked like. Four of them, waiting in the shelter of the doorway, moving in tight circles to stay warm. Not an auspicious start, Bursum told himself, and he leaned back in the chair, closed his eyes, and watched the lake sparkle in the sunlight.

"OKAY," says Coyote. "Let's see if I have this right. First, Thought
Woman floats off the edge of the world and into the sky."

"I'm very impressed," I tell Coyote. "Pretty soon you can
tell this story."

"And then she falls into the ocean," says Coyote.

"Hooray!" I says. "Hooray!"

"Did I get it right?" says Coyote.

"Not exactly," I says.

Thought Woman floats around in that ocean for a long time.
Three months. Six months. Nine months. You get the idea.

Then she floats ashore.

Where are we? says Thought Woman, and that one sits up
in the water. Where is that River? Where are those Rocks?
Where are those Trees?

Hello, says a voice. About time you arrived.

Thought Woman looks around and there is a little short
guy with a big briefcase.

Allow me to introduce myself, says the man with the big briefcase. And that one hands Thought Woman a card. That card
says A. A. Gabriel, Canadian Security and Intelligence Service.

Insurance? says Thought Woman. Burglar alarms?

Oops, says A. A. Gabriel. Wrong side. And he turns that card over. The other side says A. A. Gabriel, Heavenly Host.

That card is very white and it has gold lettering and it has A. A. Gabriel's picture on it.

That is one beautiful card, says Thought Woman.

Thank you, says that Card. And that Card begins to sing. Hosanna da.

That's what it sings. Hosanna da, hosanna da, hosanna da.

"I know that song," says Coyote. "Hosanna da, in-in the highest, hosanna da forever. . ."

"You got the wrong song," I says. "This song goes 'Hosanna da, our home on Natives' land.'"

"Oh," says Coyote. "That song."

Here we are, says A. A. Gabriel, and that one opens that brief-case and takes out a book.

Name?

Thought Woman, says Thought Woman.

Mary, says A. A. Gabriel. And he writes that down. Social Insurance Number?

"Six three seven," says Coyote, "zero one five . . . five six one."

"A. A. Gabriel wants Thought Woman's Social Insurance Number," I says, "not yours."

"Are you sure?" says Coyote. "I have a very important number."

Any fruit or plants? That A. A. Gabriel keeps reading that book.

Any firearms? Any alcohol or cigarettes? Are you now or have you ever been a member of the American Indian Movement?

Sign here, says A. A. Gabriel.

What is it? says Thought Woman.

Virgin verification form, says A. A. Gabriel. Here's a map of the city. We're here, and this is where you'll have the baby.

Hosanna da, hosanna da, sings that Card. Hosanna da.

I'm not pregnant, says Thought Woman.

No problem, says A. A. Gabriel. Sign this paper.

As long as the grass is green and the waters run, says that White Paper in a nice, deep voice.

Oops, says A. A. Gabriel, and he shoves that White Paper back into the briefcase. Wrong paper, he says. That one is for later.

What else do you have in that briefcase? says Thought Woman.

We're going to need a picture, says A. A. Gabriel. Could you stand over there next to that snake?

Snake? says Thought Woman. I don't see a snake.

"Look, look," says Coyote. "It's Old Coyote."

"Hmmmm," I says. "So it is."

"Hmmmm," says Coyote. "I don't like the sound of that."

Hello, says Thought Woman to Old Coyote. What are you doing here? Beats me, says Old Coyote. But I would appreciate it if you don't stand on my head.

Enough pictures, says A. A. Gabriel. Let's have you lie down here, and we'll get on with the procreating. Ready? Hail Mary / Full of grace . . .

Hosanna da, sings that Card. Hosanna da.

I don't think so, says Thought Woman.

Wait, says A. A. Gabriel. There's more. Blessed art thou among women / And blessed be the fruit . . .

No, says Thought Woman. Absolutely not.

"Fruit?" says Coyote.

"Relax," I says. "It's just another metaphor."

"Oh . . ." says Coyote. "So she really means yes, right?"

So, says A. A. Gabriel, you really mean yes, right?

No, says Thought Woman.

But that's the wrong answer, says A. A. Gabriel. Let's try this again.

Let's not, says Thought Woman, and that one gets back in the water.

Wait, wait, says A. A. Gabriel. What am I supposed to do with all these forms? What am I supposed to do with all these papers? What am I supposed to do with this snake?

Hosanna da, sings that Card. Hosanna da.

There are lots of Marys in the world, shouts A. A. Gabriel as Thought Woman floats away. We can always find another one, you know.

"But there is only one Thought Woman," says Coyote.

"That's right," I says.

"And there is only one Coyote," says Coyote.

"No," I says. "This world is full of Coyotes."

"Well," says Coyote, "that's frightening."

"Yes it is," I says. "Yes it is."

THE LONE RANGER, HAWKEYE, AND ROBINSON CRUSOE stood outside Bill Bursum's Home Entertainment Barn and watched Ishmael dance in a tight circle.

"That looks like it all right," said the Lone Ranger.

"I don't know," said Hawkeye. "That looks more Kiowa
to me."

"Maybe if you bent over a bit more," said Robinson Crusoe.

"Now it looks Cree," said Hawkeye. "You better keep
working on it."

Ishmael stopped dancing. "Boy, I'm getting hot with all this
dancing. Maybe Hawkeye should do some dancing now."

"Yes," said the Lone Ranger. "That's a good idea."

"Okay," said Hawkeye. "I guess I can do that."

"Yoo-hoo," says Coyote. "You may not believe this, but I
know that dance. I can do that dance."

"Ho," said the Lone Ranger. "Look, it's Coyote."

"Hello, Coyote," said Robinson Crusoe.

"Haven't seen you in a while," said Ishmael.

"Watch this," says Coyote. "Watch this."

To the west, clouds ran in low against the land with thunder at their backs, and in the distances, the world rolled up
dark and alive with lightning.

"Oh, oh," said the Lone Ranger. "I don't think that's the right dance."

"No," said Robinson Crusoe. "That's not the right dance at all."

"Watch this," says Coyote. "This is the fancy part."

The wind arrived first, warm and damp. The old Indians moved under the eaves of the store and watched the sky darken.

"You can stop," said Ishmael. "You've done enough dancing."

"Yes," said Hawkeye. "That was some very fine fancy dancing."

"Looks like it's going to rain," says Coyote. "What should we do now?"

"We're going to a party," said Robinson Crusoe. "It's our grandson's birthday."

"A party?" says Coyote. "With cake and ice cream?"

"Sure," said Hawkeye.

"And presents?" says Coyote. "And games?"

"You bet," said Ishmael.

"I love parties," says Coyote, and he dances even faster.

"Yes," said the Lone Ranger. "We remember the last party."

"That wasn't my fault," says Coyote just as the rain begins to fall. "That really wasn't my fault."

DR. HOVAUGH EASED INTO THE CONVERTIBLE into a parking place in front of the Blossom Lodge and got out.

"Maybe it was a star." Babo stayed in the car and watched Dr. Hovaugh walk to the edge of the coulee and look out over the river bottom. "Or a flying saucer. Something like that."

"Look around you," Dr. Hovaugh shouted back to Babo. "What do you see?"

"Looks like a storm coming in," said Babo. "Maybe we should put the top up."

The wind blew Dr. Hovaugh's coat up his back and rolled his hair over his face. "No," he said. "That's not what I mean."

"I'd still put the top up," said Babo.

Dr. Hovaugh spread his arms. The coat rattled around his stomach, the tie floating in the sky like a kite. "If you were the Indians, where would you go?"

Babo half turned in the seat and looked at the Lodge. Then she looked at Dr. Hovaugh and the prairies. Then she looked at the Lodge again. "Don't know," she said. "This looks like a nice place. I guess I'd stay here."

"Exactly," shouted Dr. Hovaugh, and he thrust his hands into his pockets and strode toward the motel. "Grab the bags."

Babo looked to the west. The light was still there. Westward leading. Getting close now, she thought. Getting pretty close.

When Babo came into the lobby, Dr. Hovaugh was at the front desk talking to a nice-looking man in a dark cardigan.

"Ah, yes," said the clerk. "Is that Mr. and Mrs.?"

"No," said Dr. Hovaugh.

"Do your televisions have remote control?" said Babo.

"Does the gentleman have a major credit card?" asked the clerk.

"Of course," said Dr. Hovaugh.

"My daughter tells me that most of the good places have remote controls these days."

"Does the gentleman have a car?" asked the clerk.

"The white Karmann-Ghia convertible," said Dr. Hovaugh.

"It's nice to be able to lie back and just push the buttons," said Babo.

"A lovely car," said the clerk.

"Thank you," said Dr. Hovaugh.

"I have a remote at home," said Babo.

"And does the gentleman require any assistance with his bags?" said the clerk.

"No, thank you," said Dr. Hovaugh. He turned and smiled at Babo. "We can manage."

Babo smiled back and gave the clerk a nod.

"Where are the bags?" said Dr. Hovaugh.

"In the car," said Babo.

By the time Lionel turned to walk down Fourth Street, he had divided the remainder of his life into a series of manageable goals. First, he would resign his position at Bursum's. Bursum had been good to him and he hated to leave the man in the lurch, but after he explained to Bill how he wanted to get on with his life, he was sure that Bill would understand. And there would be no need to mention that he had never received a raise in all the years he had worked there. Or that he thought Bill should consider changing the gold blazers for something that didn't suggest real estate and used cars.

"Bill, I'm going to resign and go back to school."

"Good for you, Lionel. Don't forget us when you're rich and famous."

"I won't, Bill. The years I've worked for you have taught me a lot."

"Lionel, you've been my best salesman."

The second thing he planned to do was to go back to university and get his degree. Like Charlie. Like Alberta. Like Eli. Like almost everyone he knew. Perhaps he should go back East as Eli had done. Perhaps he should talk to Eli. Perhaps Eli could help get him into the University of Toronto.

"I'm going back to university, uncle."

"That's a good career move, Lionel. Have you decided on a school yet?"

"I was thinking about the University of Toronto."

"I know the president. Would you like me to call him?"

"I'd appreciate it."

"Will you need any scholarship money?"

"I'd appreciate it."

Third, he would talk to Alberta about his new life, about commitments, about babies. See what she thought about these things. See how her ideas fit in with his plans.

"I'm going back to university. I expect to be a lawyer. Are you interested in coming along?"

"I just want to be where you are."

"What about your career?"

"It can wait. I can always pick it up later."

"And children?"

"Lionel, I'd love to have your children."

Last, he would go to the reserve and spend more time with his mother and father, help them around the house, drive them into town, maybe even go to the Sun Dance with them. His father had never insisted, but Lionel knew that it would make him happy.

"Thought I'd help out with the house."

"You're a good son."

"Maybe you and Mom would like to go to a movie in town."

"Are you sure it's no trouble?"

"No trouble at all. I'm thinking I'll go to the Sun Dance with you, too."

"You're a good son."

There were other things he needed to do, too. Five, six, seven. But four was a good number to start with.

Lionel had misjudged the walk. It was longer than he remembered. His feet were beginning to hurt and his shoulders had begun to ache. To make matters worse, a storm had snuck in while Lionel was setting up his goals, and as he looked to the sky, he realized that it would be upon him before he got to the store.

Lionel picked up the pace, striding out, swinging his arms, looking for all the world like a goose at full gallop. He was going to be late. And wet.

The storm broke hard and quick, catching Lionel as he turned the last corner and headed down the alley to the store. The rain fell in huge drops that ran through his blazer and his wool pants straight to the skin. As he puffed along, the rain slanting into him, he could feel his hair begin to come free and wash down the sides of his face.

Up ahead, at the end of the alley near the rear entrance to the store, Lionel thought he could see a yellow dog dancing in the rain.

ALBERTA SAT IN THE COFFEE SHOP and watched the steam rise from her coffee. Now she was sleepy. Lying in bed had left her wide awake. Sitting up in a restaurant was putting her to sleep.

"Have you decided?" The server smiled and rolled his pen around in a small circle. "Would you like to hear the specials again?"

Alberta sat up and reached for the cream. "Yes, please."

Nothing much sounded good. Alberta ordered half a grapefruit and some whole wheat toast and dumped most of the cream and two sugars into the coffee.

When her father got out of jail, he was still angry. Not the flashing anger Alberta had seen the day the border guards unwrapped the family's dance outfits and spread them out on the ground, but a deeper, quieter rage that Amos buried with smiles and laughter as he recounted the story.

"So here's this asshole with eyes like an owl. He looks at the outfits like he's checking prime fur and says, 'Oh, yes, these are eagle feathers, all right.'"

"What'd you tell him, Amos?"

"I told him you can't treat people like that."

"What'd he say?"

"What the hell do they ever say?"

Somehow a reporter from Medicine River heard about the incident and wrote a series of stories on the suppression of Indian religion. Within two weeks, several politicians were making speeches in the House of Commons about the abuses that Canadian citizens had to suffer at the hands of Americans.

"Will the Honorable Minister please tell the people of Canada why our citizens are no longer safe to cross the border while we continue to offer visiting Americans every courtesy?"

"I can assure the Honorable Member from Medicine River that the matter is being looked into and will be dealt with in a proper manner."

"Will the Honorable Minister explain to the people of Canada and our Aboriginal brothers and sisters why this government has done nothing to assure the return of the religious and historical artifacts that were stolen by the United States government?"

"The government of Canada has always had the greatest respect for our Aboriginal peoples and will continue to provide them with the same protections that every Canadian enjoys."

It took almost six months of articles and stories and speeches. Then, one morning, Alberta's mother got a call from a voice that said that the dance outfits were at the courthouse in Medicine River and could be picked up at any time.

"We don't get to town all that much," Alberta's mother told the voice.

"The Honorable Robert Loblaw," said the voice, "is always happy to be of assistance to his Cree constituency."

"That guy got a car?"

"And I can assure you that Mr. Loblaw has worked tirelessly on this matter."

"Maybe he could bring them out. Save us a trip."

"May I pass your compliments on to Mr. Loblaw and his staff?"

"Should probably tell that guy that me and my husband are Blackfoot."

"That's very generous," said the voice. "I'm sure Mr. Loblaw will be delighted to hear that."

Across the restaurant, a black woman and a white man were having breakfast. The man was talking, pointing out the plate glass window toward the mountains.

You didn't see many black people in Alberta, Alberta thought. For that matter, you didn't see many black people in Canada at all. A colleague of hers at Calgary, a man from New York who liked to work at being provocative, told her that Canada was an all-white country, that the only reason there were any blacks in Canada at all was because of the Commonwealth. Except for baseball, of course. "What can you expect," he liked to say, "from a country that sells citizenships to fat cats from the Middle East and the Orient?"

"The U.S. does the same thing."

"Hell, everyone knows the U.S. is sleazy. But Canada is supposed to have some integrity."

Alberta didn't care much for the man, but there was a hint of truth to his observations. In the ten years that she had taught at the University of Calgary, the only blacks she had seen had been exchange students.

The woman was probably a tourist.

Alberta watched her breakfast arrive. The grapefruit was tiny, the size of a large orange, and it had been cut so that it looked like an open mouth with teeth. The toast was cold.

"Is there anything else I can bring you?" said the server.

"The toast is cold."

"Oh, dear. Here, let me throw it in the microwave for a jiffy and get it nice and hot."

Alberta grimaced. "No," she said with a sigh. "It'll be just fine."

Amos went to the courthouse the next week to get the outfits. They were on the floor of a closet in three green garbage bags.

"I'll bet you're happy to get these back, Mr. Frank."

"You can't stick outfits in a bag like this."

"I've been to a couple of powwows," said the man. "At the Calgary Stampede. Very colorful."

"You'll bend the feathers doing that. You bend the feathers and it'll ruin the outfit."

"Let us know," said the man, "if we can be of any further assistance."

Amos brought the outfits home without ever looking at them. He put the bags on the table and sat on the couch. That evening, after the family had finished dinner, Alberta's mother got a razor blade from the cupboard and slit the bags open.

The black woman was laughing. The white man was wagging a fork at her as if he were in the middle of a lecture. Perhaps she was an entertainer, someone from the States up for a show. Or maybe she was a movie star. Alberta picked up a piece of toast, testing it with her fingers. That was probably it. She certainly wasn't a baseball player.

The grapefruit half hadn't been sectioned. Alberta glanced around the restaurant to see if anyone was watching. Locking her legs around the table, Alberta waded into the grapefruit with the spoon, slicing the fruit into a lumpy pulp, spraying her wrists with juice.

The man had stopped talking now and was staring out the window. The black woman had finished her meal and was sitting quietly with her coffee, rubbing one leg. There was something disconcerting about the way the woman drew her nails across her skin, as if she were scratching. Or shaving.

Two of the outfits were badly tattered, most of the feathers snapped off, the ends missing. Alberta's mother said the others could be repaired. As she held each one up to the light, Alberta could see the pattern of dirt on the sleek feathers where someone with boots had walked on them.

·   ·   ·

The toast had gone hard and oily. Alberta wiped her wrists, looked at the bill, and stood up. The man had begun to talk again. As Alberta passed the table, she heard him say something about the Indians being close by.

Tourists, Alberta told herself. Only tourists wouldn't know that Canada's largest reserve was just to the east of town. No, she thought, as she walked into the lobby, that was the very thing that tourists *would* know.

Alberta pushed through the front doors. There was rain in the air. She had always liked the rain, wondered if her father had liked the rain, too. For a moment, she considered driving out to Horsehead Coulee to stand on the prairie and watch the storm settle on the land.

Her car was not where she had left it. Alberta walked through the parking lot, thinking she might have forgotten exactly where she had parked. After all, it had been late. It had been dark. Things always looked different in the light.

But the car was gone. The puddle she had had to walk around the night before was still there. The car was not.

ELI FELT THE WIND FIRST, quick and full, as the storm caught the truck at the top of the rise. He had watched it in the rearview mirror for several miles as it boiled out of the mountains and out onto the prairies, dragging the rain behind it. In the distance, Blossom lay in sunlight.

The truck slid off the hill, picking up speed, and Eli let it run down into the river bottom, the wind rattling all around, the rain tumbling after him like a flood.

Lionel's birthday. He'd wish his nephew a happy birthday, maybe buy a small radio from him for the cabin. They'd have lunch at the Dead Dog and he'd say hello to Latisha as well. He had seen little of his family since he came home. Except for Norma stopping by from time to time with groceries and gossip and Sifton hiking over most mornings for free coffee, Eli had surrounded himself with space and silence.

An Indian Thoreau. Except that Thoreau had been at Walden Pond for only a year and he hadn't been serious, saw it as a social experiment, something that the semi-idle, semi–middle class could afford, the precursor, Eli supposed, to the ever popular retreat. Grey Owl was more to the point. The Englishman who wanted to be an Indian. What had Eli become? What had he wanted to be?

"People ask about you," Norma told him. "What should I tell them?"

"Tell them I'm home."

"Everybody knows that, Eli. People want to know if you're alive or dead."

"Tell them I'm dead."

"Been telling them that for years. No one believes me anymore."

"Then tell them I'm alive."

"Nobody believes that, either," Norma said. "Tried telling them you're just an old man in a cabin, but that lie's not thick enough to dry dishes."

After the first few years, Karen stopped talking about the Sun Dance and mentioned it only on those occasions when the trip appeared in conversation. It was a silent place in their lives. Eli knew Karen wanted to go back to Alberta, but he also knew she could sense his reluctance. At first Karen suggested that perhaps he felt uncomfortable about taking her along since she wasn't Indian.

"You're probably just nervous, Eli," Karen had said.

"That's not it."

"And I understand."

"That's not it."

"What you should do is go out there by yourself. Then, once you're comfortable about going home and you're not embarrassed anymore . . ."

The Indian who couldn't go home.

It was a common enough theme in novels and movies. Indian leaves the traditional world of the reserve, goes to the city, and is destroyed. Indian leaves the traditional world of the reserve, is exposed to white culture, and becomes trapped between two worlds. Indian leaves the traditional world of the reserve, gets an education, and is shunned by his tribe.

Indians. Indians. Indians.

Ten little Indians.

"I want you to be happy, Eli."

The Indian who couldn't go home.

It had been hard leaving the reserve and his mother and his sisters, and by the time he got to Toronto, it was all he could do to keep from turning around and going back. But he didn't go back that first year, knowing if he did, he would stay. Each year was easier. Each year laid more space between who he had become and who he had been. Until he could no longer measure the distance in miles.

By the time Eli got to the turnoff, the windshield was under water. The wipers labored back and forth, moving the rain from one side to the other with little enthusiasm. Inside, everything was fogging up, and Eli had to scrub circles on the glass so he could see. He remembered the general run of the road, how it climbed the hill, rocking to the right near the top, and then swinging back past the water tower.

Eli turned on the headlights and leaned forward to see out under the sweep of the blades.

"Nothing wrong with Lionel selling televisions," he had told Norma. "Unemployment on the reserve is close to eighty percent. At least the boy has a job."

"Figured you'd want to help."

"I could talk to him about university. I suppose I could do that."

"We need the young people to stay home, Eli. Figured you could tell him about that."

"The reserve's not the world, Norma."

"There are good ways to live your life and there are not so good ways."

"Nothing wrong with getting away from the reserve."

"We've been here for thousands of years."

"Tourist talk, Norma."

"Good times and bad. You ever ask yourself why?"

So he had stayed in Toronto and taught his classes. Year after year. Good times and bad.

When Karen began waking up in the mornings with nausea, Eli thought she might be pregnant. Karen thought so, too, and she was annoyed when the tests came back negative.

"Sorry," she told Eli, as if she had done something wrong. "No baby."

There were tests and pills and the nausea went away. And then it came back. Stronger and debilitating. There were more tests. And then more tests. At first the problem appeared to be anemia. And then it was supposed to be hypoglycemia. One doctor suggested that it might simply be the onset of early menopause. The nausea came and went, disappearing for months at a time, but always coming back.

"All in all," Karen told him on one of their innumerable visits to the clinic, "I'd rather be pregnant."

"Me, too."

"At least then I'd have a reason for throwing up."

It was two years before the doctors caught it. The irony was that the same doctors who hadn't been able to figure out the problem earlier on could now trace the symptoms right back to the source.

"I'm almost relieved," Karen told him. "At least I know what's wrong."

"We'll beat it," Eli told her. "Now that we know the problem."

But while the doctors finally agreed on the problem, they all had different ideas about how to deal with it, and for the next few years, Karen ran a gauntlet of medical enthusiasms, until the procedures came full circle and began to treat the cures.

"This is crazy," Karen told Eli. "These pills are to control the side effects of the treatments."

There were moments when the disease and the doctors, worn out by their long confrontation, took a break, and Karen came home.

"It's been seven months," Eli told her. "Things are going to be better."

"It's still there, Eli. I can feel it."

"That's just the pills."

"Before I die, I'd like to see the Sun Dance again."

"Nobody's going to die."

It had been a stupid thing to say, and he had known it was a lie even before he said it. They had become a melodrama. The doctors, the disease, Karen and Eli. A bad movie with absurd dialogue.

"I'd like that, Eli. I'd really like that."

Eli swung the corner and pulled into the parking lot. The storm had let up a little. It was early yet, and there were no other cars. Eli turned off the engine and leaned against the door. There was no hurry, no place else to go.

Through the blur of the windshield, Eli could make out four figures moving under the overhang, waiting for Bursum's to open, and as he watched, a scraggly dog dashed back and forth, chasing its tail, spinning in the rain, as if it were trying to dance.

"THE PROBLEM IS," said the young man, "it's not one of ours."

Charlie sat on the edge of the bed with the phone cradled against his shoulder. The sun had disappeared beneath a flood of clouds, and even with the curtains open and the lights on, the room was dark and depressing.

"We don't have a car missing," said the young man.

"I rented a car from you last night," said Charlie.

"Charlie Looking Bear?"

"That's right."

"That's right," said the young man, "and the car you rented is still in the lot. We tried to call you this morning, but we didn't have a local number."

Charlie sighed and put the phone down and looked out the window. It was going to rain. It was going to rain for quite a while. He picked up the phone.

"Look. I rented a Pinto. There was a Pinto in your lot. A rusty red Pinto. It was the only car in the lot. The keys you gave me fit the car. I drove the car to the Blossom Lodge and parked it in the lot. This morning, it was gone."

"Well, that explains it," said the young man.

"What explains it?"

"We did rent you a Pinto. But it was lime green. And it was brand new. And it's still here."

"The keys you gave me fit."

"That happens sometimes."

"Then whose car did I take?"

"It wasn't one of ours."

"Look," said Charlie, squeezing the phone, "I'm a lawyer."

The rain came in with the wind, suddenly, hard, rattling across the window. Charlie sat on the bed and waited. Nothing.

"Let's start over again," said Charlie, breaking the silence. "You rented me a car. A lime green Pinto. That car is still in your lot, right?"

"That's right."

"Okay, then I'll come out there and pick it up."

"Well, there's a problem."

"Besides the stolen car?"

"When we couldn't get in touch with you this morning—"

"It's still this morning."

"We rented the car."

"Let me guess."

"And we don't have any other cars available—"

"Because it's a long weekend."

"Because it's a long weekend," said the young man.

Charlie laid the phone on the bed and walked to the window. The parking lot was black and slick and the space where he had parked the car was filling up with water. No car. The long weekend and no car.

The young man on the phone continued to talk, something about a reduced rate off the next rental, and how sorry he was that matters hadn't worked out this time. Charlie hung up the phone without saying good-bye, waited until the line cleared, and then called the front desk.

"Could you call me a taxi?"

"Mr. Looking Bear? Room four twenty-four?"

"That's right."

"To the airport?"

"No."

Charlie put his shoes on, picked up the phone once again. He dialed the number, waited for the circuits to route the call. The line was still busy. He sat there and listened to the busy signal, as though it might change to a ring.

All right. He'd catch a taxi to Bursum's, say hello to Lionel, look around the store. He'd been thinking about a new television, anyway. It might be fun to have Lionel show him around. He'd joke around with Bill, maybe even pull his chain about the lot at the lake.

Sooner or later, Alberta would show up. And, Charlie mused as he watched the rain pour down on the town, Alberta had a car.

"COYOTE, COYOTE," I says. "Get back here. Things are happening.

"Just a minute," says Coyote. "I got to finish my dance."

"You've done enough dancing already," I says.

"Looks like I've got to go," Coyote says to the old Indians. "But I'll be back."

"It's okay, Coyote," said the Lone Ranger. "We won't start without you."

"Great," says Coyote. And that one dances back into this story.

"About time," I says. "Thought Woman can't float around forever, you know."

"Hey," says Coyote, "where did that island come from?"

"That's what happens when you don't pay attention," I says.

So Thought Woman floats along and pretty soon she hits an island. Not too hard. With her head.

Ouch! says that Island. Look where you are going.

Sorry, says Thought Woman. I was just floating.

Say, says that cranky Island, I'll bet you've come to visit Robinson Crusoe, the famous shipwrecked writer.

Does he write novels? says Thought Woman.

No, says that Island. He writes lists.

. . .

"Hey," says Coyote, "haven't we seen that guy before?"

"They all look the same," I says.

"But isn't that . . .?" says Coyote.

"No," I says. "That's Robinson Crusoe. You're getting him mixed up with Caliban."

"Who's Caliban?" says Coyote.

So pretty soon Robinson Crusoe comes walking along and that one looks at Thought Woman. And he looks at her again. Thank God! says Robinson Crusoe. It's Friday!

No, says Thought Woman. It's Wednesday.

Now that you're here, Friday, says Robinson Crusoe, you can help me with my lists. Here we go. Under the bad points, I have been shipwrecked on this island for years.

I'm Thought Woman, says Thought Woman.

Under the good points, says Robinson Crusoe, I haven't argued with anyone in all that time.

Why are you making lists? says Thought Woman.

Under the bad points, says Robinson Crusoe, all my clothes have worn out until I have nothing to wear.

Actually, I'm just floating through, says Thought Woman.

Under the good points, says Robinson Crusoe, the climate is so mild and pleasant, I do not need clothes.

"Oh, no," says Coyote. "Robinson Crusoe is naked."

"Well," I says, "at least no one can see him."

"It's still very embarrassing," says Coyote.

Under the bad points, says Robinson Crusoe, as a civilized white man, it has been difficult not having someone of color around whom I could educate and protect.

What's the good point? says Thought Woman.

Now, you're here, says Robinson Crusoe.

"He doesn't have a car," says Coyote. "That's a bad point."

"But he doesn't have to buy gasoline," I says.

"Okay, but he doesn't have a television, either," says Coyote. "That's very bad."

"So he doesn't have to watch it," I says.

"Okay, okay," says Coyote. "Old Coyote doesn't seem to be around to help."

"So what's the bad point?" I says.

"Boy," says Coyote, "this is fun."

Have you got it straight? says Robinson Crusoe.

Sure, says Thought Woman, I'll be Robinson Crusoe. You can be Friday.

But I don't want to be Friday, says Robinson Crusoe.

No point in being Robinson Crusoe all your life, says Thought Woman. It couldn't be much fun.

It would be a lot more fun if you would stop being stubborn, says Robinson Crusoe.

All things considered, says Thought Woman, I'd rather be floating. And she dives into the ocean and floats away.

"This is beginning to get boring," says Coyote. "How long is Thought Woman going to float around this time?"

"Who knows?" I says.

"I have to get back," says Coyote. "How about I call you from the store to see what's happening? How about I call you Friday? Hee-hee, hee-hee."

"Better call sooner than that," I says. "By Friday, this story will be done."

By THE TIME LIONEL MADE IT TO THE BACK DOOR, got his key in the lock, and slipped inside, he was soaking wet. His hair hung in his face. The gold blazer had turned brown and smelled like a wet dog. His shoes squeaked.

"Lionel, we got company."

Through the hair and the water that ran down his face, Lionel could see Bursum standing at the front of the store with some people. Lionel pulled the hair to one side.

"Hello, grandson," said the Lone Ranger.

The four old Indians. Lionel was in the motion of raising his hand to suggest that he would just stop at the bathroom and dry off when Bursum put his arm around the Lone Ranger and waved Lionel over.

"Come on, Lionel," said Bursum. "Don't want to keep customers waiting."

"We brought you a present, grandson." And Hawkeye held up a package wrapped in brown paper.

"That's nice," said Bursum. "More people should do things like that."

"It's his birthday," said Ishmael.

"How about that," said Bursum as Lionel got within range. "Lionel, you're all wet."

"Something for your birthday," said Robinson Crusoe. "Something to make you feel better."

"You're making a puddle," said Bursum.

"You got pretty wet," said Hawkeye.

"Yes," said the Lone Ranger. "You're all wet, all right."

"Hi," said Lionel, feeling the water drip off his sleeves. "Good to see you again."

Over Bursum's shoulder, Lionel saw another man standing by the front door. The light was at the man's back, and Lionel could not see his face.

"Hello, nephew," said Eli. "Happy birthday."

The day had not started out well, Lionel told himself. And things were not getting any better.

"Is that you, Eli?" said Bursum. "Lionel, look, it's your uncle Eli."

"Hi, Eli," said Lionel.

"Hi, Eli," said Bursum.

"Hi, Eli," said the Lone Ranger and Ishmael and Robinson Crusoe and Hawkeye.

"Is it time to sing 'Happy Birthday'?" says Coyote.

"Not yet," said the Lone Ranger.

"Where's the cake and the ice cream?" says Coyote.

"Maybe that comes later," said Ishmael.

"Nothing like having family around on your birthday," said Bursum.

Lionel shifted from one foot to the other. He was beginning to feel chilled. "So," he said to the four Indians, "how have you been?"

"Oh," said the Lone Ranger, "just fine. How about you?"

"I've been fine, too," said Lionel. "This is my uncle, Eli."

"Real good to meet you," said Ishmael, and Eli and the four Indians shook hands.

Eli shook hands with Bursum. "How's it going, Bill?"

"You know," said Bursum. "Same as always."

"How's the lot?"

"You know. Same as always."

Lionel felt as though he was anchored in one spot, and that if he didn't do something soon, he was going to have to stand there all day and listen to Eli and Bursum and the old Indians exchange greetings.

"Somebody ask me how I am," says Coyote. "Go ahead, ask me."

"Uncles are pretty important," said the Lone Ranger. "I hope you listen to your uncle."

"You bet," said Lionel. "All the time."

"I'm fine," says Coyote. "That's how I am."

"I thought I'd look around for a radio for the cabin," said Eli. "You got any good radios?"

"We got the best," said Bursum. "Lionel, show your uncle the radios. I'm going to show your other relations how The Map works."

"Of course, I'm also wet," says Coyote. "Being wet is not so fine."

"Ah, they're not really relations," said Lionel.

"Everyone's related, grandson," said the Lone Ranger.

"That's right," said Bursum. "That's the way things are with Indians."

On second thought, Lionel decided that he didn't mind standing there, dripping water on the floor. He had the disturbing feeling that if he moved, things would begin to unravel.

"Don't need anything really expensive," said Eli. "Just something that works good."

Bursum was already moving toward The Map with the old Indians in tow. It was, Lionel had to admit, pretty impressive. All those televisions piled on top of each other, all those televisions arranged in particular shapes, in particular spaces. It was more than advertising, Bursum had told him. It was a concept, a concept that lay at the heart of business and Western civilization. He had said some other things, but Lionel had forgotten exactly what they were.

Lionel squeaked over to the radio display.

"How's the cabin, uncle?"

"It's okay," said Eli. "You should come out and visit. Don't get much company."

"Sure," said Lionel. "Here's a nice Sony. It'll pull in the local stations. Should get CBC too."

"Norma tells me you're thinking about going back to school."

Lionel turned the radio on and adjusted the antenna. "That's right. I figure it's time to finish the education."

"Got any ideas?"

"Maybe law. Probably try a few things out."

"Lots of ways to live a life."

Lionel put the Sony back and brought out a larger Panasonic.

"When I was young," said Eli, "I couldn't wait to get off the reserve."

"I figure it's time I made some moves."

"Of course," said Eli, "lots of people stayed, too."

"Figure in a few days that I'll tell Bill that I'm going to be resigning soon. Give him some notice, you know."

"Norma's still here. Camelot's still here. Lots of people are still here."

"Sure," said Lionel, flipping the switches on the Panasonic. "You came back."

Eli laughed and shook his head. "You're right. After all that time, I came back."

"I came back, too," says Coyote. "You guys know where a phone is? I have to make a call."

"What do you think?" said Lionel.

"About coming back?"

"No, about the radio," said Lionel.

"No, no, no," says Coyote. "About the phone."

Bursum lined the old Indians up in front of The Map. He stood off to one side and waved the remote in a circle and then hit the button.

"Ah," said the Lone Ranger as the screens came to life. "That's very beautiful."

"Yes," said Ishmael. "Everything is so silver."

"And bright," said Hawkeye. "Everything is nice and bright."

"Boy," said Robinson Crusoe, "can you do that again?"

"Sure," said Bursum, and he turned The Map off and then on again several times.

"That's amazing," said the Lone Ranger. "What else does it do?"

Coyote dials the number several times. Busy. So that Coyote dials that number again.

"Hello," I says. "First Nations' Pizza."

"Hello, Friday," says Coyote. "Hee-hee, hee-hee."

"Hello, Coyote," I says.

"Don't hello me," says Coyote. "What's happening with Thought Woman?"

"Who?" I says.

"Is she still floating around?"

"Who?" I says.

"Stop that," says Coyote. "It's mean stuff like that that makes this world so silly."

"This one," said Lionel, "is the best we carry. On a good night you can hear New Zealand with this one."

"Don't know that I want to hear New Zealand," said Eli. "Norma says you're coming out to the Sun Dance."

"You don't have to listen to New Zealand. You can listen to France."

"I thought maybe I'd go this year. Thought you might like to come along."

"It's fairly expensive. It just depends on what you want."

"What I want," says Coyote, "is a party."

"Thought we could have lunch. Maybe say hello to Latisha," said Eli.

"Sure," said Lionel, holding up the Sony and the Panasonic. "What do you think?"

"I think we should start the party," says Coyote.

"Probably the little one," said Eli. "It's not as large a world as people think."

Lionel smiled and put the radios back in the case. As he did, the front door swung open and Charlie Looking Bear came in. The first thing that Lionel noticed about Charlie was that he was dry.

"Lionel," said Charlie.

"Charlie," said Lionel.

"Bill," said Charlie.

"Charlie," said Bill.

"Hello, Charlie," said Eli.

"Eli," said Charlie.

"Hello, Charlie," said the Lone Ranger. "Good to see you again."

Charlie looked at the Lone Ranger, Ishmael, Robinson Crusoe, and Hawkeye and smiled. "Sure," he said.

"Thought you were in Edmonton," said Lionel.

"You got that right," said Charlie, looking back at the old Indians. "Who are they?"

Lionel looked at the old Indians and then he looked at Charlie. "Beats me," he said, and he put Eli's radio in a bag.

"They look familiar," said Eli. "Maybe they're from Brocket."

"Hello, Charlie," says Coyote.

"Lionel," shouted Bursum, "when you're done with Eli, show Charlie that new television system."

"How's life in the cabin?" said Charlie, pulling the radio out of the bag and looking at it.

"Good enough," said Eli. "How you doing up in Edmonton?"

"Good enough," said Charlie. "You should get that small Sanyo. It'll catch stations as well as the Sony and it's cheaper."

"That so?" said Eli.

"Hey, cousin," said Charlie, "we going to have a party or what?"

"Now you're talking," says Coyote. "Now you're talking."

"This," said Bursum, holding up the tape as if it had some significance, "is the best Western ever made."

"Yes," said the Lone Ranger. "It's our favorite, too."

"John Wayne, Richard Widmark," said Bursum.

"Yes," said Hawkeye. "All our favorites."

Bursum put the tape into the VCR and hit the play button. "Watch this," he said, and settled against the wall. "Watch this."

"A movie!" says Coyote. "I love movies."

"Hey, Bill," said Charlie. "What's on?"

"Come on," said Bursum. "You'll love it."

"Come and join us, grandson," said the Lone Ranger. "Bring your uncle and your cousin."

"Maybe we should give Lionel his birthday present before we start," said Hawkeye.

"That's a good idea," said Ishmael.

"Yes," said Robinson Crusoe. "We don't want to forget that."

"Okay," said Bursum, and he pushed the pause button. "But let's be quick. This is a great movie."

"Here, grandson," said the Lone Ranger.

Lionel took the package reluctantly and unwrapped it.

"Look at that," said Bursum. "That's a really nice gift."

"Let me see," says Coyote. "Let me see."

Lionel held it up. It was a jacket. A leather jacket. With leather fringe. Lionel slipped on one arm and was surprised how soft and warm the jacket felt.

"Fits real good," said Eli.

"Looks old," said Bursum. "It's got a couple of holes here in the back, but nothing serious."

"That's true," said the Lone Ranger. "It's pretty old."

"But these things never wear out," said Ishmael.

"Yes," said Hawkeye. "You can wear them forever."

"And they're always in style," said Robinson Crusoe.

"We got to sing 'Happy Birthday,'" says Coyote. "We can't have a party without singing 'Happy Birthday.'"

"I guess you're right, Coyote," said the Lone Ranger. "We better sing 'Happy Birthday.'"

"Sure," said Charlie, trying to keep from smiling. "Let's sing."

"Make it quick," said Bursum, fiddling with the remote.

"Happy birthday, nephew," said Eli. "You know, you look a little like John Wayne."

ALBERTA STOOD AT THE DESK and waited for the officer to return. She had never been inside a police station, had seen them only on television. The real thing was not as depressing as she would have supposed. It looked rather like an insurance office or maybe a radio station, the kind of place you would expect to find lawyers and politicians. It was the locks and the heavy glass and the uniforms that gave it away.

"Late model Nissan, that right?"

"That's right," Alberta told the officer. "It was parked in the Blossom Lodge parking lot."

"And it was locked?"

"I always lock it."

"Well, I've got everything I need. If we get anything, we'll leave a message for you at the Lodge."

"I really need my car."

"I know what you mean," the officer said. "If I lost mine, my kids would shoot me."

"I mean, I can't believe anyone would steal my car."

The officer smiled. "Believe it, honey," she said. "The bastards will steal anything."

. . .

For a time, Amos had worked for the tribal police. Missing cars on the reserve were a common enough occurrence. Generally, the cars had been borrowed by a family member or a friend or a relative. And, generally, they made their way home. Amos's job, among others, was to hasten their return, to soothe hard feelings, and to prevent trouble.

He had been on the job for six months when his brother-in-law lost a Ford pickup truck. Milford had parked it in front of Super Sam's in Blossom and had gone in to pick up a few groceries. When he came out, the truck was gone. At first he thought someone was playing a trick on him, or that one of his sons or daughters had taken the truck. Late that afternoon, he caught a ride back to the reserve, half expecting to see the truck parked in his yard. It wasn't there, and none of his children had seen it.

After the second week, Milford called Amos.

"Hell, Amos," Milford said, "the truck is eight years old. Shocks are shot, and the steering box needs work."

"You check with all your relations?"

"Whoever took it could have done a whole hell of a lot better."

"It'll probably show up. I'll ask around."

"What am I going to do without my truck?"

The truck did show up. But not where anyone would have expected it. Milford was driving to bingo with his wife, Bernice, when he saw the truck parked at Peterson Chevrolet. There were little flags hanging from the antenna and across the windshield was painted "Runs Good."

Milford had Bernice stop the car so he could get out and take a closer look.

"Damn," he said to Bernice. "It's my truck all right."

"We're going to be late for bingo, Milford."

"They're trying to sell my truck."

"Tell Amos. He'll take care of it."

"It's not Amos's problem."

The next day, Alberta's mother got a call from Bernice to ask her if she could ask Amos to come down to the jail in Blossom and talk to Milford.

"He found his truck," Bernice told Ada.

"What happened?"

"Just tell Amos he found his truck."

Alberta stood under the overhang of the police station and watched the rain fall. The weekend had turned into a disaster, and in spite of her best efforts, she found herself blaming Lionel. Lionel's birthday. If it hadn't been for his birthday, she would be in Calgary curled up on the sofa with a book, safe and warm. Instead, she was in Blossom in the rain without her car. Alberta leaned against the wall and waited.

"Hey, you look lost."

It was the police officer who had just finished helping her. "Look, my name's Connie. You're not local, right?"

"Calgary."

"I'm really sorry about your car." Connie looked at the rain and then back at Alberta. "You can't stand here all day. How about I give you a ride back to the Lodge? It's no trouble."

Alberta started to shake her head, but Connie patted her shoulder. "Yeah, I know. It's a pain in the ass. You got any kids?"

By the time Amos got to the jail, Milford was stretched out on a cot, sound asleep.

"Crazy bugger was trying to steal a truck right off of Peterson's lot," the officer told Amos.

"It's his truck," said Amos. "It was stolen a couple of months back."

"He ever file a report with us?"

"Nope. He filed it with the tribal police."

"Hell," said the officer. "You know that doesn't count."

Milford's eyes were red and there was a nasty bruise on the side of his face.

"They got my truck at Peterson's. I tried to tell them it was mine, but they had a bill of sale with my name on it. I told them someone stole the truck but they just kept waving that bill of sale at me."

"They say where they got the truck?"

"They say they got it from me. But that's a damn lie."

"I'll see about getting you out."

"I want my truck back, Amos."

"I figured that."

"It's one thing for family to take it."

"That's true."

"They aren't family."

"Family's a great thing," said Connie as she drove down Fourth. "I got four kids. You believe that?"

"You look great," said Alberta.

"Had them when I was young. Doesn't tear you up as much if you have them when you're young. But then I was dumb, too."

"I'm thinking about having a child."

"You married?"

"No."

"No law says you got to do that. Man's a nice thing to have around but so's a dishwasher. I take it you're progressive."

"What?"

"You know, women's libber." Connie turned her head and winked. "It's okay. So am I."

Alberta started to laugh, and then she began to cry.

"Whoa," said Connie, and she guided the car into the Lodge parking lot. "We better talk about this."

Fred Peterson was all smiles when Amos came into his office.

"Afternoon," said Fred. "Haven't seen you in quite a while."

"Never been in," said Amos, and he put his tribal police badge on the edge of Peterson's desk.

Peterson looked at the badge, sucked his mouth into a

smile, and picked at the side of his nose. "Didn't I sell you a Camaro four, five years back?"

"Must have been my twin."

Peterson laid his head back and laughed as if he were trying to bring the walls down. "Didn't know we had Indian police."

"We do," said Amos.

"What do you guys do?"

"We look for stolen trucks."

Peterson shook his head and opened a drawer in his desk. He pulled out a piece of paper and slid it across to Amos. "Copy of the bill of sale."

Amos looked at the paper and then looked at Peterson.

"All up front and legal," said Peterson.

"You talk to Milford when he sold you his truck?"

"Nope. Ricky, my sales manager, bought the truck."

"Ricky around?"

"Nope. Left about a week ago. Took a job in Florida. You believe that? Florida, for Christ's sake."

Amos turned the paper around and slid it across Peterson's desk. "It's not Milford's signature."

"That's what he said," said Peterson. "But there it is. Big as life."

"Spelled his name wrong."

"How's that?"

"Spelled his name wrong. It's Milford. Not Melfred. Whoever signed this spelled the name wrong."

Peterson looked at the paper. "Looks like Milford to me." And he put the paper back in the drawer.

"Somebody stole his truck."

"Well," said Peterson, leaning back in his chair, "you know how it is."

"How is it?" said Amos.

"Well, let's say that maybe Milford or Melfred comes in here and he needs a little money. And maybe he's had a little to drink. He sells us the truck, and then, maybe he forgets about it."

"Milford doesn't drink."

"So you say," said Peterson.

"You can't sell his truck."

"So you say."

Connie and Alberta sat in the patrol car until the windows fogged up and the rain ran to drizzle.

"And those are the high points," said Alberta.

Connie leaned against the door and ran her hand across the steering wheel.

"I know what it sounds like," said Alberta. "Two men, a good job, no responsibilities. What have I got to complain about?"

"Oh, hell, honey," said Connie. "Everybody makes a mess of their lives in their own way. Look at me."

"You look okay."

"Sure," said Connie, sitting up in the seat. "I got married when I'm seventeen, had four kids before I'm twenty-three, divorced at twenty-seven. I spent three years sitting around watching television, and then I became a cop."

"It must be exciting being an officer."

"I'm not an officer, honey," said Connie. "I'm a secretary. Oh, I've got the uniform and I've got the gun and I can handcuff you and drag you off to jail, but all they let me do is sit behind that desk and take messages. I've been a cop for ten years, and the only time I've been in a patrol car is driving back and forth to work."

"I'm sorry."

"It's the shits, all right."

"What are you going to do?"

"Retire," said Connie. "Another fifteen years and I can retire. What about you? What are you going to do?"

"What do you want to do?" Amos cradled his coffee and watched Milford's face.

Bernice brought the coffeepot over and filled Amos's cup. "You want some more bread?"

"Don't know," said Milford. "I didn't sell my truck to Peterson. I don't know what the hell happened."

"Can always get a lawyer, I guess," said Amos.

"A lawyer? You remember Everett Stacy? He got himself a lawyer when that real estate agent refused to sell him that house in town. Cut and dried, the lawyer said. You remember that?"

"I remember."

"They're right behind us, Amos," said Milford. "Always right behind us."

"What do you want to do?"

"You can't stop them." Milford sipped his coffee. "How many years did they drag out that case? Four or five? Until Everett was broke and had to give it up."

"So what do you want to do?"

Milford hunkered over his coffee and stared at the table. "Sure as hell don't want to get a lawyer."

About a week later, someone set the truck on fire. By the time the Fire Department arrived, Milford's truck was gone and four other cars had been damaged. The police arrested Milford and held him for three days.

"I didn't do it," Milford told Amos. "I wish I had, but I didn't."

"Probably vandalism," said Amos.

"They kept asking me who did it, as if I really knew." Milford began laughing. "So finally I told them that it was probably Coyote."

"What'd they say?"

"They got no sense of humor."

"Too bad about your truck."

Milford took his cup to the sink and rinsed it. "So what do you figure?"

"About what?"

"How much I owe you for the gas?"

"Had nothing to do with it, Milford."

"Coyote, right?"

"I guess," said Amos.

"It won't stop them, you know," said Milford.

"I guess," said Amos.

Alberta and Connie pulled up in front of the Dead Dog Café. The rain was steady now, falling in cadence.

"Never been here. Don't get to eat out much," said Connie.

"You want to come in and get some coffee?"

"No. Got to get home. I work a half shift and then I have to come back tonight. Sort of like a waitress."

"Some other time."

"Sure."

"Thanks."

"Sure."

Alberta stood in the parking lot and watched Connie drive off. It was cold out, and Alberta wrapped her coat around herself tightly, hugging herself to keep out the chill. As she stood there, she suddenly felt fragile and very small.

DR. HOVAUGH WATCHED THE REMAINS OF HIS EGGS sink into the pool of ketchup. It was a pleasant morning and the drive had been surprisingly relaxing. But as he sat in the coffee shop, contemplating another cup of coffee, he found himself missing the hospital and, particularly, the garden. Things in Canada seemed slightly wild, more out of hand, disorderly, even chaotic. There was an openness to the sky and a wideness to the land that made him uncomfortable.

Even the eggs weren't done quite right, the ketchup the wrong brand, the potatoes shredded for hash browns with the skins still on.

And the Indians.

Dr. Hovaugh opened the book and checked his notes. It was all there. No arguing with the circumstances and the patterns, with the regularities that marked their comings and goings.

"Why'd you bring me along on the trip?" Babo tore open a packet of sugar.

"What?"

"This trip. Why'd you bring me along?"

Dr. Hovaugh squeezed his tie and pursed his lips. "Well," he began, "it's fairly simple. When patients such as the Indians escape from a hospital such as ours, it is always advisable to have someone who knows them close at hand."

"Like me," said Babo.

"That's right," said Dr. Hovaugh.

"Because they'll listen to me."

"No," said Dr. Hovaugh. "Because they know you. I want them to listen to me."

"What are you going to tell them?"

"What do you mean?"

"When we find them. What are you going to tell them?"

"I'm afraid that's confidential."

"They like it there at the hospital, you know," said Babo.

Dr. Hovaugh looked at the book again, to make sure he was in the right place at the right time. Blossom, Alberta. Yellowstone, Mount Saint Helens, Wall Street . . . Krakatau? Yes, it was indisputable. Everything fit. Everything made sense.

"They like it there a lot," said Babo.

"What?"

"The Indians," said Babo. "They really like the hospital."

"Our hospital?"

"They said they like helping out. Fixing things."

"Indeed."

"Like the world. You know."

Babo leaned back. It had been a long drive, and the bed in the Lodge was hard. She had stayed up and watched a Western on television, and now she was tired. Maybe she would just stay at the Lodge and float in the pool and let Dr. Hovaugh drive around the countryside looking for the Indians. She could have told Dr. Hovaugh to just stay at the hospital, that sooner or later the Indians would show up, but the idea of a trip to Canada had been inviting. Now it was becoming tiring, and Dr. Hovaugh was becoming boring.

"Your ancestors were slaves, were they not?" said Dr. Hovaugh. "Nope," said Babo. "But some of my folks were enslaved."

"Ah," said Dr. Hovaugh.

"There's a difference," said Babo. "Of course," said Dr. Hovaugh.

"All sorts of slaves in the world," said Babo.

"Of course," said Dr. Hovaugh.

"Drugs, television, junk food, religion, cars, sex, power, cigarettes, money—"

"Yes," said Dr. Hovaugh. "I see what you mean."

". . . fashion, jobs, designer kitchens, politics—"

"Yes, yes," said Dr. Hovaugh. "How's your breakfast?"

"Did you know that my great-great-grandfather was a barber?"

"A barber?"

"Cut hair. Shaved faces with the best of them. He worked on ships."

"Cruise ships?"

"Something like that," said Babo.

"That must have been exciting."

"I have his razor. His name was Babo, too. All firstborn in my family are named Babo. Did I tell you that?"

Dr. Hovaugh motioned for the server to bring the bill. He had lost track of what Babo was saying. Something about barbers. Something about ships.

"You should let me give you a real shave with a real razor."

"That's very kind."

"There's nothing like it. If I were a man, it's the only way I'd shave."

Dr. Hovaugh put a twenty-dollar bill under his glass. It was raining outside and it looked as though it was going to be gloomy for a while. And disorganized.

"We should drive around and see the sights," said Babo, looking at the guide she had gotten at the front desk. "Grand Baleen Dam is out to the west. So is Parliament Lake. We could stop at a real Indian reservation. There's a whole bunch of other interesting places, too. Maybe we'll find the Indians along the way."

"Perhaps," said Dr. Hovaugh, going over the notes in the book one last time.

As Dr. Hovaugh stood, he remembered the car. "Did we put the top up?"

"Top?"

"The car. The convertible top."

Babo brushed off her dress. "I don't remember, but a little water won't hurt it."

"It's a classic," said Dr. Hovaugh, and he was out and into the lobby before Babo had finished straightening herself.

Babo wandered into the lobby and stood by the large picture windows that emptied into the parking lot. She could see Dr. Hovaugh in the lot, standing in the rain, still as a statue. At first, she thought he was just enjoying the storm, but as the rain quickened, Dr. Hovaugh turned and shouted something to her that she could not hear through the glass. Then he waved his arms around, agitated, upset.

He was soaking wet now, standing between two cars, up to his ankles in water. As Babo watched, she suddenly realized that Dr. Hovaugh was standing in the spot where the car had been parked.

But the car was no longer there. There was nothing there except Dr. Hovaugh and a puddle.

Babo cocked her head to one side and smiled. "Now isn't that the trick," she said to no one in particular.

LIONEL WAS LOOKING OLDER, Charlie decided, forty-six, forty-eight, at least. And he looked silly as hell in that jacket. The old Indians must have gotten it at an antique store. Or a flea market. Eli was looking good, and Bill hadn't changed at all.

"Good to see you, Charlie," said Lionel.

"Thought I'd look at a new stereo system."

"They must have stores in Edmonton."

"Always pays to give relatives the business."

"Quiet," said Bursum. "The good part is coming up."

The movie was familiar. Charlie was sure he had seen it before. The old Indians stood transfixed in front of The Map, watching every movement on the screens.

"Boy," said the Lone Ranger, "look at those colors."

"Yes," said Hawkeye. "Black and white are my favorites."

"They could have made this movie in color," Bursum explained. "But the director wanted the brooding effect that you get with grainy black and white."

"And the horses," said Ishmael. "Those are wonderful horses."

"Look," said Robinson Crusoe. "Is that the president?"

"No," said the Lone Ranger. "That guy's too tall."

"Are there any Coyotes in this picture?" says Coyote.

"I don't think so," said the Lone Ranger. "But we should keep looking, just to be safe."

"The next scene," said Bursum, "used over six hundred extras, Indians and whites. And five cameras. The director spent almost a month on this one scene before he felt it was right."

"He didn't get it right the first time," said the Lone Ranger.

"But we fixed it for him," said Hawkeye.

Charlie's mind was not on the movie or on Lionel or Eli or the old Indians. Alberta. He would have expected her to show up at the store before this. Maybe she got halfway to Blossom, realized she had made a mistake, and had turned around and gone back to Calgary. What a bizarre joke it would be if she had been trying to call him the whole time he was running around Blossom trying to find her.

"Too bad Alberta's not here," Charlie whispered to Lionel. "She likes these kinds of movies."

"She does?"

"Hey, if she was here, we could all go out to dinner."

"Well, actually, she and I are going out to dinner tonight," said Lionel, trying to follow the action on The Map.

"Well, then you're all set," said Charlie, and he sat down on the edge of a stack of stereo boxes. "Say, isn't that John Wayne?"

"The Duke," said Bursum.

"He was a funny guy," said the Lone Ranger.

"We told him that shooting Indians wasn't too good for his image," said Ishmael.

"He didn't listen," said Hawkeye.

"And look what happened," said Robinson Crusoe.

"You mean . . . he died?" said Lionel.

"No, grandson," said the Lone Ranger. "He didn't get to be president."

"I don't shoot Indians," says Coyote. "I would make a wonderful president."

"Here we go," said Bursum. "Here we go."

As Bursum and Lionel and Eli and Charlie and the old Indians and Coyote watched, John Wayne and Richard Widmark and a few dozen soldiers dashed across a river.

"We're trapped, men," Wayne shouted. "Get behind those logs."

"Come on," yelled Widmark. "If you want to keep your hair."

Wayne and Widmark and all of the soldiers ran around, jumping behind logs, digging holes in the sand, hiding behind boulders.

"Don't shoot," shouted Wayne, "until they get to the middle of the river." And he took off his leather jacket and hung it on a branch.

How Bursum loved his Westerns, Lionel thought. Every one was the same as the others. Predictable. Cowboys looked like cowboys. Indians looked like Indians. The chief in this one was a tall man on a black horse. He was naked to the waist. His long black hair was hanging loose and tied around his head with a leather band. It was his eyes that got you and that great nose.

Lionel didn't have a great nose like that and he had always thought he looked more like John Wayne.

"Surrender, white men," shouted the chief across the river.

"Nuts to you," John Wayne shouted back.

"That's the same thing he says in that war movie he made," whispered Bursum. "It's a great line."

As the camera pulled in tight to the chief, Charlie stood up and took a step forward.

It was his father.

It was the same movie he had seen last night on television. The same stupid wig. The same stupid headband. The same stupid nose.

"Then die," shouted Portland, and he wheeled his horse around in the shallows, throwing flashing sprays of water in glistening circles.

"Damn it, Dad," said Charlie under his breath.

"Is that Portland?" said Eli.

"Who else," said Charlie.

"He's looking pretty good," said Eli.

"Is that your father?" said Lionel.

"So what?" said Charlie. He jammed his hands into his pockets and watched the screens.

Portland raced his horse up and down the river, taunting John Wayne and Richard Widmark and the rest of the soldiers. The Indians gathered on the banks of the river, waiting.

Portland brought his horse to a stop at the river's edge and looked across at the soldiers. "Who rides with me?" he shouted, and raised his lance in the air. And with one voice, on all the speakers on all the televisions on The Map, the Indians shook their lances and their rifles and their bows and yelled until Bursum had to turn the volume down a bit.

"Really gets you all excited," said the Lone Ranger.

"You bet," said Hawkeye.

"Almost as much fun as being there," said Ishmael.

"Nothing like the good old days," said Robinson Crusoe.

"Attack!" shouts Coyote.

"Not so loud," said the Lone Ranger. "You're going to scare these young boys."

"Get ready," said Bursum. "Here it comes."

Portland spun his horse around again, and then, with a yell, he started across the river. And the rest of the Indians followed.

"Here they come, men," shouted John Wayne. "Make every shot count."

And the soldiers began shooting for all they were worth. And John Wayne and Richard Widmark ran back and forth, encouraging the men, the bullets flying around them.

"Take your time and aim," shouted Widmark.

But the Indians kept coming, relentlessly, moving through the water. Then, in the background, along with the music, there was the sound of a bugle, faint at first and then louder, until it filled the speakers, and over the hill behind the Indians came a troop of cavalry charging down the hill into the river bottom.

"Hooray," shouted John Wayne, and he took off his hat and waved it at the charging troops.

"Hooray," shouted Richard Widmark, and he buttoned up his vest and ran a hand through his hair.

"Hooray," shouted the soldiers, and they all leaped from their hiding places and watched the Indians, who were trapped in the middle of the river.

"Hooray," shouted Bill Bursum, and he bounced in place, keeping time to the music with the remote.

"Hooray," shouts Coyote. "Hooray."

"Oops," said the Lone Ranger. "I thought we fixed this one."

"Yes," said Ishmael, "I thought we did, too."

"A lot of them look the same," said Hawkeye.

"Boy," said Robinson Crusoe, "this is sure a lot of work."

"Come on," said the Lone Ranger, and he began to sing.

"I didn't mean hooray," says Coyote. "I meant oh no! That's what I meant."

The Lone Ranger's voice was soft and rhythmic, running below the blaring of the bugle and the thundering of the horses' hooves. Then Ishmael joined in and then Robinson Crusoe and then Hawkeye.

"Come on, Coyote," said the Lone Ranger. "You can help, too."

"I had nothing to do with it," says Coyote. "I believe I was in Houston."

As Charlie watched, the Indians stopped in the middle of the river. Portland sat on his horse and looked back at the closing cavalry. None of the Indians moved. They sat there as if they were resting or waiting for a bus.

On the one side of the river, John Wayne and Richard Widmark and the soldiers yelled and cheered and waved their hats.

On the other side of the river, riding at full gallop, the cavalry thundered along the valley floor. And as they came, as the music swelled, there was a new sound, faint at first, but building until it lay against the cadence of the oncoming soldiers.

As the troops got closer to the Indians waiting in the river, every soldier drew a saber, and each saber caught the sunlight and flashed silver in the pale blue sky. And as the horses came, tearing at the earth with their hooves, you could see the pale yellows of the sand and the deeper greens and blues of the grass and the sage.

There at full charge, hundreds of soldiers in bright blue uniforms with gold buttons and sashes and stripes, blue-eyed and rosy-cheeked, came over the last rise.

And disappeared.

Just like that.

"What the hell," said Bursum, and he stabbed at the remote.

Everywhere was color.

Portland turned and looked at Wayne and Widmark, who had stopped shouting and waving their hats and were standing around looking confused and dumb.

Without a word, he started his horse forward through the water, and behind him his men rose out of the river, a great swirl of motion and colors—red, white, black, blue.

"Get back, men," shouted Wayne, and he began firing at the Indians. Widmark pulled both guns and began firing from the hip.

The soldiers ran back to their logs and holes and rocks, shooting as they went. But as Lionel and Charlie and Eli and the old Indians and Bill and Coyote watched, none of the Indians fell. John Wayne looked at his gun. Richard Widmark was pulling the trigger on empty chambers. The front of his fancy pants was dark and wet.

"Boy," said Eli, "they're going to have to shoot better than that."

And then Portland and the rest of the Indians began to shoot back, and soldiers began falling over. Sometimes two or three soldiers would drop at once, clutching their chests or their heads or their stomachs.

John Wayne looked down and stared stupidly at the arrow in his thigh, shaking his head in amazement and disbelief as two bullets ripped through his chest and out the back of his jacket. Richard Widmark collapsed facedown in the sand, his hands clutching at an arrow buried in his throat.

"Jesus!" said Bursum, and he stabbed the remote even harder.

Charlie had his hands out of his pockets, his fists clenched, keeping time to the singing. His lips were pulled back from his teeth, and his eyes flashed as he watched his father flow through the soldiers like a flood.

"Get 'em, Dad," he hissed.

"Yahoo!" shouts Coyote.

And then the movie ended and the credits rolled to black and all the screens ran to static.

"Now, that was some movie, Bill," said Eli.

"Well, something sure as hell got screwed up," said Bursum, looking at the remote in his hand. "Damn. You put your faith in good equipment and look what happens."

"Thought it was supposed to be black and white," said Eli.

Lionel looked at the empty television screens, and he looked at the Lone Ranger, Ishmael, Robinson Crusoe, and Hawkeye, and somewhere in the back of his mind, right on the edge of his consciousness, something told him that whatever mistakes he had made in the past, his real problems might just be beginning.

"YOO-HOO," says Coyote. "I'm back."

"About time," I says.

"Did you see that movie?" says Coyote.

"Forget the movie," I says. "We have work to do."

"Where's Thought Woman?" says Coyote.

"Floating," I says.

"Still floating?" says Coyote. "Say, is there something I'm missing?"

So Thought Woman floats around. That one floats around and makes up lists.

Under the bad points, says Thought Woman, I am floating around with nothing to do.

Under the good points, I do not have to make any decisions.

Under the bad points, says Thought Woman, I have no one to talk to.

Under the good points, it is very quiet and peaceful.

Under the bad points, I have no friends to share my travels with.

Under the good points, says Thought Woman, there are no Coyotes.

.   .   .

"Whoa," says Coyote. "That's not a nice thing to say. That hurt my feelings."

"Calm down," I says. "It's just a list."

"Under the bad points," says Coyote, "there are soldiers waiting on shore to capture Thought Woman. How do you like that?"

"Oh, no," I says. "You have done it again."

"See how Thought Woman likes that."

"So," I says, "what's the good point?"

"What good point?" says Coyote.

"Silly Coyote," I says. "There are good points and there are bad points, but there are never all good points or all bad points."

"Are you sure?" says Coyote.

"Positive," I says.

"Okay," says Coyote. "The good point is that the soldiers have flowers in their hair."

"That's a good point?" I says.

"It's the best I can do," says Coyote.

So Thought Woman floats around and pretty soon she winds up on a beach in Florida and pretty soon some soldiers with flowers in their hair come along and arrest her.

Are you the person responsible for these flowers in our hair? say those soldiers.

I'm Robinson Crusoe, says Thought Woman. I'm in charge.

Good grief, says one of the soldiers with flowers in his hair, another Indian. And those soldiers with flowers in their hair take Thought Woman to Fort Marion.

"I'm sorry," says Coyote.

"Too late for being sorry," I says.

"I got a little carried away," says Coyote. "But I've got it straight now."

"Are you sure?" I says.

"You bet," says Coyote. "But just to make sure, could we go through it one more time?"

JBPT

ЯАҺ

THIS ACCORDING TO HAWKEYE:

"Wait, wait," says Coyote. "When's my turn?"

"Coyotes don't get a turn," I says.

"In a democracy, everyone gets a turn," says Coyote.

"Nonsense," I says. "In a democracy, only people who can afford it get a turn."

"How about half a turn?" says Coyote.

"Sit down," I says. "We got to tell this story again."

"How about a quarter turn?" says Coyote.

THIS ACCORDING TO HAWKEYE:

One day Old Woman is walking around and looking for good things to eat. Something tasty. So, that one thinks. And that one makes tasty things to eat in her head. Pretty soon that one sees a big tree and she sees a tender root sunbathing near that tree. Yum, says Old Woman to herself. There is a tender root.

Eeek! says that Tender Root. It looks like Old Woman out looking for tasty things to eat.

Yes, says Old Woman. That's true. Are you tender?

But that Tender Root doesn't say anything. That Tender Root jumps back in its hole. Oh, oh, says Old Woman. Looks like I'm going to have to do some digging.

So, that one finds a digging stick and that one gets down on her knees and that one puts the stick in the ground. Under that tree. That big tree.

Eeek! says that Tree. That tickles. If you keep that up, you're going to make me laugh.

I am looking for a Tender Root that jumped in this hole, says Old Woman.

But that Tree is laughing too hard to hear Old Woman.

· · ·

"I'm not very ticklish," says Coyote.

"Can we get on with this?" I says.

"Except for feathers on my toes," says Coyote.

"It's getting late," I says.

"Then I'm ticklish," says Coyote.

"And people want to go home," I says.

Old Woman digs and digs and that one chases that Tender Root under the Tree and around the Tree and pretty soon, that one has dug a big hole.

Ooops, says Old Woman, and she falls through that hole into the sky.

"Hey, hey," says Coyote, "I know this story. I can tell this story."

"Are you sure?" I says.

"You bet," says Coyote. "This is the same story."

BILL BURSUM SHOOK THE REMOTE and turned back to The Map. He rewound the tape for a minute and then hit Play. The cavalry came riding over the hill again, and just as they got to where the Indians were waiting in the river, they disappeared. The Indians charged out of the river and massacred John Wayne and Richard Widmark. Just like before. Bursum pushed the Rewind button again.

"Boy, that was sure a good time," said the Lone Ranger.

"Yes," said Ishmael. "We got to do that again, soon."

"Something like that," said Robinson Crusoe, "makes your whole day a little brighter."

"Maybe we should sing 'Happy Birthday' again," said Hawkeye.

Lionel smiled and held up his hands in defense, but the old Indians ignored him and began singing. Even Eli joined in. Bursum stood there pushing buttons, cursing, pushing buttons. Charlie was over at the desk on the phone. There was no place for Lionel to go, and he stood there as the old Indians and Eli, who was really getting into the singing, sang four choruses of "Happy Birthday."

"Well, grandson," said the Lone Ranger, "we better get going."

"Yes," said Ishmael. "We've done all we can do right now."

"If we try to do too much," said Robinson Crusoe, "things don't turn out so well."

"We're not as young as we used to be," said Hawkeye.

The old Indians said good-bye to Lionel. They shook hands with Eli and waved to Charlie, who was still busy on the phone.

"Good-bye, Bill," said the Lone Ranger. "Real nice display."

The sky outside was beginning to clear. Lionel watched the old Indians walk down the street. Bursum was still playing and rewinding the tape.

"Come on, nephew," said Eli. "Let's get some lunch."

Bursum punched the buttons again. "Go ahead," he said. "Minnie'll be here soon. Hey, it's your birthday. Take an extra hour."

"Thanks, Bill."

"Sure," said Bursum. "And don't forget Eli's radio."

Lionel's shoes were still wet, and they squished as he walked.

"What about earphones, Eli?" Bursum shouted after them. "Lionel, see if your uncle needs a set of earphones for the radio."

THE LONE RANGER, ISHMAEL, ROBINSON CRUSOE, AND HAWKEYE walked down the street single file. They moved quickly and quietly through the town, down into the river bottom, and out onto the prairies.

"Wait for me. Wait for me."

The old Indians stopped and looked around. The Lone Ranger walked to the top of a rise and looked down into the coulee they had just crossed.

"It's Coyote," said the Lone Ranger.

"Wait for me," says Coyote, running up the side of the hill. "Where are you going?"

"We're going over there," said Ishmael, gesturing with his lips.

"Can I come?" says Coyote.

The Lone Ranger looked at Ishmael and Ishmael looked at Robinson Crusoe and Robinson Crusoe looked at Hawkeye and Hawkeye looked at the Lone Ranger.

"It's okay with us, Coyote," said the Lone Ranger.

"But you can't take any pictures," said Ishmael.

"I wouldn't do that," says Coyote.

"And you can't make any rude noises," said Robinson Crusoe.

"You mean like burping and farting?" says Coyote.

"And you can't do any more dancing," said Hawkeye.

"Okay," says Coyote. "I won't do any of that stuff."

The clouds moved away from the sun as the old Indians and Coyote made their way through the prairie grass. Ahead, the mountains rose off the prairie floor, supporting the clouds and the sky.

"This is a lot of fun," Coyote says to himself quietly. "I feel like . . . singing."

THE MORNING HAD BEEN SLOW, the breakfast crowd small, mostly regulars, except for the three men sitting near the window, watching the storm clouds grumble out of the west.

"I'm Louie," the large man in the plaid shirt told Latisha when she came to take their order. "And this is Ray. The ugly guy is Al."

Latisha smiled and nodded. "Louie, Ray, Al. Welcome to the Dead Dog."

"We're from Manitoba," said Ray. "We get together each year for a fishing trip."

"We'll have the breakfast special," said Al.

Latisha could hear Billy in the kitchen banging pots and singing. Cynthia was at the register, talking to someone on the phone.

"Louie is a poet," said Ray. "Teaches literature at the University of Manitoba. Al is a priest, but we're not supposed to tell anyone that, are we, Al?"

"He's jealous because I catch all the fish," said Al.

"I work in Ottawa," said Ray.

Latisha looked back to the kitchen. Billy was leaning on the passthrough, only his head and shoulders showing. He was smiling and pointing at the table with his chin, making happy sheep sounds. Cynthia was still on the phone.

"Friend of mine was through here ten, twelve years ago," said Louie. "Said you had some really good fishing."

"Must have been before the dam," said Latisha.

Louie took a map out of his jacket and spread it on the table. There were colored lines around several lakes in Montana and a couple in Alberta.

"Figured we'd drop down here and hang around Scott Lake," said Al, pointing to a small lake circled in orange. "Does that special come with toast?"

Cynthia was waving at Latisha. She had the phone in her hand. Latisha took the orders and hung them on the wheel.

"It was the same guy as yesterday," Cynthia told Latisha. "He was kind of rude this time. I told him you'd be free in a minute, but he hung up."

"No name?"

Cynthia shrugged. "Just said he'd catch you at the Sun Dance."

"Then it wasn't Lionel."

"Your brother? No, don't think it was him."

"It must be Eli."

"Cute," said Cynthia. "He sounded cute."

Each year Latisha's parents went to the Sun Dance. Harley had a tepee that had been his father's, and every July he would haul it to the Sun Dance camp and set it up. When they were younger, Latisha and Lionel spent most of July with their relations and friends and neighbors. Lionel stopped going as soon as he moved out of the house and got an apartment in Blossom, but Latisha went back each year, spending much of the time helping her mother and Norma fix the food and assist the women's society.

It was George's idea to get married in late June and honeymoon at the Sun Dance. Latisha had never heard of such a thing.

"I don't think anyone's ever done that," Latisha's mother told her. "It sounds progressive, I guess."

"You think there'll be any problems if I bring George?"

"Well," said her mother, "I don't know that you can leave him home."

Norma let them use her lodge, and she moved in with Latisha's parents.

"So this is it," George said as he sat in the tepee among the mattresses and blankets and cooler chests and water jugs. There was a gas cook stove near the entrance and an open fire pit in the center with a blackened grill sitting on a circle of stones.

It was strange being there in the tepee alone with George. Latisha could not remember a time when she had ever been alone with a man at the Sun Dance.

"What happens if it rains?" said George, looking up at the smoke hole.

"You close the flap. Most of the time the water will just run down the poles onto the ground."

"This is great, Country. Just like the movies. Any way you can lock the door?"

Latisha grabbed the pot of coffee and made the rounds.

"Say," said Louie when Latisha got to their table, "what's the story on the lake just west of here?"

"Parliament Lake?"

"That's the one. How's the fishing?"

"Probably very good."

"Hey," said Louie, "you guys hear that?"

"But you can't fish. Court order."

"Court order," said Louie. "Boy, you guys really take your fishing serious out here."

Latisha spent most of that first morning in the tepee with George, making coffee and stew. Almost as soon as the coffee was done, people began arriving. The flap of the tepee would open, and relatives and friends would come in without a word and sit down. Latisha would pass the coffee around, and after everyone had some, a conversation would begin. Sometimes it was about family. Sometimes it was about an upcoming marriage. Most of the time it was about children.

Just after lunch, George rolled off the bed and began taking off his shirt. At first, Latisha tried to ignore him.

"George, come on. I've got work to do."

"Come on," he said, unlacing his boots. "There must be some way to lock that door. God, these people don't even knock."

George was just undoing his pants when the flap was pulled to one side and four older women came in. George had just enough time to throw a blanket around himself and slide back against the side of the tepee.

The women hardly noticed him. They sat and drank coffee and ate stew and talked to Latisha about their grandchildren and the weather. Latisha had to keep from looking at George wrapped up in a Pendleton blanket for fear of laughing. By the time they left, George was scowling and sweating under the heavy wool.

"God," he said, "I thought they'd never leave. Does this go on all day?"

Latisha told him that it did.

"Look," she said, "why don't you go on out with the men. Some of the older people need help setting up their tepees and there's always wood to be chopped. You'll feel better if you get out and do something."

George had just gotten dressed when the next group lifted the flap and came in. George smiled and said hello to everyone, and then he slipped out. Latisha didn't see him until later that evening.

"That man of yours is a funny guy," Latisha's father told her. "Got some interesting ideas."

"Something wrong?"

"No," said her father. "Wouldn't say that. He helped Mrs. Potts with her tepee. Had a new way to get the poles up."

"Did it work?"

"Nope," said her father. "But he sure was sure it would."

"No one got hurt, did they?"

"Nope," said her father. "But it sure was interesting."

Louie and Ray and Al were still bent over their map when Latisha came around with the pot again.

"Supposed to be a dam around here," said Louie. "Guy at the Lodge said it was worth seeing."

"It's not working," said Latisha.

"Sort of like the lake, huh?" said Al.

Latisha filled the cups right to the brim, spilling a little coffee into each saucer.

"It's all tied up in court. They can't use the dam, and they can't use the lake."

"Hey," said Louie, "is this the place where people bought lakefront property figuring they would build houses and cottages, and now they can't?"

"I guess so," said Latisha.

"Yeah, it is," said Ray. "Made the papers all the way back in Manitoba. There's an old guy who lives in some cabin right under the dam."

"My uncle," said Latisha.

"Son of a gun," said Louie. "Son of a gun."

Later that night, as they lay in bed, George nuzzled up against her back and held her close.

"I'm having a great time," he said. "How about you?"

"Sure."

"How much longer is it?"

What George liked best was the men dancing. He sat at the edge of the circle with Harley and watched the dancers move in the late afternoon light.

"Why are they skipping?" he asked.

"Why are they holding hands?"

"What do they do inside the double tepee all day?"

"That man of yours," her father told her, "is sure full of questions."

"George is inquisitive, Dad."

"Yeah, I can see that," her father said. "His eyes okay?"

"Sure, why?"

"Guess his ears work, too."

George talked about the Sun Dance for months after that, and the next year, just after Christian was born, Latisha went to the Sun Dance alone.

"It just wouldn't be the same, Country," he told her. "The first time is always the best."

The guys from Manitoba finished their breakfast and left. Al bought a couple of postcards, and Louie bought a menu to send home to his daughter.

"If we come through Blossom on our way back," Louie told Latisha, "we'll bring you a trout."

Latisha watched the men get into their station wagon. The rain had started again, and the sky was darker.

Billy stuck his head out of the kitchen. "When you going out to the Sun Dance?"

"Maybe later this afternoon, when the kids get out of school. Can you work both shifts?"

"Sure. Do it every year."

"Thanks, Billy."

Latisha loaded the dishes in the tray. As she wiped the table, she noticed a woman standing in the parking lot in the rain. The woman's back was to her.

"Tourist?" said Cynthia, gesturing toward the figure.

Latisha laughed.

"Must like the rain," said Cynthia, and she took the tray of dirty dishes to the kitchen.

There was something familiar about the figure, and as the woman turned around, Latisha saw that it was Alberta.

Latisha smiled and waved Alberta in, and Alberta waved back. But she didn't move. Under the lowering sky, Alberta waited in the parking lot, in the rain.

ELI EASED THE TRUCK out of the parking lot and onto the road. The rain was falling again, not as heavily as before, but steadily, patiently. Eli turned his headlights on and waited at the corner for the light to change.

"What do you think, nephew?" said Eli.

"Probably just a weird problem with the tape," said Lionel, looking up and down the street. "It happens all the time with electronic stuff."

"No, I mean the weather," said Eli. "For the Sun Dance. Norma's going to be mad as hell if it doesn't clear up."

"You see those old Indians?" said Lionel. "They couldn't have gotten very far."

Eli rolled across the intersection and turned west. The sky was moving overhead, a gathering of clouds. "Sure doesn't look good, but you never know."

"If you see the old Indians, let me know," said Lionel.

"I remember one year, it rained for three weeks before the Sun Dance, but when things got going, the sun came out and it was beautiful."

"I can't keep this jacket," said Lionel. "I like it, but I can't keep it."

"When was the last time you were at the Sun Dance, nephew?"

"I mean, I don't even know who they are."

Karen got better. A remission, the doctors called it. Not a cure. Just a reprieve. If there were no problems for another four or five years, they said, then they could talk cure. Karen was weak for a long time, but each year she got stronger.

"Eli," she said one day when he got home from the university, "why don't you take early retirement. We could travel, do some of the things we've always wanted to do."

"Like what?"

"Like France. Maybe go to Germany. We could take a cruise to the Caribbean."

"Sounds good."

"Since I'm not going to die on you, and you're stuck with me, we might as well do something with the rest of our lives."

"Okay," Eli said. "What do you want to do first?"

"The Sun Dance," said Karen.

"You know," said Eli, "I was a lot like you when I was your age."

"No kidding."

"Norma's probably told you all about it."

"Only four or five hundred times."

"That's Norma." Eli laughed. "Got a real strong idea about how the world should look. Norma says you got plans."

"Going back to school."

"That what you want to do ?"

Lionel shifted in his seat. They should have caught up with the old Indians by now. They couldn't just disappear.

"It's a big world out there," Eli said. "Always seems like there are a lot of things to do."

"That's what I figure."

Lionel pulled the jacket around him. It was nice looking but it wasn't very warm. Maybe he'd wear it over a sweater when he and Alberta went out to dinner.

"Alberta and I are going out to dinner tonight," Lionel said, watching the side streets on the off chance that the Indians had wandered off and got lost.

"That Amos Frank's girl?" said Eli. "The one who teaches over in Calgary?"

"That's right."

"Norma says you want to marry her."

"We're just good friends," said Lionel. "Like you said. It's a big world. Lots of things to do."

Eli slowed the truck and let it drift to the side of the road until it came to a stop. He turned sideways in the cab and smiled at Lionel. "That's what I said, nephew. That's what I said, all right. And I was wrong."

"Don't tell your mother or your sisters," Karen said. "Let's surprise them."

Eli said sure, that it might be better that way. Just to show up. They could always go back into Blossom of an evening and stay at a motel.

"No," said Karen. "I want to stay in the camp. You're not worried about my health, are you?"

"No."

"And you're not embarrassed?"

Karen told all of their friends that they were going to go back to Alberta to the Sun Dance that summer, and Charlie Catlin and his wife organized a little going-away party.

"Charlie, we're not going until the summer. It's only February."

"Sure, Eli, we know that, but it's as good an excuse for a party as we'll get."

The night of the party, Karen picked Eli up from the university. The night was slippery and wrapped in snow and ice. Karen had the heater going full blast.

"I think I'm going to melt."

"Just getting you ready for summer."

As Karen worked her way through Toronto traffic, Eli tried to think of what he was going to say to his mother. It had been over twenty years since the last visit. He had no excuses, no good reasons why he had stayed away so long. Even Karen's illness couldn't cover over his absence.

"Are you afraid, Eli?"

"Of what?"

"Of going home."

Eli shook his head and watched the lights of the city pool up on the wet sidewalks and slide across the road. "I am home," he said.

Eli saw the car before Karen did, a dark flash of purple and black, glistening as it came, plunging through the intersection.

At first Lionel thought that Eli had seen the Indians, but as he looked around, Lionel saw nothing but empty streets. Eli leaned over the steering wheel, and for a moment Lionel thought his uncle might be sick. Or worse.

"You okay?"

Eli nodded.

"You sure?"

"Just thinking," Eli said, and he straightened up and checked the side mirror. "Tell me, nephew. If you could go anywhere in the world, where would you go?"

Lionel shrugged. "I've been to Salt Lake City. Don't want to go back there again."

"Anywhere you want to go."

"The rest of the time, I've been here. In Blossom."

"Okay," said Eli, and he pulled the truck into gear. "That's what we'll do."

Dr. HOVAUGH STOOD IN THE PARKING LOT and stared at the empty space where his car had been.

"Dr. Hovaugh." Babo stood at the door to the lobby. "It's raining."

"Where's my car?" shouted Dr. Hovaugh.

"Looks like it's gone," said Babo. "Maybe you better come back inside."

"Not until I find my car," said Dr. Hovaugh, and he pulled his collar up around his neck and marched up one end of the parking lot and stomped down the other, oblivious to the rain and to the puddles and ponds.

From where she stood, Babo could see Dr. Hovaugh sliding through the water, could hear him spitting as he thundered among the rows of cars. Until he came back to where he had started. Wetter. Angrier.

"Where's my car!"

It took Babo a while to talk Dr. Hovaugh back into the lobby. He stood at the window, dripping, and watched the empty spot as if he expected that the car would reappear at any moment.

"It's the country," said Dr. Hovaugh. "Look around. Just look around."

Babo held up the towel she had gotten from the front desk.

"Same thing happened to me," she said. "I know just how you feel."

"It's the Indians," said Dr. Hovaugh.

"What about the country?"

"Same thing."

Babo draped the towel over Dr. Hovaugh's head. "Well, the good point is that whoever took it probably put the top up."

Dr. Hovaugh snorted and turned away from the window. "I'm going to get changed. See if you can rent us a car."

"Another good point is that a rental car will probably have more room, in case we find the Indians and have to give them a ride."

"After that, call the police."

"The bad point is a larger car will use more gas."

Dr. Hovaugh ran the towel through his hair and wiped off his shoulders and chest. "Just get us a car."

When Dr. Hovaugh returned to the coffee shop, Babo was sitting at a large table with a map and several brochures spread out in front of her.

"What's all this?" he said.

"You want some tea?" said Babo. "They have some great cinnamon tea."

"Did you get a car?"

Babo ran her finger along the map and then looked at one of the brochures. "Not exactly."

"What do you mean?"

"Well," said Babo, looking at another brochure, "none of the rental places had any cars left. It's a holiday."

"What holiday? There's no holiday."

"In Canada there is. Everyone gets Monday off. It's a three-day weekend. So there aren't any cars."

"So what did you get?"

"A bus," said Babo.

Dr. Hovaugh bent forward and rubbed his forehead. His

hair was still wet, and drops of water ran out on his neck.

"It's actually a tour. I figured if we can't get a car, we can tour around the countryside. Maybe we'll spot the Indians that way."

Dr. Hovaugh picked up one of the brochures. "A tour of a dam?"

"That's the tour I signed us up for. See, it takes us near a real Indian reservation and then up to this place right here, Parliament Lake and the Grand Baleen Dam. The dam's supposed to be something to see. It's not working right now, but the woman at the desk said it's a beauty."

Dr. Hovaugh looked at the brochure, spread it out in front of him. And then he looked at the map.

"The dam!" he said.

"That's right," said Babo. "Tour leaves at eight in the morning. We get lunch at the dam itself. Should be a great trip."

"Of course," said Dr. Hovaugh, turning the map so he could read it. "The dam."

"Look," says Coyote, "I haven't much time. The old Indians need my help."

"I thought maybe you would like to tell this story," I says. "But if you're too busy, I guess I can do it myself."

"No, no," says Coyote. "I want to do that. I'll just tell it fast."

"Okay," I says. "Just get it right."

"Okay," says Coyote. "Where were we?"

"Well," I says, "Old Woman just fell through that hole into the sky and then she fell into—"

"I know, I know," says Coyote. "A whale!"

"We already had a whale," I says.

"A fiery furnace!" says Coyote.

"No," I says. "Not that either."

"A manger!" says Coyote.

"Nope," I says. "Old Woman doesn't fall into a manger."

"Give me a hint," says Coyote.

"Old Woman falls into the water," I says.

"The water?" says Coyote. "That's it?"

"That's it," I says.

"Okay, okay," says Coyote. "Old Woman falls through the hole, falls through the sky, and falls into the water."

"That's right," I says.

"Great," says Coyote. "What happens next?"

"Well," I says, "Old Woman falls into that water. So she is in that water. So she looks around and she sees—"

"I know, I know," says Coyote. "She sees a golden calf!"

"Wrong again," I says.

"A pillar of salt!" says Coyote.

"Nope," I says to Coyote.

"A burning bush!" says Coyote.

"Where do you get these things?" I says.

"I read a book," says Coyote.

"Forget the book," I says. "We've got a story to tell. And here's how it goes."

So Old Woman is floating in the water. And she looks around. And she sees a man. Young man. A young man walking on water.

Hello, says Old Woman. Nice day for a walk.

Yes, it is, says Young Man Walking On Water. I am looking for a fishing boat.

I just got here, says Old Woman. But I'll help you look.

That's very kind of you, says Young Man Walking On Water. But I'd rather do it myself.

Oh, look, says Old Woman. Is that the boat you're looking for over there?

Not if you saw it first, says Young Man Walking On Water.

So there is a boat. A small boat. And there are a bunch of men in that boat. A big bunch. And that boat is rocking back and forth. And those waves are getting higher.

Rock, rock, rock, rock, says that Boat.

Whee, says those Waves. We are getting higher.

Help us! Help us! shout those men.

Pardon me, says Young Man Walking On Water. But I have to rescue my . . . rescue my . . . ah . . .

Factotums? says Old Woman. Civil servants? Stockholders?

You must be new around here, says Young Man Walking On Water. You don't seem to know the rules.

What rules? says Old Woman.

"I know, I know," says Coyote. "Young Man Walking On Water is talking about Christian rules."

"Yes," I says. "That's true."

"Hooray," says Coyote. "I love Christian rules."

Christian rules, says Young Man Walking On Water. And the first rule is that no one can help me. The second rule is that no one can tell me anything. Third, no one is allowed to be in two places at once. Except me.

I was just floating through, says Old Woman.

But you can watch, says Young Man Walking On Water. There's no rule against that.

Well, says Old Woman, that's a relief.

So that you're not confused, says Young Man Walking On Water, I am now going to walk across the water to that vessel. I am going to calm the seas and stop all the agitation. After that, I will rescue my. . . my. . . ah . . .

Deputies? says Old Woman. Subalterns? Proofreaders?

And they will love me and follow me around.

"That's a really good trick," says Coyote.

"Yes," I says. "No wonder this world is a mess."

"Maybe the . . . ah . . . would follow me," says Coyote.

"Now that's a really scary thought," I says.

So Young Man Walking On Water walks on the water to that Boat. With those men.

Help us! Help us! says those men.

And Young Man Walking On Water raises his arms and that one looks at those Waves and that one says, Calm down!

Stop rocking! He says that to the Boat. Stop rocking!

But those Waves keep getting higher, and that Boat keeps rocking.

Help us! says those men. Help us!

Whee, says those happy Waves.

Rock, rock, rock, rock, says that Boat.

Calm down! Stop rocking! Calm down! Stop rocking, says Young Man Walking On Water.

But that doesn't happen, and those men on that Boat begin to throw up.

Yuck, says that Boat. Now look what happened.

Well. Old Woman watches Young Man Walking On Water. She watches him stomp his feet. She watches him yell at those Waves. She watches him shout at that Boat. So, she feels sorry for him. Pardon me, she says. Would you like some help?

There you go again, says Young Man Walking On Water. Trying to tell me what to do.

Well, says Old Woman, someone has to. You are acting as though you have no relations. You shouldn't yell at those happy Waves. You shouldn't shout at that jolly Boat. You got to sing a song.

Sing songs to waves? says Young Man Walking On Water. Sing songs to boats? Say, did I tell you about our Christian rules?

It's a simple song, says Old Woman. And Old Woman sings her song.

Boy, says those Waves, that is one beautiful song. We feel real relaxed.

Yes, says that Boat, it sure is. Maybe I'll take a nap.

So that Boat stops rocking, and those Waves stop rising higher and higher, and everything calms down.

Hooray, says those men. We are saved.

Hooray, says Young Man Walking On Water. I have saved you.

Actually, says those men, that other person saved us.

Nonsense, says Young Man Walking On Water. That other person is a woman. That other person sings songs to waves.

That's me, says Old Woman.

A woman? says those men. Sings songs to waves? They says that, too.

That's me, says Old Woman. That's me.

By golly, says those men. Young Man Walking On Water must have saved us after all. We better follow him around.

Suit yourself, says Old Woman. And that one floats away.

"Not again," says Coyote.

"You bet," I says.

"Hmmmm," says Coyote. "All this floating imagery must mean something."

"That's the way it happens in oral stories," I says.

"Hmmmm," says Coyote. "All this water imagery must mean something."

ALBERTA WAS SOAKED right through to her underwear. She pulled the blanket around her and watched Latisha try to keep from laughing.

"You want another blanket?" Latisha said, and she had to put a hand over her face and turn away.

Alberta's hair had fallen in wet clumps around her face, and she could feel the first waves of shivering roll up her body. She clutched her hands tightly in her lap and rubbed her thighs together to try to get warm.

"You want some more coffee?"

"Why don't you just pour a pot over me."

"You know," said Latisha, "my granny had a story about a woman who didn't have the sense to come in out of the rain."

"Your granny ever tell you it was impolite to laugh at people?"

"Yes, she did," said Latisha, and she burst out laughing.

Alberta snuggled deeper into the blanket and considered the cup of coffee in front of her, trying to figure out a way to get the cup to her lips without opening the blanket.

Latisha was still giggling. "You want a straw?"

Alberta thrust a hand out of the blanket and picked up the cup. Her skin had a slightly blue tint to it and the skin between the fingers looked transparent.

"I could have hypothermia," Alberta said.

"I've got an idea," said Latisha, biting her lower lip to keep her mouth quiet. "Billy, that old hair dryer still in the back room?"

Alberta felt a little weird sitting at the table, looking out the window at the parking lot, wrapped in a heavy blanket, holding a hair dryer on her lap. But it felt wonderful. And it was drying her clothes. Already she was beginning to feel her breasts again, and her panties had lost that awful clammy texture. In fact, working the nozzle of the hair dryer in particular directions felt slightly erotic.

"So," said Latisha, seeing the color return to Alberta's face. "Besides wanting to play with my hair dryer, what brings you to town?"

"Lionel's birthday."

"You drove down from Calgary for Lionel's birthday?"

"I promised him I would come."

"Well," said Latisha, a smile edging its way out of her mouth. "I love my brother, but standing in the rain in the parking lot makes a lot more sense now."

Alberta shook her head. Latisha was right. What was worse was that as she got warmer, she began to feel nauseous and her breasts began to hurt. They felt swollen and hot.

"You okay?"

"I'm just wet and a little dizzy."

"I used to get like that when I was pregnant. For the first few months, I'd be sick all the time. And my breasts would just ache."

Alberta looked at Latisha, who was looking at her expectantly.

"I'm not pregnant."

"Just wet, right?"

"That's right."

Latisha leaned back in the chair and drank her coffee. "Well, it's not all it's cracked up to be anyway."

Alberta sipped her coffee. The hair dryer continued to purr on her lap. The nausea was beginning to subside, but her breasts still hurt. She could feel every seam in her bra, could feel the sides chafing and squeezing. She tried to adjust herself, but it didn't help.

"So," said Latisha, "what's new with you?"

It was an hour before Alberta stopped talking and realized that the blanket had slipped off her shoulders and that the hair dryer was burning a hole in her skirt.

"All that and your car gets stolen, too?" said Latisha.

"I can't believe it," said Alberta.

"Neither can I."

"That I would just rattle on like that. I'm really sorry."

"Hey," said Latisha, "what are friends for. The artificial insemination part was wonderful. With alternatives like Charlie and Lionel, it makes perfect sense."

"It probably seems a little crazy," said Alberta.

"No, not at all," said Latisha. "Now let me get it straight. Attractive university professor. No, that's sexist. Successful university professor seeking employment as a single parent desires discreet short-term relationship with attractive, considerate person. Men need not apply. Intercourse not required. Willing to drive great distances. Own car essential."

Alberta started to laugh.

"Is that about it?" said Latisha.

"That's about it," said Alberta.

Billy stuck his head out of the kitchen. "Food's up and packed. Ready whenever you are."

"Thanks, Billy."

"If you're about done with the dryer," said Billy, smiling at Alberta, "there are other customers waiting for it."

Latisha picked up the coffee cups. "I've got to go. Why don't you stay here and have lunch. When you see my brother, wish him happy birthday for me."

"Where you going?"

"Sun Dance," said Latisha. "I take food out for the dancers and their families every year. The men begin dancing this afternoon."

"You taking the kids?"

"Always do."

Alberta looked out at the sky. It was clearing to the west. "You staying with your folks?"

"Kids'll stay with them. I'll stay with Norma."

Alberta draped the blanket over the chair and wrapped the cord around the dryer.

"You mind if I come along?"

"What about Lionel?"

Outside, the rain had slowed to a gentle mist, and Alberta could almost see the vague shadow of the Rockies on the horizon. Alberta pulled her hair out of her face and straightened her dress.

"Let him get his own hair dryer," she said.

THE LONE RANGER, ISHMAEL, ROBINSON CRUSOE, AND HAWKEYE
sat down in the grass on a rise and waited for Coyote to catch
up.

"Boy," says Coyote, "this is a lot of running back and
forth. Has anything happened?"

"Nope," said the Lone Ranger. "We didn't want to start
without you."

"Yes," said Ishmael. "We always feel better knowing where
you are."

"Nothing to worry about," says Coyote. "I'm right here."

"Look," said Robinson Crusoe. "The grass."

"Look," said Hawkeye. "The light."

The clouds had moved away from the mountains, opening a
path to the sky. From where they sat, the old Indians and Coyote watched the prairies lean away and turn blue and green
and gold as the edges of sunlight touched the storm. It was as
if a bright fire had sprung up in the deep grass, running before
the wind, seeking the world ablaze with color.

"How beautiful it was," said the Lone Ranger.

"Yes," said Ishmael. "How beautiful it is."

"It is ever changing," said Robinson Crusoe.

"It remains the same," said Hawkeye.

"Hey, hey," says Coyote. "That's all very profound, but I'm a little cold, you know. Maybe we could look and talk as we walk."

The old Indians got to their feet. The Lone Ranger gestured toward the mountains. "You can see them now."

Coyote looked toward the west, but all he could see was the mountains and the sky and the land.

"See what?" says Coyote. "Say, is this a trick?"

"We should hurry," said Ishmael, "or we'll be late."

"Late for what?" says Coyote, and he looks across the land again.

"And that wouldn't be polite," said Robinson Crusoe.

"No," said Hawkeye, starting down the slope. "It certainly would not."

MINNIE LEANED ON THE COUNTER and watched Bursum put another tape in the VCR and fast-forward it to the big scene at the river.

"Damn," said Bursum. "How many more copies of the movie do we have?"

"That's it," said Minnie. "Is it just the one movie?"

Bursum looked at the tape in his hand. He looked at the VCR. He looked at The Map. He looked at Minnie.

"What do you mean?"

"Well," said Minnie, "we have lots of other Westerns. What if they all have the same problem?"

It was time to go to the lake. Time to spend a day in the sun and enjoy the quiet of nature. Time to forget about Lionel and Charlie and Eli and the old Indians. And the movie.

"Of course," said Minnie, "it could be a computer virus. You can make a virus do anything."

Time to relax.

"It's still weird, though," said Minnie. "Who would want to kill John Wayne?"

ELI TURNED ONTO THE LEASE ROAD and felt the pavement give way to gravel.

"Dead Dog's the other way," said Lionel.

"I've got just the place to eat," said Eli.

The road was a long run of potholes and washboards, dusty and slippery in the late summer and fall. But in the spring and early summer, when the rains came, the water spread out across the low places in the road until all you could see was the water, and you were left to guess where the danger lay. The truck lurched and plunged through the holes, sending Eli against the wheel and Lionel onto the dash.

"Council's going to pave the road," Eli shouted.

"So I hear," Lionel shouted back. "Where are we going?"

"Thought we'd go Native."

"Where are we going?"

"Nephew," said Eli, "did I ever tell you why I came home?"

Lionel watched his uncle negotiate the road, swinging around the potholes that he could see, diving into the ones he could not, riding out the bone-rattling teeth of the washboards. The Dead Dog Café and Blossom were disappearing behind the truck, and as Lionel held himself in the seat, he discovered that he was hungry.

Eli leaned against the wheel and settled into how he had left the reserve as a young man and had gone to Toronto and on to the university.

"Those were good days, nephew. Everything was new. There weren't enough hours in the day to see everything. I'd always lived on the reserve. When I got to Toronto, well, I'd never seen anything like it."

The first few years had been lonely, Eli told him. But he finished his degrees and got a teaching job, and then he met Karen.

"Did Norma ever tell you that Karen and I came out for the Sun Dance one year?"

"Turned your life around. That's what she says," said Lionel.

"Says that, does she?" said Eli. "Not surprised."

"Did it?"

"What?"

"Change your life?"

Eli swerved around a pothole and wound up sideways for a moment on a washboard. "No," he said. "Can't say that it did."

"So why'd you come home?"

"Can't just tell you that straight out. Wouldn't make any sense. Wouldn't be much of a story."

Karen really liked the Sun Dance, Eli told Lionel, wanted to go back the next year. But they didn't. And they didn't go back the year after that.

"Karen got sick," said Eli. "She was sick for a long time."

"Norma said she was nice."

"Then she got well."

"That's great," said Lionel.

"Then she was killed in a car accident."

Lionel was sorry that Eli had started the story. He could see that it was going to be depressing.

"A drunk ran a red light."

"Well," said Lionel, looking at the clearing sky, "it's sure turned into a nice day."

"Good day for a birthday, nephew. You hungry?"

"A little."

The cab of the truck was hot. Lionel rolled down a window, but it didn't help. The jacket had become uncomfortable, tight, as if it were slowly shrinking around him.

"After she died, I thought about coming home," Eli continued. "But I didn't."

The road ran on in front of them, a pitch of hills and coulees that dipped and rose on the land. It had been a long time since Lionel had traveled the lease road. Normally, he came in through Medicine River on the road that ran to Cardston. That road was all asphalt and mileage signs and billboards. This road was a wild thing, bounding across the prairies, snaking sideways, and each time they came to a rise, Lionel had the uneasy feeling that just over the crest of the hill the road would vanish, and they would tumble out into the tall grass and disappear.

"I stayed in Toronto. My friends were there, and I had the university."

"Then Granny died, right?"

"That's right," said Eli. "You know, Norma was so mad at me for never coming home that she didn't tell me my mother had died until almost a month after the funeral."

"That's Norma."

"That's the truth."

"So you came home."

"So I came home."

"Well," said Lionel, "it sounds like a good reason to me."

The truck labored up a steep hill, and as they got near the top, Eli slowed down.

"That wasn't the reason, nephew," said Eli. "That wasn't the reason at all."

The truck gained the crest, and Eli ran it out on the flat for a way and pulled off on the shoulder.

"Karen and I stopped right here when we came out that

time. She thought it was the most beautiful thing she had ever seen. What do you think?"

Below in the distance, a great circle of tepees floated on the prairies, looking for all the world like sailing ships adrift on the ocean.

Eli turned sideways in the seat. "What about it, nephew? Where would you want to be?"

Lionel could feel his neck begin to sweat. The jacket was pulling at his arms, and the cuffs were chafing his wrists.

"Anywhere in the world, nephew. Anywhere at all."

Eli sat in the cab. It was much as it had always been. The camp. The land. The sky.

"Maybe we should stop at the band office cafeteria and get some lunch," said Lionel.

"Not the kind of place for a birthday lunch, nephew," said Eli. "Come on."

As they got closer, Lionel could see the pickups and station wagons and cars, the square canvas tents that sat next to the tepees, the pressboard outhouses set outside the perimeter of the lodges. Children dashed around the camp chasing dogs, chasing gophers. Chasing themselves.

Eli circled the camp, occasionally stopping to say hello to someone. Lionel could see Norma's tepee at the eastern edge of the circle. At first he hoped that she had gone to town, but her car was parked off to one side, and as Lionel watched, he saw her step out of the tepee, pick up a stick of wood, and go back in. Eli maneuvered the truck around the camp and parked it beside Norma's car.

"Your auntie makes one hell of a stew," Eli said, opening the truck door and getting out.

Lionel sat in the truck for a moment. It was a bad idea. He could feel it getting worse, and he was tempted to slide behind the wheel and drive back to town by himself. But he was too late. As Eli walked to the tepee, Lionel's father came around the side of the lodge, and all Lionel could do was to smile and wave.

"Lionel," his father called, "come on in. We're just going to eat. Happy birthday, son."

Norma was all smiles and compliments. She dished up stew and bread and coffee, the conversation running to community news and gossip.

"We need more wood," she said. "Maybe you and Lionel can pick some up."

"I have to go to the cabin tonight," said Eli. "I'll bring some back first thing in the morning."

Lionel's father put his hand on Lionel's shoulder. "It's my boy's birthday today. He's just about a man."

Norma nodded. "Nice shoes, nephew. But you should have worn your boots."

"Where'd you get the jacket, son?"

It was awkward sitting cross-legged on the blanket, trying to keep from spilling stew on his pants. "After lunch," Lionel said, "I'll have to go back into town. I'm working today."

"Not anymore, nephew," said Eli. "Seems to me Bill gave you the rest of the day off."

"That's not exactly what he said."

"Besides," said Eli, dipping his bread in the stew, "we still have to talk."

"After lunch," said Norma, waving a ladle at Lionel and Eli, "you two should go over and get your faces painted. Make you feel better."

"That's a good idea, son," said his father. "Get your face painted on your birthday."

"And," said Norma as she filled Eli's cup, "Camelot said you can dance with her family if you want."

"That's right, Eli," said Harley. "We always got a place for you."

"Wouldn't hurt you to dance, too, nephew," said Norma. "You want some more stew?"

It was late afternoon by the time the stew and the coffee ran out, and Eli and Lionel and Harley left the lodge.

"Too late to go back anyway, nephew," said Eli. "The men will start in another hour or so. Might as well stick around for that."

"Bill's going to be mad as hell."

"I'll buy those earphones," said Eli. "He won't be that angry."

"What do you think, Eli?" said Lionel's father.

Eli looked at Harley. "Sure," he said. "I'd like that."

"How about you, son?"

"Think I'll just hang around here, Dad. You know, just hang around."

"Sure," said Harley. "You do that."

Lionel watched his father and his uncle walk across the circle to a large tent. Lionel felt completely out of place, standing there in the jacket and slacks and dress wing tips.

The ground was wet and spongy. In places around the entrances to the lodges, it had run to mud. Lionel tried to stay on the grass, but by the time he got halfway to the outhouse, he had collected a fat layer of gumbo that curled up and over the soles of his shoes. He could hear the mosquitoes at his back. And the flies. He could feel them flash across his face as he walked and tried to wave them away.

The afternoon sun was high and in the west. The wind was beginning to blow, a gentle current in the grass. Beyond the camp, the mountains towered above the world, black and bright. Lionel felt the wind in his face and watched the light play across the camp in shifting patterns. It was beautiful, he conceded. If you didn't mind the flies and the mosquitoes, the summer heat and the wind.

As he stood next to the outhouse, Lionel felt peaceful, as if the rest of the world, the store, the town, the dam, had all disappeared. And he was sorry that Alberta wasn't here to share it with him.

And the old Indians.

For just a moment, Lionel wondered where they had gone.

"Hello, grandson," said a voice behind him. "Are we late?"

Even before he turned around, Lionel was sorry he had asked the question.

LATISHA STOPPED AT THE PETRO-CAN in Medicine River and got gas and six bags of ice.

"What about us?" said Christian. "Elizabeth would really like a pop."

"Yes, I can," said Elizabeth.

"Me, too," said Benjamin.

"The little creep wants one too."

"Christian called me a little creep."

"It's a joke, you little creep."

Alberta got a ginger ale and a box of soda crackers.

"Still feeling lousy?"

"Everything aches."

"When I was pregnant with Benjamin," said Latisha, "that's how I felt."

"There's no way I can be pregnant."

"That's what I said, too."

Alberta curled up against the door and watched the clouds through the side window. The nausea was back, and she felt like throwing up. Christian and Benjamin were wrestling in the back seat. Elizabeth was bouncing in her car seat.

"What was marriage like?"

Latisha looked at Alberta and shook her head. "You were married."

"Not even a year. It didn't count."

"They all count," said Latisha. "Look, with George the sex was great until I got pregnant, which was almost immediately. And the companionship was nice for the first couple of years."

"And then?"

"Then things got ordinary and predictable."

"After just a couple of years?"

"Nothing wrong with ordinary and predictable." Latisha lowered her voice. "George beat me. You knew that."

Alberta nodded and drew her feet up under her on the seat. "I don't know what to do."

"You're doing just fine. Having a child on your own is not a bad idea. Look at me. That's what I did."

"You had George."

"It was easier without George than with him. He took off when I was pregnant with Elizabeth, and I haven't seen him since."

"Not at all?"

"Oh, he writes me letters. I get one or two a month. You ought to see them. They go on and on. Ten, twelve, sometimes twenty pages."

Alberta closed her eyes for a moment, but it only made matters worse. With her eyes open, she could keep track of the horizon. With them closed, the car began to spin.

"What do they say?"

"I stopped reading them about a year ago. I just stick them in a box in the closet."

"What for?"

Latisha gestured toward the back seat. Christian and Benjamin had stopped wrestling. Benjamin was comparing his hands and fingers with his brother. "For the kids. In case they ever want to know what their father was like."

Alberta leaned in toward Latisha. "Why'd he beat you?"

Latisha turned into the town site and drove past the band office and the community center. Just beyond the school, the pavement stopped and the gravel started.

"Thought they were going to pave this thing," said Latisha. "They say that every year."

Latisha pushed herself back from the wheel and sighed. "Well, I figure it was because he was bored. George wanted each day to be a new adventure. Men get bored easy, you know. Most of them don't have much of an imagination."

Christian and Benjamin were playing a game that involved slapping each other's hands as hard as they could. Benjamin was squealing with pain and delight. Elizabeth was asleep in her car seat.

Alberta shifted her feet. "So what do you think? Lionel or Charlie?"

Latisha reached over and rubbed Alberta's leg. "No wonder you're sick."

Latisha turned off the lease road and rode the deep ruts and high centers out on the prairies toward the camp. For as long as Latisha could remember, Norma's lodge was always in the same place on the east side of the camp. And before that Norma's mother. And before that.

When Latisha was in high school, her history teacher asked her to give a short presentation on Indian culture. After the class, Ann Hubert, a white girl who wore a new dress to school each week, asked her if the Sun Dance was like going to church. Latisha tried to think of ways to explain exactly what the Sun Dance was, how the people felt about it, why it was important. Ann stood there smiling while Latisha searched for the words.

"We sit in pews and listen to the priest and then we receive communion, which is the body and blood of Christ," Ann told her. "What do you do?"

Latisha started to tell her about the women's society, but Ann jumped in and asked her if she had ever heard of the Catholic Women's League. "It's famous," Ann said. "They organize the big church supper and welcome new families to the parish."

Latisha started again, remembering the women's lodge and then the men's lodge, the dancing, the giveaway, but Ann continued to hobble her with questions.

"Nine days seems a long time," she said. "What exactly do you do?"

Latisha stood there in the corridor of the school and worked her hands in her lap. Finally Ann said that it was probably a mystery, something you could never know but believed in anyway, like God and Jesus and the Holy Ghost. Latisha wanted to tell Ann that that wasn't it, but in the end she said nothing.

As soon as Latisha parked the car and opened the door, Christian and Benjamin were off like rabbits.

"Mind your relations," Latisha shouted after them.

"What about Elizabeth?"

"I hate to wake her. She's such a grump when she first wakes up. Feeling any better?"

"Nope."

"Come on," said Latisha. "Why don't you lie down inside."

Latisha got Elizabeth out of the car. She woke up for a second, looked around, opened her mouth to yell, and then fell back to sleep.

"Hooray," said Latisha. "If I can get her down, she might sleep for another hour."

Norma was inside cleaning the plates and the cups. "You guys are right on time."

"Brought some food," said Latisha.

"All the work is done," said Norma.

"Alberta's not feeling too good."

"You got your period?"

"No," said Alberta. "I just don't feel very good."

"Nausea," said Latisha. "And sore breasts."

Norma looked at Latisha and cocked her head to one side. Then she looked hard at Alberta.

"I'm not pregnant," said Alberta. "There's no way I could be pregnant."

"Like to have a dime for every time I've heard that," said Norma. "Here, give me my granddaughter. Where are the boys?"

"Somewhere out there," said Latisha.

Norma settled down in a lawn chair with Elizabeth and rocked her. "They'll come back when they get hungry."

"Is it okay if Alberta stays here for a while? I've got to take the food around."

"Maybe get that brother of yours to help," said Norma.

"Lionel?" said Latisha. "Is Lionel here?"

"Him and Eli drove in about an hour ago. Ate most of the stew all by themselves."

"Lionel's at the Sun Dance?" said Alberta.

"Must be snowing in hell," said Latisha.

"No point pouring water on a spark," said Norma. "Eli and Lionel are probably over getting their faces painted."

Alberta and Latisha looked at each other. Norma caught the movement and squeezed her lips in a scold. "It's his birthday. Most men don't even start to get smart until after they turn forty."

Latisha put her purse on the bed. "Then what happens?"

Latisha got the boxes of food from the car. The prairies were aglow with light. For as many times as she had seen it, Latisha still marveled at the land in the late afternoon, the way it moved under the sky, the way it caught the light, the way it turned to follow the sun.

Latisha worked her way around the camp, leaving food with relatives and friends, staying for coffee and conversation, but never staying long. In the center of the camp, people were setting their chairs and blankets in a circle, getting ready for the dancers. Latisha stood there at the far edge of the circle and watched the people gather.

"Hello, Country."

Even before she turned, Latisha's arms instinctively came up and she stepped back, setting a distance between herself and the man behind her.

"Hello, George," she said.

CHARLIE LAY ON THE BED and thumbed through a copy of *Alberta Now*. The phone sat on the pillow beside him. He tried the number. Busy.

There was an article in the magazine on how old movie Westerns were finding a new life in the home video market and what this meant for the industry as a whole. Another article was on how small specialty restaurants were developing new ways to sustain themselves during a recession. A third was a demographic study of the number of lawyers in western Canada.

Charlie tried the number again. Busy.

He didn't read any of the articles. He skimmed through them, catching a phrase here, a graph there, glancing at the photographs, considering the illustrations.

Busy.

At the back of the magazine was a real estate section for luxury properties. Immaculate rambler with water glimpses in Vancouver. Elegant studio brownstone in Toronto. Panoramic lakefront property in southern Alberta. Stunning three-bedroom condo in the West Edmonton Mall.

Busy.
Busy.

Charlie rolled over. The storm had passed and sunlight was leaking in under the curtains. But in the room, everything was dark and cool. Charlie put the magazine on the floor and tried the number again.

Busy.

Busy. Busy. Busy.

ELI WALKED WITH HARLEY AROUND THE CAMP. When he was a child, the tepees had stood six and seven deep. Now the circle was only two or three deep. At the south side of the circle, two young men worked on tying down a cook tent.

"That's Martha Oldcrow's grandkids. The oldest boy was in prison for a while. The youngest was on drugs. Almost killed him."

"So they come back," said Eli.

"Some do," said Harley. "Some don't. There are a few more jobs on the reserve now, but most everybody has to work off reserve."

"Hasn't changed much."

"Nope," said Harley. "You see that young couple over there? That's Eaton Redbow's son and Bertha Morley's daughter. They started coming out about four years ago."

"In the old days," said Eli, "everybody had to leave the reserve to get work."

"Jason First Runner is a lawyer in Vancouver. He and his family haven't missed a Sun Dance in eight, ten years."

Harley pulled up a seat on the bumper of a red pickup truck. "What about you, Eli?" said Harley. "You still living out at your mother's place?"

"That's right."

"Must have one great view of that dam."

"If you like that kind of thing."

"Emmett over at Brocket figures that the dam is killing the river."

"Not doing it any good."

"He was on the radio the other day. Said if the river doesn't flood like it does every year, the cottonwoods will die."

"Hadn't heard that."

"That's what he said. When the river floods, it brings the cottonwoods . . . you know . . ."

"Nutrients?"

"That's it. No flood. No nutrients. No cottonwoods."

"Emmett ought to know."

"And if the cottonwoods die, where are we going to get the Sun Dance tree? You see what I mean?"

"Emmett write his member of Parliament?"

Harley turned his face away from the wind and began to laugh. "What do you think? You figure the dam's going to make us all millionaires?"

Eli looked at Harley and shook his head. "Maybe we should give the Cree in Quebec a call."

"Yeah," said Harley. "That's what I figure, too."

Eli reached down and pulled up a long stalk of grass. The sun felt good on his face. More cars and trucks began to arrive. Families unpacked chairs and blankets and dragged them toward the circle. Eli leaned back and watched the people gather.

"Just like the old days," said Harley. "Only then, we were younger."

ALBERTA LAY ON THE MATTRESS with the blankets piled around her and tried to sleep. The nausea had passed, and she didn't feel as uncomfortable as she had.

"How you feeling now?" said Norma.

"Okay."

"It'll come and go until you get past the third or fourth month," said Norma, setting the coffeepot on the fire.

"I'm not pregnant."

"You'll probably have to pee a lot."

Alberta sat up, the blankets still wrapped around her. "Maybe I should find Lionel. You know where he went?"

Norma put the pot of stew next to the coffeepot. "After that, you'll feel great. For a while."

Alberta shook off the blankets and tested her legs. "I feel better."

"But it won't last," said Norma.

When Alberta stepped through the entrance, the first thing she noticed were the people. More than there had been when they arrived. The center of the camp was filling up. Alberta looked around the circle, but she did not see Lionel.

"Hello, Alberta."

Eli and Harley were leaning against a pickup, watching the people gather.

"You looking for Lionel?"

"No," said Alberta, looking around. "Have you seen him?"

"He was here," said Eli. "But he's not now."

"Have you seen Latisha?"

"No," said Harley. "Haven't seen her, either."

Alberta left Eli and Harley and worked her way through the lodges to the open ground. It was going to be a beautiful day after all, and she had almost forgotten about standing in the parking lot of the Dead Dog. Her car was another matter.

As she came around the side of a tepee, she saw Latisha standing across the circle. She was talking to a man, and at first Alberta didn't recognize him.

And then she did. George Morningstar. And across the distance between the two women, Alberta could feel Latisha's body tense up, could feel her hands clench as she set her feet hard into the ground and waited.

Alberta turned quickly and went back to Norma's tepee. Eli and Harley were still at the pickup truck. Even before she reached the men, they stood up and began moving toward her.

LATISHA LOOKED PAST GEORGE to the mountains. The sun was above the mountains now, and they had softened to deep blues and purples.

"I called a couple of times, but you were busy."

"What are you doing here?"

"I wrote you to say I was coming. Thought I'd say hello and see the kids. You get the letter?"

"Sure."

George hadn't changed much. He still had that innocent, vulnerable look to him. His hair was shorter and he had grown a weedy mustache. He was carrying a thick black case, the kind that salesmen use.

"I got a new job."

"That's nice."

"I'm a photojournalist. Just had a story published in *New Age*. Maybe you saw it?"

Latisha looked around, hoping she would see Norma or Alberta or her parents.

"They're crazy about Indians," George said, watching Latisha, trying to catch her eye.

"Who?"

"The magazine. The magazine is crazy about Indians."

Latisha moved so that the sun was not in her eyes, so she could see George better.

"Look," he said, "I wanted to ask you if you thought people would get upset if I took a couple of pictures."

Latisha felt her face flush.

"Be nice to get inside the big tent," he said, pointing to the double lodge. "But a couple of shots of the men dancing around would be okay."

"You know cameras aren't allowed."

"Sure, but that's for strangers. Not family."

Latisha shifted her weight and locked her knees. As she did, there was a faint clicking sound as if she had stepped on something brittle. "That's for everybody, George."

George looked at the crowd that had gathered around the circle. He swung the case around as he looked. "That's pretty old-fashioned talk," he said. "You're not just mad at me, are you?"

"George," said Latisha, "I don't even think about you. I don't even read your letters."

"Well, there," said George, smiling. "See. That's why you're surprised to see me. If you had read the letters, you would have known I was coming. I even called the restaurant a couple of times, but you were busy."

"I'm still busy," she said. And Latisha tried to maneuver past George.

But he moved with her, small movements, nothing aggressive, cutting her off from the rest of the people. The sound returned just at the edge of her hearing.

"I've got work to do, George. Nobody cares if you stay. But you can't take pictures."

"It's almost the twenty-first century, Country. Look, they let you take pictures in church all the time. Hell, everything the pope does is on television. People are curious about these kinds of things. And the more people know, the more they understand."

"George—"

"I mean, it's not exactly sacred, is it? More like a campout or a picnic."

"George, go away."

George set the case on the grass. He fiddled with it for a moment, getting it to stand upright. "I really want to see the kids. If that's okay."

"I don't know where they are." Latisha motioned toward the people. "They're over there somewhere."

"Well," said George, working a smile out of his mouth, "maybe I'll just stay here out of the way and watch. If you see them, send them over."

The sound returned, louder. Clicking. Like an insect. Hard. Metallic.

Latisha looked at George. He shrugged and looked off at the people.

"George!" said Latisha. "Damn it, George."

George continued looking at the people and he continued smiling. "Looks about the same, Country," he said in that soft, singsong manner he had. "Hasn't changed much at all."

"WE WOULD HAVE GOTTEN HERE SOONER," said the Lone Ranger, "but Coyote knew a short cut."

"Who?" said Lionel.

"It wasn't my fault," says Coyote. "Everyone wants to blame me."

"How's the jacket, grandson?" said Ishmael.

Lionel rolled his shoulders around in the jacket. "Look, it's very nice. I mean, I like leather. And the fringe is . . . elegant. But I really can't keep it."

"It looks a little tight," said Hawkeye.

"Well, it is a little tight."

"It looks hot, too," said Robinson Crusoe.

In fact, Lionel felt as if the jacket was suffocating him. Worse, the jacket had begun to smell. A stale, sweet smell, like old aftershave or rotting fruit.

"It's okay, grandson," said the Lone Ranger. "We got to take it back, anyway."

"Take it back?"

"We just borrowed the jacket," said Ishmael.

"To see if it would make you feel better," said Robinson Crusoe.

"Sometimes it works, and sometimes it doesn't," said Hawkeye.

Coyote sat in the grass and spread his ears. "Listen," he says to the old Indians. "You hear that?"

The Lone Ranger, Ishmael, Robinson Crusoe, and Hawkeye turned their faces into the wind.

"There," says Coyote. "Hear it?"

"Oh, oh," said the Lone Ranger. "We got a problem."

Lionel looked around, but all he saw were the mountains and the camp and the people. "What's wrong?"

"Come on, grandson," said the Lone Ranger. "You can give us a hand." And the old Indians began walking back to the camp.

"See," says Coyote. "See. I can be helpful."

Lionel trailed after the old Indians. As they got near the edge of the camp, the old Indians turned and headed for the south side. And as they entered the cluster of lodges, Lionel saw a man and a woman standing, talking. The man was carrying what looked to be a large briefcase, and the woman was standing back with her arms folded across her chest.

"Can you hear it, grandson?" said the Lone Ranger.

Lionel couldn't hear a thing, just the sound of the drum and the wind, but he recognized Latisha. Then he saw George, and he began walking faster, closing the distance between himself and his sister.

"Wait up," says Coyote. "Wait up."

Lionel was almost to Latisha when George felt the motion and turned around.

"Hello, Lionel," said George.

"Hello, George."

"Nice-looking jacket," said George. "Where'd you get it?"

"Haven't seen you in a while," said Lionel.

"Looks a lot like my jacket."

"Yes," said the Lone Ranger. "It's your jacket all right."

"If you look closely," said Ishmael, "you can tell."

"We let Lionel borrow it for a while, but it didn't help," said Robinson Crusoe.

"Sometimes it works, and sometimes it doesn't," said the Lone Ranger.

George looked at Lionel, and he looked at the old Indians. "Who are you?"

"I'm the Lone Ranger," said the Lone Ranger. "And this is Ishmael and Robinson Crusoe and Hawkeye."

"Right," said George. "And I'm General Custer."

"I'm Coyote," says Coyote. "I really am Coyote."

Latisha moved toward Lionel and the old Indians. "He's taking pictures."

George laughed. "Come on, Country."

"I don't know how he's doing it, but he's taking pictures. With that case."

"I think you should probably give me my jacket back," said George.

Lionel looked at Latisha, and he looked at George. And then he heard it. A hard snap, a click, a mechanical movement.

"I won't even ask how you got it," said George. "Just give me the jacket, and I'll get going."

"What about the case?" said Lionel.

"What about it?" said George.

"About the right size for a couple of cameras."

"Come on," said George. "Do you see me taking pictures?"

"I don't mind if you want to take my picture," says Coyote.

"What's in the case?" Lionel said again.

"Look," said George, picking up the case and retreating one step, "you guys have your beliefs, and I have mine. Nothing wrong with that."

"Open the case," said Lionel.

"No problem," said George, and he began moving toward the edge of the camp.

"Better open the case, George," said Eli.

Lionel turned to see his uncle and his father. And Alberta.

"Hi, Alberta."

"Hi, Lionel."

"Open the case!" shouts Coyote. "Open the case."

George was surrounded. For a moment he looked as if he wanted to run. Instead, he smiled and shrugged and released the snaps on the case.

There was a camera inside on a mount. The lens was pressed against one side of the case, and as George raised the flap, the shutter clicked and the motor drive automatically advanced the film.

Eli looked in the case and nodded.

"So what," said George. "No harm in a couple of pictures."

"You can't take pictures at the Sun Dance," said Eli. His voice was flat and hard.

"No law against it," said George. "What are you going to do, scalp me?"

"Scalp!" says Coyote. "Yuck! Where did you ever get an idea like that?"

"Get the film, nephew," said Eli.

As Lionel moved toward the case, George stepped in front of it.

"I'll do it," George said. "This is expensive gear."

George bent over the case and rewound the film. He took his time, making each movement slow and exaggerated, shielding the case with his body.

"Here," he said, and he tossed Lionel a canister of film. "Now what about my jacket?"

Lionel turned to the Lone Ranger. "What about it?"

"Oh, yes," said the Lone Ranger. "That's a good idea. It's time he got his jacket back."

Lionel slipped out of the jacket and handed it to George. George snapped the lid on the case and smiled at Latisha.

"Good to see you again, Country," he said.

Lionel didn't even see Eli move until he was on George, pushing him back, snatching the case from the man's hand.

"Hey, come on," George shouted, and he came forward, reaching for Eli. But as he did, Lionel stepped in between the two men, forcing George back.

{ 385 }

"That's mine, damn it." George looked past Lionel. Eli was bent over the case.

"Hey!" George yelled. "Hey, get out of there." And he tried to shoulder his way through Lionel. But Lionel moved with him, blocking, keeping himself between his uncle and George.

Eli released the camera from its mount, opened the back, and took out a roll of film.

"You can't do that!"

Eli got to his feet and turned to face George. He held the film canister in his hand. "What's this?"

George was florid, a mottled yellow and orange. "Undeveloped film. Just blank film."

Eli reached into his pocket and pulled out a ten-dollar bill. "Then this should cover it," he said, and he caught the end of the film between his thumb and forefinger and stripped it out of the canister in a great curling arc.

Eli dropped the exposed film into the case, turned, and walked back to where the dancers were beginning to come out of the main lodge.

George watched Eli go. The case had tipped over on its side, was lying in the grass like a dead animal.

"You can't believe in this shit!" George shouted after Eli. "This is ice age crap!"

Lionel moved forward, and George fell back several steps.

"Probably time to go," said Lionel.

"Come on," said George. "Come on! It's the twentieth century. Nobody cares about your little powwow. A bunch of old people and drunks sitting around in tents in the middle of nowhere. Nobody cares about any of this."

"Go away, George," said Latisha. "Just go away."

"You're a joke!" George's lips were wet with spit. "You all act like this is important, like it's going to change your lives. Christ, you guys are born stupid and you die stupid."

Lionel picked up the case and set it on its feet. "There's nothing for you here."

George's arms were cocked at his side, quivering, as if they were hanging on springs. He stared at Lionel for a moment and then he grabbed the case and the camera and stomped off, staggering across the soft, uneven ground. As he got to the car, he turned and shouted, his mouth snapping open and shut like a trap. But the words vanished in the distance and the wind.

Lionel and Alberta and Latisha and Harley and the old Indians and Coyote stood their ground and watched George throw the case into the trunk and climb into the car.

"Well, grandson," said the Lone Ranger, "that's about as much as we can do for you. How do you feel?"

Lionel jammed his hands into his pockets. "I feel fine."

"Fixing up the world is hard work," said Ishmael.

"Even fixing up the little things is tough," said Robinson Crusoe.

"Try not to mess up your life again," said Hawkeye. "We're not as young as we used to be."

"Let's fix up some more things," says Coyote. "I have lots of good ideas."

George's car shot out from behind the lodges. It roared down the track to the lease road, throwing dirt and dust into the air. Lionel watched as the car hit the gravel, slid sideways, and bounced over the first rise and disappeared.

Lionel looked at the old Indians. "That's it?"

"You bet," said the Lone Ranger.

"This is how you help me fix up my life?"

"Pretty exciting, isn't it?" said Ishmael.

"Have I missed something?"

"In the years to come," said Robinson Crusoe, "you'll be able to tell your children and grandchildren about this."

"You do this a lot?" said Lionel.

"You don't have to thank us, grandson," said Hawkeye.

"Come on," said Lionel's father. "Let's go watch the men dance."

"Happy birthday," said Alberta.

{ 387 }

"That's right," said Latisha. "Happy birthday, brother."

The circle was tightly formed now, the older people sitting in lawn chairs along the front edge, the younger people standing at the back, the children constantly in motion. Norma caught them as they got to the circle.

"Eli's going to dance," she told Lionel.

"It's okay, auntie," said Lionel. "I need to calm down."

"No one's begging you, nephew."

The sun was just above the mountains when the families gathered. Lionel watched as his mother and father made a space for Eli.

Lionel looked around at the people. "Where'd the old Indians go?"

Alberta looked up. "Who?"

Lionel searched the camp again, but they were nowhere to be seen. "Never mind," he said.

Lionel stood with Alberta as the afternoon cooled and ran to evening. In a while, the dancers would return to the center lodge and the families would go back to their tepees and tents. And in the morning, when the sun came out of the east, it would begin again.

DR. HOVAUGH SAT IN HIS HOTEL ROOM in a sea of maps and brochures and travel guides. The book was lying open on top of the pile, and he hummed to himself as he consulted the book and then a map, the book and then a brochure, the book and then a travel guide. And, of course, there was the star. All the while, he plotted occurrences and probabilities and directions and deviations on a pad of graph paper, turning the chart as he went, literal, allegorical, tropological, anagogic.

Slowly and with a great deal of self-assurance, Dr. Hovaugh took out a purple marker and drew a deliberate circle around Parliament Lake.

"Tomorrow," Dr. Hovaugh said, leaning back in the chair. "Tomorrow and tomorrow." And he drew a second circle around the lake. And a third.

"And tomorrow."

CHARLIE READ THROUGH THE MAGAZINE AGAIN. He was intrigued by the stunning three-bedroom condo in the West Edmonton Mall. Who would want to live in a mall? Perhaps you got free tickets for all the rides or a season pass for the wave pool. As he remembered, there was a car dealership in the mall and that would probably be handy if you lived there. And the restaurants and the bars and the movie theaters and the hundreds of stores.

A three-bedroom condo in the West Edmonton Mall. Intriguing.

Charlie looked at the phone, measured the distance for a moment, and picked it up. He knew the number by heart now, and he hit each key as if it were a musical composition.

It had become such a routine—the dialing, the waiting, the busy signal—that he was already in the process of hanging up when he realized that the number was finally ringing.

Three, four, five, six.

"Hello."

"Hello . . ."

"Hello . . . Who's this?"

Charlie sat up straight on the bed and drew a deep breath. "Dad?" he said. "Is that you, Dad?"

"I GOT BACK AS SOON AS I COULD," says Coyote. I was busy being a hero."

"That's unlikely," I says.

"No, no," says Coyote. "It's the truth."

"There are no truths, Coyote," I says. "Only stories."

"Okay," says Coyote. "Tell me a story."

"Okay," I says. "You remember Old Woman? You remember that big hole and Young Man Walking On Water? You remember any of this at all?"

"Sure," says Coyote. "I remember all of it."

"I wasn't talking to you," I says.

"Who else is here?" says Coyote.

So.

Old Woman leaves Young Man Walking On Water and his apostles and floats around for a while. She floats in rivers. She floats in bays. She floats in bathtubs. She floats in lakes. One day she is floating in a real nice lake. This lake is so smooth you can see the sky when you look in the water.

My name is Glimmerglass, says that Lake. What's yours?

I'm Old Woman, says Old Woman. And I am floating.

It's a nice day for that, says that Lake.

Old Woman floats, and pretty soon she floats ashore.

Is that you, Chingachgook? says a voice. Is that you, my Indian friend?

Old Woman sits up in the water and looks around. There are some beautiful trees and some excellent rocks and some splendid clouds. And there is a short, skinny guy in a leather shirt with fringe standing behind one of the trees.

Chingachgook! That skinny guy says that. Chingachgook! That's what he says.

Hello, says Old Woman. I'm Old Woman.

That skinny guy in the leather shirt with fringe stays behind that tree, and all Old Woman can see is a big rifle. A really big rifle.

That's a big rifle, says Old Woman.

You bet, says the skinny man. I'm Nathaniel Bumppo, Post-Colonial Wilderness Guide and Outfitter. You must be Chingachgook.

No, says Old Woman, I'm not Chingachgook.

My friends call me Nasty, says Nathaniel Bumppo. Chingachgook is my friend. He's an Indian. But he is my friend anyway.

But I'm not Chingachgook, says Old Woman.

Nasty Bumppo runs to the next tree and hides behind it. Nonsense, he says. I can tell an Indian when I see one. Chingachgook is an Indian. You're an Indian. Case closed.

I'm sure this is embarrassing for you, says Old Woman.

Indians have Indian gifts, says Nasty Bumppo. And Whites have white gifts.

Gifts? says Old Woman.

That Nasty Bumppo keeps running from tree to tree as he is talking, dragging that really big rifle behind him.

Indians have a keen sense of smell, says Nasty Bumppo. That's an Indian gift.

"I have a keen sense of smell," says Coyote. "I must be an Indian."

"You're a Coyote," I says.

"No, no," says Coyote. "I have an Indian gift."

Whites are compassionate, says Nasty Bumppo. That's a white gift.

"Wait a minute," says Coyote. "I'm compassionate, too. I must be a White."

"You're still a Coyote," I says.

"Boy," says Coyote, "this is confusing."

Indians can run fast. Indians can endure pain. Indians have quick reflexes. Indians don't talk much. Indians have good eyesight. Indians have agile bodies. These are all Indian gifts, says Nasty Bumppo.

Interesting, says Old Woman.

Whites are patient. Whites are spiritual. Whites are cognitive. Whites are philosophical. Whites are sophisticated. Whites are sensitive. These are all white gifts, says Nasty Bumppo.

So, says Old Woman. Whites are superior, and Indians are inferior.

Exactly right, says Nasty Bumppo. Any questions?

"Oops," says Coyote. "We have a problem."

"Only if you're an Indian," I says.

"You're right," says Coyote. "I'm probably a Coyote."

And, says Nasty Bumppo, Whites are particularly good killers. Do you see that deer over there?

Oh, dear, says Old Woman. That's not a deer. That's Old Coyote.

What's an Old Coyote? says Nasty Bumppo, and that one shoots at Old Coyote.

Stop shooting, says Old Coyote. You could kill someone with that really big gun.

Stand still, Nasty Bumppo tells Old Coyote, so I can shoot you.

Boy, says Old Coyote, I was safer in that other story. And Old Coyote jumps into a hole by a big tree.

Phooey, says Nasty Bumppo. Now I'm going to have to kill something else.

Well, says Old Woman, there's no one here but you and me.

Well, that sure is a problem, Chingachgook, says Nasty Bumppo. That sure is a problem.

Maybe, says Old Woman, it would help if you knew that I'm not your friend Chingachgook.

Yes, says Nasty Bumppo, that does help a lot. If you're not my friend Chingachgook, then I should go ahead and shoot you and get it out of my system.

That's not exactly what I had in mind, says Old Woman.

Gut shot or head shot? says Nasty Bumppo.

"I'm going to need a few minutes to figure this out," says Coyote.

"Just pay attention," I says.

"No, no," says Coyote. "This is deep. This is very deep."

So that Nasty Bumppo hides behind a big tree and that Nasty Bumppo loads that really big rifle and that Nasty Bumppo aims that really big rifle at Old Woman.

Here we go, says Nasty Bumppo.

And there is a really big explosion. And there is a lot of smoke.

Boy, says Nasty Bumppo, that was a really good shot. And that one falls over.

What happened? says Old Woman.

I've been shot, says Nasty Bumppo. You must have shot me.

No, says Old Woman. I didn't do that.

What did you say your name was? says Nasty Bumppo.

Old Woman, says Old Woman.

That's a stupid name, says Nasty Bumppo. We have to get you a better killer name than that. How about Daniel Boone?

I don't think so, says Old Woman.

How about Harry Truman? says Nasty Bumppo.

Not that either, says Old Woman.

Arthur Watkins? says Nasty Bumppo.

No, says Old Woman.

We got to get this settled before I die, says Nasty Bumppo, and that one takes a book out of his pack. Here we go, he says. Hawkeye. That's a good name. Hawkeye.

Hawkeye? says Old Woman.

Good name, huh? says Nasty Bumppo, and that one drops dead.

"Hawkeye?" says Coyote. "Is that a good Indian name?"

"No," I says. "It sounds like a name for a white person who wants to be an Indian."

"Who would want to be an Indian?" says Coyote.

"Not me," I says.

"Not me, either," says Coyote.

Hello, says a voice. Are you all right?

Old Woman looks around, and there is an Indian standing by a tree.

Hello, says Old Woman. You must be Chingachgook.

That's right, says Chingachgook. Have you seen a skinny guy in a leather shirt with a really big rifle?

"Wait, wait!" says Coyote. "Who shot Nasty Bumppo?"

"Who cares?" I says.

"Maybe Old Coyote shot him," says Coyote.

"Anything's possible," I says.

"Maybe there was more than one gunman," says Coyote.

"Anything's possible," I says.

"Maybe," says Coyote, "it was a conspiracy."

. . .

Oh, oh. While Chingachgook and Old Woman are talking, some soldiers come along and they see the dead Nasty Bumppo.

Okay, says those soldiers. Who shot Nasty Bumppo?

Not me, says Old Woman.

Not me, says Chingachgook.

Not me, says Coyote.

Well, I didn't shoot myself, says Nasty Bumppo. And that one dies again.

Ah-ha! those soldiers says. This looks like a mystery.

Well, says Old Woman, it's sure a mystery to me.

Names? says those soldiers, and they all take out a book from their packs.

I'm Chingachgook, says Chingachgook.

Yes, says those soldiers. There is a Chingachgook in this book. And they check Chingachgook's name off the list. Next!

I'm Old Woman, says Old Woman.

No Old Woman in this book, says those soldiers. You'll have to do better than that.

Daniel Boone? says Old Woman.

Not on the list, says those soldiers.

Harry Truman?

Nope.

Arthur Watkins? says Old Woman.

Not even close, says those soldiers.

Is there a Hawkeye in that book? says Chingachgook.

Yes, there is, says those soldiers.

Well, says Old Woman, I guess I'm Hawkeye.

Ah-ha! shouts those soldiers. Then you're going to prison for a long time.

And they grab Old Woman.

For killing Nasty Bumppo? says Old Woman.

No, says those soldiers. For trying to impersonate a white man. And those soldiers put Old Woman on a train and send her to Florida.

. . .

"That sounds like Fort Marion," says Coyote.
  "Yes, it does," I says.
  "So that's what happened," says Coyote.
  "That's what always happens," I says.

ELI DIDN'T GET BACK TO THE CABIN until well after midnight.
Just as he crawled into bed and was arranging the pillows,
they turned the floodlight on. Sifton's revenge, no doubt. Eli
hung a blanket over the window, but it could not block out
the hard white light that came in around the edges and flowed
through the blanket itself and set it aglow.

He did not sleep well that night, and before dawn he got up
and put on a pot of coffee. Then he backed the pickup up to
the woodpile and threw blocks of wood into the truck as he
waited for the sunrise. He was sweating when first light filled
the sky.

Eli went back to the cabin and brought out the coffeepot
and set it on the porch. The air was cold and he felt tired. He
leaned back against the cabin and waited for the sun.

THE NEXT MORNING, Babo rose early, showered, and dressed for the adventure. It wasn't such a bad thing to have lost Dr. Hovaugh's car, she concluded. He was so set on finding the Indians that he would never have stopped at the many out-of-the-way places in the area, would never have taken the time to see them.

But a bus. Well, there was no place to go. All you could do was to sit back and relax and enjoy the view. They would find the old Indians in good time. No sense in missing the other points of interest.

When Babo got to the restaurant, Dr. Hovaugh was waiting for her. He looked as if he hadn't slept at all. The book was open and sitting on top of a map. "Good morning, Dr. Hovaugh," said Babo.

"I ordered some breakfast for you."

"That was nice. What did you order?"

Babo and Dr. Hovaugh ate in silence. Dr. Hovaugh ran down the pages of the book, occasionally looking at the map. Babo found the chili omelet a touch on the dry side, but the potato chips were tasty.

Babo had just started to drink her second cup of coffee when Dr. Hovaugh shut the book, folded the map, and stood up.

"Come on," he said. "Time to go."

"The bus doesn't leave for another half an hour."

"We have to get good seats," said Dr. Hovaugh. "At the front. So we can see everything."

"Plenty of time."

"It happens today," said Dr. Hovaugh, and he caught up the book and the map and disappeared out the front door.

Babo sighed and finished her coffee. This didn't bode well for some leisurely sightseeing. Perhaps Dr. Hovaugh would relax once the bus got going and just forget about the Indians.

When Babo climbed on the bus, Dr. Hovaugh was sitting in the front seat, the book open, the map spread out on the seat next to him.

"Sit there," he said, pointing to the seat across the aisle. Other people began to get on, but the bus wasn't very full.

"Hi," said the bus driver. "My name is Ralph, and I'm your driver for today. If there is anything I can do to make your West Wind Tour more enjoyable, please let me know."

"Let's get going," said Dr. Hovaugh.

Ralph adjusted his seat and turned on the microphone. "We'll be seeing a number of interesting places today. If you have any questions, just shout them out, and I'll do my best to answer them."

"How long before we get to the dam?" said Dr. Hovaugh.

"Remember," said Ralph, "no smoking is permitted on this bus. There's a bathroom to the rear of the bus and there are reading lights above your seats."

Babo reclined her seat and put her hands in her lap.

"On behalf of the management of West Wind Tours," said Ralph, "thanks for traveling with the Wind. So, sit back and enjoy the adventure of a lifetime."

That would be nice, thought Babo. That would be very nice, indeed.

CLIFFORD SIFTON SAT IN HIS OFFICE at the dam site and read through the pile of reports on his desk. A waste of time. A damn waste of time. Sifton loved building dams, but he hated the paperwork. Loved watching the forms being built and the concrete being poured. Hated the dinners and the speeches and the reports.

Lewis Pick opened the office door, letting in the cold air behind him.

"Hey, Cliff," said Lew. "You better come and see this."

"What is it?"

"Don't know," said Lew, "but you better come."

Sifton pushed the report aside. What he should have done was walk down to Eli's. Coffee with the old man in the mornings was always a high point, and he hated missing it.

Lew was standing at the railing, looking out over the lake, when Sifton got outside.

"So what in the hell's the problem?"

"No problem," said Lew. "Just weird."

"Okay," said Sifton. "What's weird?"

"Look," said Lew, and he pointed off across the lake.

At the far end, just beyond the range of sight, Sifton thought he saw something. Dots on the horizon. Nothing more than that.

"Here," said Lew. "Use the glasses."

The binoculars didn't help much, but Sifton could now see that there was something out there.

"Kids probably," said Sifton. "They know they're not supposed to be on the lake, so they do it anyway."

"Yeah," said Lew. "Could be kids."

Sifton looked through the binoculars again. The dots were beginning to take shape, to pull closer. There were three of them, and Sifton could almost make out what they were.

"Here," he said to Lew. "You've got younger eyes. What do you see?"

Lew took the binoculars and leaned on the railing. He stayed there for a long time, watching. Finally, he stood up and shook his head.

"So?" said Sifton.

"You're not going to like this, Cliff," said Lew, handing the binoculars back to him.

"Make my day," said Sifton.

"Cars," said Lew.

"Cars?" said Sifton.

"That's right," said Lew. "And they're coming this way."

Bill Bursum parked his car at the lake's edge and unloaded his lawn chair and the large cooler. He set up a folding table and put the portable radio and television on it. It was cold and Bursum wore a heavy jacket, but as soon as the sun came up and the day warmed, he would change into shorts and a light shirt.

The lake was spectacular, quiet and so calm you could see the sky in the water. Bursum stretched out on the chair and pulled his tuque down over his ears.

He could see the world from here. To the east was the dam. Bursum could just see the lip of the structure and the control tower, and he imagined the engineers moving back and forth, checking the turbines, running tests, drinking coffee. Beyond that was the prairies, a wondrous landscape that ran all the way to Ontario.

To the west, beyond the lake and the trees, the mountains ran north to Banff and Jasper and south into Montana.

Bursum sat up and adjusted the chair. He started to turn on the radio when a flash of light caught his attention. The sun was not yet up, but in the early light Bursum could see three objects on the lake. He walked out on the peninsula where he planned to build his house once the business with the dam and

Eli was resolved, marched right through the master bedroom and the living room until he stood at the edge of the water.

They were still a way away, but even from this distance, Bursum could tell what they were. Cars. Three cars.

"Good God!" said Bursum.

Bursum stood there as the cars sailed past the peninsula and continued on down the lake toward the dam.

THE LAKE WAS BEAUTIFUL. Babo leaned against the glass as the bus ran along the embankment road.

"Parliament Lake," said Ralph. "The eleventh largest man-made lake in Alberta."

Dr. Hovaugh was bent over the book and the map.

"Dr. Hovaugh," said Babo, "look. It's the lake. The dam is just ahead."

"About time," said Dr. Hovaugh, and he turned in his seat to look out the window.

"The lake probably looks a little deserted right now," said Ralph, "but in the near future, you can expect to see houses and condominiums along the shore and boats and swimmers enjoying the water."

"What's that?" said one of the passengers.

"What?" said Ralph.

"Over there," said Babo. "What's that over there?"

Ralph slowed the bus down and then brought it to a stop. "Well," he said, "I don't know. Anybody got some binoculars?"

Several people had binoculars. An older man gave his pair to Ralph, who looked through them and began to laugh.

"Well, folks," he said, "this is certainly a highlight of your tour. If you'll look to your right, you'll see three cars floating on the lake."

"Cars?" said Dr. Hovaugh.

"Don't ask me how they got there," said Ralph. "But someone is sure going to catch hell."

"Let me see," said Dr. Hovaugh. "I'm a doctor." And Dr. Hovaugh snatched the binoculars out of Ralph's hands.

The cars sailed past the bus, and Babo could see each one clearly now, and she recognized the red Pinto that her brother-in-law had sold her.

"So that's where you've gotten to," she said to herself. And she recognized the car next to it.

Dr. Hovaugh squeezed the binoculars. He knelt on his seat and rocked back and forth. "That's my car!" he shouted. "That's my car!"

Babo leaned around Dr. Hovaugh and watched the cars sail along. "Well, isn't that the trick," she said. "Isn't that just the trick."

CLIFFORD SIFTON AND LEWIS PICK WATCHED as the cars floated into view.

"Let's see," said Lew. "There's a red Pinto. And . . . a blue Toyota, no, no . . . a Nissan, a blue Nissan. And a . . . hey, that's nice. Look, it's a Karmann-Ghia. The white one. A convertible, too."

"A Nissan, a Pinto, and a Karmann-Ghia?" said Sifton. "What the hell are cars doing on my lake?"

"Sailing," said Lew. "And they're headed this way."

Sifton leaned on the railing and watched the cars bob along on the lake. "Did I ever tell you I could have had the project in Quebec?"

"They can't get very far," said Lew. "If they keep coming, they'll just run into the dam."

"Did I ever tell you that?"

ELI HELD THE COFFEE CUP in his hands and watched the sun appear. He was sorry he was not at the camp to see the sun come among the lodges, to be among the people as it came, and he wondered if Lionel and Latisha and Norma and Alberta and Harley and Camelot were awake to see it, for it truly was a thing of wonder.

At his back, he could feel the dam, cold and ponderous, clinging to the geometry of the land. At his front, the sun filled the sky and drove the chill west.

"Morning, Eli," said the Lone Ranger.

Eli looked up and saw the Lone Ranger, Ishmael, Robinson Crusoe, and Hawkeye standing in front of the porch.

"Good morning," he said. "Come on up. You want some coffee?"

"Oh, boy," said Ishmael, "that would be good."

"Yes," said Robinson Crusoe. "Hot coffee would be wonderful."

"Do you have any sugar?" said Hawkeye.

"Sure," said Eli. "Got lots of sugar. You want cream too?"

"I want cream," says Coyote. "I want lots of sugar and cream."

The old Indians turned to watch the sun rise. It was above the horizon now, too brilliant to look at directly.

"This is a nice place to live," said the Lone Ranger.

"Is that the dam?" said Ishmael.

Eli turned and nodded. "That's right. Government built it to help Indians. There's a lake that goes with it."

"Is the lake for Indians, too?" said Robinson Crusoe.

"So they say," said Eli, turning away from the dam. "We're all supposed to be millionaires."

"It doesn't look like an Indian dam," said Hawkeye. "It doesn't look like an Indian lake."

"Perhaps it's a Coyote dam," says Coyote. "Perhaps it's a Coyote lake."

Eli went into the kitchen and brought out more coffee cups. "Here," he said. "Just brewed."

"It's going to be a good day," said the Lone Ranger. "I can feel it."

"You bet," said Eli, and he arranged the coffee cups on the porch. But as Eli reached for the coffeepot, it began to rattle and then bounce. Eli grabbed the railing of the porch and tried to stand up. And as he did, the land began to dance.

"Oh, oh," said the Lone Ranger. "Things are getting bent again."

"You haven't been dancing again, Coyote?" said Ishmael.

"Just a little," says Coyote.

"You haven't been singing again, Coyote?" said Robinson Crusoe.

"Just a little," says Coyote.

"Oh, boy," said Hawkeye. "Here we go again."

As Eli steadied himself against the porch post, he felt the wind explode at his back, and he heard the sound of thunder rolling down the valley.

Above him, the sun continued in a clear sky.

"Earthquake," yelled Clifford Sifton.

"Earthquake," yelled Bill Bursum.

"Earthquake," yelled Dr. Joseph Hovaugh.

"EARTHQUAKE, EARTHQUAKE!" yells Coyote. "Hee-hee-hee-hee-hee-hee-hee-hee."

LIONEL WAS WAKENED BY THE NOISE. He sat up and looked around. Norma was feeding wood to the fire and cutting up bacon. Lionel's back hurt. The mattress was lumpy, and a cold breeze had come in under the flap of the tepee all night. Alberta's bed was empty.

"Where's Alberta ?"

"Outside throwing up," said Norma.

"Is she sick?"

"Nope," said Norma. "Pregnant."

"Pregnant? Ah . . . Did she . . ."

"Didn't say. Better ask her yourself."

Lionel got his shoes on. The mud had dried, and the leather near the toe was starting to curl. He heard the noise again.

"Sounds like she's about done, nephew," said Norma. "Tell her breakfast will be in about half an hour. If she feels like it."

It was the air that caught Lionel, cold and sharp. The horizon floated in soft light and then in fire as the sun rose out of the land.

Alberta was standing between two lodges bent over, her hands on her knees.

"Morning, Alberta," said Lionel, his hands jammed into his pockets for warmth.

"Morning, Lionel," said Alberta. "Do you have a tissue?"

Lionel fished around in his pocket and felt his good linen handkerchief. "No," he said. "Want me to get you one?"

"No," she said. "It's okay."

Lionel turned away as Alberta began spitting and watched the sun rise. "So," he said. "Norma tells me you're pregnant."

"I'm not pregnant."

Lionel turned back. "You're not?"

"I can't be pregnant."

"Charlie?"

"That's hardly your business," said Alberta.

"I'm just trying to help," said Lionel. "I guess it's not mine."

Alberta looked at Lionel. Her nose was running and her eyes were wet. "I'm not pregnant."

"Norma said that breakfast would be ready in a little while," said Lionel. "Bacon."

"Oh, God," said Alberta, and she turned back and bent over.

"If you're up to it," said Lionel.

Alberta put her hands on her knees, braced herself, and rocked back and forth. "It's getting worse. I feel as if the whole world is moving."

Lionel didn't feel the motion at first. He watched Alberta leaning over and debated how he should try to comfort her. Wondered if he should hold her or talk to her. Tell her a joke. Or just stay out of the way.

He had decided on a joke when he felt it. A gentle surge, a rolling motion, as if he were on the ocean.

"Bill told me a pretty funny—"

Lionel was knocked off his feet with the first shock. The land buckled and snapped and rose around him like waves. The lodges in the circle were shaking and swaying, and there were cries everywhere as the people felt the earth move beneath them.

CLIFFORD SIFTON AND LEWIS PICK watched the Nissan, the Pinto, and the Karmann-Ghia float into the dam just as the earthquake began. Almost imperceptibly, the waters swelled and the cars were thrown into the dam, hard, insistent. And before either man realized what was happening, a tremor rolled in out of the west, tipping the lake on its end.

Pick and Sifton were knocked to the ground, and as they tried to stand, they were knocked down again. It was comical at first, the two men trying to find their footing, the cars smashing into the dam, the lake curling over the top.

But beneath the power and the motion there was a more ominous sound of things giving way, of things falling apart.

Sifton felt it first, a sudden shifting, a sideways turning, a flexing, the snapping crack of concrete and steel, and in that instant the water rose out of the lake like a mountain, sucking the cars under and pitching them high in the air, sending them at the dam in an awful rush.

And the dam gave way, and the water and the cars tumbled over the edge of the world.

From the tour bus, Dr. Hovaugh and Babo watched the dam

burst. Several of the passengers took out their cameras, but as they were at lake level, there was little to see.

"It must be a spectacular sight from down below," said a man near the back.

Dr. Hovaugh sagged against the bus, took out the book, and held it up. "It's all here," he said to Babo. "I was right, after all."

"Sorry about your car," said Babo.

"The dates."

"Looks like I lost mine, too."

"The places."

Babo looked at Dr. Hovaugh, and then she turned and watched the lake race for the breach in the dam.

From the vantage point of his lot, Bill Bursum watched his shoreline disappear. He stood transfixed for a moment, and then he began walking toward the lake, trotting after the retreating water.

"Now what's gone wrong?" he shouted, breaking into a run across the immense mud flat that appeared beneath his feet and slowly curved out in all directions. "What the hell has gone wrong now?"

Below, in the valley, the water rolled on as it had for eternity.

"I DIDN'T DO IT," says Coyote.

The Lone Ranger and Ishmael and Robinson Crusoe and Hawkeye looked at Coyote.

"It's a lot of work fixing up this world, you know," said the Lone Ranger.

"Yes," said Ishmael. "And we can use all the help we can get."

"The last time you fooled around like this," said Robinson Crusoe, "the world got very wet."

"And we had to start all over again," said Hawkeye.

"I didn't do anything," says Coyote. "I just sang a little."

"Oh, boy," said the Lone Ranger.

"I just danced a little, too," says Coyote.

"Oh, boy," said Ishmael.

"But I was helpful, too," says Coyote. "That woman who wanted a baby. Now, that was helpful."

"Helpful!" said Robinson Crusoe. "You remember the last time you did that?"

"I'm quite sure I was in Kamloops," says Coyote.

"We haven't straightened out *that* mess yet," said Hawkeye.

"Hee-hee," says Coyote. "Hee-hee."

"WELL," says Coyote, "here we are at Fort Marion again."

"That's right," I says.

"And there is the Lone Ranger and Ishmael and Robinson Crusoe and Hawkeye," says Coyote.

"That's right again," I says.

"Am I missing something?" says Coyote.

"Think about it, Coyote," I says. "Just think about it."

So those soldiers get to Fort Marion and they throw Old Woman off the train and they throw her in Fort Marion.

And they says, Here's another Indian. How many is that now?

No limit on Indians, says the Soldier In Charge Of The Fort. Keep them coming.

So those soldiers keep bringing Indians and stuffing them in the fort. And pretty soon, things get crowded.

Boy, says Hawkeye, this place is crowded.

Yes, says Robinson Crusoe. It is getting uncomfortable.

Perhaps, says Ishmael, we should move.

Sounds like a good idea to me, says the Lone Ranger.

So that Lone Ranger puts on the Lone Ranger mask and walks to the front gate.

It's the Lone Ranger, the guards shout. It's the Lone Ranger, they shout again. And they open the gate. So the Lone Ranger walks out of the prison, and the Lone Ranger and Ishmael and Hawkeye and Robinson Crusoe head west.

Have a nice day, the soldiers say. Say hello to Tonto for us. And all those soldiers wave.

Who's Tonto? says Ishmael.

Beats me, says the Lone Ranger. Keep waving.

So the Lone Ranger and Ishmael and Robinson Crusoe and Hawkeye walk west, and pretty soon they come to a river. Big river. Big muddy river.

Ho, ho, ho, ho, says that Big Muddy River. I suppose you want to get to the other side.

That would be nice, says the Lone Ranger. We are trying to fix the world.

Is that what we're doing? says Ishmael.

Nobody said anything to me about that, says Robinson Crusoe.

Well, says Hawkeye, I suppose somebody has to do it.

Okay, says that Big Muddy River. Hang on.

And right away the ground starts to shake and the trees start to dance and everything goes up and down and sideways.

"Earthquake! Earthquake!" yells Coyote.

"Calm down," I says.

"But it's another earthquake," says Coyote.

"Yes," I says. "These things happen."

"But we've already had one earthquake in this story," says Coyote.

"And you never know when something like this is going to happen again," I says.

"Wow!" says Coyote. "Wow!"

So along comes this earthquake. Rumble, rumble, rumble, rumble, says that Earthquake. This is fun.

And the Lone Ranger and Ishmael and Robinson Crusoe and Hawkeye and that Big Muddy River get bounced around for a while and when all the bouncing is done, the Lone Ranger and Ishmael and Robinson Crusoe and Hawkeye are on the other side of the river.

Boy, says the Lone Ranger. That was pretty good.

Yes, says that Big Muddy River. But it's pretty tiring. Good thing I don't have to do that every day.

"So," I says, "that's what happens."

"What?" says Coyote.

"The Lone Ranger and Ishmael and Robinson Crusoe and Hawkeye keep walking until they get here," I says.

"Oh," says Coyote. "I can see that."

"Good," I says.

"But I don't get it," says Coyote.

IT WAS A LITTLE OVER A MONTH before the waters went down. The cabin was gone, the logs scattered along the course of the flood. Norma walked the flat where the cabin had stood and poked her stick at the debris. Latisha and Lionel trailed behind her. Christian and Benjamin and Elizabeth ran up and down the banks, sliding in the mud, running through the water.

"The cabin used to stand right here," said Norma.

Latisha watched her children play. "I'm going to miss Eli."

"Going to miss him, too," said Norma. "But he had a good life, and he lived it right."

"He was a nice guy all right," said Lionel.

"Hope you took notes, nephew," said Norma.

"I did. I liked him."

"Good ways to live a life and not so good ways," said Norma.

Above the flat, a car came down the road. It was coming fast, dragging a huge plume of dust and dirt behind it.

"Dam doesn't look too good," said Lionel. "Read where they're going to have to tear the whole thing down."

"Never needed a dam," said Latisha. "And it never worked, anyway."

The car stopped on the rise above them. It was a red Porsche, and Lionel knew who it was even before Charlie got out. Alberta was with him.

"Hey," shouted Charlie, "what's happening?"

"Norma's just looking around."

Charlie and Alberta made their way down the bank, Alberta moving cautiously, Charlie slipping in the soft mud.

Latisha grabbed Alberta's arm and helped her down the last, steep incline. "How you feeling?"

"Still yucky in the mornings," said Alberta.

"It doesn't get much better." Latisha laughed. "And then they turn into that." She gestured to where the kids were wallowing in the mud.

"Not much left," said Charlie.

"Everything's still here," said Norma.

"Well, the cabin's not here," said Charlie. "And neither is Eli."

"Charlie!" said Alberta. "God, you can really be sensitive."

Norma waved Charlie off. "Eli's fine. He came home. More than I can say for some people I know."

"Yeah," said Lionel, "but he didn't come home because of the Sun Dance. And he didn't come home because Granny died. He told me that."

Lionel looked at the dam. It had a long ugly crack running all the way down the face. At the top was a huge hole. Water was running out of the crack and down the face, the river slowly coming back to life.

"Lost my job yesterday," said Charlie.

"Duplessis suddenly discovered that they didn't need a hot-shot Indian lawyer anymore," said Alberta.

"No dam," said Charlie. "No job."

"Can you cook?" said Latisha. "Got an opening for a cook."

"That's too bad," said Lionel. "What are you going to do?"

"Actually," said Charlie, "I'm going to take a vacation."

"He's going to Los Angeles," said Alberta.

"Going to see my father," said Charlie. "Hey, he's a big star again."

"You big, strong men," Norma shouted, "give me a hand with this."

Norma was digging in the ground with her stick, clearing the mud away from a log stuck in the ground.

"The porch post," she said. "You see where Eli and me and Camelot carved our names in the wood."

"You want that thing?" said Charlie.

"Use it on the new cabin," said Norma. "No sense letting it go to waste."

"What new cabin?" said Lionel.

Norma picked up a car antenna and tossed it to one side. "Eli tell you why he came home?"

"He was going to. But he never did."

"Just as well," said Norma. "Always best to figure those things out for yourself. Come on, give me a hand."

It took Norma and Lionel and Latisha and Alberta and Charlie the better part of an hour to dig the post out.

"Now, that wasn't too bad," said Norma. "The rest of the logs will probably be a lot easier."

Charlie smiled and rocked back on his heels. "I'll think about you when I'm on the beach."

"You'll be back," said Norma.

"But in the meantime," said Charlie, "it's time to get going. Just came over to say good-bye."

Lionel looked at Alberta. She didn't look pregnant, but then, he guessed, you couldn't tell this early.

"So," Lionel said, "I guess you're going with Charlie."

Norma stopped what she was doing and hit Lionel on the shoulder with the stick. "Why would she do something like that?"

Latisha shook her head and laughed. "Why on earth would she do something like that?"

"Why would I do something like that?" said Alberta. "I haven't got time to be running after lawyers in Los Angeles. I work for a living."

"You sure got a way with women, cousin," said Charlie, and he began climbing back up the bank. When he got to his car, he turned and waved. "Send me pictures of the new place when you get it finished."

"When you get to Los Angeles, Charlie Looking Bear," said Norma, "tell your father hello for me. Tell him about Eli."

Lionel waited until Charlie's car disappeared down the road. "So," he said to Alberta, "you in town for the weekend?"

"That's right," said Alberta. "Figured I'd give Norma a hand."

"With what?"

"With the cabin," said Norma. "You can help, too."

Lionel stopped what he was doing and looked at Norma and then he looked at the dam. "You're not serious?"

"Sure she is, brother," said Latisha.

"Won't take much," said Norma. "We'll get Harley's truck and drag as many logs as we can back up here, and what we're short, we can cut and bring in."

"That's a lot of work," said Lionel.

"My mother did it," said Norma. "Did it all by herself."

Alberta set her feet in the mud and put her hands on her hips. "You can help or you can sell televisions."

"What's it going to be, nephew?"

Lionel squatted down and tentatively stuck a finger in the ground. "It's pretty wet."

"In or out?" said Latisha.

Lionel stood up and looked at the sun. "Well, maybe when the cabin is finished," he said, "I'll live in it for a while. You know, like Eli. Maybe that's what I'll do."

"Not your turn," said Norma. "It's my turn. Your turn will come soon enough."

Latisha put her arm around Alberta. "Come on," she said. "We'll catch lunch at the Dead Dog, get changed, and get to work."

"Lunch?" said Alberta. There were tiny beads of sweat on the sides of her nose.

"Something greasy," said Latisha.

"Don't start," said Alberta.

"Of course, I should probably go back to school," said Lionel. "Maybe that's what I'll do."

Norma stuck her stick in the earth. "We'll start here," she said. "So we can see the sun in the morning."

DR. JOSEPH HOVAUGH sat at his desk and rolled his toes in the soft, deep-pile carpet. In the garden, the willows were beginning to get their leaves, the cherry trees were heavy with pink and white blossoms, the evergreens stood dark and velvet against the stone. Yellow daffodils lined the front of the flower beds, and the wisteria and the lilacs around the arbors were greening up nicely.

Dr. Hovaugh sat in his chair behind his desk and looked out at the wall and the trees and the flowers and the swans on the blue-green pond in the garden, and he was pleased.

The knock, a sharp rap, barely gave Dr. Hovaugh time to swivel back toward the door and bring Mary into focus.

"Good morning, Mary. What do we have today?"

"F Wing," said Mary.

"F Wing? The Indians?"

"Yes, sir. They're back."

"Again?"

Dr. Hovaugh turned back to the window. He stretched both his hands out on the desk and pushed down as if he expected to move it. "Look at that, Mary. It's spring again. Everything's green. Everything's alive. You know, I thought I might get a pair of peacocks. What do you think?"

Mary stood in the middle of the room, unsure of what to do. Dr. Hovaugh seemed to shrink behind the desk as though it were growing, slowly and imperceptibly enveloping the man.

"It's too bad about the Indians," he said.

"They're back," said Mary. "They always come back."

Dr. Hovaugh turned away from the window. Perhaps he should move the desk out and get another that didn't seem so rooted and permanent.

"I need John, Mary." Dr. Hovaugh leaned on the desk and spoke each word slowly, as if he was trying to remember exactly what he wanted to say. "Find me John."

BABO PUSHED THE HEAVY DOORS open and stuck her head into the room.

"Hi," she said. "Everybody okay?"

"Hello, Babo," said the Lone Ranger.

"Good to see you again," said Ishmael.

Babo slipped into the room and put her mop against the wall. "So how was the trip?"

"It was very good," said Robinson Crusoe.

"Yes," said Hawkeye. "We fixed up part of the world."

"All right!" said Babo.

"It wasn't a big part," said the Lone Ranger. "But it was very satisfying."

"Unfortunately," said Ishmael, "part of it got messed up, too."

"Well, you got to expect that to happen from time to time," said Babo.

"Yes," said Robinson Crusoe. "That's the way things happen all right."

"Well, it's good to have you back," said Babo. "Dr. Hovaugh was very concerned about you."

"That's nice," said Hawkeye. "Maybe next time, we'll help him."

"What a wonderful idea," said Babo. "I think he'd like that."

"We could start in the garden," said the Lone Ranger.

Babo smiled and rubbed her shoulder. "Now, wouldn't that be the trick," she said. "Wouldn't that just be the trick."

"Boy," says Coyote, "am I sore."

"Coyote," I says, "you are all wet."

"Yes," says Coyote, "that's true."

"And you're covered with mud." I says that, too.

"Just here and there," says Coyote.

"So," I says, "what happened?"

"It wasn't my fault," says Coyote. "It wasn't my fault."

"Oh, boy," I says. "It looks like we got to do this all over again."

"GHA!" said the Lone Ranger.

"Wait a minute," said Ishmael. "Wait a minute. Before we begin, did anyone offer an apology?"

"Wasn't Coyote going to do that?" said Robinson Crusoe.

"Apologize for what?" says Coyote.

"In case we hurt anyone's feelings," said Hawkeye.

"Oh, okay," says Coyote. "I'm sorry."

"That didn't sound very sorry, Coyote," said the Lone Ranger. "Remember what happened the last time you rushed through a story and didn't apologize?"

"Yes," said Ishmael. "Remember how far you had to run?"

"Yes," said Robinson Crusoe. "Remember how long you had to hide?"

"Ooops!" says Coyote. "I am *very* sorry."

"That's better," said Hawkeye.

"I am really *very, very* sorry," says Coyote.

"That's fine," said the Lone Ranger. "It sounds very sincere."

"*Sorry, sorry, sorry, sorry,*" says Coyote.

"Okay," said the Lone Ranger. "We believe you."

"Hee-hee," says Coyote. "Hee-hee."

"OKAY, OKAY," says Coyote. "I got it!"

"Well, it's about time," I says.

"Okay, okay, here goes," says Coyote. "In the beginning, there was nothing."

"Nothing?"

"That's right," says Coyote. "Nothing."

"No," I says. "In the beginning, there was just the water."

"Water?" says Coyote.

"Yes," I says. "Water."

"Hmmmm," says Coyote. "Are you sure?"

"Yes," I says, "I'm sure."

"Okay," says Coyote, "if you say so. But where did all the water come from?"

"Sit down," I says to Coyote.

"But there is water everywhere," says Coyote.

"That's true," I says. "And here's how it happened."

About the author

About the book

Read on

Ideas,
interviews
& features

Author Biography

THOMAS KING is one of Canada's most beloved and critically acclaimed writers. He is an award-winning novelist, short story writer, children's author, scriptwriter, radio personality and photographer.

In the early sixties, King got a job on a tramp steamer and spent three years working as a photojournalist in New Zealand and Australia, where he made a first attempt at a novel he describes as "real pukey stuff." His attempts at short fiction were no better— "Blithering messes and romantic slop."

He returned to North America in 1967, and after finishing a B.A. and an M.A. at California State University, Chico, then went to the University of Utah to complete a Ph.D. During his last year there, he got a job offer from the University of Lethbridge and, in 1980, arrived in Canada.

It was at the University of Lethbridge that King began to develop as a writer. "I met this woman, Helen Hoy, at the university," says King. "I had nothing to impress her with, but because she was in literature, I thought I might impress her with my writing. Maybe it was Helen or maybe it was coming to Canada. In any case, suddenly I could write." King and Hoy have been together ever since.

In 1989, Thomas King received a one-month writer's residency at the Ucross Foundation in Wyoming. During that intensive month, he finished work on his first novel, *Medicine River*, and wrote the first draft of his second novel, *Green Grass, Running Water*.

Medicine River was published to critical

AUTHOR PHOTO: BOB HOUSSER

Thomas King

2

acclaim. *The New York Times* described it as "precise, elegant ... a most satisfying novel." It won the 1990 Writers Guild of Alberta Best Novel Award, the PEN/Josephine Miles Award and was also shortlisted for the Commonwealth Writers' Prize. Later, the novel was made into a CBC television movie, starring Graham Greene, and a three-part radio play for CBC Radio.

Green Grass, Running Water, King's second novel, was shortlisted for the Governor General's Award in 1993 and won the Canadian Authors Association Award for Fiction. A national bestseller, it was also named to *Quill & Quire*'s Best Canadian Fiction of the Century list and was the runner-up in CBC Radio's 2004 "Canada Reads" contest.

In 2003, King delivered the prestigious Massey lectures from *The Truth About Stories*, a book that investigates North America's relationship with its Aboriginal peoples. The lectures went on to win the Trillium Book Award.

King has also written three acclaimed children's books, garnering a Governor General's Award for *A Coyote Columbus Story*. His highly praised story collection *One Good Story, That One* became a Canadian bestseller in 1993. *Truth and Bright Water*, his third novel, was a bestseller as well. In 2002, King published *DreadfulWater Shows Up*—the first book in the DreadfulWater Mystery Series—under the pseudonym Hartley Goodweather. The second book in the series, *The Red Power Murders*, was published in 2006, only months after the release of his second collection of short stories, *A Short History of Indians in Canada*.

Recently called to the Order of Canada, ▶

Author Biography (*continued*)

King has also received an Aboriginal Achievement Award from the National Aboriginal Achievement Foundation and a Distinguished Achievement Award from the Western Literature Association.

Thomas King is a professor of English at the University of Guelph, where he teaches creative writing and Native literature. He is currently working on a new novel, *The Back of the Turtle*, as well as episodes of *Dead Dog in the City*, an extension of his popular CBC radio series Dead Dog Café Comedy Hour.

An Interview with Thomas King

Your work draws upon a wealth of traditions—Native, Christian, literary, pop culture. Can you speak a bit about the traditions that you were raised in?

I was raised in all of those traditions. No one tradition was dominant. My mom was Greek-Orthodox and she was part of a community that was Orthodox, Methodist, Presbyterian and Catholic. I went to Greek-Orthodox services, I went to Methodist Sunday school and I spent two years at a Catholic boarding school. It was kind of schizophrenic.

What it taught me is that there is a certain meanness and arrogance in religion, and in society in general, that prevails. The questions that we ask are not the kind of questions that we should ask. We ask, how will this profit me? How will this increase my prestige? Will this give me more power?

Religion is this way because it is run by humans, created by humans and inhabited by humans. In my early training, what I saw were the underbellies, but I tend to look for those imperfections. I am not a person who is full of faith.

Reserve life plays a role in your novel, yet you weren't raised on a reserve. You taught at the University of Lethbridge near the Blood Reserve. Is that where you draw your understanding of reserve life? ▶

> **❝** What I saw were the underbellies, but I tend to look for those imperfections. **❞**

I have worked on reserves all over the place. I worked with Natives in northern California and at the University of Utah, although Lethbridge was the primary place of inspiration. I have met a fair number of people on reserves and in and around reserves, kind of on the edges of those places. It's true, though, I wasn't raised on a reserve.

In a 1993 interview about *Green Grass, Running Water*, you mentioned that you felt free to ask questions such as, "Who is an Indian? How do we get this idea of Indians?" Are you still exploring these questions?

These are questions that still need exploring. Treaty rights in Canada, Native tax status and who decides how Native communities are organized and run—these are still live questions. I engage them in my novels because it is an ongoing debate. It's a dangerous debate. People out there might not like it. But I try to present sticky issues from all sides.

These questions still plague us. They are important issues. The Canadian government has no interest in Native rights. It doesn't matter who is in power. There is a lethargy. No—that's too kind a word—there is a turning of the political back to Native people.

I engage in these kinds of debates, like a nasty little blackfly buzzing around. In person I am sweet and shy, but if you put a computer in front of me, I become a bit of a radical.

Was becoming a writer a conscious decision, or did it just happen?

> People out there might not like it. But I try to present sticky issues from all sides.

I always wrote and told stories in one way or another. Even lies. Lies are forms of stories—good liars are reasonably good storytellers. I also wrote poetry. But since I was a guy, I had to hide it. What would my He-man friends think of me writing poetry? I was also a voracious reader. I spent a lot of time at the library. I was a journalist for a while. All of these things played into it. But it was like plucking at the strings of a guitar. I just played here and there—until 1980 when I started writing seriously. There was nothing organized about it, I was just thinking—how can I make a living?

Are there any writers who inspired your work?

I can't say that any writers inspired me. As a kid I read dog and horse books and the entire Oz series by L. Frank Baum. I would go down to the library in the summer, especially on hot days. The basement of the library was cool, and I would just work my way along the shelves. I'd go to the "f" section and choose a book. You could tell where I was in the alphabet by where I was seated. There were reading programs at the library and you could earn stars. I was one of the top kids in reading.

When I was older, there were writers who came along and demonstrated that literature by other peoples is available. Although there was damn little, they didn't teach literature by other peoples at school. I was living in California when N. Scott Momaday won the Pulitzer Prize for *House Made of Dawn*. I enjoyed his book and was encouraged by his success.

But there wasn't one writer or book that inspired me; it's not that cut and dried. It's rockier and more disjointed than that. ▶

> " I always wrote and told stories in one way or another. Even lies. "

An Interview with Thomas King (*continued*)

Your stories are a hybrid of styles and traditions. You weave in pop culture, aspects of Native and Judeo-Christian traditions, and imaginary or fantastic landscapes. How did writing in this manner come about? Was it a conscious decision or do your stories unfold this way?

Satire has always been a tool that comes from distrust. I am happier and stronger as a writer when I'm pointing out imperfections. I wouldn't write a piece that is laudatory. Calling attention to those things that are problematic, that mark us as human, is what I do.

You weave together humour with issues such as the plight of contemporary Natives. How would you describe the role of satire in your work?

Satire is sharp. It is supposed to hurt; it is never supposed to make you feel comfortable. I hope that when readers laugh, deep in their hearts they are uncomfortable, uneasy and looking over their shoulder, watching. That if they read something that they too have done, they feel like someone watched them do it. Maybe me.

There is a lot of writing that is complacent and soothing, and there are a lot of good writers out there—but that's not of much interest to me.

How did the CBC series Dead Dog Café Comedy Hour come about? Did the CBC approach you or did you send in a proposal?

> ❝ I am happier and stronger as a writer when I'm pointing out imperfections. ❞

I have no idea. I can't remember how it started. There are probably four or five versions of the story floating around out there. A producer that I'd done some other work with called me and asked me about doing it. But why I came up with what I did is lost in the mists of time. Sometimes I have to look at old scripts to remember what I've written and to make sure future episodes make sense.

You have also been teaching at universities for over thirty years. When did you decide to teach? How does it influence your writing?

Being around other academics and a body of information provides some of my material. But teaching doesn't improve or hurt my writing. If I wasn't teaching, I'd miss the incisive kinds of discussions about various things and the bizarre things that happen at universities. It's a lot of fun. But I think of writing and teaching as two different activities.

Even when you're drawing the past into your stories, they are still set in contemporary North America—is there any particular reason for that?

I hate historical novels. History is a dead issue. One version of it is told and is taught, and that's the version that everybody knows and the version that everybody is expecting. But it's only one of the stories told of an event. And I hate doing research for novels. I like contemporary stuff and that's what I write.

Your characters often speak along separate tangents. They end up talking around subjects ▶

> " I hate historical novels. History is a dead issue. "

An Interview with Thomas King (*continued*)

instead of talking to one another—what is the intended impact of this kind of dialogue?

It's the way people talk to each other. Take a political forum. When a politician is asked a question, they answer with something else. People don't answer questions. Much of what I hear is people speaking off on different tangents. Literary conversations like "How are you?" "I am fine" are boring.

❝ Literary conversations like 'How are you?' 'I am fine' are boring. ❞

Web Detective

To listen to CBC's interview with Thomas King about his Massey lecture:
http://www.cbc.ca/ideas/massey/massey2003.html

To listen to an interview with Thomas King about his background and writing:
http://wiredforbooks.org/thomasking/

To read an interview with Thomas King about
Medicine River:
http://www.unb.ca/CACLALS/chimo21.html#_
Interview_with_Thomas

To learn more about the Assembly of First Nations: *http://www.afn.ca/*

For information on the history of the Sun Dance: *http://www.psyeta.org/sa/sa1.1/lawrence.html*

❧